A
Charm
of
Finches

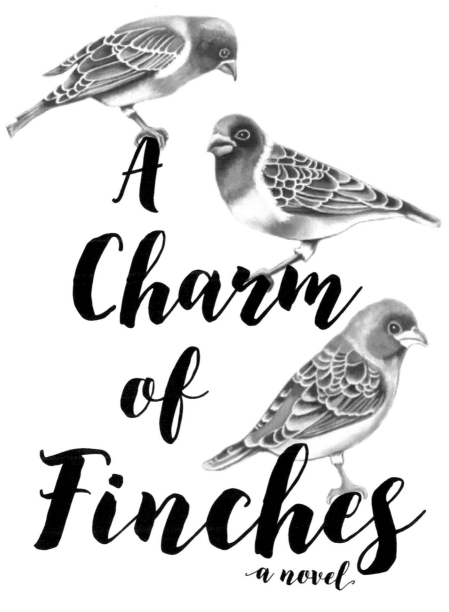

A Charm of Finches

a novel

SUANNE LAQUEUR

CATHEDRAL ROCK PRESS | NEW YORK | 2016

Suanne Laqueur/Cathedral Rock Press
Somers, New York
WWW.SUANNELAQUEURWRITES.COM

Publisher's Note: This is a work of fiction. Names, characters, places, and incidents are a product of the author's imagination. Locales and public names are sometimes used for atmospheric purposes. Any resemblance to actual people, living or dead, or to busi-nesses, com-panies, events, institutions, or locales is completely coincidental.

Book Design by Ampersand Bookery
Cover Design by Tracy Kopsachilis

A Charm of Finches/ Suanne Laqueur. — 1st ed.

ISBN 978-1-9775731-6-2 (paperback)
ISBN 978-1-7379814-4-2 (hardcover)

Author's Note

THIS BOOK CONTAINS ADULT SUBJECT matter including adult themes of sex and sexual violence, written in adult language. *An Exaltation of Larks* spoke of The Disappeared Ones of Chile. *A Charm of Finches* speaks to a different group of disappeared. An invisible demographic who often suffer in misunderstood silence. Geno Caan speaks as one who knows, but he also speaks for men who will never tell their stories. Or for men who told their stories and weren't believed. These extraordinarily brave and resilient males possess strong hearts and I stood in awe of them during the writing of this book, knowing there was a lot more I could get wrong than right.

It's my sincere hope I got it right.

—SLQR
Somers, New York
October 7, 2017

For Rach, who saw me from beginning to end on this important book. Inspiring, challenging and not letting me get away with anything. You're one of my toughest critics, one of my wisest readers and one of my dearest friends.

I write, you read, I drop.

"Because I've been lying asleep at this little farm where you were born, and to wake up I had to have the warmth of a fire only you could light."

—Chilean saying

"Listen and learn it. Learn to tell it. And tell it to teach it."

—Latin American saying

"And if I had a boat
I'd go out on the ocean.
And if I had a pony
I'd ride him on my boat.
And we could all together
Go out on the ocean.
Me upon my pony on my boat…"

—Lyle Lovett

PROLOGUE

FEED YOURSELF

*T*HE MANHATTAN NEIGHBORHOOD of Chelsea buzzed under a brilliant blue sky. Greenwich Street was closed from Gansevoort to Jane, its curbs lined with vendor booths. The air juggled a dozen tantalizing smells and sounds. The crackle of grilled sausage and chicken, falafel, burgers and kebabs. Buttery popcorn, sugary fried dough and honey-roasted almonds. A Babel of languages wove with street musicians playing jazz on one corner, reggae on another and classical in between.

Over on Horatio Street, smack in the middle of the festival, the Bake & Bagel hummed with a productive energy bordering on frantic. Already one of the neighborhood's most popular joints, it was packed today, the line curling through tables and easing out the door.

The owner Micah Kalo had been up since three in the morning, making dough. His daughter and co-owner, Stavroula, was a blur behind the counter. She hustled from display case to register, calling orders back to the double-staffed kitchen.

Assembling and wrapping sandwiches, Geno Caan moved with the automated purpose of one who has reached the tipping point of fatigue. He'd been up since three as well, first helping Micah with the dough prep, now working the line. Coffee couldn't touch him anymore. He revived himself with strong mint chewing gum and icy swallows of water, coasting on waves of disjointed thought.

The orders were piling up and Javier Landes came in the back to lend a hand. He and the bakers immediately began giving each other friendly hell in Spanish. The one female cook smoothed her hair in the reflection of the stove's hood, looking back over her shoulder, eyes full of undeclared love.

Everyone loved Jav. No secret that two-thirds of the crowd out front came for the food, while the other third came hoping for a look at the gorgeous hunk who worked here sometimes.

"Move, fucky," Jav said, hipping Geno out of his way and reaching for the big cutting knife.

"Did you just call him fucky?" one of the bakers said, laughing.

Jav reached the hand not holding the knife around Geno's neck and smacked a kiss on his crown. "He's my wittle fucky."

"Get out of here." Geno hipped him back with his own collection of Latino put-downs. His Spanish went rusty after his mother died three years ago. But since he became friends with Jav, it flowed again fluently, laced with words his mother wouldn't approve of.

"I finished that book you gave me," Geno said. "The biography of Genghis Khan."

"How was it?"

"I liked it. You know anything about him?"

Jav ripped a sheet of butcher paper off the roll. "Only what I learned in school. Emperor of half the world. Badass motherfucker."

"When he was about fifteen, his father died, and the tribe kicked him out. Him and his mother and brothers and sisters. They were wandering around in exile. Starving. Then he was captured by his father's friends. And they made him a slave."

"Yeah?"

"They put him in a cangue. It's kind of like a yoke. A flat piece of board you put your head through. You know, like Puritans would put you in the stocks, but this was a portable stock you could walk around in." Geno's hands shaped a square frame around his head. "You could walk and work, but you couldn't feed yourself because your hands couldn't reach your mouth."

"Wow."

"I was surprised to learn how much of his youth was spent being hungry and a captive. Anyway, he finally escaped, and the escape earned him a reputation. Men began to join with him. They became his generals. That's how it started."

"With escape," Jav said. His dark brown eyes slowly blinked. "And getting your hands back to your mouth to feed yourself."

They were quiet as they finished up the last of the orders. The pulse of the shop slowed, and the buzz of the crowd settled into a lull. Everything in the hot kitchen seemed to exhale and deflate.

Geno took a long swig of ice water and asked Jav, "Do you believe everything happens for a reason?"

"I do," Jav said. "But not everyone gets the privilege of liking the reason. Of feeling the reason was worth the ordeal or the experience."

"Never thought of it that way."

"What, that you don't have to like it?"

"Yeah."

Jav looked at Geno a long moment. "You're going to be a huge voice in the world."

Geno's heart curled away shyly. "You think?"

Jav nodded. "You have an important story to tell. A story with a lot of power. It can be the kind of thing that…"

"What?"

"The kind of thing that builds an empire."

JULY 2007

(ONE YEAR EARLIER)

THE BOOK OF IF

"IF YOU COULD trade places with anyone for a day, would you?"

Geno closed his eyes to consider the question. "No," he said.

Beside him, Kelly Hook turned the page of a small square tome titled, *The Book of If.*

"If you could spend a day with anyone who is now deceased," she said, "who would it be?"

"My mom, I guess."

"Same," Chris Mudry said, from his sprawl in the leather recliner.

"You'd spend the day with my mom?"

"And night."

"Chris," Kelly cried as Geno let out a howl and fired a throw pillow at the recliner.

"Spend that, asshole," he said, flipping Chris off.

Grinning, Chris fired the cushion back. Geno crossed his arms over it and the two motherless boys locked understanding gazes an instant before looking away. Membership in this unfortunate club allowed them to crack dead mom jokes. But only with each other.

Kelly slouched deeper in the couch cushions and stretched her long legs next to Geno's on the coffee table. Her smooth calves and pale blue toenails made him swallow hard. Until this year, Kelly Hook had been nothing more than background noise. One of the dozens of girls he'd known since kindergarten.

Extras in the drama of his life. Overnight, it seemed, her volume went up. Her presence blocked Geno's path at every turn. Getting in his way, derailing his train of thought, occupying his waking time and monopolizing his dreams.

This girl is wrecking me.

He kind of loved it.

She had the look. A soap-and-water clean beauty. Long red hair she didn't do a thing with and a smattering of freckles across her nose. She couldn't be bothered with makeup, and she didn't need it. She was standalone gorgeous, right down to those blue toenails so close to Geno's sneakers and the hint of perfume tickling his nose.

It was becoming a bit of a problem.

Resisting the urge to adjust himself, Geno moved the cushion a little lower into his lap.

"Were you there when your mom died?" Kelly asked.

"No, school."

"But she died at home."

"Yeah," Geno said. "She was in hospice at that point."

"Freshman year, right?"

"Sophomore. I was in geometry class. The principal came to get me in the middle of a test."

"Maybe your mom timed that on purpose," Chris said.

"Thanks, mom," Geno said, laughing. "It was weird how Dr. Stanton didn't say anything. Everyone looked up and he was in the doorway looking right at me. We just held eyes and… I knew." He freed a hand and held it out to Kelly, his thumb gesturing toward the base of his pinky. "That dot there? Can you see?"

Kelly peered close, her breath tickling his palm. "Yeah."

"I had my compass in my hand. I sort of slammed my fist down on the desk and the point stabbed into my palm. Right there."

"Ouch."

"Show her what's in your wallet," Chris said.

Kelly's copper eyebrows raised. She'd turned more in Geno's direction. A subtle shift in body language that gave him courage. He fished his wallet out of his pocket and, from its folds, drew a small square of denim. The blue was smeared across with maroon.

"I wiped my hand off on my jeans," he said. "Got blood on them. I cut this piece off and threw the rest away. Been carrying it with me since."

"Wow," Kelly said. Her shoulder was touching Geno's now, pushing against it. In another minute, she'd meld right into him. The idea made his belly coil like a snake in the sun. Hiding his burning face, he put the scrap of fabric and his wallet away.

"Who did Dr. Stanton tell first?" Kelly asked. "You or your brother?"

"Me," he said. "Then I went with him up to Carlito's class."

"That must've been awful."

"Yeah," Geno said. "He looked at me a few seconds and then closed his eyes and nodded, like he'd been expecting it."

"Do you guys ever feel the same things or have a psychic moment?"

"No," he said, brave enough to give her a playful shove. "I don't read his mind, he doesn't feel sad when I do."

He was lying. He did sometimes feel what Carlos felt. But it was too hard to explain the twin bond and now Kelly was shoving him back. They were nearly wrestling, each trying to knock the other off the couch.

"Get a room," Chris mumbled, aiming the clicker at the TV.

Kelly laughed and laughed, her hair tumbling over her face and getting in Geno's mouth. She was writhing to get out of his grasp, but not too hard. All of his skin jumped up and down in curious excitement, wondering what this would be like if he and Kelly were alone. In the dark. Lying down. And naked.

She's luscious, he thought. One of those words that sounded exactly like what it meant. She was warm and luscious, her muscles firm under his palms, yet soft and springy. Her flesh *gave* under his touch. He could knead her like dough. Butter her up and eat her.

He chuckled under his breath. *Butter* was a word that made him giggle since he was a little boy. Butter and pickle.

"You laughing at me?" Kelly said.

"No."

"Don't lie, Geronimo."

"I'm not."

"Geronimo," she shouted, holding the O long as she gave him one last shove to tumble onto the floor. It was an overused joke that came with having a famous name. He didn't mind it coming from Kelly, though.

Not at all.

He rolled on his stomach, head on his crossed arms, calculating how he could make his move at the party tonight. The logistics were tricky. Kelly Hook's father was the Stockton Police Chief. Which made him Captain Hook. Which meant Geno couldn't fuck around with his daughter's luscious honor.

As he turned scenarios over in his mind, Kelly was on and off the phone, talking to kids coming over that night to swim and cook out. A combined party for the Fourth of July and her birthday.

"Stacey's coming," she said to Chris.

Chris' eyes didn't leave the TV. "Mm."

"Stacey likes him?" Geno asked.

"Big time. Is your brother coming?"

"Why, do you like him?"

Her eyes held his like a challenge. "Is he?"

"I told him it was happening, but he said he was doing…something. I don't know."

He put his head down again and let his mind drift to the right, to the vague place where he stopped and his twin brother began. An imaginary land under a field of glittering stars, where two became one.

Nos, he thought. It was the password to within.

His head turned more to the right. Waiting for the reply which took longer and longer to come these days.

Nos.

Nos…?

The Caan twins had been tangled so intricately in the womb, it took doctors half an hour to sort out arms and legs and cords during the C-section. Put down to sleep in separate swaddles, they worked their arms free while dreaming. Migrating, drifting and turning toward each other. Within minutes, they would be nose to nose, each with a little hand pushed under the other's cap.

Growing up, they spoke in first person plural. We went. We did. We want. We are. They patted heads to say hello, say goodbye, get each other's attention. To say without speaking, *Brother mine.*

Only in adolescence did their paths of interest diverge and their separate selves evolve. Carlos was purely visual, taking in life through his eyes or the lens of his camera. Geno was led by the ear, following talk radio and music and spending his allowance on MP3 players and expensive headphones. The world beckoned like a siren to Carlito, who kept a world map over his bed and stuck pins in the lands he wanted to visit. Geno got slightly anxious when the family traveled. He liked being at their destination but *getting* there made him feel cut loose in space. For him, the best part about going somewhere was coming back home.

Home was We. Although he and Carlos were in separate kindergarten classes, they came home with the same self-portrait: two boys, dressed alike, with a field of stars between them. The stars were their third entity. Their two states united in us-ness. They had a name for their shared space, and within it, they had secret identities. Carlos was Los. Geronimo was Mos. Los and Mos lived in the starry world of Nos, Spanish for *we*. Nos rhymed with *dos*, Spanish for *two*.

"Nos," one would say when they parted ways for the day.

"Dos," the other replied.

They promised their mother no tattoos until they were in college, but they had it all planned out. A field of stars inked on their sides, creating Nos when they stood together. In a shifting, changing world, Carlito's presence was constant and immutable. Either he was physically there, standing next to Geno. Or he was there as Los, tangible in the air to Geno's right. He only had to turn his head the tiniest bit in that direction to dial into his twin.

Nos, he'd think, and toss it into the star field. Carlito said he could sense it like a flickering light in his peripheral. He'd send his reply back and moments later, it would touch Geno's ears like a single wind chime.

Dos.

Us two. Together.

"¿Dónde están mis pollitos?" their mother would call when she got home from work.

Where are my little chicks?

Born in Mexico, Analisa kept her maiden name, Gallincro, which was Spanish for *henhouse*. Geno often envisioned his mother's love as a little red house, nestled in a glade of trees. Golden light spilling from the windows like a beacon and Analisa waiting within, plump and warm and soft like feathers.

Then she died.

Cancer came the first time when the boys were eleven. Analisa made it a game, letting her chicks dye her hair pink and purple and shave it into a mohawk. Carlos was allowed to photograph her bald scalp close-up, to frame her lash-less, brow-less eyes and capture her hard days. Geno sat with her long hours, listening to NPR. Saturday afternoons with Jonathan Schwartz, who played the music Analisa loved—oldies and show tunes—but had the most God-awful delivery. A slow, gravelly drawl that tried to make everything *deep* and *significant.*

As Analisa's health deteriorated, Geno tried to be brave, but the lights were dim in the henhouse, filling him with anxiety. Of the twins, he was the more introverted and homebound. He'd always had his mother's love of kitchens and food and hospitality, but when she became ill, the love became a purpose. He took over meals and shopping and laundry, fervently believing if he could keep things running the way they always ran, Analisa would get well.

"You're the only one around here with a lick of common sense," she said, sitting in her clean kitchen with a cup of tea, watching Geno chop vegetables and stir soup, burn the rice and grate his own knuckles. Sometimes coaching him through recipes, sometimes too tired to do anything but watch him figure it out.

He basked in the simple compliment, knowing it wasn't lip service because he'd overheard her say it to a friend on the phone: "Nathan and Carlito are like two deer in the headlights sometimes. Geno's the sensible one."

She went into remission and everything was fine again.

Until it wasn't.

Until cancer came back to finish the job.

Until Analisa was too weak to sit in the kitchen and too sedated to make jokes about Jonathan Schwartz's voice. Music made her fretful. Talk shows made her agitated and she couldn't sip anything more than water.

One day, Geno walked into geometry class a normal kid and walked out under the arm of the principal with bloodstains on his jeans.

He discovered death hurt like hell. He was unprepared for the sheer physicality of sadness. His skin, bones, teeth, hair follicles and fingernails ached with the loss. Grieving was like being in a really bad car accident. All day long.

Every day.

It was in the midst of this physical ordeal that Geno realized Analisa was right: While he had sensibly braced himself for her death, his father and Carlos had stared into its blinding light and let themselves be sideswiped.

Nathan Caan was there for his boys. Physically there, although overnight he seemed two inches shorter and twenty pounds thinner. His diminished body was present but his twinkling eyes had gone flat, burned out by death's headlights. He stared into space for long stretches of time. His sentences trailed off as if he forgot what he was saying as he was saying it. Worst of all, he began to mix up his sons. Once he boasted he could tell them apart blindfolded. Now he'd be mid-conversation with one twin and realize he thought he was talking to the other. It started out amusing. Then became disconcerting and finally, hurtful. Because after Analisa died, Geno and Carlos became utterly unalike.

In the first months of mourning, Geno was afraid to leave the house while Carlos seemed afraid to be *in* it. Carlos threw himself into his photography. Disappearing until dinner, saying he had an after-school job. Busy, busy, busy. While Geno sat alone in blood-stained jeans, listening to the radio.

He reached out. *Nos.*

The reply took forever. It hit his ear like a squeal of tires or a needle-scratched record. A burst of static heralding a disinterested *Dos.*

Geno wore his same jeans to death while Carlos was taking great pains with his appearance. Monopolizing the bathroom and taking innumerable selfies. He started dressing almost exclusively in black and sporting an expensive leather jacket.

"Where'd you get that?" Geno asked.

Carlos hitched it a little higher on his shoulders and turned in front of the mirror. "Bought it."

Everything was changing.

The henhouse was empty, and Carlos was harder and harder to find in the Land of Two. Only a few weeks ago, Geno was doing laundry, emptying pants pockets of loose change and other junk, and he drew a handful of folded-up notes from Carlos' expensive jeans.

> *Come see me soon.*
> *I don't feel alive if you're not around.*
> *—A*

> *I could barely let you go yesterday.*
> *My cells cried after you were gone.*
> *I love you so much, I need two of you.*
> *—A*

"Holy crap," Geno said under his breath, eyebrows raised. Carlos had a girlfriend? He was always surrounded by chicks at school, but he seemed unfazed by their company to the point of boredom. Had one of them broken through his aloof facade? Geno ran a roll call of female classmates with A names but none turned on a lightbulb. He couldn't reconcile any of the Amys, Amandas, Andreas or Ariannas with these passionate sentiments.

> *Your body is so beautiful.*
> *Your soul is a double helix.*
> *I want to gather it to both sides of me.*
> *—A*

Geno rolled his eyes. He was no poet, but he was sure he could do better.

It hurts when you deny me
What I want so badly.
What I need if I'm to love you completely.
It's all or nothing.
You know this yet you keep half back.
Nothing is finished because you don't love me.
Don't come here anymore.
—A

"High maintenance," Geno mumbled. "And she definitely wants to get in your pants, dude."

His eyebrows wrinkled at the next bit of crumpled paper. Carlos' handwriting this time:

Please let me come back.
I can't live without you.
You're the only one who knows me.
The only one who sees me.
Please.
Please.
—C

This one leaned on Geno's stomach, like being punched in slow motion. *I know you,* he thought, wounded. *I see you. I was born tangled with you. We started as one cell before becoming two.*

His relief was almost smug when he read the reply, written directly below:

No.
—A

"Harsh," he said. He stuffed the notes back in the jeans pocket and threw them into the washer. The ink would run and be rinsed away. The paper would disintegrate to shredded bits in the lint trap. Carlos would get over it.

Until then, Geno would be waiting for him in the Land of Nos, keeping the lights on in the little red henhouse.

KNIFE SKILLS

*I*N HIS LILTING Irish accent, Captain Hook laid down a strict no-alcohol rule for tonight's shindig. Being no dummy, he also set up a bowl for keys and a breathalyzer.

"*Dad,*" Kelly said, mortified but resigned.

"Yes?" he said, standing in his shirt sleeves at the kitchen counter, mixing a gin and tonic. "Geno, we got a lime in the fridge?"

Geno found one. His father liked a vodka tonic in the evenings, and Geno had learned how to score a lime with a paring knife, cutting off a spiral of peel to float among ice cubes.

"Now that makes a drink handsome," Hook said, holding up his garnished glass before taking a long sip. "You got some knife skills, kid."

Geno flipped the knife and caught the handle in his palm, then went back to cubing vegetables. Chris threaded the cubes onto skewers, alternating chicken and beef and shrimp. At the far end of the counter, Mrs. Hook was frosting a two-layered chocolate cake.

"Where you boys headed next fall?" she asked.

"Lewis and Clark," Chris said.

"Oregon?" Above his glass, Captain Hook looked impressed. "You're flying far from the nest."

Chris gave a slow nod but made no other comment. Hook's eyes flicked to Geno.

"Brooklyn College," Geno said.

"Poor man's Harvard," Chris said.

"Beautiful campus, I hear," Hook said. "How about your brother, where's he off to?"

"He got into Parsons but he's going to take a gap year."

"Geno, how's your dad doing?" Mrs. Hook asked.

"Good. Busy. He's in Singapore until Monday."

The police chief raised an eyebrow. "Why isn't the party at your house?"

Geno pointed the knife at him. "Because you have the best breathalyzer in town."

Carrying the mixing bowl to the sink, Mrs. Hook brushed her lips against her husband's broad shoulder. At the same time, Kelly passed by Geno and casually scratched his back. As if they were a couple. He looked around the domestic scene and a contentment drew the walls of his heart in, close and warm, like hands cupped around a flame.

"You'll find joy again," so many people said after Analisa's death. "You'll smile again, feel good again, laugh with friends again. It will happen."

Chris definitely helped make it happen. He was largely responsible for breaking up Geno's agoraphobia, getting him out of the lonely henhouse into other people's homes. Sticking by him through nervous episodes, pushing him to keep participating in life.

"You're allowed to have a good time," he said. "She'd want you to."

The truly good times happened in kitchens, Geno thought. Life was conquered and feted in the triangle of stove, sink and fridge. The room where people came both to cry and celebrate. Here he could be social while keeping a barrier of little tasks between him and the guests. Cooking and prepping occupied his hands and smoothed out his awkward, shy edges.

Guests began to trickle into the Hooks' house and yard. Mrs. Hook lit the grill and a meaty smoke hovered over the smell of the cut lawn and the chlorine haze from the pool. As dusk fell, Captain Hook lit the tiki torches. Three guys brought out guitars, and singing wove with the laughing and splashing. Flames danced in Kelly's eyes and made her perfect skin glow as she and Geno fed each other cake, laughing between chocolate bites. They shared one lounge chair while Chris occupied the other, the besotted Stacey at his feet. He was kind and attentive to her, but a blind man could pick up the *He's just not that into you* vibe. Finally, with a dignified hair flip, Stacey moved on.

Kelly heaved a sigh, threw Geno an apologetic look and then followed her friend, leaving the boys alone.

"Not feeling it?" Geno said, scraping the last bit of cake frosting off his plate.

Chris made a vague noise, half apology, half explanation.

"What about Jenny Steenberg?"

Chris cracked his knuckles. "I don't know."

"She totally digs you. Never understood why you didn't ask her to prom. You could've—"

"Dude, *stop.*" Chris's voice split open on the word.

Fork poised in the air, Geno froze, staring, realizing his friend was practically in tears. Chris seemed to realize it, too, and with a scrape of the chair legs on concrete, he bolted, striding toward a far corner of the wide lawn. Geno set his plate aside and went after him. "Yo. Chris, wait up."

"Just leave me alone."

"Hey. Come on. Talk to me."

With a small groan, Chris leaned on the split-rail fence at the far end of the property. Fireflies lit up the scrub beyond. "Please just fucking leave me alone, G."

"What's wrong?"

"You gotta back off with that shit. Enough already."

"What shit, what did I do?"

Chris squeezed everything. Eyes. Face. Fists. Wringing the answer out of himself. "Look, I don't like any of the girls at school, okay?"

"Okay, I just—"

"I don't like *girls,* G."

The confused moment twinkled with fireflies.

"I don't like girls," Chris said again.

"You're...?" Geno couldn't get his mouth to wrap around the word.

"Gay."

"You?"

"Yeah. Me." Chris crossed his arms, jaw tight and eyes narrowed. "I'm gay. The date I wanted to bring to prom was impossible. Okay? I just... I can't take it anymore. I can't stand this town and this school and this fucking *act* I have to put on for everyone. I can't be me anywhere I go. It's like I want to kill myself sometimes, my life is such a phony crock of shit. Jesus, I can't wait to get the hell out of here. Start somewhere new."

"Dude, I—"

"Don't." Chris held up a palm. "If you're gonna walk away, do it now. I get it if you feel threatened." A snorted, resigned chuckle made his shoulders hitch. "No offense, man, but you're not my type."

Geno blinked a few times, wetting his dry lips. "Nobody knows?"

Chris shook his head.

"Only me?"

"Yeah." A bit of soft laughter. "I always thought if anyone would understand, it would be you."

"Me? Why?"

"Because of Carlos."

The lawn seemed to expand, growing longer, wider, leaving Geno a small speck in the center. "What do you mean?"

"Nothing," Chris said quickly.

"No, not nothing. What?"

Even in the dimness, he could see Chris had gone pale. "Oh fuck, I really put my foot in it now." A hand through his hair, a rough exhale. "Shit. I thought you knew. I mean…"

"Carlos is gay?"

Chris' hands lifted, then fell. "I thought you *knew.*"

"How do you know?"

"Well, I—"

"You've talked to him about it? He told you?"

"No," Chris said. "But I saw him once… Couple weeks ago. I was getting some stuff at Target. And… Oh man, I feel like shit now. *Fuck.*"

"Tell me," Geno said.

Chris's face twisted up with something that looked like shame. "You don't understand. Outing someone is so fucking *uncool.*"

"You saw him with someone?"

Chris groaned. "It was a crowded day, I was parked around the side. Walking back to my car I saw him. Actually…" He gave a weak laugh. "For a second I thought it was *you.* Then I saw the leather jacket. Anyway. They were standing together by the loading dock. They were, you know, making out."

Silence, punctuated by peepers and splashing and laughter.

"Who was it?" Geno said, his voice dry.

"I don't know. No one from around here. He looked like an older guy."

A hand slipped around Geno's chest and squeezed. And he remembered. *Come see me soon. —A*

"I almost wondered if it was that photographer," Chris said. "The one your parents had some kind of trouble with? All those years ago?"

Geno slumped against the fence as the night cracked open and caved in on his head. Realization piling up on realization, edges aligning and corners shifting into place. The clothes. The vain streak. The posturing and the selfies. The female entourage.

The notes.

The letter A.

"What was his name again?"

From far away, Geno heard his voice answer. "Anthony Fox."

I could barely let you go yesterday. —A

"Right," Chris said. "He did the after-school photography program, my sister was in it. But what ended up happening with Carlos?"

I love you so much, I need two of you. —A

"He was in that program for years," Geno said. "Then Anthony took some pictures of him and wanted to enter them in a competition. Carlos was only fourteen, so he needed parental consent. Instead he forged my father's signature on the release form."

"Who forged it? Anthony?"

"No, Carlos signed my father's name."

"Damn, that's a federal offense."

"No shit," Geno said. "Then Anthony won and the exhibit was in the paper. Giant double-spread of my brother in the Sunday *Times* magazine. My parents fucking flipped."

"Were they nude shots?" Chris said, eyes wide.

"No, but still kind of sexualized and weird…"

Your body is so beautiful. —A

"That's fucked up," Chris said. "And it was when your mom was going through chemo, right?"

It was. Adding insult to debilitating injury. His mother had been weak and fragile, and Fox had *upset* her.

"That goddamn Fox was in my henhouse," Geno heard her mutter to his father. And Nathan, usually so cool and implacable, had a look on his face Geno had never seen before. The warm blue eyes hardened to icy slate, two hatchets poised to chop the enemy in the midst.

"Yeah," Geno said, his voice still disembodied from his thoughts. "They yanked him out of the course and it was basically a clusterfuck. They got a restraining order. Anthony's not supposed to have any contact with him. Or vice-versa."

I could barely let you go yesterday. —A

"Look, dude," Chris said. "I didn't mean to plant it in your head it was *him*. It was a total knee-jerk assumption." He crouched down, elbows on knees and hands in his hair. "I feel like ten kinds of crap. I'm sorry. I'm making it all worse."

"It's all right."

"No, it's not. Shit."

Inked words running, rinsed away in the wash. Paper bits in the lint trap.

A for Anthony.

"G, I'm sorry."

"I'm…" Geno couldn't finish, all at once unsure what he was. Because if Carlito, his brother, his twin, his mirror and the other half of his soul… If Carlito was gay, what did that make *him*?

A border dropped onto the topography of Nos. A red dotted line of demarcation defining where Geno could not go.

Why are you going where I can't follow? I can't be one with you there.

Then, from far away, beyond the hills and within the walls of the little red henhouse, Geno heard Analisa speak up.

This is not about you, querido. Just be kind.

It was all she wanted from her boys, she said. More than grades, more than success, she wanted them to be kind. To be good men. Empathetic and compassionate. Aware of the secret battles others were fighting.

Just be kind.

Geno shook his head, hard enough to make Chris blur into two boys, then back into one.

Be kind.

Geno's eyes focused from inward to outward. From him to his friend. "Are you all right?" he asked.

Chris' brows furrowed. "Me? Yeah."

"Literally nobody knows?"

"My sister knows. Just her. My dad wouldn't take it too well."

"Nobody else?"

Chris shook his head. "Well," he said. "This guy I've been secretly seeing. Obviously he knows."

"He from around here?"

"No. And no offense, G, but I'm not going to talk about him. It's already too much tonight."

"I got it. It's cool."

"C'mon, let's head back," Chris said, smiling. "Before they start talking about us."

How It's Supposed to Be

As they walked across the lawn in step, Geno's eyes kept flicking to his friend. Noting the set of his shoulders and the rolling lope of his stride. He was taller than Geno, more built up. He was always working out. For vanity or for protection?

Geno's mind slid puzzle pieces around, twisting and rotating them. Chris was gay. Things that Geno imagined doing with Kelly, Chris did with men. Geno's eyes kept sliding sideways, trying to imagine it. Chris and another guy around the side of Target, arms around each other. Chris pressing his mouth to another boy's mouth.

"Dude, quit *staring* at me," Chris said. "Jesus."

"Sorry. My head's all over the place."

"Yeah, I know. Welcome to my world."

"Here you are," Kelly said, coming toward them, her hand extended. "G, you left your phone on the chaise. It's been lighting up."

Three text bubbles from Carlos were on the display.

Mos.

A few minutes later, **You there?**

And then, **Ping me back.**

"I just need a minute to talk to him," Geno said, and headed toward the side of the house.

Hey, he typed. **Where are you?**

Be kind, he thought.

He waited a long, anxious moment, looking from the phone up to the stars.

Los, he typed. **What's up?**

Carlos replied: *My car won't start. Can you pick me up?*
Where are you? Geno typed.

A longer moment, sharp-edged and sinister, before Carlos answered:
I'm at Anthony's.

Geno closed his eyes. When he opened them, more texts had piled up: *AND DON'T GIVE ME SHIT. I just came to buy some old lenses and stuff he had.*

Geno gathered together all his common sense. All his empathy and compassion and sensibility, and he pulled it on like a jacket. Zipped it tight to his throat.

I won't give you shit, he typed, *but Dad will fucking kill you if he knows you're there.* It was a lame threat. Nathan was on the other side of the earth in Singapore.

He won't know unless you tell him, Carlos texted. *Just come pick me up, OK? Is the party still going on? I want to hang.*

Yeah, everyone's here. Chris and I will come.

No. Just you come.

Why?

Because I want to talk to you about something.

Geno drew a deep breath in and let it out slow. Then typed: *OK. Give me the address.*

17 Lantern Street in Heading.

Be there soon.

As he stuffed the phone in his back pocket, it pinged once more.

Love you, Carlos texted.

Geno stared. Carlito had never said such a thing. Not out loud, anyway. Never in a text. The words popped from the screen, not so much a sentiment as a coded message: *Please love me.*

Love you, Geno typed. His fingers were clumsy, making mistakes and backspacing through the two simple words. *No matter what,* he added. *Dos.*

Good boy, Analisa whispered. *You're the only one around here.*

"Everything okay?" Chris appeared around the corner of the house. Geno looked from the phone to him. Tested the moment and found he trusted it. "You were right. He's at Anthony's house."

"Fuck," Chris said. "Oh boy. What's going on?"

"He wants me to come get him. Alone. Says he needs to talk to me." Geno turned the phone. "He said I love you. He… Dude, he's never said that."

Chris looked, chewing his bottom lip. "Think he's trying to tell you something?"

"Yeah. I know this sounds weird, but I can kind of feel it."

"Man, everything about tonight feels weird." Chris's eyes met Geno's and held on. "But maybe this is how it's supposed to be."

"Yeah."

"C'mon, I'll walk you out."

A big show in the adult-occupied kitchen as Geno blew the breathalyzer. Hoots and laughter as Captain Hook demanded explanation for the .009 reading.

"Maybe it was the red wine vinegar," Mrs. Hook said, looking genuinely concerned.

"Or a swig of mouthwash," the chief said. "Plan on kissing someone tonight, Mr. Caan?"

"*Dad,*" Kelly cried.

As he handed over the key fob, Captain Hook ruffled the top of Geno's head. His hand rested warm and heavy a moment on Geno's back. "Drive safe," he said.

Tonight feels weird, Geno thought. *But maybe this is how it's supposed to be.*

Chris walked him out to the car, carrying his backpack. "You still want me to sleep over tonight?"

"Yeah, why wouldn't I?"

Chris shrugged, then handed the pack over. "My wallet's in there so lock up if you leave it in the car."

"Sure."

The pack was exchanged as if it were something much more valuable. The weight of it settled in Geno's hands and he felt, for the first time in a long time, a sense of purpose. A responsibility. A job. His mind couldn't wrap around Chris' sexuality, but it hooked into Chris' pain like Velcro.

"I'll do whatever you want," he said slowly. "I don't…get it. But it's not something for me to get." He hefted the backpack a few times, hoping Chris understood.

Chris looked away, his lips rolled in, nodding a little.

"What I *do* get is putting on an act when you really feel like jumping off a bridge," Geno said. "So this is safe with me, okay? You want it hid, it's hid. You want to come out, I'll be there."

I'll be with you. You and I will be We.

Us.

Nos.

A different Nos.

"Thanks," Chris said. "Keeping a secret, it's exhausting."

"I know."

"Fucking hell," Chris said, his voice shaking. "I'm so tired."

"I know," Geno said. "Me too. We can talk more about it later. Or not. Whatever you want."

He took a step just as Chris did. Each reached an arm around the other, gave a pull in, landing a fist on the shoulder blade.

You've hugged before, Geno thought, conscious of the press of Chris' chest against his. *You hugged before tonight, and it wasn't a thing. It's not a thing now.*

Except it was. Kind of. And it filled Geno with enough shame to make him flatten his fisted hand and rub a circle on Chris' back.

"I'll be back in a few," he said.

He wouldn't.

The next time he saw Chris was in the hospital.

THE GAME

*G*ENO DROVE TO Heading, the car window rolled down and the soft summery air blowing over him. Eagles singing "Take it Easy." Thinking about the exhaustion of secrets. Slippery secrets that didn't like holding still in his mind, let alone being dressed in words. The raw open knife wound of his mother's death. The persistent, worry rash that was his father's workaholic distraction. The black hole vacuum where once his brother's stars shone.

Maybe all that would end tonight.

At 11:14, he pulled up to the curb outside 17 Lantern Street and texted Carlito he was there.

On the radio, the Eagles "Take it Easy" ended and Heart's "Barracuda" began.

By 11:20 he was getting annoyed. He texted his brother again. **Dude, you coming?**

Carlito replied, **Come inside.**

Geno sucked his teeth and typed, **I'm not in the mood to be social. I just need you to help carry some shit, okay?**

Exhaling, eyes rolling, Geno turned off the engine, got out of the car and headed up the walkway.

His memory of that night would always be fractured, shards and slivers scattered across his mind like broken glass. Some were crystal clear and sharp. Others blurred and scratched. Some had turned to obsidian, blacked-out and useless.

He remembered whistling "Barracuda" as he went up the walkway. His shoe kicked a pebble that bounced and skipped ahead of him on the flagstone path.

He remembered ringing the bell and the two-tone chime from deep within the belly of the house.

He remembered the scent in the front hall. Like the place had just been cleaned. Lemon and pine. Plus a faint, sweet smell curling around the air, like cookies in the oven.

"Carlito's downstairs," Anthony Fox said. "Want a drink?"

Geno remembered staring a moment at the man, annoyed by his easy use of Carlito, a family endearment. It suggested intimacy he had no right to.

Fox was in his early forties. A friendly, normal-looking guy, but the possibility he'd been making out with Carlos behind Target made a wary suspicion twist in Geno's stomach. A prejudice already rooted in unpleasant memories from the time his mother was ill.

That goddamn Fox was in my henhouse.

"Get you a beer?" Anthony said, looking off to the kitchen a moment. Geno remembered his stare intensifying at Anthony's ear. It looked inside-out. Squashed and deformed and weird.

Anthony caught him looking and smiled. "Nice, huh?" he said, touching it. "Souvenir from my wrestling days. They call it cauliflower ear."

"Oh."

"Get you a beer?"

"I'm driving," Geno said pointedly.

"How about a Coke?"

"Sure," Geno said, to be polite. To be *kind.*

"Go downstairs, I'll bring you one."

Geno remembered the smell of the downstairs TV room was thick and hoppy, like someone had thrown a keg party recently. Couch and recliners were arranged before a big flat screen TV. At the far side of the room, Carlito and two other men were standing around a pool table. Not playing. They were looking at black-and-white photographs spread across the green felt. Various shots from around Manhattan.

Anthony came down and gave Geno a Coke.

Geno remembered the can was opened. He thought nothing of it at the time. If only he had. But why would he?

If only he'd paid more attention to the curl of distrust in his gut.

Paid more attention to the dreadful conviction when Anthony leaned to look at a photograph and slid his hand along the back of Carlito's neck.

The way the other men stared as he drank the Coke, then exchanged glances.

The way Carlito wouldn't meet his eyes. Wouldn't acknowledge Geno's repeated throat-clearing and the mental nudges of, *Can we go now? Come on. Let's go.*

But by then it was too late. The walls of the room were growing blurry. The blacks and whites of the pictures morphing into grey then popping with color. Geno's fingers stroked the green felt. Soft. It tickled. Everything was giggling. Geno's eyes stared at Anthony's ear, fascinated with its weirdness.

"What's happening?" he remembered saying, tongue thick and sweet in his mouth. The cookie-laden air from upstairs had come down to play. It filled his lungs. He was baking.

"You better lie down, okay?" Anthony said, like a 45 record slowed down to 33.

"Don't hurt him," Carlito said, playing at 78.

"Don't worry, he'll love it," Anthony said. "Won't you, baby boy?"

His hands settled on Geno's shoulders, like two warm loaves of bread.

With butter, Geno thought. Butter and pickle always made him laugh.

Anthony's ear was pickled.

Cauliflower pickle, Geno thought.

Piccadilly clutter butter.

"Fluffernutter," he said, and laughed. Everyone joined in. Except Carlos, who stared down at the grassy green pool table. Geno's laughing brain looked back as Anthony led him toward a room, but Carlos turned away.

The walls of Geno's mind were closing in, pressing him small and tight, folding him up into a letter. He laughed and laughed, thinking it was a game and Carlito was missing out on the fun.

He was tingling and burning. His skin so soft and warm. It *gave* under Anthony's hands, like warm, buttered bread dough.

"Wait," he said, thinking so much of his skin shouldn't be showing. Not in this place. Not with this man.

"It'll be fine," Anthony said, unbuttoning Geno's shorts. "You'll do great. We're just going to play."

"Is it a game?"

"Yeah. It's fun. You'll be good at it."

"I don't think I…"

"Shh," Anthony said. "Let me do the thinking, baby boy."

Geno's brain shrugged.

The last clear thing he remembered was Anthony saying, "You'll love it."

He was so high. So up, up, up, high in a buttery, sugary haze.

Then he was down.

A bunch of mixed up, mashed up and fucked up things happened.

Things were on him and in him. In his mouth and against his back and shoved deep inside.

His mind scattered like a startled flock of birds.

He didn't love this.

It wasn't a game and it wasn't fun, but his fractured mind couldn't wrap around what was happening. It was a dream. It had to be a bad dream. He'd wake up soon.

Through the shapeless hours of the night, the game went on. Different players came on and off the field, in and out of the room. In and out of Geno. Whatever was in the Coke wore off, then Geno started to fight. He lashed out and hit whatever he could. He was hit back. Hard. The sides of his head clanging back and forth like a bell.

"Don't fucking hit his *face*," Fox yelled. "Jesus Christ, what are you thinking? Give him another shot, you moron."

A sharp stab in Geno's leg and he went all blurry and giggling again, the rules of the game sliding and slipping around his mind like a wet bar of soap.

"Smile for me, baby boy," Fox said, his hand stroking up and down Geno's toasty skin, flicking off grains of sugar. "That's it."

It was the game. Men came and went and played until time turned inside-out. Sugar turned to salt, running wet and stinging from Geno's eyes into his mouth. Now his hands were cuffed to the bed and the panic rose up in the back of his throat. He fought harder. Yelled and yanked at his wrists, cried for help, screamed his lungs apart.

No help came, only more men.

From far away he heard Carlos yelling. "Let him go. I did what you wanted, now let him go. You *promised…*"

His voice was full of rage. Then it was full of pain. When they dragged him into the bedroom, Carlos was crying. "You promised. You promised."

He was cuffed to the leg of Geno's bed and Anthony started playing with him. Another man held Geno's head, making him watch. Another man took pictures.

Geno kicked and bucked in his prison bed, trying to hide his face, twisting and writhing against the rules of the game.

Then it was Geno's turn, but nobody made his brother watch.

Lying on the floor, his hands still restrained, Carlos turned his head away.

Geno begged his brother.

He babbled and bawled like a baby, imploring his twin to look at him.

Carlos stared off at nothing. As if none of this were happening.

Forty-four hours, the Caan twins were held captive at Anthony Fox's house.

It never stopped happening.

THE LAND OF NOS

*N*OW THE LAND of Nos was under attack. A foreign power had invaded, laid siege to the stars and tore apart the sacred bonds of Two.

In the face of such war machines, the human spirit can only take so much before it breaks.

Or adapts.

Survival depends on resiliency while escape relies on common sense.

You're the only one around here with a lick of common sense, Analisa said to one of her twin sons.

Common must become extraordinary to survive what cannot be understood.

Geno was still common and still trying to understand when Anthony was on him for the second time.

Or maybe the third.

With so many men, and so many times, it was hard to keep track.

He was so tired. He wobbled and flopped when Anthony yanked him up on his knees. Geno's arms stretched out long, slack and weak, no longer able to pull against the cuffs. He had no fight left in him. His leg muscles ached and buckled, and he slumped this way and that.

Anthony held the deadweight easily, pulling Geno back against him. He was so strong. So much better at this game.

"Well, look what we got here," he said. His arm curved around Geno's waist. "Someone's enjoying this."

Geno made a noise like "Nuh." Garbled and unintelligible, like his tongue was too big.

"Sure you are," Anthony said, laughing, his breath warm on Geno's shoulder. "Can't have one twin be gay without the other."

"Nuh…"

"Just give into it. It's okay to want it. I can feel how bad you want it."

As his penis stiffened into Anthony's grip, Geno started crying.

"It's okay, baby. Don't feel bad. Say you want it."

"Nuh."

"Say it." Anthony's voice grew harder. He had one hand wrapped around Geno's erection while the other slid into Geno's hair. "Say it, baby boy."

Geno yelped like a frightened puppy as his head was yanked back.

"Say it or I won't stop until you're dead. Say it or you'll never get out of here alive."

"Nuh."

"You'll say it and then you're going to come in my hand, baby boy. Understand? You'll say it and then you'll show it."

"Nuh."

"Oh yeah, you will. They all do for me. All my baby boys are loyal to me. Including your brother. He brought you here. I said I wanted you and he brought you to me. I had to wait until Daddy was away until I could get my present."

Geno moaned like one who wished he were dead.

"Now show me what a good boy you are. Say you want it." His hand fisted tighter in Geno's hair. "Say it."

"I…"

"Say it, you little bitch. Before I fuck you in two."

"I…wan it."

"Say it."

"I wan it," Geno said, sobbing.

"Yeah," Anthony said. "You do. You want it so bad. You're a whore just like your brother. Say you like it."

Geno said it.

"Now say you love me, baby boy."

Geno said that, too.

"Tell me to fuck you."

Geno said it all. He said everything Anthony told him to say. He let his mouth go on without him.

When Anthony told him to come, Geno let his body go on without him, and he came.

When he came, he became extraordinary.

When Anthony scooped up semen and rubbed it on Geno's face, the last tattered shreds of his mind looked around and became aware of the impossibility of the situation.

He stopped trying to understand.

He started trying to escape.

This is not happening to me.

It's happening to someone else.

Anthony was done. He won the game again. He pulled out and left, the door clicking shut, leaving Geno alone. Carlos was gone. The other twin bed was empty, a single cuff still clasped to the head rail.

Lying face down in the soiled sheets, Geno kept plotting his escape.

Go away. Go away from this place. This thing happening will not stop happening so you must leave it.

It must happen to someone else. Not you.

I am not here. I am not me. This is all happening to someone else.

The room had a single transom window, high in the wall. If Geno tilted his wrist, he could see it reflected in the shiny surface of the handcuff. It was dark outside. He couldn't see the stars, but he caught a slice of the moon, a metallic crescent marred by the small keyhole.

The portal.

The door.

Geno made himself small.

He crawled through the keyhole, into the moon and toward the stars.

He went into Nos. The shared place of Two.

Mos faced Los and declared, *You are not welcome here. Not anymore. You are dead to me.*

Like a conqueror, Mos planted his flag in what had been his brother's part of the land.

I am Mos. The one with sense.

From this mirror-reflection vantage point, he looked over at his bodily self, cuffed in the twin bed. He observed neutrally and felt nothing. He had nothing to feel. It wasn't happening to him.

The new universe and its rules swayed on wobbly legs, confused who was who and uncertain this was going to work.

This is how it is, Mos said firmly. *I am Mos. I only watch the things that happen to Geno. This is my job as ruler of Nos.*

Mos was tired. Such secrets were exhausting to carry. It was good to finally rest. He drifted in and out of consciousness, always waking on the other side of Nos, where nothing felt.

It's happening to him. Not me.

I just watch.

Sometimes Mos noticed pain when things happened, but he dismissed it as not his.

Sometimes he sensed fear, but he quickly learned to be sensible about it.

It's unfortunate, he thought. *But it's not happening to me.*

DEADWEIGHT

*S*OMETHING NEW WAS happening.

Mos watched, dispassionately, as a man burst into the room, wielding a gun. Like a scientific researcher, Mos made a careful note on a clipboard.

Someone is here. He seems different than the others.

From across the divide came an explosion. The stars of Nos put down their swords, turned their heads toward the sound.

Another explosion. Instead of being blown back, Mos was pulled in, through the stars, back to Geno. He crashed into his body and was immediately sucked into an airless vacuum of agony. Pain ripped his young bones apart while an impossible, immeasurable weight fell on his back.

He's on my back, he's on me and in me, on my back, get him off me, get him out of me…

Deadweight smashed him into the earth, crushing his ribs around his heart and lungs. Sending a dirty spike of pain through his backside and up his spine.

Get out get out get out get out get out.

His body and brain screamed for air as the room beyond filled with a crackling, shouting energy.

"You goddamn son of a *bitch*," someone cried.

Another voice, one that made Geno's ears prick up, yelled, "Jesus fucking *Christ*…"

The weight lifted. It took a moment for Geno's lungs to realize it. Then he sucked in air, choking and coughing on the ragged exhale.

It is quite difficult to breathe, Mos thought.

"I got you," the man with the familiar voice said, down on his knees at Geno's side. "Geno. Son, look at me."

How interesting, Mos observed. *Our friend Captain Hook is here.*

"It's over," the police chief said. His hands cradled Geno's face. "I got you. We're getting you out of here, okay? Look at me. We'll get these things off you and get you out of here, I promise. Look at me. I won't let you go."

Geno's body bucked and heaved. Hook held his head as the past forty-four hours came up and over and onto the floor.

"That's it," Captain Hook said. "Let it go. Let it out. It's all right." He let go long enough to pull off his jacket and drape it over Geno's body. "We'll get you out of here. Hang on, buddy. I won't leave." He turned his head and his voice raised into authority. "Bukowski, ETA on the ambulance?"

"Chief, we need you in here," someone yelled from the other side of the wall.

"Where's EMS?" Hook called back.

"Just turned down Lantern."

"Bukowski, I want a cuff key or a bolt cutter in here *now.*"

Many interesting things are happening, Mos thought.

"Chief, they need you," another voice said, closer. "He's in the bathroom."

"Get those fucking things off," Hook said, rocking back on his heels. A rattle and a crunch and Geno's hands dropped down from the head rail, his shoulders howling in relief.

"Easy, bud," Hook said. "EMS is here now, they're going to take care of you. I'll be right back."

The paramedics gently rolled Geno onto his side. He cried and cried. A silent weep. Air moved through his throat, but no sound emerged. His voice was gone.

Mos turned his head and retreated far into Nos, not watching or listening anymore. The world went deaf, dumb and blind for a long time, only re-emerging when Geno was carefully moved onto a gurney. Captain Hook held his hand as he was wheeled out, then climbed into the ambulance with him.

"Dad," Geno said, but no sound came out. His mouth must have made a recognizable shape because Hook put a rough palm on his head.

"We'll get him," Hook said. "He's in the air right now but we're getting in touch with his office, they'll send someone to the airport to bring him straight to the hospital. I promise. He'll be with you real soon."

Geno's mouth shaped another silent name.

He's dead to us, Mos said sternly.

A ripple of something crossed the captain's face. "Shh. Lie still and rest. It's all over."

We are leaving now, Mos thought, as the ambulance pulled forward, making the gurney vibrate.

This is good.

Mos held his clipboard tight and went along with Geno. It was his job.

Someone has to be in charge. I am Mos, rhymes with dos, and I'm in command here. I have the strength of two now. I'm the one with the common sense in this family.

Things happen to Geno.

I only watch.

He felt nothing but conviction he was right. This was how it had to be. He knew no other way to survive what couldn't be understood, other than to have it happen to someone else.

What Else We Found

The New Jersey Star-Ledger

July 7, 2007

"MISSING TEENS FOUND, ONE DEAD AND ONE ALIVE, IN CHILD PORNOGRAPHY RING BUST"

Two missing Stockton teens were found at a residence in Heading last night. One was being held captive in the basement of the house. The other was found dead in a bathroom, police said.

Two men were arrested, a third fled and a fourth was shot dead by police.

Utility worker Milton Johns, 27, of Morristown, and Carl Ferri, 35, a swimming pool installer from Summit, were found at 17 Lantern Drive, sexually assaulting one of the teens. The men face felony charges including sexual assault, sexual exploitation of a child, dangerous crime against a minor, and possession of child pornography.

FBI and U.S. Marshals are currently searching for a third suspect, Anthony Fox, the homeowner, who fled the scene. A fourth suspect, Ty Pelletier, 33, a contractor from Summit, was shot dead by police.

A search for two missing Stockton brothers first led police to Lantern Drive Sunday afternoon. The boys had been missing since Saturday night, last seen at a party at a classmate's home.

"We knew one of the boys had been at Fox's house Saturday night," said Stockton Police Capt. Daniel Hook. "He sent a text message to his brother saying his car wouldn't start and he needed to be picked up. The brother left the party and that was the last time anyone saw him."

Police said they questioned Fox Sunday afternoon. He cooperated and provided an alibi.

"We had no cause to search the house at that time," Hook said.

Sunday night, cash withdrawals from one of the missing teen's ATM cards gave police a new lead. Video surveillance showed a license plate. Monday, police traced the plate number to a vehicle parked at the Fox residence.

"I can't describe what else we found in that basement," Hook said. "The worst kind of sexual abuse imaginable."

Police said the FBI shut down more than two dozen child pornography websites directly connected to what they found at the property. They also seized thousands of pictures and hundreds of videos connected to an international pornography ring that was discovered by Austrian authorities in February. Austria's Federal Criminal Investigations Bureau is lending their full support to the FBI.

Fox, a professional photographer who once worked at Franklin Middle School, fled as police arrived, officials said. His car was later found in a commuter lot in Morris Plains. His smashed cell phone and wallet were left inside.

U.S. Marshals in New Jersey, New York and Pennsylvania are working together with the FBI to locate Fox. He is described as six-foot, two-inches tall and 170 pounds. He has greying brown hair and blue eyes. His left ear is disfigured and misshapen, known as a "cauliflower ear."

Anyone with information on the whereabouts of Fox is encouraged to contact the U. S. Marshals Service or the FBI. Callers can remain anonymous.

LIFE ADVICE FROM A WHORE

*T*HE LINE TO the deli counter snaked along one wall, nearly to the door. Those who had ordered and paid clustered in a small scrum by the display of bagged chips, keeping an ear peeled for their number and an eye out for projectiles. Here, your sandwich was literally thrown over the counter, so you had to be ready.

One of the Puerto Rican cooks bellowed, "Twenty-four, turkey club." An oblong in white paper sailed into the crowd. Its owner was reading a newspaper and nearly missed the catch. He fumbled, but Javier Landes caught it up in time.

"Thanks, bro," the guy said to Javier. "Want the paper while you're waiting?"

Jav, whose number was in the forties, took it. The cover of the none-too-subtle *NY Post* demanded attention in three-inch letters:

MODERN MENGELE.

Below, in only slightly quieter type: *PORN RINGLEADER - PIMP GROOMED AND TARGETED TWINS. MANHUNT CONTINUES.*

> *The leader of a child prostitution ring is still at large, despite a manhunt by U.S. Marshals in four states and the FBI.*
> *Anthony Fox, 32, fled his house in Heading Monday when police arrived to investigate two missing brothers from Stockton. The brothers were discovered at the scene, one dead, the other held captive in the basement.*
> *Police arrested two men at the house, Milton Johns, 27, and Carl Ferri, 35, now being charged with multiple felonies. A third suspect, Ty Pelletier, 33, was shot dead by police. The FBI found*

evidence of child prostitution and seized pictures, video, comput-
ers and flash drives, which police said fetishized twins and, in
some instances, triplets.
Police said the material has been linked to a larger, internation-
al child porn ring busted by Austrian authorities earlier in the
year…

Jav grimaced at the sordid details, the newsprint slimy in his hands. A hor-
rific story in general, yet his eyes kept sliding back to one word in particular.

Prostitution.

The word was a vocal workout. Pushing the klutzy double-consonant "pr"
took effort. The "sti" and "tu" blocked the way like bouncers, trying to get you
to stutter or trip. The "shun" sound was an apt ending. Soft, almost genteel, yet
loaded with judgment and disdain for the world's oldest profession. The low-
lifes shunned from decent society.

Javier Landes would know. He was in the business.

Prostitute, he thought, his mind hefting the syllables like dumbbells.

Hustler. Gigolo. Rent boy.

Or, as he preferred to call it, escort. A high-end, highly paid, highly sought-af-
ter escort who did business in extremely decent society and made a boatload
of money.

Pimp.

Now that word was ugly. Swollen and unproductive. Like pump, but no air
or water for your trouble. A pimple that wouldn't pop. Jav never had a pimp.
He'd been in control of his own destiny since he started escorting at age twenty-one.

As his eyes skimmed over the newspaper again, his stomach curled in a nauseous realization he was a there-but-for-the-grace-of-God escort. He was lucky
to have such control. Lucky he could count up dates with sketchy clients on one
hand. Lucky he could be picky about the clients he chose and had the mature
judgment and strength to diffuse or abandon a bad situation.

But what if he didn't have that luck? What if, after being thrown out of his
home at seventeen, he bounced off the dirty sidewalks of Queens, straight into
the hands of a modern Mengele?

Such retroactive, hypothetically dire scenarios weighed heavy on his mind
these days. He had a nephew in his care. The only son of Jav's late sister, Naroba.
If Jav hadn't been around to take guardianship of Ari when Naroba died, who
the hell knew what might've become of him? Jav's overactive imagination had

zero trouble what-if-ing worst possible scenarios. Especially since he adored his nephew. He freaking *loved* that kid, his one and only blood relative. His sister-son. A magnificent eighteen-year-old boy on the cusp of manhood. Ari was no sheltered innocent, but he looked to Jav for direction. And now he knew what Jav did for a primary living:

"Don't tell me what I know and want, Jav. I don't take life advice from a whore."

Whore. Another word that took effort to eject from your mouth. One Jav never heard applied to him personally. Certainly not one he expected coming from his nephew. Ari went pale and apologized, genuinely contrite. Jav brushed the outburst off as impulsive passion in the heat of the moment.

It was actually kind of funny now.

Yet the word hung around. It went along on Jav's next date, tucked in his heart like a suit's pocket square. Glaring at him when he slid the envelope with the evening's earnings beside it.

You whore.

The word never bothered him before. Now it made him flinch. Not with shame, but with dread. He was forty-five years old. Late to the party already.

You're nearly halfway through your life, he thought. *What are you doing?*

You're worth more.

His friend Alex had thrown the remark out in passing. *You're worth more.* Like a spot of spilled Crazy Glue, it stuck in Jav's mind and he couldn't pick or peel it off.

Worth.

You have worth.

You have more value *than this.*

He tossed the newspaper onto an empty table, unable to read what a modern Mengele had done.

The counter man called: "Forty-five, roast beef sandwich."

That's me all right, Jav thought.

He took a step and deftly caught his lunch.

THE KVATER

*M*OS HOVERED IN a corner of the hospital room, quiet and invisible. Much had happened and much needed to be done. Observations to make. Notes to take. Experiences to keep separated. Feelings not to feel.

Nathan Caan was dead. Every time Geno went to sleep, he forgot. He awoke and learned the news all over again. Sleep to forget. Wake to remember. It took a long time for his father's death to put down roots in the rocky soil of Geno's short-term memory. It made so little sense. A man receiving shocking news and keeling over worked fine in the movies and on TV. The reality was much harder to accept.

The reality was Nathan's heart broke. First tested by a fourteen-hour flight with radio silence, while the fate of his missing boys wound like a snake around his aorta. He landed to find the twins were found, but *found* was a deceitful classification. *Found* was tragedy cloaked in optimism and relief.

The police found Carlos dead, hung from the shower head in the basement bathroom. They found Geno still cuffed in the bedroom, a two-hundred-and-sixty-pound man fucking him. That guy was dead now. Dispatched from the world by Captain Hook.

Found kept racking up points. Cops searched the Caan house. They found clues in Carlos' dresser that expanded the story. Pictures. More love notes from Fox. Letters documenting love's turn to psychological abuse and blackmail. They found out Fox was one nest in an underground hive. He had dozens of baby boys, trapped in honey-slick cells, buzzing for nobody to hear.

The police put the pieces together and found out what Carlos was willing to do for love. He posed for the pictures. He let his image be sold, then his body. He kept the secrets. He waited until Nathan was away and then offered up Geno as a gift. All for love.

Then *found* had the last laugh. Because Fox was on the run. And they couldn't *find* him.

Nathan's heart broke at Geno's bedside. His wellspring sprang, uncoiled and fell to the floor limp and defeated. He was raced into surgery, where he flatlined. Doctors brought him back, but only for a minute, then the line went flat again.

And he died.

It will be addressed later, Mos thought, carelessly throwing Nathan on the scrapheap of Geno's life. What was one more tragic scene in this story? You piled pain on top of pain and eventually it plateaued. The only thing to do was not care. When it became clear Geno wasn't going to die anytime soon, it became clearer never living again was the only way to survive.

Geno slept and woke briefly, then slept again. On one side of the bed stood Vern Kastelhoff, Nathan's best friend and lawyer. Now he was Geno's lawyer.

Zoë Caan-Douglas, Nathan's daughter from his first marriage, sat on the other side. She was nineteen years older than Geno. Her relationship with Nathan's second family was somewhat strained. Geno assumed because Analisa was the other woman, but he wasn't sure. He didn't know Zoë that well.

Did anybody really know anyone well?

While Geno was in emergency surgery at Overlook Medical Center, Vern made a dozen calls, looking for the best colorectal specialist in the tri-state area. Everyone pointed to Miranda Bloom at Mount Sinai. Once Geno was stabilized, he was air-lifted to Manhattan. He slept through the helicopter ride. He slept through much of the first week after his rescue.

He woke from drugged slumber, broken and battered and confused. Nurses touched him gently and labeled his pain. His wrists chafed raw, partially flayed from where he yanked against the handcuffs. A sprained jaw and a torn rotator cuff. Multiple muscles in his back pulled and wrenched and strained. His voice reduced to less than a whisper because he screamed enough to make his vocal cords give up. The doctors said he just needed to rest them. It was temporary, as was the transverse colostomy, which stopped all fecal matter before it could reach his descending colon and rerouted it to a bag outside his body. It would only be necessary a few weeks, the doctors assured him. Enough time to give the injured anal tissue time to heal.

They really did a number on him, Mos thought, rather unprofessionally.

Anal tissue might recover from that kind of thing, but could a man?

Geno didn't know.

Carlos might have known.

But Carlos was dead.

It's of no importance, Mos wrote. *He was dead to us long ago.*

Then Geno remembered Nathan was dead, too. Mos watched as Geno wept into his hands, falling into smaller and smaller pieces. Vern put his arms around Geno, which was a mistake. Vern was a big, strong man. He smelled of aftershave and pipe smoke. Masculine scents that only made Geno remember things. He shied from Vern's arms, twisted out of the embrace. Then he felt terrible and cried harder.

Feeling is illegal in Nos for a reason, Mos thought.

A nurse put morphine in Geno's IV. The lights in the room dimmed.

"I'll be right here," Vern said. He sank wearily in a chair next to the bed, loosening his tie. "You rest now. I'll take care of everything."

Geno put his hand against one of the flat bars of the bed rail. Vern put his palm against it, the cool, smooth metal keeping their skin separated.

"I won't let anyone near," Vern said. "No one will touch you while you sleep."

Geno closed his eyes and let Vern's voice carry him away. Vern was the kvater at Geno's bris. It was the kvater's job to take the baby from his mother's arms and carry him to the mohel. Then carry him back to his mother.

We don't want him to carry us, Mos thought. *We don't want his arms now. They feel like the things we're not supposed to feel.*

Geno opened his eyes.

"Right here," Vern said. "You're safe with me." He sniffed once and his jaw trembled.

Poor Vern.

Geno could count on one hand the number of times he saw Vern in casual clothes, and each time, Vern looked weird. He belonged in business attire. He wore expensive, classy suits and pocket squares. In the hospital room, he took off his jacket and rolled up his shirtsleeves, but still looked sharp and shrewd with his suspenders and Rolex watch. His iron-grey hair all combed back from his face.

Good old Vern.

"If you're ever in jail," Nathan said to his boys. "Call Vern first. *Then* call me."

Now Geno only had Vern to call.

We are the only ones left.

The stars of Nos became one star. Its boundaries loosened, threatening to set Mos adrift toward the border of Geno. Go back inside him, where things felt.

Mos stayed far back from the edge, regarding the regrettable situation and feeling nothing.

It's unfortunate, but this is how it is.

DUMB OR GREEDY

"**I**'M DETECTIVE MACKIN," a woman at his bedside said. "I understand it's difficult for you to speak, but it's important I ask you some questions."

"Do you think you can write answers?" Captain Hook said. He stood at the other side of the bed, holding a pad and pen.

Geno had a few questions of his own. "Who find me?" he wrote in a sloppy curve. "How find me?"

Hook pulled up a chair and sat so he was at eye level. "Chris Mudry knew where you were headed, so we went to Fox's house to question him. He said your brother came by to buy some photography equipment. He showed us the check Carlos wrote and said the whole exchange happened in the garage. Said Carlos never came into the house and when he went to leave, his car wouldn't start. You came and got him and that was the last he saw of either of you. Said he spent the rest of the night with a friend, gave us a name and address to confirm."

"Carlos's car was parked at the curb," Mackin said. "Police couldn't start it. Your car wasn't there. It all checked out. We had no probable cause for a search warrant. No reason to think anything was off."

"We found your car parked at the Short Hills Mall," Hook said. "Stripped down to floor mats. Not a clue left. We thought the trail was dead, but then Chris Mudry called me. His bank's fraud department contacted him about suspicious charges on his credit card. He remembered you'd taken his backpack and his wallet was in it."

"A lot of cases are cracked because a criminal was dumb or greedy," Mackin said. "Or both. Whoever ditched your car took Chris's wallet. Charged five hundred dollars worth of booze at a liquor store a block from Fox's house.

Surveillance cameras in the strip mall got him on film. Then we had a plate number. The rest was legwork."

"I'm just sorry it took two days," Hook said, curling a hand around Geno's fingers. "Geno, I'm so sorry."

Geno turned his head and threw up between the bars of the bed rail. He spiked a fever and the questions had to wait. An infection right now could kill him.

He wished it would.

The days fell into a pattern. Geno ate a little, slept a lot and answered questions. Three or four times a day he rolled over for whichever doctor or nurse wanted to take a look up his ass. Everybody was respectful and compassionate. Still, every exam made him wish he were dead.

His half-sister Zoë came occasionally. Vern was there constantly.

And of course, Mos watched. It was his job.

Dr. Bloom, the surgeon who operated on Geno, came every day. So did a gastroenterologist. And a cadre of nurses whose faces and names started to fall into predictable shifts.

"You're one lucky kid," a male nurse said, taking vitals one morning.

Geno hit him.

It was a feeble swipe, the back of Geno's hand making a weak thud on the nurse's chest. Apologies were made, but after that day, Geno only had female nurses, and nobody called him lucky again.

One day Captain Hook brought Chris Mudry with him. The chief beamed as Chris approached the bed. As if Chris were a *present*.

Geno didn't make eye contact with his friend. He bit his lip hard as he and Chris clasped right hands. He leaned forward a bit to accept the fist tap on his shoulder blade, then disengaged quickly.

Captain Hook slipped away to give them privacy. Silence squeezed the room in an awkward fist as Mos watched Chris take in the healing raw circles at Geno's wrists. The IV with antibiotics fighting a persistent Chlamydia strain from one of his attackers. The feeding tube because he was struggling with cyclical vomiting and couldn't keep anything down. The colostomy bag to handle all the unpleasant output.

"Dude, I don't know what to say," Chris said.

"Don't say anything." Geno's broken voice was gaining strength, although it still slid into a rasp when he was tired or upset.

"I'm so sorry."

"Don't. Say. Anything." Geno measured out the words like medicine. "You came, you saw the freak show, you know what happened to me. You can go now."

Chris stayed still, breathing slow through his nose. "Kelly really wants to see you."

"No," Geno said.

"She's crazy worried about you and she—"

"I don't want anyone to see me like this. Least of all her." Geno's hand reached and closed around the front of Chris' shirt. "Don't you fucking tell anyone what you saw here today."

"Jesus, G, I wouldn't—"

"I swear to God, I'll rip your tongue out if you say anything."

Chris reached up, ostensibly to work Geno's fist off his shirt. Geno yanked his hand away first. "Go," he said. "Just fucking go and leave me alone."

Chris' mouth opened and shut a few times. "G," he said, his voice filled with broken glass. "I'm so fucking sorry. It's killing me. I should've gone with you."

"Why? So you could've gotten the shit fucked out of you too? At least you would've enjoyed it."

The color drained out of Chris' face and his mouth pressed into a tight line. His eyes misted and something within Geno unfolded in delight, pleased someone else was hurting.

"I suppose you want the details," he said, relishing the feel of a knife handle as he twisted it. "I'd tell you, but you might be jealous. Hope you didn't come here with any ideas about me coming over to the dark side. I'm not your type, remember?"

"Dude, stop," Chris said. His hands were shaking.

"Why don't you get out of here? Seeing your faggot face isn't making me feel any better. In fact, it's making me sick. Should've been you in that house."

"G, what are you—?"

"Just leave me alone. Go blow your boyfriend or whatever it is you do to each other. Bunch of sick fucks."

Chris stood still. His lips parted but nothing came out.

"What part of 'leave me alone' do you not understand?" Geno yelled over his frayed vocal cords. "Leave? That's easy. You get the fuck out of here."

The last words were barely a whisper, so Geno threw an emesis basin to drive the point home.

Chris was crying as he left.

Mos stayed. It was his job.

A DISTINCTIVE SCAR

*M*OS LISTENED CAREFULLY as doctors and police came and went. He was incredibly busy sorting information into bins. Things Geno didn't want to know. Things he wanted to know. Things he might want to know later but couldn't handle right now.

So much to process. Dr. Bloom talked and talked, dropping words like anal fissure, perineal tear, stoma, collection apparatus and rehabilitation protocol. Mos heard HIV mentioned, followed by, thank God, negative. The chlamydia was stubborn, requiring a host of antibiotic names. Then the really magic words: morphine, Vicodin, Percocet, fentanyl. Mos wanted them all for Geno. As much as Geno wanted. Anything and everything to make it go away.

Mackin and other police dropped words like perp and alleged and leads. They talked about swabs, evidence, blood, semen, saliva, fingerprints. And pictures.

Amazing how many pictures could be taken in forty-four hours. No way of knowing how many were right-clicked and saved before the FBI shut the websites down. No way to determine how many of those shots were posted elsewhere. Or emailed. Or texted.

Somewhere, someone was hunched over a screen or device, jerking off to Geno's pain.

He wished he were dead.

The Fox was still at large. The manhunt extended to five states. The FBI had his prints and his DNA. They had a ton of DNA. They scraped it off Geno's skin and combed it out of his pubic hair and swabbed it out of his mouth and ass. Grand total came to seven separate profiles. Seven different men raped him over the course of forty-four hours. One dead. Two headed to jail. Fox and three others were out there. Laying low until they could strike again.

The bust of the porn ring and the FBI investigation was front page news. Because Anthony's cell targeted and fetishized twins, people called him a modern-day Josef Mengele.

"Sons of bitches," Vern said to the TV, where one of the morning talk shows was discussing the Mengele Ring. "Like that momzer's name needs to be resurrected for any reason? My grandparents were gassed at Auschwitz. You don't know *shit* about Mengele."

Vern. What a mensch.

The cause of death in Nathan's obituary was kept vague. Geno's name was kept out of all the papers. Pretending to be asleep, he listened to Vern pace and berate a journalist on the phone.

"He is seventeen fucking years old," he said through the wall of his teeth. "I don't know how you got this number, sonny, but I give you my word: If I see his name in conjunction with this story, if I see a goddamn capital G in one of your stories, I will *bury* you."

Good old Vern. Fighting the little battles even though Geno lost the war.

Police asked again and again if Geno could remember anything, *anything* about his other attackers. Even the smallest detail could help. If they'd called each other by name. If one of them had an accent. If they wore a class ring, a wedding band, any other kind of jewelry. Tattoos. Piercings. Did he remember a mole? A birthmark? A distinctive scar? Anything?

Mos put his hands around Geno's throat and squeezed, swearing he'd strangle both of them before he'd let Geno remember or say one word about what *did not happen.* Geno ripped a sheet off the ever-present pad of paper and wrote, "I was on my face. I didn't see ANYTHING."

He practically threw the note at Mackin, then sank back in his pillows and wished he were dead.

I saw nothing.

I never saw it coming.

I never saw this.

Never.

DR. FRANKENSTEIN

*G*ENO AND HIS stomach reached cordial relations and the feeding tube was removed. The stoma to his colostomy could be capped for short periods of time. After weeks of bedridden sponge baths, he finally got a hot shower.

A *private* shower.

The nurse gave him soap and a washcloth and he wished it were bleach and steel wool. He felt dirty at a cellular level. Lathering up again and again, he remembered terms from tenth-grade biology and felt their lament in every particle of his body. He was tainted to the mitochondria. His Golgi complex stained. His ribosomes ruined. He once heard that in seven years time, every cell in a human body replaced itself, essentially making you a new person.

In which case, he'd be twenty-five when the last cells of this experience were out of his body.

He leaned a hand against the wall and vomited into the drain. Then he turned the water as hot as he could stand. Eased himself to the cold tile floor, wrapped his arms around his knees and let himself be scoured.

We will address it later, Mos said, taking over all thought and feeling again.

A psychiatrist from Mount Sinai's adolescent health center started coming to Geno's room. To talk about things that didn't happen.

Geno refused to be alone with Dr. Stein. Not because he didn't like the guy, but Geno had so little control over things. Being able to say who got to be with him was a scrap of dignity he clung to. And Stein respected it. So Vern sat in a chair by the window with his noise-reduction headphones. In view, but out of earshot, he worked on papers while Dr. Stein talked and Geno said nothing.

Stein honored Geno's right to say nothing. He was a decent guy. Geno overheard him telling Vern bad jokes. Gags so cornball, you had to laugh while you groaned.

Vern laughed hardest when he found out Stein's first name was Franklin. "Franklin Stein?"

Stein turned up his palms. "Go ahead. Take the next step."

"Dr. Frankenstein."

"My grandfather's name was Igor. You can't make this stuff up."

Stein didn't joke around with Geno. He was easy and gentle and attentive, even in the silences. He used words like anxiety, depression, anger, flashback, nightmares. He mentioned Prozac, Zoloft and Clonazepam. A word he really liked to throw around was *feel.*

How are you feeling, what are you feeling, how do you feel about that, how did that make you feel…

Annoyed, Mos waved copies of local ordinance NOS-34726: "Feeling is prohibited by law."

Leave him alone, Mos thought. Geno was working hard to feel nothing, and all this talk wasn't helping. The poor kid stared at Vern's headphones like they were the only thing he wanted in the world.

Mos wanted them, too.

So much noise.

He finally understood how sound made Analisa so crazy when she was nearing the end of her life. How the music and talk shows she always loved became a distraction, and finally a torment.

So much to process. So much not to think or feel.

Sometimes it was hard to be a good citizen of Nos.

"It's exhausting carrying around a secret," Chris Mudry had said, the night of Kelly's party. Now so long ago, it seemed a past life.

Because it is, Mos said. *It's someone else's past life.*

Sometimes, though, Mos had to let Geno reveal a few things. Like the notes found in Carlos' jeans pocket. How Geno thought they were from a girl. Until the night of the party, when Chris hit him with a right, then a left hook.

"You must have been stunned," Stein said.

"I had no idea," Geno said.

Stein looked down at his hands, twisting his wedding band around his fourth finger. "Carlos never hinted anything?"

Geno shook his head.

It is not our concern, Mos wrote on his clipboard, but not with his usual strictness. He was tired. Even Stein seemed tense and drained, at a loss for words. Unusually, it was Geno who filled the silence this time.

"I don't know why he didn't tell me," he said. "We told each other everything. Well. We used to. Things changed after my mother died."

"Can you talk about that?"

Geno's chest expanded as he filled his lungs with air and courage. "It was hard," he said. "Everything hurt."

Stein slowly nodded. "I was sixteen when my father died. I remember feeling like I had the flu for about a year."

For the first time, Geno met the doctor's eyes and held on. "It was like getting beat up every day. It was hard. For all of us. We kind of…drifted. I don't know how else to say it."

We don't like to speak of it.

What else could be said? Their little red hen died. Life got hard. Nathan was broken-hearted and distracted. He buried himself in work and emerged blinking and squinting, as if expecting to get mowed down in the glare of headlights. Geno was broken-hearted, but he picked up his common sense and figured out how to cook, clean, shop and keep order in the nest Analisa left behind.

Carlos took his broken heart where he wasn't supposed to be. He walked out of the henhouse and left the door wide open, letting the Fox in. Giving him access to little chicks.

I said I wanted you and your brother brought you to me.

Mos cleared his throat. *We know nothing and feel nothing about this. It is inconsequential to the case at hand.*

"Do you think your brother had an idea what Anthony was planning?" Dr. Stein asked.

Geno's fists clenched and his anger splashed against the walls of the hospital room.

Feeling is against the rules, Mos reminded everyone. *Feeling is illegal in Nos.*

"I know he did," Geno said.

"How?"

"Because Anthony told me. I was a fucking present. Carlito lured me into an ambush. He fucking sold me."

Stein only nodded, his face haggard. He and Geno fell silent. Frankenstein and his broken, wretched creature. The unspoken questions circling between them.

Why? Why'd he do it? How could he do it? What made him do it? What drove him to do it?

Geno didn't know.

Only Carlos knew.

And Carlos would never say.

Despite the laws of the land, Mos felt terrible. This job was exhausting. Geno was vomiting again. Would it ever end?

Mos let his clipboard fall to the charred, smoking ground of Nos. He waited until the bed linens were changed and morphine was starting to close like a loose fist around Geno's mind. He crept to the bed and got in. He snugged up against Geno's back. Close. Closer. Pressing and easing. Until finally, he slid past the boundary and dissolved, oozing through the fingers of the morphine fist, floating away like fog.

Geronimo Caan slipped between the stars of Nos and back inside himself. And slept.

AUGUST

SON RISE

*T*HE BATTERY CHARGED on vacation never lasted long. The laptop was still booting up and Steffen Finch hadn't yet swallowed the first sip of coffee when his boss, Ronnie Danvers, put her head in his office.

"Need you," she said.

"I missed you, too."

"I'm sorry, welcome back. You look well-rested, well-fed and well-laid."

Stef laughed. "You don't get laid at an ashram."

"Sorry, I meant well-prayed, not laid."

"I did pray a lot, yes."

"I'm glad you're back," Ronnie said. "And I need you."

Stef made a futile gesture to his laptop with one hand, a more urgent gesture to his foil-wrapped breakfast sandwich with the other. "It'll get cold."

"I'll buy you another."

Stef slapped both palms on his desk and got up. "I take it back. I didn't miss you."

He followed Ronnie out of his office and down the open stairwell. The Coalition for Creative Therapy occupied one half of a sprawling brick building on Eleventh Avenue. Once, during the gritty, dirty and bloody reign of Manhattan's meatpacking industry, this was the slaughterhouse and packing plant of Kraus & Brothers. Family-owned for three generations, Kraus eventually migrated from Chelsea to the new Hunt's Point Market in the Bronx, leaving a void in New York's west side that 1960s gay culture rushed to fill. The plant became a club called Manhunt, packing a different kind of meat in an era that was a different kind of gritty, dirty and bloody.

Manhunt was forcibly shut down in the 1980s at the height of the AIDS scare. For two decades it crouched like a haunted misfit at the river's edge, occasionally rising up in the hands of new renters with new ventures and new money, only to be abandoned again.

Optimism moved out and the wretches of Manhattan's underworld moved back in. When the Whitney Museum of Art began scoping Chelsea for a new location, it seemed the slaughterhouse's sordid days were numbered.

Salvation came in the form of a Hollywood actor, a native New Yorker who went public with a shocking story of how he was raped by his agent. Crediting art therapy as being key to his recovery, he bought the Kraus plant with the intention of creating a residential and therapeutic facility for male survivors like himself.

The residential side of the building was called the Exodus Project. It provided housing and inpatient mental health services for up to thirty men. The Coalition for Creative Therapy provided outpatient rehab for sexual assault survivors of all ages and genders.

"Max Springer," Ronnie said, reading from a file. "Six years old. Born Upper East Side. Biological father died when he was three, his mother remarried a year later. She's active army, deployed to Iraq seven months ago. As far as we can tell, the abuse started shortly thereafter."

"The stepfather?"

Ronnie nodded. "Max's teacher noticed behavioral issues. Coupled with stomach pains and bathroom troubles. He fainted after passing blood in his stool and enough of the story came out that the school called CPS. Temporary foster care until grandparents could get here from Florida and the mother could get discharged. He's living with her now."

"Jesus."

"He was treated at Mount Sinai. Your esteemed mentor Franklin Stein referred Max here, just after you left for vacation. He made a point of putting your name in the write-up."

"Dr. Frankenstein likes to overestimate me."

"Well, his estimate of Max was spot-on," Ronnie said. "Nobody can do a thing with this child."

"No?"

"The mother, God bless her, has brought him here every day. First few sessions, he screamed and wouldn't leave her side. Next few he cried and wouldn't leave her side."

"Skip ahead a little," Stef said.

"Two accomplishments. He'll let his mother out of his sight for an hour. And he's stopped screaming."

"Good. Is he verbal?"

"He talks mostly to himself," Ronnie said. "Bare minimum to the staff. Hello. Goodbye."

"Does he say *no?*"

She shook her head. "He hasn't gotten his *no* back."

Sexual assault robbed a child of the power of no, a power they were only just beginning to understand. Getting their no back was one of the first milestones of recovery.

"Who's been working with him?" Stef asked.

"Being that he was abused by the stepfather, we started with the obvious and had both Aedith and Katie try."

Stef nodded. It was logical to have the juvenile victim of a male abuser work with a female therapist. But this kind of trauma had no logic. It never liked to do what you expected. "No go?"

"Wanted nothing to do with either of them. So we tried Beau, but one look and Max was out the door. Nothing wrong with his motor skills, I'll tell you. We found him under a bed over on the residential side."

Stef found himself smiling. *Good for you, kid. You couldn't escape before, so run like hell now.*

"Poor Beau," he said. Beau deBrueil was a gifted therapist, but some clients couldn't get past his six-six, three-hundred-pound presence. Many who did found they never wanted to leave it.

"So as usual," Ronnie said, pausing outside the main art room door. "You're my only hope, Obi-Wan."

As usual, when she said this, Stef felt a blend of pride and apprehension. While his reputation for cracking tough cases preceded him like a showy parade horse, the fear of failing was hitched behind like a rusty trailer. It dragged hard today, when half his game was still meditating in California, and the other half sulked in his rumbling stomach. He was pretty useless when he was hungry.

"Do what you can," Ronnie said. "And welcome back. I mean it."

Stef drew a resigned breath and went into the art room. It stretched along the building's west side. High ceilings exposed vents and duct work. Tall windows overlooked the ongoing construction of the new elevated High Line park. A handful of men occupied the long wooden worktables. Aedith Johnson supervised a group of young girls at a round table in the corner. In one of the partitioned private spaces, Katie Bernstein worked one-on-one.

"What's up, my man," Beau said, striding over to give Stef a rib-crunching hug. "Glad to be back?"

"No," Stef said to the wall of Beau's chest.

"I missed your stupid face. How was the monastery?"

"Ashram."

"God bless you."

Stef managed to turn his face free. "I can't breathe."

Like a loving python, Beau gave a last squeeze and released his coils. "Ronnie tell you about Max?"

"Where is he?"

Beau pointed to an empty table at the room's far end. "Under there."

Stef regarded the boy through narrowed eyes. Someone had put a Do Not Disturb placard on the tabletop. Common practice for a new client whose primary goal was getting used to the space and the staff and feeling safe. The people who came here for therapy were not amenable to closed doors or situations where they felt penned in. By design, the art room's partitions were only six feet high. More improvised constructs of privacy—a folding screen, a wall of chairs, a Do Not Disturb sign—were held sacrosanct.

Max lay beneath his empty table. Plaid pajama pants and a baseball T-shirt. Brown hair, cut short. He curled on one side, a hand reaching toward the underside of the table.

"He talks to himself," Beau said. "Constantly. But yesterday as he was leaving, he said goodbye. Unprompted. Today he made a little eye contact. I see him peeking out from underneath the table every now and then, looking curious. He's definitely more *here* than he was two weeks ago."

"Mm."

"Good luck," Beau said. "Everyone's glad to see you back."

"Thanks," Stef said absently, his focus drawing in tight.

He circled the room a few times, weaving around the tables, saying hello to residents and giving a few highlights of his retreat in California. He walked by Max's table a few times, letting the boy notice him from the knees down. He crouched in eyesight, letting the rest of him be seen as he collected some scrap paper, a book of mosaic designs and a pack of magic markers. He whistled as he roamed. Finally, he put another Do Not Disturb sign on the table next to Max's. Without making eye contact, he crawled beneath, stretching out on his stomach.

Still whistling, he began to color. He resisted the urge to look Max's way. Instead he listened.

Beneath the table, Max nattered away to himself. Total gibberish, yet the sounds had pattern and inflection. Strings of chatter rose up at the end, asking a question. He paused between babbles, as if waiting for an answer. It was definitely a conversation.

Who are you talking to, Stef jotted on a scrap of paper. *Imaginary friend? Hero? Mom?*

Secret language. Nobody else can know. Nobody understands.

Private universe. Private language.

Real privacy taken away. Construct it however you can.

Max lay on his back now, soles of his feet pressed to the tabletop. Over and over, he sang a two-note warning. Like "Uh-oh" but with different syllables.

From beneath his table, Stef whistled the same tones, mimicking the high-low.

Max sang again, sounding like, "Ear cook."

Stef whistled. High-low.

"Ear cook," Max said.

They went back and forth a few times. When it came to his turn, Stef inverted the notes, low to high.

A long pause.

Stef whistled low-high again, slower.

"Bye gee," the boy said, copying.

Low-high whistle.

"Bye gee."

High-low whistle.

"Ear cook."

They went on chatting this way, each under a table, barricaded behind chair legs. Stef whistling. Max singing. He followed Stef's tones, but never changed the words.

Ear cook? Stef wrote. *Bye gee? Mean anything or nonsense?*

On one of his whistled replies, Stef sent a marker rolling across the floor, aiming between chair legs and under Max's table. He didn't follow it with his eyes. He kept his gaze on his work and kept coloring. The small of his back was starting to howl. Drawing prone was hard on a grown man's body. He'd have to move soon.

He allowed himself a glance. Max was still on his back, one knee crossed over the other. He was babbling again, drawing in the air with the blue pen. Stef rolled a second marker over. Red this time. The boy picked it up and waved both above his head. Grandiose, sweeping motions, like a conductor with two batons. Then he made little scooping movements, tossing an invisible salad. One pen fought the other in sword play. He put the blue cap on the red pen and the red cap on the blue pen. He rubbed them between his palms, then switched the caps back and began to conduct again.

Without making any sudden or abrupt movements, Stef collected his supplies and crawled out from beneath his table. He sat in one of its chairs, stretched his lower back, cracked his neck, then went back to work. He waited, but expected nothing more from Max. This tiny bit of connection was a good start.

Out the corner of his eye, he saw Max peeking at him from between the legs of a chair, red and blue markers clutched in a tight fist. A dagger at the ready.

Stef kept working, whistling softly through his teeth now. Building trust was like building a fire. If you hovered over the baby flames, you'd cut off the air and kill them. It required an anxious blend of feeding and benign neglect.

Tiny bits of fuel.

Let him catch if he wants.

Max came crawling out and crouched at the back legs of Stef's chair. Then he crawled to the other side of the table. Only his hair showed above the edge at first. Then two eyes. Then his chin. A little floating head on the tabletop.

Slowly Stef looked up.

Max ducked.

Stef made the two-tone whistle. High-low.

No answer.

Stef made it again.

"Ear cook," Max said.

"Just checking," Stef said.

Little by little the head reappeared, like a rising sun.

Son rise, Stef thought, a sadness stirring at the backs of his eyes.

Rise up, brave son.

He folded the feeling up and put it away for later.

Standing now, Max pushed the red magic marker across the table. Stef looked up again. The boy met his eyes for two seconds, then dropped them and pushed the marker further.

"You want me to use this?" Stef said.

A quick nod.

Stef turned the coloring book around and slid it toward Max. "Which shape?"

Max breathed through his mouth as his eyes swept the geometric design. A grubby finger pointed, reached and touched a hexagon.

Keeping the book upside-down, Stef colored it red.

Max handed him the purple marker and pointed to a triangle.

"You want to do one now?" Stef asked.

Max shook his head. He pushed a brown marker and pointed.

As Stef colored, he eased the rest of the markers toward the center of the table. He waited for directions. Max gave him a green marker. Then an orange one. He pointed. There, with this color. Here, with that one. Now do this. Now do that. Stef followed orders, capping each pen carefully when he was done and putting it back in the pile.

Max stopped then, staring at Stef's left arm. Wrist to elbow, it was tattooed with mythical horses. Centaurs and pegasi. Stef rolled his arm back and forth so the boy could see both sides. Max picked up a black marker and handed it to Stef. Then he pointed to himself.

"You want a tattoo?" Stef asked.

Max nodded.

"What would you like?"

The boy's shoulders stiffened. Stef's heart kicked up a bit. This was the real test. Did Max know what he wanted and, more importantly, could he say it?

"I'll draw whatever you want," Stef said, wondering when was the last time this boy was given a choice.

Max wet his lips. "Pain," he whispered.

Stef stared. *Jesus Christ, he wants me to draw pain?* He turned an ear toward Max and made his voice just as soft. "Sorry, I didn't hear?"

A big, deep inhale. "Plane."

"Oh, a plane. Sure. Where do you want it?"

Max examined one arm, then the other, then laid his left arm on the table, hand in a fist.

"Point to where," Stef said, uncapping the black marker. "Tell me exactly where."

Max pointed and Stef sketched a plane. Ideally he'd put his free hand on top of Max's arm to steady the surface, but touching without permission was against the rules. So he had to hold the marker like a brush and sort of paint the picture with the tip.

"What color do you want it?"

Max handed him a blue pen.

"You ever been in an airplane?" Stef asked.

Max shook his head.

"Where's this plane going?"

Max's open-mouthed, huffed breaths blew warm on Stef's wrist. "Away."

Stef nodded, making lines from the back of the aircraft, indicating it was taking off. "Away's a good place," he said. "I go there a lot."

BATTERIES DRAINED

"I WAS STATIONED IN Kirkuk," Colleen Springer said. "Ear cook."

"I see," Stef said. "Of course."

"I don't know what bye gee is." She sighed heavily, her eyes welling up.

"You're not to blame for this," Stef said.

Colleen pressed the back of her hand into one eye, then the other, and gave a short, brisk nod. At her feet, Max was busy playing with the straps of her sandals, babbling under his breath. Seemingly oblivious to the conversation taking place over his head.

"You're a good person and a good mother," Stef said. "And you've got to take care of yourself. I can't press this point harder. If you're not all right, Max isn't all right. Do you understand?"

Colleen nodded again, her shoulders pulling back and squaring. Stef worked with enough veterans to know they liked clear, direct instructions and a set goal.

"Find a counselor," he said. "You need to have someone to talk to, too. Don't tough this out alone. Do you need a name? I can help you find someone."

"I've already made some calls," she said.

"Good. Excellent. You have people to help you? Family?"

"My sister's moved in with me for a little while. My parents are in Florida but they're looking for a short-term rental. My brother's in Stamford. He's close by. Close enough."

"Good. Gather your people around and don't be afraid to lean on them."

"Oh, I'll lean," she said, laughing a little as the tears dripped down. She drew a tremendous breath and blew it out. "God, this is a nightmare."

"We'll get through it," Stef said.

"We," she said faintly, pressing fingertips under her eyes.

"Listen. This didn't just happen to Max. It happened to you, too. It's traumatizing. Don't brush your pain aside. All right?"

Another huge exhale. "I'd hug you right now, but Max gets upset when…"

Stef put his palms together and looked in her eyes. After a moment, she put hers together and looked back.

"Thank you," she said.

"Take care of yourself," he said, pausing between every word. Making it an order, not a farewell.

After the Springers left, Stef dodged his colleagues, told Ronnie he needed to eat or die, and left the art room.

Away. We're getting on a plane and going away.

His feet led him to the other side of the building, which was the domain of Exodus Project. Down more stairs, through the dining hall and into the large industrial kitchen. Betty, the head cook, was taking her post-breakfast coffee break while three residents washed dishes. Everyone housed at EP had to contribute, either in the dining room, the kitchen or the laundry.

At one of the large butcher block counters, Stavroula Kalo chopped vegetables, her head tilted toward the radio perched on a shelf, tuned to NPR.

"Come here often?" Stef said, sliding an arm around her shoulders and giving a squeeze.

"Hey, welcome back," she said. "How was the retreat?"

"Enlightening."

"How was your morning?"

"Dark."

Stavroula sighed. "Batteries drained already?"

"Big time. I didn't even get breakfast."

"That's not good. Sit." She reached a leg out long and pulled a stool near.

Stef sat, exhaling heavily. Stavroula wiped off her hands, lit a burner and put a small skillet down. She poured Stef a cup of coffee. He dragged a folded copy of the *NY Post* closer, unfolded it and read the headlines.

> *MENGELE MANHUNT CONTINUES.*

"Mengele manhunt," he said. "Really?"

"My mother is still furious about it," Stavroula said. "You want eggs or egg whites?"

"Eggs."

Stavroula cracked two in a bowl and started scrambling them. "Did I tell you she called the *Post* and gave them an earful?"

"No, but I can imagine." As one of the few surviving twins of Josef Menge-le's heinous medical experiments, Lilia Kalo had strong opinions about the use of his name as a modern noun.

"Apparently she dropped an F-bomb," Stavroula said.

"Shut the fuck up."

A crackle of hot butter as a waterfall of pale yellow slid from bowl to skillet. "She was quite proud of herself."

"She should be," Stef said, skimming over the paper.

> …*News of the porn ring bust shook up members of the Stock-ton community.*
>
> *"It's incredibly upsetting because Anthony Fox was well-known in our neighborhood," said Stockton resident Marc Lowenstein. "This wasn't a stranger lurking in the shadows. He's done after-school photography programs for years. He's photographed sports events and public events, you see his byline in the paper all the time. Adults knew him. Kids trusted him. When I think of what he was doing to those boys all this time, I'm just shocked and sickened."*

Stef folded up the paper before his mind could fill its tank with imagery and gun the engine down the long road of all the therapy those boys were going to need.

They're not your cases, he thought. *You can be sympathetic to the pain, but you don't have to feel it.*

"You want cheese with these eggs?" Stavroula said.

"Bless you, sister."

The youngest of three sons, Stef had always wanted a kid sister, but he'd acquired this one under bizarre circumstances. Ten years ago, Stef's mother and Stavroula's mother left their husbands for each other.

It was an interesting conversation starter now, but at the time, the announce-ment left two families stunned. While Stavroula's parents, both Holocaust sur-vivors, managed their separation with quiet dignity and grace, the Finches' marriage went down kicking and screaming. Like a whirlpool, it sucked in their three adult sons, chewed thoroughly and spit out everyone's latent issues.

Reeling in the wake of their own failed marriages, Stef and Stavroula found more reason to ally than be hostile to each other. Once parental emotions cooled down and plates stopped being thrown, the quasi-step-siblings discov-ered they got along well.

Stavroula was an only child, adopted late in the Kalos' lives. Stef often felt like an only child. He was a late delivery from the stork, a surprise third child who grew up alienated from his older brothers, both in years and in nature. The divorce drew particularly harsh battle lines through the Finches, with Rory and Stef on one side, Marcus and his two eldest on the other.

Stef liked Stavroula. He also relied on her in little ways. She and her father owned a bagel shop on Horatio Street, and she volunteered a few days a week at EP. Stef often went to see her after a grueling appointment. She made him a little snack. Or gave him a few mindless but meditative tasks to do. Or just gave him her quiet presence and a place to rest and think.

Now she put the plate with the egg sandwich in front of Stef and got him some ketchup.

"Thanks."

She smiled, turned up the radio and went back to her chopping.

"You're listening to *Moments in Time*," came the female voice through the grubby, flour-dusted speaker. "I'm Camberley Jones, thanks for joining us. Author Gil Rafael is best-known for the short story 'Bald,' which was made into the critically acclaimed movie in 2004, starring Kristin Scott Thomas…"

Stef licked ketchup off his pinky finger and tilted his ear. Weird. A friend recently lent him a copy of Gil Rafael's short story collection, *Client Privilege*. Stef had been pissed about forgetting to bring it with him to California. It was home on his bedside table, spine still unbroken.

"I met up with Gil in the Sunset Park area of Brooklyn," Jones said. "Where he's doing field research for his next book, a collection of Latin American folktales. He's going to all the Latino neighborhoods of New York City, collecting stories and legends from the elders of these ethnic enclaves.

"Sunset Park has one of the highest concentrations of Mexican immigrants in the city. Gil's made no appointments nor scheduled meetings. He simply walks the neighborhood streets, looking for oral traditions on the stoops and corners. The abuelos and abuelas who remember storytelling occasions of their childhood."

"I just walk around," Gil Rafael said. "I always find someone and I'm always touched by how willing they are to talk to me."

Stef rested on his elbows, chewing thoughtfully. He did a lot of walking in the city. Usually when he was troubled. One of countless New Yorkers wandering the streets on any given day, troubled or otherwise, looking to find connection.

Most people are looking for someone to listen to their story, Stef thought. *This guy is looking for someone to tell.*

OUT OF MY HAIR

"THE TALES DON'T always leave you satisfied," Jav's recorded voice said from the computer. "They're often unfair. But always they have a little saying at the end, like a curtain call for the teller. It goes, 'Listen and learn it, learn to tell it, and tell it to teach it.' I love that. It just beautifully describes the work I'm doing right now. Listen to learn. Learn to tell. Tell to teach."

Now Camberley Jones's voice came through the speakers: "Gil Rafael's novel *The Trade* comes out in September. You can read an excerpt on our website, along with another Latin American folktale he collected from the immigrant neighborhoods.

"For *Moments in Time,* this is Camberley Jones in New York City."

Camberley reached to stop the sound file, then turned to Jav with a smile. "What do you think?"

"I love it," Jav said. "Holy shit, it came out great." He spun in his chair and looked at his new publicist, Donna. "What do you think?"

She leafed through her pad of notes. "It's excellent. And I think we found your mission statement." She turned the pad around and showed a quick sketch of a website header. A long rectangle with his pen name, Gil Rafael, in block letters. Beneath it, she'd written *Listen to learn. Learn to tell. Tell to teach.*

"Boom," Camberley said, holding a fist out to Jav.

"I can't thank you enough," Jav said, touching his knuckles to hers.

"It was a pleasure. I'm so glad we got a chance to work together. Again" Her voice was crisp, but a rosy blush crept up from her throat. Her eyes flicked surreptitiously to Donna before she winked at Jav.

He blinked back. He remembered the way she blushed, hairline to heels, obscuring her freckles.

When Camberley won the Peabody Award in 2002, she hired Jav to accompany her to the awards ceremony. And accompany her home afterward. She was emerging from a nasty divorce at the time, and decided a night devoted to her bruised ego was well worth the money.

She was one of a few one-time clients who stuck in Jav's memory. While he didn't see her again after their date, he heard her all the time on the radio. A few weeks ago, they ran into each other at a Starbucks. They caught up over coffee and next thing Jav knew, Camberley was trailing him on one of his jaunts to Latino neighborhoods.

The Trade would release in September, followed by Jav's first book signing tour. A three-week trip along the entire east coast that by turns, thrilled and terrified him.

"Got time for lunch?" Cam asked Jav.

"I don't." He checked his watch. "My nephew's coming home from Vancouver. I need to head to LaGuardia." He leaned to kiss her cheek and the pink blush swept over her face again.

Jav didn't kiss the introverted and formal Donna. A smile and a nod sufficed, then he was on his way.

A sappy anticipation coursed through his heart as he drove to the airport to collect his nephew. After a lifetime of each not knowing the other existed, Jav and Ari were tragically introduced a little over a year ago, when Jav's sister died and named him guardian for her seventeen-year-old son. Instead of uprooting Ari and causing further disruption, Jav shut down his city life and moved north to a little town called Guelisten. He found an apartment for them and found building a relationship with Ari to be a complicated but ultimately rewarding experience. So much so that when Ari went out to Vancouver for a film school workshop this summer, Jav missed him. A lot. He'd gotten used to having a buddy around.

"I keep looking for you," he said when Ari called him after a week.

"Oh my God, T, are you *crying?*" Ari said. He called Jav T, for Tío. Spanish for *uncle.*

"Shut up."

"Come on, I bet you have an absolute *surplus* of toilet paper now."

"This is true," Jav said. "One box of cereal lasts forever and I only have to buy a half-gallon of milk."

"See? You don't miss me at all."

"You're right. Glad to have you out of my hair. Don't ever come home."

Ari was back in Jav's hair now, looking an inch taller and a few pounds heavier when Jav got arms around him. The traffic on the Grand Central Parkway was obscene and Jav used the delay to play the MP3 of the radio piece.

"Man, T, that is awesome," Ari said when it was over.

"Thanks," Jav said, turning off the car stereo. "I can't believe how great it came out."

"I can." Ari scrubbed a hand through his hair and yawned. "Working on any other projects?"

"I'm thinking about writing a memoir called *Life Advice From a Whore*."

Ari groaned and slouched in his seat. "I *said* I was sorry."

Jav laughed, shoving him. "I'm just giving you shit."

"Yeah, I missed you too."

"Anyway, I've retired from escorting."

Ari sat up a little. "You kidding?"

"Nope. I'm done."

"Not because of me. What I said, I mean."

"Because it was time."

"Oh." Ari went quiet. Typically, he soon dozed off, his body sliding until it was curled like a shrimp against the passenger window. Jav quelled the urge to pat him and sighed heavily instead.

It was time.

He didn't second-guess the decision. But it was supposed to be liberating. He was completely unprepared for this soul-sucking emptiness in his heart and guts. Overwhelming emotions of confusion and regret often dissolving into a panicked fear.

I'm too old.

I'm too late.

What have I done?

It happened at night. When so many things happened to him. By day Jav wrote, ensconced in his apartment, unshaven in ball caps and ratty jeans, ears plugged against distraction. At night he unfurled like a flag and hit the streets in a hustler's confident strut. Sleek and groomed, his ears attuned to his date's verbal cues, his eyes laser-focused on her non-verbal ones.

One night, he was just done with it all.

It wasn't the woman. She was perfectly lovely. Like Camberley, a recent divorcée needing validation and a date to a family wedding. He gave her everything she paid for. Attention. Flirting. Dance after dance after dance. He listened to her. His eyes lingered on her. He made her feel beautiful.

"I'm having such a good time," she said, a hint of tears in her eyes.

They went to her place and he gave her an even better time. It wasn't his A game. Not that she would know. She was an incoherent heap in the sheets by the time he was done. Jav on the other hand, couldn't get his thoughts to shut up. He was distracted. Tired to his bones.

A little bored, frankly.

And ever-so-slightly disgusted with himself.

You're worth more.

When time was up, Jav kissed the woman goodnight. He dressed, making sure the envelope with his payment was safe in his jacket pocket, and saw himself out.

It took all of four blocks to realize he didn't want to do this anymore.

No lightning bolt revelation. No breakdown. No fed-up fist shaking at the sky. The thought was quiet but resolute. An almost laughably easy decision.

I've had enough. I've done enough.

He sighed, remembering a promise he'd made not too long ago. A pledge to give himself another chance at being friends with love. It was an empty promise if he continued selling himself.

I'm worth more.

He passed a homeless man sleeping in the recessed alcove of a building's service doors. Jav's fingers closed around the envelope in his pocket.

You gonna keep on fucking to make money and then just sit around and count it?

You did a good job. Whether it was a hundred an hour, or a thousand an hour, you always treated a woman like she was paying a million an hour. You're not a whore.

You're just better than this.

It's time. Go spend the dough. Go love someone.

Jav crouched and carefully tucked the envelope beneath the snoring man's shoulder.

"I will do this," he whispered beneath the night. "And you will give me nothing."

When Ari woke, he was hungry and eager to see his dog, Roman. Soon he'd be bored with Jav's company and itching to get up to Guelisten to see his girl-friend, Deane.

Jav had two of three matters under control. He'd ended the sub-lease on his longtime apartment on St. Nicholas Avenue and moved to a new building on Riverside Drive that allowed dogs. It was also a block from Fairway, where he'd been this morning to fill the fridge and stock toilet paper. If Ari wanted to get laid, he'd have to put his own horny ass on a train.

They had couch dinner that night, balancing plates in front of the TV, watching baseball. Ari licked his plate clean and set it on the coffee table, then held out his arms to Roman, who climbed up and into the boy's lap. Roman, a Duck Tolling Retriever, turned his sleek, coppery head toward Jav with a smug expression.

Master is home. You're dismissed.

"Check it out," Ari said, reaching around Roman to push up his T-shirt sleeve. An eye was tattooed on the cap of his shoulder.

"Nice," Jav said, leaning in to get a closer look. The pupil was heart-shaped, a tiny white question mark making a highlight in the black.

"Deane and I both got it," Ari said, his fingers rubbing the skin.

"What's the meaning?" Jav asked.

"Love each other and see what happens," Ari said.

"I like it," Jav said. "Good philosophy for the moment and in the long-term."

He suppressed an apprehensive sigh. When you had the misfortune to fall in love with your own cousin, loving and seeing what happened were your only options.

They talked away the innings, gradually lowering the volume on the TV until it was barely background noise.

"Were you ever afraid when you were escorting?" Ari asked as they dug into ice cream.

"Afraid?"

"Yeah. You know, the cliché story of the hooker getting offed by some psycho trick. Did you ever have that fear?"

"Not so much fear as an awareness. I couldn't get lulled into a false sense of security just because it was a woman. Only takes one female with a knife or a gun and then I'm floating in the river or something."

"Anything like that ever happen?"

"No," Jav said. "But a couple times I walked into a date and my gut told me to leave the money and walk out. It's one of the rules. Always trust your instincts."

"What's another?"

"Always let someone know where you're going, even if you write it down and tape it to your bathroom mirror. Leave a trail with someone you trust."

Ari stared at him a moment. "Who was it when we were living in Guelisten?"

"Alex."

Alex Lark-Penda was Deane's father and, for all intents and purposes, Jav's best friend.

And lover for all of twenty minutes. If some sloppy kissing and grappling qualified one as a lover.

Alex's wife qualified it that way.

"You been back to Guelisten much?" Ari asked, cuddling with Roman again.

"Technically the lease on the apartment lasts through the end of August. Some of our stuff is still there."

A smile played around Ari's mouth. "That wasn't the question."

"I haven't been up there in about three weeks."

"Did you and Alex have a fight?"

Jav glanced down the couch. Two human eyes, two canine eyes and one tattooed eye met his.

What happened between Jav and the Lark-Pendas was none of Ari's adolescent business. Still, Jav had rules about lying to his nephew and he finally answered, "Kind of."

Roman yawned and Ari's gaze grew troubled. "What about?"

"It's complicated," Jav said. "It wasn't really a fight. Just a…thing. A thing between us we're taking some time and distance from. It's going to be fine."

Ari seemed satisfied, and he reached for the clicker to turn the game back up.

JEALOUS IN THE CITY

1 *I*T WASN'T A *fight.*
Just a thing.
Me trying to seduce your girlfriend's father. That kind of thing.
Hey, I was half successful.
Not that it's something to brag about.
Shit…

The nauseating shame and heavy heartache Jav first felt in the affair's wake had downgraded to embarrassment and functional melancholy. He missed Alex, yet every time he reached for the phone to text or call, he froze, not knowing what to say. Afraid anything he said would only make things worse. He wrestled with conscience and sentiment and ended up doing nothing. Then he glared at the phone for hours, pissed Alex wasn't calling or texting. Wondering if he was going through the same mental gymnastics. The same bicep curls using the phone as resistance.

Do you miss me?
Jesus, he was lonely.
I knew a ton of women, but I didn't know anyone.

Ari bounced around the tri-state area, hooking up with friends old and new. He headed up to Guelisten for weekends with Deane, leaving Jav alone and jealous in the city. Realizing what a reclusive life he'd led during the daytime hours, he forced himself out of the apartment from nine to five. He stuck a finger into a map of Manhattan and picked a neighborhood at random. He took his laptop, took Roman if the venue allowed, and hopped the subway. A different office every day. Coffee shops and diners and libraries. He changed his workouts from mornings to evenings so he could hit the gym at a more crowded and somewhat more social time.

Get out there, man. Meet someone.

Roman was an excellent wingman and icebreaker. Jav met a lot of dog lovers. His laptop, notebook and pen invited overtures from grad students and free-lancers.

"Hi," they said.

"Hi," Jav said. "How are you?"

"Good, what are you working on?"

"A book. You?"

An article, they answered. A research paper, a dissertation, a novel or short story they'd had in a drawer for years.

He met Oneida this way, when a Yorkville cafe's outdoor seating area was crowded, and Jav shoved things aside so she could sit at his little table. Beneath it, her bulldog began to sniff Roman enthusiastically.

She was pretty. Smart. Getting her master's in literature at City College. A voracious reader. Cuban American, and it was a treat to converse in Spanish, her throaty accent like honeyed cognac. He shared some of his folktale research with her. She shared a story her abuela used to tell at bedtime. Their brains connected, and the atoms between their bodies definitely crackled with physical chemistry. They exchanged cards.

A few nights later, they went to a movie. Tonight, they went out to dinner. The chemistry was still crackling and after dinner, they went to her place.

They had sex.

Jav couldn't understand it. Once in Oneida's bed, his body and brain disconnected completely. Below the belt, he was in the game. Upstairs, he was a thousand-yard stare.

What am I doing? What do I want?

What does she want?

He made up an early meeting commitment and left her apartment. Down the hall, into the elevator and out on the street to hail a cab, with a nagging feeling he'd forgotten something. His hands patted his person. Wallet, yes. Keys, yes.

Oh.

The envelope.

Which wasn't there anyway.

"This is harder than I thought," he said, staring down First Avenue.

"You ain't kidding, brother," said a homeless man shuffling by.

Jav lay in bed that night, eyes fixed on the ceiling. He pulled a pillow partly onto his chest, one palm smoothing it as if it were someone's head. First it was the rough, coiled dreadlocks belonging to Flip Trueblood. A golden dream that slipped through Jav's fingers, boarded a plane on 9/11 and disappeared forever. Then it was the thick softness of Alex's hair beneath Jav's palm. A dream that shouldn't have been in Jav's hands in the first place.

He pulled the pillow to his face, remembering a jaw rough with beard growth. He hugged it again to his chest. It became a tattooed arm, first olive-skinned with a silver globe, then black with a dragonfly.

Open your pants for me, rude bwoy, Flip whispered.

Come closer, Alex echoed.

Feel this and want it.

I want this.

Your voice gives me a hard-on.

I get a hard-on every time I think about your fingers between mine.

I wanted…but I left before I could get greedy.

I wanted it bad and letting it go is tearing me up inside.

I'm kind of missing you already.

I miss you.

Come here, Javier.

Come on, don't make this harder…

Clutching his pillow, moaning into the dark behind his eyes, Jav came in his hand with the two men he loved in his head. A thousand times more engaged and aroused than he was mere hours ago, in bed with a woman.

"Maybe this will be easier than I thought," he said softly, his chest heaving hard, his palm damp with desire.

It'll be worth more, Alex silently agreed.

LOLLYPOP

"**A**NY PAIN THERE?" Dr. Bloom said.

"Little bit," Geno said.

Her finger probed deeper. "How about here, along the scar tissue?"

"Yeah, that's still sore." Geno closed his eyes and turned his head on his crossed arms. The paper on the exam table crackled. His kneecaps were starting to howl from contact with the hard platform at the table's foot.

Should bring my pads next time, he thought, as he always thought, but never remembered to actually bring them.

He closed his fingers around the cuff of the nurse's cardigan. She lay her palm across his knuckles.

"Doing great," she said quietly. Her name was Mary Pat and she had the unflappable air of a veteran mother. Incapable of being shocked or grossed out. She could catch vomit with one hand and wipe an ass with another.

She'd done both for Geno on occasion.

Her touch was heavy and still. She knew he didn't want to clutch her or be patted through these exams. He just needed a Valium and a little bit of contact with someone who wasn't afraid of shit.

Literally.

"Don't ever retire," he said.

She smiled, showing her crooked incisor. "With five kids? I'll be working until I'm eighty."

"Almost done," Dr. Bloom said. "Deep breath in now. You'll feel pressure, bear down against it. On three, exhale hard. One. Two. Three…"

The paper crackled again as Geno pushed his breath out. The scope slid in, cold and rigid.

At least buy me dinner if you're going to do that.

"It's all healing beautifully," Bloom said. "You're using the suppositories? Morning and night?"

"Yeah."

"And soaking?"

"Yeah."

"Good, good. This is excellent." The scope withdrew, leaving a smarting burn in its wake. Geno let go of Mary Pat's cuff as Dr. Bloom tugged the exam gown closed over his exposed ass.

"Come up here," Dr. Bloom said, patting the table. She and Mary Pat walked over to the counter, Bloom to peel off her gloves and wash her hands and the nurse with some kind of busywork. Geno sat, a little KY jelly oozing out of him, his feet icy cold and clammy in their socks.

Bloom looked in his eyes, nose and ears. Listened to his heart and tested his reflexes. He didn't know if this was all truly necessary, or if she did it to convince him he wasn't just another asshole to her.

A corner of his mouth flickered, wondering how many asshole jokes a colorectal surgeon heard in any given day. Miranda Bloom had a dry sense of humor, as well as gentle hands. She probably gave as good as she got.

He imagined asking, *How'd you get into this line of work, doc?*

She'd answer, *You start at the bottom and work your way up.*

But seriously, folks.

Bloom had him lie back and she palpated the skin around the stoma scar on his abdomen. Ten days ago she'd reversed the colostomy and all his plumbing was reconnected. Not since he was three was such a fuss made over him taking a crap all by himself.

Didn't even get a gold star or anything, he thought, studying the ceiling tiles.

"Bowel movements are all right?" she asked. "Any pain?"

"Sometimes. Not terrible."

The cold disc of her stethoscope traced paths on his stomach. "You're taking the stool softeners?"

"Yeah."

"Blood when you pass stool?"

"I haven't seen any."

"Excellent."

He trusted her use of excellent. Hers was the only compassion Geno trusted lately. Which made it difficult to lie to her.

"You're still seeing your psychiatrist? Dr. Stein?" she asked.

No. "When I need him."

"Any side effects from the Prozac?"

I quit taking it. "No."

"Sleeping all right?"

No. "Good nights and bad nights."

"What do you do on the bad nights?"

Cry, throw up, pace. "Ambien helps."

"You're living at your sister's still, correct?"

"Yeah." The truth was cool relief on Geno's lying tongue.

"Sit up," Bloom said. "Everything is looking good. Keep up with the baths and the suppositories. I'm going to graduate you to monthly exams so make an appointment for four weeks. Any abdominal pain or rectal bleeding, you call in. Especially if it's accompanied by a fever. Don't screw around if you're running a temperature."

"I won't."

She gathered up his chart and closed it. "I'll see you next month then." She reached in her lab coat pocket and came up with a lollypop.

Geno smiled as he took it. "Thanks."

Her eyes were soft and steady on his face. "You call me if you need me, all right?"

"I will."

She left, followed by Mary Pat, who gave Geno a smile before shutting the door behind her.

He wiped up with some tissues and got dressed. Hanging at the appointments desk, waiting for the receptionist to find him a slot, he felt the eyes of the waiting room on his back. He was the youngest patient by several decades, and it was no thrill having senior citizens check out his ass, wondering what his ailment was. He ground his molars together, pressing his mouth into a tight line. The lollypop dropped from his hand into the wastebasket.

"Take care now," the receptionist said, handing him his card.

Care is always taken, Mos said.

After five weeks living at Zoë's house, Geno couldn't say he was any closer to his half-sister, yet his life was now inextricably bound up in her household. With nobody suggesting or asking or arranging a thing, Geno had made himself into an au pair.

"You don't have to," Zoë said, when Geno first started cooking a meal, cleaning a bathroom, running the vacuum, changing a diaper.

"I want to," he said, sweeping and dusting and scrubbing the dirt from the world, putting things back in order and making them stay there. Wiping up the spills and splashes and mess and making it seem they'd never happened.

I need to.

Tom, Zoë's husband, drove a truck and was on the road four days a week. Zoë worked long hours as an administrator at Seton Hall. She had three kids, the youngest an eleven-month-old boy. Summers were particularly challenging for her, a jerry-rigged schedule of daycare, playdates and babysitters that varied from week to week and often fell apart. Meals were thrown together on the fly, she was always running out of staples. Weekends were crammed with laundry, chores and errands. Wanting family time and wanting time alone with Tom.

Geno made himself scarce when Tom was home. While Zoë's husband was a perfectly decent guy, Geno got the feeling Tom Douglas wanted his family to himself on his days off. More than once, Geno looked up to find Tom staring at him. Not with hostility, more the opposite. A nervous uncertainty, as if he were examining a grenade he found, unsure if it were live or a dud. The first few times it happened, Geno ducked into the bathroom to make sure his colostomy bag wasn't leaking.

Tuesday mornings came around quickly, then Tom was gone again. The kids needed a thousand things. Zoë needed help. Geno needed to be kept busy. The busier, the better. It made him feel normal, and normal was one of the few feelings allowed in Nos.

Now the Douglas house was an immaculate paragon of domestic organization, law and order.

"It's like a miracle," Zoë said, practically in tears when she came home to dinner made, toys picked up, clothes folded, pantry stocked and clutter removed. "I can see my countertops," she said. "I haven't seen my countertops in months."

Geno smiled and dodged her effusive gratitude. He had no reason to dislike her and he didn't. He just didn't like adult company these days. He wanted to work and be useful, not make relationships. He didn't like being around people who knew what had happened to him, and he arranged his life to avoid them.

Phone calls and texts from school friends were ignored. The pile of condolence cards, to which he hadn't yet responded, filled him with an uneasy guilt. Analisa wouldn't be pleased at him ignoring acts of kindness. He hid them in a shoebox in the closet with a vague promise to deal with them later.

He didn't like later.

He did, however, like being with the kids. He could breathe easy around them. Nine-year-old Madeleine was shy with him, turning red when he made eye contact. Stephanie, six going on twenty-two, was fearless, asking a hundred frank, curious questions about his colostomy equipment. As for the baby, Matthew, it seemed he'd been waiting all his short life for Geno to show up. He beamed when Geno came into a room. He locked arms around his half-uncle's leg, or held them up in a demand to be carried. Any time Geno sat down, the boy came crawling or toddling to get in his lap.

"He's a mushy one," Zoë said. "He needed a fourth trimester, I swear. For three months after he was born, he was only happy when he was attached to me. And he's still happiest when he's canoodling."

Tom's disconcerting looks grew more intense when Matthew was canoodling with Geno. Geno chalked it up to possessive, alpha male jealousy, and tried to keep his distance from the baby on weekends. It was hard. He found the innocent, trusting weight of the little boy was the only touch he could bear. When Matthew hugged him, Geno felt his heart slow down and his muscles relax. He'd exhale completely. All the rigid rules and laws of Nos would suspend. Mos shut up, and Geno could be completely autonomous.

With Matthew in his arms or asleep on his chest, Geno felt good.

And *good,* along with normal, was allowed in Nos.

DOUGH

AUGUST HELD THE world in a sweaty fist. You could run a knife through the air and watch a slice fall away with a damp thud. Inside the Douglas house was cool and quiet. Tom was on the road, Zoë at work, the girls at an all-day camp.

In the kitchen, Geno was trying his hand at making pizza dough. He'd never done it before, but he was following Alton Brown's directions, which never led him wrong.

Matthew cruised around the island, hanging onto cabinet handles. When Geno blocked his path, the boy held onto Geno's legs to get around, often stopping to squeeze them before setting off on the next lap.

Geno scraped the gloppy ball of dough out of the bowl and onto the floured countertop. He started kneading, clumsy at first, frustrated with the dough sticking to his fingers. Finally it started to incorporate. His hands fell into a rhythm, folding and pressing and rolling. The dough was warm against his palms. Tactile. It filled his hands like…something. He couldn't quite think what. Something familiar. Something nice.

He slowed down. His eyes closed. His hands grew still around the dough a moment, then his fingers started to sink into its mass. It was alive and warm in his hands. Like…

He didn't know.

This is crazy.

Something about the texture and warmth and *give* of the dough was making his throat get all tight. Something he thought he lost was now back in his hands.

But what?

What? What are you? What are you reminding me? What is this?

He filled up with feeling and Mos allowed it. These were good feelings, even if he didn't understand, and good was allowed in Nos.

Matthew made his way down the cabinet fronts and got his arms around Geno's leg. He pressed his cheek tight to Geno's knee and hugged.

"Na na na na," he sang, which meant he was getting sleepy.

Eyes still closed, Geno let the dough fall from one hand to the other. Fingers sinking and pulling and pushing. Swaying a little on legs that weren't exactly shaking, but vibrating in a weird way. All of him was buzzing. The feeling wasn't unpleasant. He just couldn't recognize it.

He leaned against the counter.

"Na na na," Matthew said, his smooth fat belly pressed against Geno's leg. Damp hands slid on Geno's skin. A wet mouth left little kisses like presents.

The dough squeezed through Geno's fingers.

His eyes opened.

He had an erection.

For a moment he felt ten years old. At a total loss, freaked out, wondering what the hell his body was doing, was it *supposed* to do that?

Then he exhaled a small, tentative laugh.

Holy shit.

Sexual thoughts weren't tolerated in Nos and it was barely an effort to obey that particular law. Once upon a time, he had sex on the brain and couldn't go seven hours without jerking off. He hadn't touched himself in seven weeks, nor had a single thought that made his dick even want to twitch.

It still works.

He leaned a little harder against the counter, intensifying the thrumming sensation now taking over his groin and belly. He stared at the dough in his hands.

Dough made me get hard? Seriously?

He glanced down at Matthew hanging on his leg.

Or was it something else?

The thrumming wasn't so pleasant now. He filled up with a sense of inappropriateness. And no small amount of danger.

Mos spoke up. *We shouldn't think about this.*

"No, this isn't right," Geno said. His hands felt dirty, the dough's texture now grotesque and repulsive. He dumped the ball into the mixing bowl. It was supposed to rise for two hours but no way was Geno going to *eat* it tonight. Nor watch the family sink their teeth into his gross, perverted thoughts.

To get to the garbage can, he had to plant one foot and drag the other leg with Matthew behind. Step, drag and pull. Step, drag and pull. Nathan used to do this with his twin boys. One on each leg until they got too heavy, then they had to take turns.

"Dad, do Quasimodo," they'd say. "Do the hunchback, Dad. I go first."

"Sanctuary," Nathan would groan, hunched over, dangling a limp and crippled arm. A laughing boy clinging to his leg as he hobbled down the hallway.

Matthew laughed and laughed as he was dragged across the floor. Geno dumped the dough in the garbage, then lurched to the sink. He scrubbed his hands, getting off every shred and speck of dough.

That was fucked up.

Mos nodded in vigorous agreement.

"Na na na," Matthew said, then yawned. It was nap time. Geno took him upstairs. Usually they snoozed together in Geno's bed, but it didn't seem right today. Perhaps it was never right, letting a little boy be in his bed.

Boys weren't supposed to be in beds with boys.

Say it, baby boy.

Geno put his nephew in the crib. Matthew's lower lip pushed out and his eyes filled up. "Na na na," turned to "No no no."

"Go to sleep," Geno said, pulling the shade.

"Nuh."

Geno backed away, eyes bulging, head shaking back and forth on his neck. "Stop."

Nuh.

Say it.

Nuh…

Say it, baby boy, before I fuck you in two.

Mos slammed a fist down. *We do not* talk *about that in Nos.*

Geno backed miserably out of the room, leaving the wailing baby behind. He went to his room. The kids used it as a playroom, so he had to share space with all their toys and games and clutter. But it was either this or the second guest room in the musty basement where Tom had his TV, his bar and his pool table. And no fucking way was Geno sleeping down *there*.

Matthew was in full-blown meltdown now. Geno lay on his bed, a pillow wrapped around his ears, but he could still hear the crying. It made him remember how he cried. He cried like a fucking baby.

Cry all you want, baby boy. Your daddy's not coming. Your brother waited until Daddy was across the big ocean.

Nathan went away. First in spirit after Analisa died, then for real that July weekend.

He flew away and left the henhouse door open.

He came back, saw what he'd done, and died.

"You were supposed to rescue me," Geno whispered against his pillow.

Instead it was Captain Hook who came swashbuckling in, guns ablaze. Hook who killed the last man to fuck Geno. Hook who held Geno's head and yelled an order to get those handcuffs off *now*. Hook who gripped his hand tight in the ambulance and promised Nathan was coming.

He came too late.

Matthew screamed from his crib. His voice broke at the apex, making Geno sit up.

What, are you going to leave him crying in there? Alone in the dark with his father a thousand miles away? Trapped like you were, thinking nobody was coming for you?

Geno ran down the hall.

"I'm sorry," he said, reaching into the crib. "I'm sorry. It's all right. I'm here."

Matthew was red-faced and sweaty, tears and snot running in his mouth. He pushed his wet, streaming face into Geno's neck, hiccupping and whimpering. One fist closed around Geno's T-shirt, the other around Geno's hair. A dual death grip.

"Shh." Geno rocked him side to side. "I got you."

Dad's here.

It's over now.

It's all over. I rescued you.

The little hitching breaths grew into longer breaths. "No" became "Na" again.

Back in his room, Geno carefully lay down with Matthew on his chest, the little fists still clenched on his person.

"It's all right."

His hand ran circles on Matthew's damp back. He was so warm. Soft and springy. Like dough to be made into warm bread.

With butter.

A tiny yelp of laughter burst from Geno's throat, followed by the hot sting of tears. Crying again. All he did these days was cry. He was such a fucking baby.

Aren't you, baby boy?

"Na na," Matthew sang.

"Shh," Geno said. "We don't talk about it. Go to sleep."

HERE TO HELP

*T*HE MINUTES DRAGGED by, measured in breaths.

Geno waited until Matthew's mouth went slack around his little thumb, then carefully set the boy down on the mattress, making a little nest of covers.

Then he shook.

His limbs quaked, his teeth rattled. He shook so hard the bed moved and Matthew stirred in his sleep. Geno slid off the mattress to sit on the floor, arms wrapped tight around his knees. He didn't sob, but the tears soaked the knees of his jeans.

Cry all you want, baby boy.

"I can't do this," he said. "I can't do it anymore."

He waited for Mos to answer but Mos was gone. Sometimes it got so bad, even Mos went away, leaving Geno to fend for himself.

He needed help. He should call Dr. Stein. But how could he, after skipping so many appointments, not returning messages and basically flaking out on therapy? Stein was no doubt pissed at him. He'd give a lecture about commitment to recovery or some bullshit. Geno didn't have time. He needed help. Now.

He could call Vern. No, Vern was at work. He'd already taken too much time off for Geno.

Zoë? She was working too. She worked so damn hard. She, too, had already done so much.

Somebody help me. Please.

People had to be out there who could help. He couldn't be the only one. He *knew* he wasn't. The bust of the Mengele Ring was scandalous, front-page news because Anthony was one ring in a larger network. Which meant Geno was one of many victims caught in the coils. He wasn't alone. He couldn't be.

Nobody's coming for you, baby boy.

He squeezed his eyes tight. Opened them again and reached for his phone. His shaking fingers typed "rape hotline" into a search box. He added "New Jersey" and scanned the results. His heart smashed a fist against the inside of his chest. His stomach pulled tight like a knot.

Call. Just call. It's what they do. They wait for people to call and they help.
You can do it.

Again his fingers tapped the screen. The phone trembled as he held it to his ear.

"You've reached the Rape Crisis Hotline. My name is Ruby and I'm here to help."

Geno pressed his teeth together, swallowing hard against the gorge rising in his throat.

"Are you there?" Ruby said. "I'm listening. I want to help."

Geno pulled in a long breath.

"I know it's hard," she said. "Just start with your name, okay? Can you do that?"

His breath held tight against his stomach, Geno managed to push out. "Hi."

A pause. "Hello."

"Yeah…um… This is hard."

"Take your time." Her voice had changed. The softness had gone out of it. It was measured and cool.

"So I was…raped a couple months ago," he said, and immediately broke out in a cold sweat. "And I'm having a tough time right now."

"I see," Ruby said. "Can you tell me what happened?"

Geno panicked. He'd never told anyone what happened. For two months he'd only been in the company of people who knew. He had no story composed. No short and sweet version.

What do I say?

"Well," he said. "I was at this guy's house. I mean, I didn't know him. He was a friend of my brother's. Not a friend. More like a…"

It was all wrong. He was doing this all wrong. He should hang up.

"More like a what?" Ruby said.

"Never mind. It doesn't matter. I was over there and they put some shit in my drink. Like they slipped me a roofie and—"

"They who?"

"My brother's friend. And some other guys that were there. Then it started happening."

"*What* started happening." It wasn't a question.

"I woke up and I was cuffed to a bed." The words were picking up steam now. "Men were in the room. Different men and they kept on coming. It went on and on and it wouldn't stop, and the whole time my brother was watching. They made him watch while I got—"

"Okay, that's enough," Ruby said. Or rather, she snapped it. Curt and dismissive like a mother fed-up with her child's bullshit. "I'm not letting you do this. Too many people in the world need legitimate help for me to waste my time."

Geno's mouth fell open. "What?"

"You heard me. You're not the first pervert to call this hotline and jerk off to a twisted story. Call a sex line or a prostitute or something. Or better yet, get a fucking life. Men like you are the reason we need rape hotlines in the first place. You sick piece of shit."

The line went dead.

Geno's face was numb as he stared across the room. The phone toppled from his hand and fell with a thud on the carpet.

She didn't believe him.

Of course not, he heard Anthony laugh. *You love it. Come on. Say it.*

"I loved it," Geno said.

He scooped Matthew up and put him back in his crib. The baby whimpered a little in his sleep, but didn't wake. Geno raised up the side with a soft click and resisted the urge to lay his hand on Matthew's back.

He loved it too much.

MY FATHER'S CHILD

*H*E WAS OUT of Ambien. Geno found Tylenol PM in Zoë's medicine cabinet and dry-swallowed two caplets. It was a mistake. The pills did the trick of knocking him out, but they lacked Ambien's power of suppressing dreams.

He was in the basement again. His hands cuffed, his wrists dripping blood. He yanked at the metal restraints, sometimes trying to get free, sometimes trying to get them to cut him deeper. Slice through skin and sinew, tear open veins and slice off his life. End this already because it couldn't possibly go on. Yet it went on. And on. And on. Crushing him. Tearing him. Pulling and pushing his body apart. Yanking his head by the hair. Wrapping an arm around his waist and finding the truth.

"Well, look what we have here. Someone's enjoying this."

"Nuh," Geno cried. He cried and cried and cried…

His eyes opened.

Matthew was crying.

Hands were on Geno's shoulder blades. By their shape and weight, Geno instantly knew they were male. He whipped around, rolled over and sat straight up, a fist exploding. He'd never punched another human in his life, but not a shred of hesitation was in the blow. A straight, expert shot to the jaw with a hurricane of rage behind it. Tom Douglas went sprawling into the dresser. The mirror leaning on its back edge slid behind, straight down to the floor.

Glass fractured.

Matthew screamed from his crib.

Out in the hallway, two little girls cried at the top of their lungs.

Geno stared at Tom, breathing hard. "What are you doing here?"

"I live here, asshole," Tom yelled. "What the hell is *wrong* with you?"

Zoë came running down the hall, the baby on her hip. "What happened? What happened?"

"Are you out of your mind?" Tom said, getting to his feet, eyes blazing. "Are you fucking *drunk?* Passed out drunk while my son's screaming his head off?"

"Tom, stop," Zoë said. "Stop yelling. Calm down. Everyone, please." Her voice shook, cracking at the edges. "Calm down."

"You can't wake me up like that," Geno said, on his feet with fists still clenched. "You can't come up behind me that way. You can't fucking *touch* me like—"

"Geno, *please,*" Zoë said, chugging the baby on her shoulder. "Shh. Shh. It's all right."

Geno sank onto the bed, head in his hands. All around him, screaming and crying, broken glass, a family clutching at each other.

"I'm sorry," he said, his voice falling apart.

"No no no," Matthew cried.

Geno looked up. The baby was leaning far out of Zoë's arms, his fat little hands reaching for Geno.

"Ghee," he said, reaching. "Ghee. No."

"He's talking," Stephanie said, gulping back her tears. "He said your name."

Geno's hands hesitated, then started to reach for Matthew. Tom stepped between them and plucked the baby out of Zoë's grasp.

"No no," Matthew cried, squirming over Tom's shoulder. "Ghee no."

"Come on," Tom said to the girls. "Downstairs. Now."

The crying and protesting dwindled away, down the hall and down the stairs, leaving Zoë and Geno staring at each other.

"I'm sorry," he said. "I'm so sorry."

"What happened?"

"I… I fell asleep. I woke up and his hands were on my back. You can't *do* that."

"All right, it's all right," Zoë said, crouching down by the bed. "He didn't know."

"How could he not know? What the fuck does he think happened to me down there?"

"Geno."

"What, does he think I'm making it up?"

"No. No, he just doesn't…understand." She put her hands on his knees.

"Please don't touch me."

Her hands flew off. "I'm sorry."

Geno put his face in his palms again. His mouth was dry and his head ached. He could hear Matthew crying downstairs. Calling Geno's name. It crowded the air in Geno's ears. He shook with wanting, his arms craving to hold the little boy. He wanted it so bad.

Do I like little boys?

Is this how it starts?

Zoë walked over and closed the door, cutting off the sound. "God, he really loves you," she said softly.

All my baby boys are loyal to me.

"I need to go," Geno said.

"What?"

"I need to leave."

"What are you talking about?"

"I can't stay," Geno said, on his feet again. "It's not safe."

"Stop," Zoë said. "Tom was just upset. He's not going to hurt—"

"I don't mean not safe for me. I mean it's not safe for…"

Zoë crossed her arms. "For who?"

"Nothing. Never mind. It's just better if I go."

"Go where? You're being ridiculous."

"You don't understand. I can't explain. I can't explain any of this to anyone, nobody understands, nobody…" He exhaled. "I need to go. If I stay here, it'll make things tense and miserable. You need to take care of your family first."

"You are family," she cried. "You're my goddamn half-brother. You're my father's *child.*"

"But I'm not your child. Or Tom's. I'll be fine."

"You're serious about this."

"It's just better," he said, picking up a backpack.

"Don't… Put that down. Don't leave tonight. You're making an impulsive decision after something upsetting. Sleep on it." Her hand reached to him, then remembered, and she took one of the backpack straps instead. "Please. Don't leave tonight. Let everyone calm down. Things will look different in the morning."

He sighed. He let go the backpack. He tried to smile. "All right."

"Promise me."

"I promise."

She ran a hand through her hair. Something within her seemed to crumple. "I feel terrible."

He replied with another weak smile and the truth. "I don't feel anything."

He stayed in his room the rest of the night. The light off, to make it appear he was sleeping. Really he was packing. And when he sensed the house was in a deep sleep, he left.

CURVING TO THE EAST

*T*HE TWO WEEKS between Ari's return from Vancouver and his departure for college didn't just fly by. They *dissolved.* Jav thanked God Trelawney Lark let him carry the lease of the Guelisten apartment through the end of the month. It allowed him to use it as a staging area for all the art supplies and dormitory clobber that wouldn't fit in his apartment.

He ferried things upstate with a bizarre furtiveness. Sneaking in and out of the town like a thief.

Or an illicit lover, he thought sourly.

He texted Alex a couple of times. Variations of *hey, I'm in town, dropping some stuff off. Got time for a beer?*

Both times Alex made one excuse or another and Jav found he was more relieved than disappointed. But one weekend, Alex came to the city and made an overture to get together. Jav was about to reply yes, when all at once, he knew it was no.

I can't, he thought. *Not yet anyway. I'll feel like shit. I'll say or do something stupid. I'll get depressed.*

He tried to let it go, offer it up. Keep his heart and eyes open, loving and seeing what happened. The last days evaporated and then Jav and Ari were in the loaded car, heading for New Paltz.

"You got a title for your next book?" Ari asked.

Typically Jav didn't share titles of his works in progress. But Ari had been the first person he told about *The Trade.* He liked the symmetry of telling him now, *"The Chocolate Hour."*

"What's that from?"

"It was a line I heard while I was out collecting stories. 'And then it was the chocolate hour.' It stuck in my head and wouldn't let go."

Ari nodded, his mouth silently moving around the title. "I like it. You get a lot of imagery in just three words." He unzipped his hoodie and wiggled out of the sleeves. "Roger's going to come see me next weekend," he said. Meaning his biological father, Roger Lark. Val and Trelawney Lark's brother.

Because life couldn't be weird enough.

"Yeah?" Jav said. "What's he in town for?"

"No reason." Ari glanced toward Jav with a grin. "He's just coming to see me."

"Well, that's all kinds of cool."

"He wants to help pay for college."

"Ah," Jav said. "He and I had a chat about that."

"Mm." Ari laced hands behind his head and his grin grew broader. "Dig me with two fathers."

Jav laughed, but the remark kind of cuddled up to him. Laid its head on his shoulder and took his hand.

Silence for a few miles before Ari asked, "Been on any dates?"

"A few."

"You don't sound enthused."

Jav exhaled heavily. "Twenty-three years I had this perfect social life. Perfect date after perfect date. I'm really becoming aware of what an *act* it was. What a repertory of roles I played and none of them were really me. It's kind of put me in a mini existential crisis. I have moments when I don't know who the hell I am." He looked over at his nephew. "That got heavy. Sorry."

"No, don't be. Weird how you got to have a hundred girlfriends without really *having* a girlfriend."

"Yeah. Serial love affairs, but only the good parts. And because of the arrangement, it was leaping right into romantic behavior no one in their right mind would do on a first date. Women telling me *I love you* an hour after meeting."

"Did you say it back?"

"Yeah," Jav said. The word stung his mouth. "It… I was playing a part. Getting paid to say what they wanted to hear. To be the love of their life for a few hours. I guess it's no wonder now that I'm trying to date women for real, I'm numb to it. Trying to be real feels like an act. I just have no spontaneity. Everything feels calculated and fake. I spend more time wondering what the hell this woman *wants* from me, rather than what I want from her."

"You don't exactly trust her motives."

"Exactly."

Another interval of silence. A small elephant lounged on the console, tapping the end of its trunk.

Go ahead, Jav thought. *Just ask.*

"Think you might date guys?" Ari said, chewing on his thumbnail.

"I'm open to it. Would you be all right with that?"

Ari's head flicked to him. "Me?" A chuckle made his shoulders twitch. "Why does what I think matter?"

"Because it does," Jav said.

The air in the car swelled with a strange, emotional bewilderment. Each man realizing the other's opinion meant something.

"I hope you find someone," Ari said. "You deserve it. Male or female, it's about time you had someone you can be yourself with."

"Thanks."

Ari was quiet a minute. "Either way, don't be screwing in front of my dog. Okay?"

The car wobbled in its lane as Jav burst out laughing. "Shut up," he said, smacking the back of his hand against Ari's shoulder.

Ari whacked him back. "I'm *just* saying, T. He's young and very impressionable. And do we need to have a talk about safe sex? A different condom every time?"

"Back off, punk. I was having safe sex before you were even born."

The laughter died away as the car rolled onto the span of the Newburgh-Beacon bridge. Both Jav and Ari glanced to the right, looking up the Hudson River. The mighty waterway began curving to the east here. Even on the most crystal-clear day, neither man could even pretend to see the Mid-Hudson Bridge and the little town of Guelisten sheltered beside it. Still they gazed upriver, thinking of the place where they'd both found love.

SEPTEMBER

BEN HIERONIM

*G*ENO LIVED AT Vern's house the rest of the summer.

"Nothing happened," he said. "It's not Zoë's fault. She's great. It's me. I just feel better here with you. I've known you longer and it's like being near Dad."

Behind his glasses, Vern looked concerned, but also touched. He didn't ask Geno many questions. If he had his own conversation with Zoë about what happened, he never said so. He made arrangements and helped Geno get ready for college.

"You're sure you're ready to go?" he asked.

"Yes," Geno said, only sure he was ready to go somewhere where nobody knew him.

At freshman orientation, he introduced himself as Mo. One short, tough syllable. The bare minimum. A suit of armor he pulled on in the morning and laid in a drawer at night.

"It's going all right," Geno said to Vern on the phone. "I like the campus. Classes are cool. I'm getting involved in the radio station."

"Good, good," Vern said. "Making any friends?"

"A few."

"And you like your roommate? Bill?"

"Ben."

Vern tried hard to get one of the residence hall's single rooms for Geno, but enrollment at Brooklyn College was up and first come was first served. So Geno was sharing digs with a sophomore boy from Connecticut.

"He's okay," Geno said, truthfully. "Good guy. So far, we don't annoy each other."

"How do you feel physically? Everything all right?"

"Yeah. I still don't sleep all that great, but I have the Ambien. I saw Dr. Bloom and she green-lighted me to start working out. The campus has a fitness center, but she wants me to work with a certified trainer. The school helped me find someone. He's a physical therapist but he also does personal training at the Flatbush YMCA. It's just a few blocks away."

"Excellent, sounds like a perfect fit."

"Yeah, maybe if I'm getting some regular exercise, I'll sleep better."

"I bet you will."

"Sorry it's another expense, but—"

"Don't give it a thought," Vern said. "The money is yours to do as you wish."

Geno rolled to his back on his bed, slinging a forearm over his eyes. "Any buyers for the house yet?"

"No, but the listing only just went live. The realtor's having two open houses this weekend."

"Okay." He swallowed. "Have you talked to Detective Mackin?"

Vern's voice softened. "Regularly. But no updates."

Geno exhaled.

"You know I'll tell you the minute I hear anything."

"I know. Just…" The next inhale hurt his throat and chest. "Those pictures are out there and…*he's* out there."

"I know. And after you, no one wants him taken in more badly than me."

"I gotta head to class now," Geno said. "I'll talk to you next week?"

"Talk to me anytime."

Geno hung up and collected his backpack. He stepped into the hall just as his roommate, Ben, was arriving with a couple buddies.

"What's up, my man," Ben said, coming in high for a handshake.

"Mo," the other guys echoed. Like people greeted Norm in *Cheers*. Handshakes around, bit of chit-chat and Geno was out of there. Feeling eyes on his back but no hostility. By now, at the end of September, he'd established himself as the residence hall's weird loner.

The afternoon was chilly, and a brisk wind ran a hand over Geno's head. Before coming to school, he clipped his hair to an eighth-inch buzz. He thought it made him look tougher. Also, nobody could grab a handful of stubble and yank your head back. Of course, his head got cold, especially at night. Being cold often triggered his anxiety or made it worse. He started wearing wool hats while he was studying. Inevitably, his left hand would creep up under the ribbed brim, fingers rubbing against the thick, soft nap of short hairs. Words would blur in his eyes and he'd be gazing off, into the past, full of memory so distant, yet so deep. A soul memory of little hands on his head.

Brother mine.

From his crown, his hand would drift down to his right side, where stars were supposed to be inked when he got to college. Then his fingers would drift a little more to the still-tender scar where the colostomy used to empty out, and he vowed no stars would be at his side.

Ever.

Which didn't stop him from getting tattoos. His first design was a little red hen inside a house. He put it on the cap of his shoulder, with *Gallinero* in pretty script beneath. On his other shoulder, in stronger letters, he had *Nathan* inked. A week later, he went back and had the Hebrew name put under it, *Natan ben Hieronim.* Nathan, son of Jerome. In the ancient lettering, it felt like a protective charm as well as a tribute. He believed fervently in the power of names, just as he believed the persona of Mo kept Geno safe.

He wanted more ink. Wanted to cover himself in wards and spells and magic. He didn't mind the pain of being tattooed. It was the vulnerability in taking his shirt off and lying down while the artist worked, *together* with pain. Maybe when his body got stronger he'd feel differently. For now, he had his parents' hands on his shoulders.

It was enough.

CLIENT PRIVILEGE

*T*HE LAST DAY of a program was always tough. This program was the first of its kind at the Dutchess County Family Shelter, and its graduates—as Stef liked to call them—were incredibly emotional. They cried as they hugged Stef goodbye. He had to hold on tight as he hugged back, assuring them it wasn't goodbye, and what they learned through art therapy was only the beginning. With it they could both express the pain of the past and create a vision of the future.

"Come back," the kids said. "Come back and do it again."

"Do this again," the women said, mothers and wives and girlfriends who had fled unspeakable abuse. "Even if we're not here anymore, keep doing it."

Exhausted, Stef lingered in the empty art room. It was once the shelter's kitchen, but when they got a grant to renovate and build new dining facilities, the director called the Coalition for Creative Therapy and inquired about creating an art space. Stef couldn't get up to Poughkeepsie fast enough, teeth itching to sink into a project.

The kitchen's industrial sinks, worktop surfaces and shelving were perfect for artwork. It was a space conducive to making a mess. Now Stef walked around returning supplies to their proper places. Brushing off the counters, straightening materials and taking his time letting this adventure come to its end.

"I can't thank you enough," Adrienne, the director said as she walked in.

"It was a privilege," he said.

"I wanted to talk to you about doing an exhibit," she said. "I think it would be an incredible opportunity to raise awareness, both for the shelter and for art therapy."

"Absolutely," he said. "Would you do it here?"

Adrienne sighed. "We could. But I'd love to find a nicer space. The work deserves it."

"I'll poke around," Stef said. "See what's available in the area."

"You want to grab a cup of coffee?"

Stef checked his watch. "I need to get over to Marist College. My mother's doing a lecture there this afternoon. We came up on the train together."

"A lecture on what?"

"Sexual fluidity in the modern age. Give or take a few tangents."

Adrienne's eyebrows rose. "I'll call you a cab."

Stef got to Fusco Recital Hall just as the Dean of Liberal Arts was making his closing remarks, thanking Rory for her time and fascinating expertise. The applause was generous and sustained. A few people even stood to clap. From her easy chair onstage, Rory smiled, composed and gracious. She put the palms of her hands together and made a tiny bow of her head. Stef smiled. She got that little namaste gesture from him.

He sat down, knowing the post-talk schmooze could be a while. People were coming up to Rory, shaking hands, talking earnestly. A few of them had copies of her books they wanted signed. Stef yawned, now wishing he'd grabbed that coffee. He half-dozed in the back row, people-watching. Finally the crowd thinned out to just a handful, and he made his way down the steep stairs.

Rory was chatting with a fascinatingly androgynous woman. Slender and pale, cropped blonde hair and a silver nose ring. She held a plastic-bound sheaf of papers in one hand.

"Oh Stef, you're here," Rory said. "This is my son," she said to the blonde woman, who reached to shake Stef's offered hand.

Rory pushed her purple glasses up her nose. "This young lady… Forgive me, I'm terrible with names."

"Trelawney Lark."

"She did a paper on me while she was at Brown."

Rolling her eyes, Trelawney waved the bound papers. "Usually I keep the memory and let go of the thing. This I had to keep for some reason. Now I know why. Would you mind terribly…?"

"You got an A, of course I don't mind." Rory signed the front page and handed the pen back. "How did the last day go?" she asked Stef.

"Emotional."

"I can imagine." Rory turned to Trelawney. "Stef's an art therapist."

"Really?" Trelawney's eyes were pale, icy grey.

"I just finished a program at a domestic violence shelter," Stef said. "Almost finished, actually. The director wants to do an exhibit of the work. We need to look around the area for a space, though."

"A gallery?" Rory said.

"That would be nice, but it doesn't necessarily have to be."

"I have a space," Trelawney said.

"Where?"

"I own a building in Guelisten. The upstairs used to be my mother's gallery. It's empty at the moment. I'd be more than happy to let you look at it."

"Why don't you go now," Rory said. "I have people I want to see. I'll get a car service home."

"Are you sure?" Stef said.

She kissed his face and dismissed both of them, drawn into another conversation.

"You sure you have the time?" Stef asked Trelawney.

"It's no problem at all. I'm going there anyway. It's across the street from the station. You can hop the train right after. Plus a fabulous coffee shop is under the gallery, if you're in need of caffeine."

"I'm in," Stef said.

The gallery was on the second floor of an old brick building, its windows facing the train station with a gorgeous view of the river.

"My mother made dollhouses," Trelawney said. "They were displayed here until about two years ago, then we sold or donated them."

"All of them?"

"My sister and I each kept one. She owns the dress shop downstairs."

"You both stayed in your hometown, then."

"Minus a few youthful jaunts. It's a great town to come home to. My older brother owns the apartment on the other side of that wall. I rent it out for him. He's the globetrotter in the family."

"Where does he live?"

"Everywhere," Trelawney said. "You might've heard of him. He has a show on HGTV, *Home in a Tree.*"

"Your brother is The Treehouse Guy?"

She smiled. "Yes, he is." Her eyes flicked over Stef's shoulder and her chin rose. "Hey there, handsome…"

Stef looked back. A man was at the top of the gallery's stairs. Tall and built, wearing jeans and a black blazer. Taking off aviator shades to show his face.

Whoa.

As Stavroula Kalo would say, this was a guy who made your underwear sit up and beg. Stef blinked as his hand reached in slow motion, extending a shake and his name.

"Javier Landes," the man said. "Hi." The handshake was brisk and firm, but his smile wobbled a little, as if he were shy.

"Jav's my favorite ex-tenant," Trelawney said. "And among other things, a marketing specialist."

"Only free marketing," Jav said. His eyes were deep brown under sleek brows. Stef felt his own gaze widen, just a hair, before he glanced away.

Don't stare, Finch.

"Stef's an art therapist," Trelawney said.

"Really?" Jav said.

"Yeah," Stef said, his eyes still averted, looking casually around the empty walls. "I've been doing a program with women and kids at a domestic violence shelter in Poughkeepsie." Now he turned back toward Jav. "I'm looking for space to do an exhibit of their work. Raise money for the shelter."

"And awareness." Jav was looking straight at him, not blinking.

"That's right." Stef's awareness was raised to the apex of attention. Every hair on his body sticking out like an antenna as Jav looked in his eyes.

May I help you? Stef thought. *Please?*

"Come down for a cup of coffee," Trelawney said. She put her hand on Jav's arm. "You, too."

Her hand stayed tucked in his elbow as they went down the stairs, Stef following. The hair on his nape was falling back into place, noting Trelawney's chummy lean against Jav and the way Jav opened the door for her, his hand grazing her lower back. He didn't look around as he held the door an extra second for Stef, no longer.

Oh well. It was fun while it lasted.

Trelawney led them next door to what appeared to be a reader's paradise. The space stretched the entire depth of the building, lined with shelves crammed full of books. A fireplace at one end. A maze of couches, easy chairs and small tables. A line of tall stools at the long chrome bar. And all through the air, the intoxicating smell of coffee.

"Holy crap," Stef said. "I want to be held hostage here."

Jav stopped short and looked back at him. "That's literally what I said the first time I walked in."

"I think I just came."

Zero reaction. Not a smile, not a smirk.

Definitely straight, Stef thought. *Glad we cleared that up.*

As Stef's eyes went on circling the bookshelves and the artwork, he grabbed quick details of Jav. He looked in his forties, only a little bit of grey at the back of his head and in his sideburns. Unlike Stef, who was more salt than pepper. It was the Finch genes. The men kept their hair all their lives, but it went white by the time they were fifty.

Jav slipped off his black sport coat and laid it on an empty stool. He wore a plain white T-shirt under it, which made his dark skin a weapon. He had a large dragonfly tattoo on one forearm. On the other forearm, a ship's wheel. No other decoration. No jewelry of any kind, just a wristwatch. This guy had a master's degree in Less is More.

"Who drew all the comic strips?" Stef asked, peering at the long wall next to the bar.

"My nephew," Jav said.

"No shit. Where'd he go to school?"

"He just started at New Paltz."

"Visual arts?"

"Yeah."

"He'll love it. They have a great program."

His voice seemed amplified in his ears. He took his coffee cup and walked over to the wall. Both out of curiosity and the need to distance himself from the thick attraction. He could keep cool when a woman he was digging gave him the brush-off, but when guys made him nervous and he couldn't do anything about it, he tended to say stupid things. Loudly.

Trelawney came around the bar and wiggled back between Jav's knees, pulling his arms around her from behind.

Well, you're awful cute together, Stef thought. *You must lay around naked and stare at each other all day.*

Like he needed that visual.

Behind him, Jav mumbled something and Trelawney laughed. "Aren't I lucky then," she said.

Stef turned and smiled at them. "I'd say she's lucky."

"He's the best hugger," Trelawney said. "He really should get paid for it."

Over her shoulder, Jav mouthed, "I do."

Then he winked.

Stef's chest dropped into his shoes as the attraction yanked him in and French-kissed him.

Jesus, get a grip.

The bell on the jamb rang and customers came in. Trelawney went back behind the bar. Stef slid onto his stool as Jav swiveled to face forward and their knees collided.

"Sorry."

"My bad."

"You live in town?" Stef said.

"I did. I rented the apartment upstairs from Trelawney. Which reminds me." He reached in his pocket and pulled out a set of keys, which he pushed across the counter to Trelawney.

"Thank you, sir," she said.

"I'm in Manhattan now," Jav said. "Riverside Drive. You?"

"I'm down in Chelsea."

They stared again.

Chelsea, Stef thought. *You know, the big, fat, LGBT neighborhood?*

Jav said nothing and Stef looked away, checking his watch. His train was in fifteen minutes, but he needed to get out of here already. He was starting to feel toyed with. Not by Jav, but by fate. He wouldn't give it the satisfaction. He had a nice bit of eye candy, now it was time to leave. He took a last sip of coffee, then reached for his messenger bag. "Listen, it was good to meet you."

"Same." They shook hands, Jav's grip holding a nanosecond longer than Stef thought necessary.

Screw it.

"You got a card?" he asked.

"Sure. Give me yours?"

Jav smoothly drew a card from the inside pocket of his jacket while Stef had to set his bag on the stool and dig around in its jumbled mess. "You can see I'm hopeless at selling myself. I never have a card when I need one. Goddammit…" He unloaded notebooks and his paperback, trawled through a tangle of ear bud cords, broken pencils and gum wrappers.

"Hey, that's a great book," Trelawney said, spinning Gil Rafael's *Client Privilege* around to face her. Jav was staring at the black and green cover, his face completely expressionless. Like he didn't know what a book was or why anyone would carry one around. Finally a strike against Mr. Perfect.

Dude, if you don't read, Stef thought, *we ain't go no future anyway.* "Ah. Here you go." He slid the card down the counter toward Jav. "Don't lose it."

He packed up, shouldered his bag and tucked the book under his arm. "I'll be in touch," he said to Trelawney. He raised a palm to Jav who barely lifted his fingers off the countertop in return. It seemed a mile to the door, which closed behind him with another jingle of bells. Stef exhaled and glanced down at the card in his hand. Plain white stock and simple black letters. *Javier Landes.* A phone number and an email.

"Landes," Stef said softly.

He couldn't shake a weird feeling that something important had just happened.

You found a venue for the exhibition, he thought. *You got a cup of great coffee and a very nice deposit in the spank bank. That's all that happened. Now get on the train and don't be stupid.*

How did Trelawney put it before?

Keep the memory, let go of the thing.

With a brisk flick of his head, Stef slipped the card into the pages of his book and set out across the street, shading his eyes against the sun that was starting to dip toward the west bank of the Hudson.

"Hey," someone called as he reached the steps to the platform. He had a foot on a tread when the voice called again. "Stef."

He looked back. Jav was crossing the street. His stride long, his body tight. The sun in his hair and eyes.

"I'm actually driving back into Manhattan," he said. "Want a ride?"

CUSHMAN ROW

"**W**HY DOES IT say 'curator and sailor' on your card?" Jav asked.

"It's dumb," Stef said.

"No really. Why?"

"Well, curator is from the Latin *curare*. Means to take care. In Old English, a curator is a guardian."

"Are you someone's guardian?" Jav asked.

"In a sense. I work at the Coalition for Creative Therapy and the past two years, I've been working almost exclusively with male survivors of sexual assault."

Jav's eyebrows rose above the frames of the aviator shades. "That has to be intense work."

"But important work."

"Why do you do it?"

"Why?"

Jav's shy smile unfolded. "Asking people what they do is boring. Asking why they do it is so much more interesting."

"Why do I do it?" Stef chewed on the question.

"Personal experience?" Jav said tentatively.

"No," Stef said. "I just… I guess I seem to have the right kind of…" He wracked his brain, which looked back at him, clueless. Jav sat quietly, a hand on the wheel, the other rubbing his chin. Stef leaned on the patience as his mind relaxed into the question.

"I want to say I have a knack for it," he said. "But knack isn't the right word, it makes it sound like a trick to master."

"Only so much of it is skill, I would think."

"Right. The rest is insight and… Well, like any true vocation, it just *is.*"

"Are these victims of child abuse?"

"Some of them. Long-term abuse by a family member or someone in the community. For others it was a one-off event. They were raped by a stranger. Or strangers."

Jav took off his shades and set them in the little cubby beneath the radio. Stef waited. Whatever Jav said next would be a clear indicator of the kind of guy he was.

"That has to be a somewhat invisible demographic." Jav's gaze was intent on the windshield. "I mean, how many male victims come forward?"

"Not many," Stef said. "If a woman is afraid or ashamed to tell her ordeal, a man can be twice as reluctant."

Jav glanced at him, then looked away again, his shoulders giving a small twitch. "I'm fighting against the urge to say it's worse because it's not. Rape is rape. There's no better or worse scenario for men or women. But for a man, it's got to have *some* truly different psychological effects."

"Oh yeah," Stef said. "It fucks with their identity on a whole lot of levels."

"Back to what I said: that has to be intense, complicated work."

"It is."

Jav smiled. "But now 'curator and sailor' make sense."

"I take them from one place to another place."

"Using art."

"It helps express the things that can't yet be spoken out loud."

Jav raised and lowered his chin in a single nod, his eyes blinking. "You're a captain."

"Kind of. Anyway, enough about me. Why do you do whatever it is you do?"

"I'm a writer," Jav said. "I do it to keep from talking out loud to myself in public."

"Books?" Stef said. *So you* do *read?*

Jav flipped a thumb over his shoulder, toward the back seat. "Just picked up the proofs of my latest."

"No shit." Stef twisted around and saw a large cardboard box on the floor. He loosened the seat belt and reached, plucking out a heavy paperback. A brand-new book in all its exhilarating, pristine glory. The edges square and trim. The cover glossy and crisp, its corners unmarred, the spine unbroken.

Stef turned it in his hand. *The Trade* printed in white above a grainy photo of the Twin Towers. His eyes lowered to the author name. Doubled back and read it again.

"What the fuck?" he said.

Jav chuckled, running a hand through his hair. "I'm having the weirdest day."

Stef scrambled between his feet to reach into his messenger bag. He pulled out his paperback and held both books side by side.

Client Privilege, by Gil Rafael.

The Trade, by Gil Rafael.

"You're him?"

"Yeah."

"Are you shitting me?"

Jav shook his head. "This never happens. Swear to God."

Stef looked at the covers, then at their alleged author. "Can I see some ID?"

"Gil Rafael is my pen name. I don't have ID for him."

Stef put the books down in his lap and crossed his arms. "I don't know about this, man. Could be a line you lay on people."

"Fair enough." Jav reached into his inside pocket, then handed Stef his phone. "Open my email, search for Lorraine Merril. She's my agent. Look for something from her back in July. With 'contract' in the subject line."

Stef took the device with a weird thrill. It was a startlingly intimate overture. These days, being granted access to someone's phone was like being invited into their pants.

Easy, Finch.

He scrolled through Jav's email, finding dozens from Lorraine Merril. He tapped on an attachment and a PDF opened. Turning the phone horizontally, he read the first lines under his breath.

"*Book publishing contract for agreement between Javier Landes, 'author,' a.k.a. Gil Rafael, 'pseudonym,' and…* Holy shit."

"Nice to meet you."

"It's weird to meet you. I never met an author in my life."

"I never met anyone carrying my book in their bag."

Stef held up *Client Privilege.* "I'd love to say I'm a big fan but so far, I've only read half of this. And became annoyed when I had to put it down. So…"

The color was up high along Jav's cheekbones and his head bobbled around like he was looking for a graceful exit from the conversation. "What happened to your eyebrow?"

Stef reached up to touch the scar that bisected through his left brow, intrigued Jav had noticed it. "Knife fight."

"For real?"

"No. I fell and hit my head against a filing cabinet."

"I like the knife fight better."

"It's more badass."

"You said you live in Chelsea?"

"West twentieth," Stef said. "I kind of live with my mom, which isn't as pathetic as it sounds. She owns the townhouse. I rent the garden apartment."

"What does she do?"

"She's retired now, but she was a psychologist and a sociology professor at NYU."

"Why d— sorry, I ask a lot of questions."

"I don't mind."

They asked, answered and talked all the way down the Saw Mill, across the Henry Hudson Bridge and along the length of Manhattan. When the conversation took a rest, they sat still, listening to classic rock. When Springsteen's "Out in the Street" came on, Stef leaned to turn up the volume.

"This is so high school," he said. "Friday night theme song."

"I haven't heard this in years," Jav said. But naturally, any Springsteen song heard once was coded in your DNA forever, and soon they were both singing lustily, letting their voices go all rough and raspy to get to the high notes. An excitement coursed in Stef's veins. Curious, but tempered. On tune, but a little rough on the high notes.

"I like your ink," Jav said, flicking his chin toward Stef's forearm.

"Thanks." Stef turned it up and then back again, letting Jav see the intricate sleeve of winged horses and centaurs.

"Does it have a story?" Jav asked.

"More like a lifelong fascination. I guess because I was born both a Finch and a Sagittarius. Something in me digs winged horses."

"I'm a Taurus," Jav said. "I dig making up bullshit."

"You always been a writer?"

"Been bullshitting on paper since I was a kid. Then I did a lot of web copy. Speaking of which, if you need a website for the exhibit, I can hook you up with my friend Russ."

"Great, I'd appreciate that." They were moving beyond the blocks of the Upper West Side, where Jav said he lived. "Dude, you don't have to take me all the way downtown."

"I don't mind."

Stef didn't either, already constructing a casual way to feel out if Jav was interested in getting together.

Following Stef's directions, Jav turned off Eleventh Avenue onto 19th Street. Up Tenth Avenue for a block and onto West 20th Street. The General Theological Seminary loomed on the left side of the car.

"It's four-twelve," Stef said. "The red brick cluster on the right there."

"Are you kidding me," Jav said. "You live on Cushman Row?"

Stef laughed. "Mom prefers to say I squat on Cushman Row."

Jav double-parked and leaned on the wheel, looking past Stef at the seven red-brick townhouses. They were among the oldest homes in Chelsea and considered to be the best examples of Greek Revival architecture in the city.

"You grew up here?" Jav asked.

"No, on Roosevelt Island. This was my maternal grandparents' townhouse. Mom inherited it when they died."

"Jesus."

Stef hesitated. "You want to come in?"

Still leaning on the steering wheel, Jav looked at him. "Maybe someday." His full lips parted in that shy smile, and Stef's own heart curled inward, hiding behind his ribs, just as bashful.

"All right," he said. "Well, great to meet you. In a lot of ways."

"Same."

They shook hands. "I'll give you a call about that website?"

"Sure."

Stef got out and shut the door. Both men threw a palm up in a wave and Jav drove away.

Stef watched the SUV reach Ninth Avenue just as the light turned green. It crossed the intersection and slowly disappeared in traffic. Stef counted to thirty, then took his phone out of one pocket and Jav's business card from the other.

Thanks for the ride, he texted to the number on the card.

Five seconds later, from the depths of his messenger bag, came an electronic chime he'd never heard before.

"Oh shit," he said, digging around inside. He found Jav's phone sandwiched between the two books, Stef's text flashing on its display.

"I took his fucking phone," he said.

He looked down the block, then back at his hands, each holding a phone. Slowly he sank onto the front steps, laughing under his breath. "This could either be brilliant or a disaster."

He waited, following a hunch and fighting the temptation to snoop in Jav's phone. It felt heavy and sleek and sensual in his palm.

Five minutes passed.

He wondered what Jav would feel like in his palm.

You're insane.

After ten minutes, the black SUV came down 20th Street again and Stef felt a smile crack his face open.

Gotcha.

The passenger window slid down as Jav pulled up. He sat back from the wheel and crossed his arms, eyebrows raised. Stef got up and approached, wiggling the phone in front of him.

"Yours, I believe?" he said.

"Mine."

"I lied about the art therapy thing," Stef said. "I'm a professional thief."

"I'm not a writer," Jav said. "I'm an assassin."

Laughing, Stef handed the phone over. "Let's try this again. I'll give you a call."

"Okay."

They both paused, holding eyes. The evening was a beautiful thing. A golden New York moment full of promise.

"Get out of here," Stef said. He thumped his fist on the car's roof and stepped back. Once more, he watched until the car disappeared past the intersection, then he turned to go up the stairs.

Lilia Kalo, his mother's partner, was coming up the street, wearing her grubby red quilted jacket and carrying a cloth tote bag in each hand.

"Hello, Pony," she said, using his childhood nickname.

"Mom went to dinner," he said, taking the bags from her. "She'll get a car service home."

"Yes, she told me. They had beautiful apples at the market. I brought you some."

Stef loved apples. "You're my favorite."

"You look happy." Her thick Hungarian accent made a goulash of *happy*.

I met someone, he thought.

BETTER THAN THIS

*T*HE CUSHMAN ROW townhouses were each five stories high. Most owners rented the uppermost floors and Stef's mother, Rory Finch, was no exception. She and Lilia lived on the parlor and third floors, while Stef had the garden apartment. The fourth and fifth stories were rented to professional couples without children or pets. The attic had a small bathroom and technically could be used as living space, but it was filled with Rory's junk and she had no desire to haul it out.

The townhouse had been in Rory's family since the 1850s. Stef's father, Marcus, had no claim to it during the divorce, but brotherly tensions were tight and bitter from the unspoken understanding the property would be left to Stef someday. Stef knew it was just as likely Rory could leave the house to some charity or turn it into a museum. It was best never to get too set on what you thought Rory would do with her life.

Still, it was a beautiful apartment and Stef took exceedingly good care of it. In turn, it soothed and comforted him after long, hard days at sea, navigating terrified young men.

The American Finches who made pianos descended from Danish Finks who made cabinetry and furniture. An eye for a clean, classical line was in Stef's DNA, and his minimalist taste let the open floor plan and garden view speak for themselves. Clutter and frills irritated him. The only reckless mess he liked was the creative process. Where he lived, ate and slept, he liked it neat.

He popped a beer and took to the sectional couch with his laptop, answering a few emails. He always sat on the side oriented toward the fireplace, not the one facing the TV. Stef didn't watch much primetime. His job was stressful enough without getting bogged down in the problems of fictional characters. His visual nature sucked him into a storyline while his analytical, insightful nature started digging into and sorting out imaginary angst. Internalizing all the drama and brooding about it far beyond the final credits. It was like working a second shift he didn't get paid for and could never cure. He stuck to books, which he could put down, or the radio, which he could turn down. More often than not, he chose silence.

He jumped in his skin when his phone rang, thinking it could be Jav. It was Deborah Cenk, an optometrist he'd met at a party last weekend. Did he want to have dinner tomorrow? Catch a movie?

"Sure," he said, remembering shiny curls, big breasts and an infectious laugh.

He dealt with a few more emails, then shut his laptop, put it aside and closed his eyes, exhaling. His mind combed through the day's images, sorting and lingering on little details. The couch put arms around him. His mind unraveled at the edges and he slept.

The ping of an incoming message dumped him out of the snooze. He lunged for the phone. It squirmed out of one hand and through the other, laughing in his face as it slid between two sections of the couch and clattered onto the floor beneath. He had to shove aside the coffee table and hit the deck on his stomach, thrust an arm under to drag it out. All that hassle and it was only Thomas, wanting to hang out.

Still foggy with sleep, Stef chewed his bottom lip and ran fingers through his hair. He knew Thomas from grad school days. They networked professionally and their social circles overlapped in a few places.

He was also something of a fuck buddy.

Stef considered the invitation. The buzz of meeting Jav was still crackling in his veins. It was so random. So weirdly coincidental. They hadn't been introduced or set up. No Grindr match or gym crush. They just wandered into the same place at the same time. Stef to look at the gallery, Jav to return his keys. And they met. The Gil Rafael thing took it from a cool story to a *crazy* story, one worth chewing on a little longer.

If you go chew on Thomas, it'll kind of end the story, Stef thought. *It feels cheap.*

Honestly, it felt like cheating.

Which was the dumbest thing he'd ever heard of.

I don't know, he typed back, hedging. **Long day. Kind of beat.**

Thomas persisted, as Stef knew he would. **Come on, it's been forever since I saw your cute ass.**

A sucker for being validated, Stef agreed to meet up for a beer. Just one. Maybe two.

Of course, some other buddies showed up and he had about five. A good time, but he kept catching himself watching the door, as if Jav were due to show up as well. Typically annoyed by people who couldn't keep their noses out of their devices in public, he kept reaching for his phone, wanting to text Jav. Wanting to make sure Jav hadn't texted him.

Christ, who is this guy?

With each beer and every unsatisfying phone check, Stef's euphoria gave way to an itchy, frustrated and fretful burn. He was hungry.

Thirsty.

"Want to split?" Thomas said, sliding a hand down Stef's spine, into a back pocket and squeezing.

The *yes* stumbled on the tip of Stef's tongue, looking over the edge into the abyss. Instead of beckoning with a seductive, crooked finger, the maw of desire crossed its arms and gave him a long, considering look.

You're better than this, it declared.

Stef squirmed under the reproach. At the same time, something deeper within his consciousness agreed.

Wait. Just wait. Walk away. Go home. Give it a chance.

Give what *a chance,* he argued to himself. *Jav's probably straight. It was a meet, not a…thing.*

But it feels like a thing.

His shoulder twitched the exchange off, annoyed. He didn't need this shit, he needed to get laid. Yet as he stared over Thomas's edge, into the depths beneath, he knew what he sought wasn't down there.

He smiled at Thomas and gently shook his head. "I'm beat and I've got work in the morning," he said.

"Wow, you've never turned me down before."

Stef flicked his eyes toward the ceiling and finished the last of his beer.

"What's his name?" Thomas said, his hand still caressing Stef's ass.

"Deborah," Stef said. "She's an optometrist."

Now the hand came out of the pocket. "I see."

Stef laughed and punched Thom's shoulder. "Good one."

THE OPTOMETRIST

STEF SAT WITH Max Springer at the art room's sand table. After five weeks of therapy, he was beyond pleased with the boy's progress. He was less moody, more verbal. But today, with the unveiling of the new sand table, Max was...*Max*.

He plunged both hands in, up to the elbow. He practically climbed into the sand to push and dig and build and demolish. Round and round the table he moved, talking nonstop, a field general plotting a war. He gave Stef constant orders: mix this, spoon that, dig here. Stef followed directions and waited between tasks. He only touched and participated with permission. He listened as Max made rules for the elaborate games and justified them with, "Because I said so."

"Your game, your rules," Stef said, the game of course being a metaphor for Max's own body.

"My rules."

Max buried a dozen fake gold coins in the sand, then had Stef help him heap more sand on top, building a mountain. Pouring water and packing it down before adding more, they made it high.

"Now we dig a tunnel," Max said, handing Stef a spoon. "You go that side, I go this side. We meet in the middle and find the treasure."

Each started burrowing from their side.

"In, in, in," Max chanted, flinging spoonfuls.

Stef was hyper-attentive. All the creations in this room, all the structures made from sand, or paint, or clay, or collage—all were stand-ins for the human body. When any client started cutting holes, poking holes, or digging holes in their projects, Stef's antennae went up a little. But if his youngest clients started *putting* things into those holes, his antennae went up a lot.

"It will go in and you will feel it," Max said.

"Does it hurt the mountain when we dig?" Stef asked.

"Yes, but it's a secret."

"Is the mountain afraid?"

"It's really afraid and it wants to run away but it can't."

"Can anyone help the mountain?"

"No. Nobody comes."

A clatter as Max threw his spoon aside and started digging and scraping into the tunnel with his hands. Stef did the same, up to his elbow, until through the wall of sand, he felt wiggling. The tiny round tips of Max's fingers poked through and touched his. Stef went still, letting the boy feel him out.

Max giggled as he wrapped his hand around two of Stef's fingers. "Is that your peepee?"

"No," Stef said.

"You're lying."

"I always tell you the truth."

"You're not supposed to tell."

"What will happen?"

The grip around Stef's fingers tightened. "She'll die," he said. His voice sank into a strange monotone. Older. Deeper. Speaking scripted lines he'd memorized. "She'll die in the war. She'll get blowed up into pieces. You can't tell or the bad soldiers in ear cook will win."

"But she didn't die," Stef said. "You told the truth and she came home."

Max stared at him. Unblinking. Like a snake about to strike.

"You told the truth," Stef said again. "It was the bravest thing in the world. As soon as you did, your mother came home and started to make it stop. She came home as soon as she knew. Right?"

A long pause. "Take it out," Max said, his voice transformed into a hiss. "Take it out right now. You're not supposed to touch. Get out."

Stef pulled his hand back through the tunnel.

"You don't ever go in again," Max said, punching the top of the mountain. Stef squinted against the flying sand as the tunnel collapsed and the mountain imploded beneath Max's onslaught. With fists, spoons and cups, Max hacked and chopped at the hilltop.

"We need some water," Max said. "We need to make a river."

For another forty minutes, they dug holes in the dead mountain and poured water. Holes expanded to join with other holes and become ponds. Then lakes. Then a river cutting the sandy land in two and exposing gold coins. Stef had to dig out every one and deposit them in the bank of Max's hands. Max counted them, then washed them carefully. The coins went back into their net bag. Then Max directed Stef in raking all the sand flat within the box. The floor was swept and the collected sand sifted through a sieve, like a fine sugar coating.

Stef checked his watch. "It's time to pick a word."

At the end of every session, Max picked a word for the upcoming week, and Stef drew it on his arm with Sharpies, making a semi-permanent tattoo. He could ask questions about the word picked, but he couldn't try to change Max's mind or suggest another one. Those were the rules. Max picked the word and where it went. Max made the rules about who and what got to touch his body.

"Spiderman," Max said today, putting his forearm on the table, palm to the ceiling.

Stef found some images on his phone, Max picked one, and Stef got to work with his markers. First, he folded up a towel lengthwise and laid it across Max's arm. A compromise that let Stef rest his free hand on Max's wrist without touching Max's skin.

"Spiderman's the bomb," he said, outlining the figure.

"I wish I had nets in my fingers."

"What would you do with them?"

"I could shoot them up and make them stick to nothing and get away from the bad guys."

Stef drew nets from both Spiderman's hands. "Crazy how he always finds something to grab onto with his web."

"He can stick to the sky."

"This is a good word," Stef said. "When you feel bad and feel like you can't get away, you can look at Spidey and remember you always have something to grab onto."

Max was quiet, breathing through his mouth. "I wouldn't ever grab a person."

"No, you wouldn't," Stef said, coloring Spiderman's suit blue and red.

"If someone said to me *no*, then I'd do no. I mean I wouldn't do it."

"Because you're one of the good guys."

"If I saw a friend say no and the other person kept doing it, I'd shoot my nets out and make them stop. But I still wouldn't grab them."

"You'd just leave them there in the net?"

"Yeah. And then I'd shoot another net and stick it on the sky and get away."

"Would you take your friend with you?"

"Yeah."

"See?" Stef said, capping the pen. "You really are a good guy. You're one of the best guys I know."

Max watched as Stef filled in Spiderman's eyes with yellow. "He said I was bad."

Stef looked up. "He was wrong."

Max's fingers closed into a fist, then opened again. "Are you sure?"

Stef leaned forward a little. Not too far, but enough to make Max pay attention. "Any guy, any adult, who does something bad to you and tells you to keep it a secret? That's not a good guy. If anyone hurts you and says you can't tell or someone special will die? They're lying. You tell. You tell your mother, you tell me, you tell anyone who will listen. You tell the truth, because that's how it stops. You know this. Right?"

Max's chin rose and fell, mouth still open and breathing a little harder.

"He did a really bad thing to you," Stef said. "He made you and your mountain feel terrible. But that doesn't mean you *are* terrible. You, Max, are *awesome*. And brave. And good."

Slowly Max's mouth closed and the next breath he took was through his nose. It widened across his little chest and he appeared to sit straighter.

Stef uncapped a fine-tip black Sharpie. "Can I write the other words by Spiderman? So you remember?"

Max nodded and went on breathing through his nose as Stef lettered all around the edges of the nets: *awesome, brave, good.*

"That's what you are," Stef said. "Even if you feel lousy in your head and your stomach. Even if you feel afraid or angry or confused or sad. You're still awesome and brave. You always tell the truth. You're one of the good guys."

"Do you have a mommy?"

"Sure I do," Stef said. He was judicious about the personal information he shared with adult clients, but young kids' nosy questions served a purpose. With everything Max knew about family and homes and marriage now destroyed, the boy was simply trying to figure out what was normal.

"Do you have a dad?" Max asked.

Stef nodded.

"They live here?" he asked.

"Here in the city? Just my mother. My dad lives in Germany."

"Did he die?"

Stef blinked. "No, he's alive. He just lives somewhere else. He and my mother aren't married anymore."

"Then who do you live with?"

"I live by myself."

"You don't have a married girl in your house?"

Stef's throat grew warm. Max not knowing the terms for spouses ought to have been cute. Instead, it seemed incredibly sad. "You mean a wife?"

"Yeah."

"No. I don't have a wife. I did once. But we're not married anymore either."

"Oh. You don't have anybody?" Max's expression was concerned.

"I have lots of people," Stef said. "Lots of family. Lots of friends."

And I met someone.

"It's unbelievable," Ronnie said. "I'll be the first to admit I was skeptical about the sand technique but, holy crap, I was wrong."

Slumped in one of Ronnie's office chairs, Stef slugged half a bottle of water and wished it were gin. Max was always his last appointment on Wednesdays, and it wiped him out. Left him a container bulging with Max's mess.

"You're a wonder," she said.

"I'm a wreck."

"But really, how are you these days?" she said. "Dating anyone?"

"No," he said, thinking, *But I met someone.*

"What about that woman you met a couple weeks ago? The optometrist?"

"Oh. Yeah. I'm seeing her tonight, actually."

She laughed. "Good thing I reminded you."

He laughed along, then said goodnight and headed to the other side of the building, downstairs to the kitchens, where Stavroula was making meatballs.

"Well, you look fresh from a breakthrough," Stavroula said.

"Do I?"

"You have that definitive air of 'Now *that's* how you do it, motherfuckers.'"

Stef laughed and pinched a piece of meatloaf mix.

"Oh my God, don't," Stavroula said. "You'll be dead of salmonella later."

"I'll take my chances."

"How's the optometrist?"

"I'm seeing her tonight."

Stavroula's sideways glance was wicked. "What about that auditory specialist you were nailing?"

Stef crossed his forearms on the butcher block table. "I haven't heard from her."

"Weren't you dating a speech therapist for a while?"

"Her conversation sucked."

"Then there was the ENT nurse."

"He kept ramming his political views down my throat."

"And the proctologist."

"She had a real stick up her ass."

"What about that male stripper you picked up?"

Stef sighed. "I couldn't get his clothes off."

Stavroula groaned and hip-checked him off the counter.

I met someone, Stef thought, falling onto a nearby stool. He kept the words under his tongue. Something about the meeting seemed fragile, yet filled with strong possibility. Like an expecting couple not wanting to share the news until the uncertain first trimester had passed, he didn't want to talk about it yet.

Plus he had an optometrist to see.

Because we're being sensible about this.

Deborah's curls were blown out straight tonight, but her laugh was exactly as Stef remembered. Back at her apartment, the breasts that spilled out of her black lace bra were magnificent. Her body was crazy. Her sex was even crazier.

And it was taking him for-freaking-ever to come.

"Jesus," she said, breathless. "You jerk off earlier today?"

"No," he said, rolling her over. He'd jerked off twice today, not thinking about Deb either time.

I met someone.

He turned her this way and that. Fucked hard and fast, slow and soft. Whispered obscenities. Laughed her name. Sighed something sweet.

It was good.

It just wasn't taking him anywhere.

Frankly, he was a little bored.

Because I met someone…

Jav's face swam into focus. The shy smile under a deep brown, unblinking gaze. The tight, unadorned body, indolently sexy in jeans and a white T-shirt. Skin like a weapon.

What would his back taste like under Stef's dragging tongue? How would his wrist bones roll in Stef's hands? How would the curve of his ass feel pressed against Stef's hips?

He wanted to know.

It was hard not to think he was *supposed* to know.

I heard him on that radio show. I walked around with his book in my bag. I lay in bed reading his words. Then I met him. Things like that don't happen to me.

Christ, a guy is loitering in my head while I'm fucking a woman.

This isn't like me.

Guys don't do this to me.

Wait, what?

"What?" he said.

"I said, you got Superman complex," Deb said.

Spiderman complex, he thought. *I need something to stick to so I can get out of this.*

He ran his hands up her spine. "You need to tap out?"

"Hell no. You just seem distracted."

"Hell no," he said. "Come on top of me."

Hidden between the curtain of her hair and the wall of her breasts, he managed to sledgehammer his way to an orgasm. But rather than a soulful satisfaction, it was the grumpy, exhausted achievement of finally getting a computer glitch fixed. Relief, but more trouble than it needed to be.

"I can't stay," he said after a bit of cuddling and pillow talk. "Early meeting tomorrow."

He opted to walk back to Chelsea, feeling like an unfaithful lover going home to nobody. The September evening had turned chilly and its gaze on him was full of reproach.

What are you doing?

He sighed. Parts of his life were so full of excellence, while others were barely mediocre.

For the gazillionth time that day, he took out his phone, wanting to text Jav. Just to say hi. See what was going on. Did he want to get naked?

He put the phone away. *He's straight, you jackass. You're only setting yourself up to be shot down.*

Home in his dark apartment, he showered for the third time that day, then got into bed. It was a little past ten. Good. He'd get some quality shut-eye for once.

At 10:45, he was still wide-eyed and full of thoughts. Picking up his phone and composing texts to Jav. Deleting them and putting the phone down again.

He was forty years old for fuck's sake. Forty-one in December.

So what are you waiting for?

He picked up the phone, typed, **What's up?**

"I am fourteen," he muttered, and hit send. He tossed the device aside, flopped back in the pillows and flipped the covers over his head. "Don't say I didn't warn you."

In the dark cave of the blankets he sighed. He stayed under until his own exhales were smothering him, then moved the blankets off. He stared at the ceiling, mindfully breathing, trying to bring back the serenity he'd cultivated at the ashram in California.

It took discipline to quiet the monkey mind. To be bigger than your own train of thought.

Focus on being present.

If you're frustrated, be frustrated. You can deal.

Compartmentalize want from need.

When your needs were met, you were comfortable. When your wants were met, you were happy. You could be uncomfortable yet happy. You could want for the sake of wanting. You could want without having.

Visualize. Sort the desire.

What do I want to want and what do I want to have?

The phone pinged. He made himself count to twenty before picking it up.

Hey, just got home, Jav replied.

Same, Stef typed.

Then nothing. After a minute, Stef put the phone face down on his chest, delaying gratification. He wanted Jav to reply, but he didn't have to have it.

What do you want then?

His chest rose and fell beneath the slick weight of the phone. It had the means to disrupt electrons and magnetic waves in just the right way to convey a bit of emotion, if only the circuits would...

Connect, he thought. *I want to connect.*

His heart closed around the thought like catching a firefly.

I'm lonely and I want to connect with someone. Mind and body. Something that means...something.

This I want.

This I want to have.

"Have" sounded an awful lot like Jav...

The phone pinged: *Sorry,* Jav wrote. **Needy dog demanding attention.**

What kind? Stef texted.

Duck Tolling Retriever. He's my nephew's dog but he lives with me.

I see.

Another long pause. Stef held still. "Come back," he said, a fingertip tracing the edge of the screen. "Just keep talking. That's all."

A text came in: *We're taking a walk now.*

Last call?

Exactly.

What you have going on tonight?

I had a date.

Stef lobbed a shot over the bow and typed, **With Trelawney?**

LOL, shit no. Trey's like my sister.

Stef grinned like an idiot even as worried jealousy refused to budge. **Oh. Someone new?**

Yeah. Met her at a bar the other night. As one does. This was the follow-up.

Stef chewed his bottom lip and knitted his brows. **How'd it go?**

Eh? Between you and me, I don't think there's another date in the future.

Not feeling it?

No. Was kind of bored, actually.

Weird, Stef typed. **I had a date tonight and felt the same way.**

I guess it happens.

He pulled in a deep breath, aimed his nets toward the sky and willed them to stick. **What are you doing tomorrow?**

Working, Jav replied. **Gym. Research. Phone interview. Errands. Typical Thursday. Want to grab a beer and bore each other?**

A relieved joy cascaded from Stef's eyebrows to his heels. He pulled against the net's strength and swung out into the night. **Sure. Your lame neighborhood or mine?**

LADDER

"**H**ow'd your date go?" Stef's co-worker, Aedith, asked the next morning.

He grunted. "Eh?"

"Not feeling it?"

"I'm not sure we're compatible."

"Did you figure this out before or after you nailed her?"

Stef looked up. "You're not cute."

"Oh, but I am." She perched on the edge of his desk. "Want to catch a movie with me and Katie tonight?"

"Can't. I'm meeting a guy for a beer."

Aedith raised her eyebrows. "A meet or a date?"

"A meet."

"I don't know, Finch. You got a funny look going on."

"What are you talking about?"

"This is totally a date."

"No, it isn't."

"Shut up. Tell me everything. What are you going to wear?" She leaned into his space, eyes dancing behind her glasses.

He gently pushed her back. "It's not a date. We met, we're having a beer."

"Who is he?"

"He's a straight writer who might help me build a website for that exhibition in Poughkeepsie. We're having a beer to talk about it." Stef closed his laptop and got up.

"You are blushing."

"You are a pain in my ass. Move. I'm late." As he walked out of his office, the back of his neck flamed.

"Wear blue," she yelled after him. "It makes your eyes pop."

He was wearing a grey shirt today. It would fucking have to do. He went straight from work to the bar. No going home to shower, shave, pick a blue shirt and hang out in front of the mirror like a twink.

Dig me, dig my crappy shirt.

He walked the few blocks north on the High Line, New York's new aerial greenway. Built on an elevated spur of the New York Central Railroad, it ran from Gansevoort to 20th Street in Chelsea. The stunning views of city and the Hudson were enhanced by naturalized plantings along the meandering walkway. By the end of construction, it would reach the West Side Yard at 34th Street.

Stef was five minutes early, but Jav was already there, sitting at the bar with a beer and a book. Cargo pants, worn along the seams and a hole in one knee. A dark green T-shirt. Unshaven as well. Attractive in a way that felt foreign in Stef's veins. He was no stranger to appreciating a good-looking guy's body, but not to the point where it stopped him in a doorway. Made him stand still and pick out holes in knees and the color of a shirt. Note the length of sideburns and the curl of a foot around the stool leg. This keen, detail-oriented interest was what he experienced with women. So was this goofy coil of warm excitement in his gut, a double helix of sexual and cerebral interest lassoing him across the floor to the bar.

"Hey," Jav said, closing the book and extending a hand.

Stef shook it. "What's up?"

"Good to see you."

Stef drew the book closer and spun it around. *The Magic Orange Tree: Haitian Folktales.* "Is this required reading or pleasure?"

"Bit of both. I'm working on a book of Latin American folktales."

Stef slid onto a stool. "You know, I think I heard you on NPR some time ago."

"I was on *Moments in Time* back in July."

"Were you going around different Latino neighborhoods and collecting stories?"

"That was me," Jav said, looking pleased.

"You do a lot of that kind of thing to promote your books?"

The bartender came by and Stef ordered a Guinness.

"I've never done any mainstream promotion of my books," Jav said. "But it's about to change with *The Trade.*"

"When does it release?"

"Tomorrow morning," Jav said. "And Saturday afternoon, I'll be drunk on an airplane, kicking off a three-week signing tour."

"What's the itinerary?" Stef kept his face neutral, thinking *three weeks?*

"Miami first," Jav said. "Atlanta, Charleston, Raleigh, Virginia Beach, DC, Baltimore, Philadelphia, Providence… I'm forgetting something before Providence. Boston, somewhere else I think, then home."

"Your agent coordinates all this?"

"Publicist."

"Is she good?"

"She's expensive," Jav said. "And so far, good."

"Does she come with you?"

"Oh God, yeah. She tells me what to do."

Stef pictured a young, nubile PR rep with mile-long legs, telling Jav exactly what to do. "Is she cool?"

"For a sixty-two-year-old woman, she's extremely cool."

Stef laughed, mostly at himself. "What are the venues? Book stores?"

"Yeah. Some just signings, some will be readings."

"Nervous?"

Jav paused, taking a deep breath. "Yes."

"I predict by Charleston, it'll be easy."

"Here's hoping."

Stef's beer arrived and they clinked glasses. "To the next phase of your career."

They drank.

"So your card says Javier Landes," Stef said. "Your book covers say Gil Rafael. Who's the real you?"

"Technically neither. I was born Javier Gil deSoto. I left home when I was seventeen and became estranged from my family. The woman who eventually became my mentor, her name is Gloria Landes. I changed my name to hers when… Well, that's a story for the third or fourth date."

"Is this a date?"

Jav barked a laugh. "No. It's just a line."

Satisfied now? Stef thought. *Let it go already.* "How did you come up with Gil Rafael?"

"I was submitting a short story to *The New Yorker,* I wanted a pen name. I took my dad's name, Rafael, and the Gil part of my original surname. It sounds like 'heel' but it's spelled g-i-l. I put them together, but at the last minute, I reversed them and made it a hard G. Gil Rafael. And that's who I've been writing as since."

"Why use a pen name at all?"

Jav took a drink and stared straight ahead.

"Or is it for date six or seven?"

Jav glanced sideways and his shy smile opened up. "It's no one asking me before, actually. Not even sure what the answer is."

"Were you hiding?"

"Kind of. Or maybe if I bombed, no one would know but me."

"Same if you succeeded."

Jav nodded. "I guess I was okay with that."

"Are you still estranged from your family?"

"Sadly, my nephew and I are the only Gil deSotos left."

"This is the nephew at New Paltz?" Stef asked.

"Ari. He's my sister's son. Until two years ago, neither of us knew the other existed. But when my sister died, she named me his guardian. And we met."

"What was that like?"

"Surreal," Jav said. "But he's a great kid. I'd think so even if I weren't related to him. I doubt I'll be having any kids of my own at this point, so it's like finding a son. No. Not really. More like finding a little brother."

"I see."

"You have siblings?" Jav asked.

"Two older brothers."

"Are you close?"

"Not particularly."

The bartender came by. "You guys hungry?"

Stef and Jav exchanged glances.

"I haven't eaten," Jav said.

"Me neither."

The bartender slid over some menus.

"You're not close with your brothers?" Jav said, perusing his.

Stef smiled. "I'll tell you about it on date nineteen."

"Fair enough."

"Short version is my parents divorced when I was thirty. If divorce is tough on young kids, it makes adult children into total lunatics. It resulted in a lot of sides being taken and a lot of bitterness. It also didn't help that my mother left my dad for another woman."

"Shut up."

"It was a blurry year in my life. Going through my own divorce made it even more hazy."

Jav gave him a long, appraising look. "I think we're gonna need a bigger bar."

Stef laughed. Through another two rounds of beers and burgers, they laughed a lot, trading bits of stories, asking and answering questions. Even it if wasn't a date, it still felt like a really *good* first date. The kind that made you wonder when the next one would be. Keeping a running tab of the things they'd talk about at a later time made Stef optimistic this wasn't a one-off.

Except the three-week tour was going to delay next time. Damn it all to hell.

"Crap, I gotta get going," Jav said, checking his watch. "I got eight thousand things to do."

"Who watches the dog while you're away?"

"I have a neighbor who dog sits, but not for this length of time. I'm going to drive him up to Guelisten, leave him with some friends. Trelawney Lark's sister, actually."

"How did you meet her?"

Jav pointed the neck of his beer bottle at Stef. "Dude, you have no idea how complicated that story is."

Stef raised his eyebrows. "Date sixty-two?"

"At minimum."

"Are you keeping track of what gets talked about when?"

Jav tapped the beer bottle against his temple. "I got this."

"Well, good luck," Stef said, after they squared up and headed outside. "You'll have to sign my copy of *The Trade* when you get back. If your hand isn't paralyzed."

"My nightmare is nobody shows up."

"Dude, not to cheapen your talent, but if you stand in the middle of Barnes & Noble, they'll show up."

Jav chuckled at the ground, scraping at the pavement with his foot. "Buddy of mine once described me as a marketing man's wet dream."

"He was right."

Jav looked about to say something, then stopped.

"What?" Stef said, crossing his arms.

"Nothing. I'll call you when I get back."

"Give me a call from the road," Stef said, he hoped casually. "If you want."

"Sure."

"All right. Knock 'em dead."

They shook hands, touched right shoulders and bopped each other on the back. Then walked off in separate directions.

After six steps, Stef ventured a look back. Just as Jav looked back. They each raised a palm before turning away again.

❧

HELP, he texted Stavroula.

Speaking, she replied.

He called her. "I met a guy."

"You need help with this?"

"I'm pretty sure he's straight," Stef said.

"Not one hundred percent sure?"

"No."

"You want me to seduce him and report back?"

"Cute," Stef said, exhaling heavily as he waited on a red light. "Anyway, we had a beer. I can't tell if it's on."

"Where'd the evening end? Wait, are you calling from his bathroom?"

"I'm walking home, smartass," Stef said. "We floated the idea we'd hang again. I got an 'I'll call you.'"

"The kiss of death."

"You think?"

"That's just my experience."

"I got a look back as we walked away."

Stavroula laughed. "Oh my God, I've never seen you like this."

"Dude, me neither."

"So talk to me," she said. "What do you need?"

"I don't know. Do I tell him I'm bi now or later?"

"Hm. Think you'll talk to him while he's away?"

"I have a hunch yes."

"Well, is he cool?" she said. "You think if you tell him and he's straight, it'll be the end of everything? Even potential friendship?"

"I have a hunch no. It's really my own sanity I'm thinking of."

"Oh, if this is a sanity thing then tell him now. Otherwise you'll create a big three-week buildup. He'll come home, you'll tell him and when he says he's straight, it'll be beyond a bummer."

Stef scowled at the sidewalk. "You could've said *if*, not *when*."

"I'm sorry. I'm off my optimism meds."

"No, you're right. I'll tell him now. Get it over with."

"I'll be up late. If I don't hear from you, I'll assume it went well."

"Thanks, sis."

"Good luck."

He ended the call. But didn't text Jav. He put it off and put it off.

"Don't be a pussy," he muttered, and finally reached for his phone around eleven o'clock.

So listen, he typed. ***Now that you're going away for three weeks there's something I need to throw out there.***

Jav replied almost immediately. ***Is it date 2 already?***

This is date 1-A.

Sub-dates are a thing?

Yeah. Where have you been?

Out of touch, apparently, Jav typed. ***Fire away.***

"Sweet gods and goddesses, let me down easy," Stef mumbled. Then he typed: ***Within the context of dates and joking about dates, I just want to mention I'm bisexual. So I'm not entirely joking.***

He almost hit send, but decided to barrel through to the end, then hurl his phone into the Hudson River.

If I'm barking up the wrong tree, it's cool, he added. ***I just figured it's better to be honest from the get-go. Anyway. That's all for 1-A. Any reply will be considered 1-B.***

"I hate everything," he said, as he hit the button and burned the boat. He went in the bathroom and brushed his teeth, but when he returned to the counter, no reply had come in.

"Shit, I blew it," he mumbled. He leaned on his hands, head hung between, staring at the phone.

The phone stared back.

"Come on," he said, closing his eyes. "Easy answer. Right tree or wrong tree. It doesn't matter. It does but it doesn't. I just want to know now."

The phone pinged.

Stef opened his eyes.

A picture was flashing on the phone's screen. He blinked a few times before he realized it was a rope ladder dangling down from a tree branch.

Stef stared, his mouth slowly falling open. "No way," he said.

A text popped up beneath the picture. **Stop barking, you'll wake the neighbors. Just come up.**

"No fucking way," Stef breathed, picking up the phone. He typed **LOL**, because he couldn't think of a damn thing else to say.

I like this sub-date thing, Jav texted. **Will there be a 1-C?**

I'll have to consult the guidebook, Stef typed, **but I think the change of venue officially makes it date 2. And may I say, nice tree?**

You may. It's new.

Stef blinked, not sure he was understanding. **New?** he wrote.

Jav replied: **Never been on a date with a guy.**

Shut up.

And here I was worried we wouldn't have anything to talk about while I was on the road.

"This isn't happening," Stef said, hitching up to sit on the counter. He looked around his apartment, around at his life, as if he'd walked into a surprise party. "This is *not* happening…"

AN AMATEUR LOVER

JAV RANG THE doorbell of Gloria Landes' home in Riverdale. He didn't wonder why, after twenty-odd years, he still rang. He liked to. Ringing her bell had changed his life. Now, as then, she opened it with a delighted expression and the same words she always spoke.

"Jav, darling. How wonderful you came."

He was still called Javier Gil deSoto the first time he stepped over this threshold. Twenty-one and broke, living hand-to-mouth in a minuscule studio in Washington Heights. Gloria found him tending bar at a wedding. She offered him a business proposition with an open-ended contract. She said with his looks and the way he behaved with women, he could make a lot of money.

He didn't trust many people at that time in his life. But he trusted this woman. She groomed him. Taught him everything he knew about being a champion date and a professional lover.

And he made a shit-ton of money.

Gloria went on to guide him through his early writing career. She encouraged him to submit "Bald" to *The New Yorker*, and then helped him negotiate the sale of the movie rights. Rarely a week went by when he didn't spend a well-paid, enjoyable night in Gloria's bed. After 9/11, though, their sexual relationship ended. When Jav lost Flip, he found in Gloria the one person who loved him unconditionally. The woman who had taken him in when his own people cast him out. He went to court and legally changed his surname to Landes. He would never think of her as his mother. He chose her name because it was the thing he respected most in the world.

"So," Gloria said, as they sat in her study with coffee. "You leave tomorrow. Are you excited?"

"Excited and terrified," Jav said.

"Excellent combination. I highly recommend it."

"I usually do what you recommend."

Gloria smiled at her protégé. "It's going to be fantastic. I'm thrilled for you. And proud. You dropped Roman off with the Larks?"

"This morning."

"What was that like?"

"Quick."

"Quick?"

"I said 'hello, how are you, thank you for doing this.' Val said, 'no problem, good luck, have a great time, keep us posted.' And we said goodbye."

"Sounds cold."

"No, it wasn't cold, it was just…quick."

"Well, you did sleep with her husband."

"I didn't *sleep* with him," Jav said.

"I'm sorry, let me rephrase," Gloria said. "You did kiss and grope naked with her husband."

"When you call me out on my bad decisions, at least get the details right."

"I take it you didn't see Alex in this fast transaction?"

"No."

Gloria set her cup down. "You miss him."

It wasn't a question.

"Yes, I do," he said. "In other news, I met someone."

Gloria's eyebrows raised. "Is he married?"

Jav pointed a finger. "Now you're being mean to me."

"Well?"

"No, he isn't married. Yes, he's bi. And ironically, after we've established mutual interest, I'm the one getting on an airplane this time."

The teasing fell out of Gloria's expression and her hand dropped onto Jav's knee. "I won't tell you not to think about it," she said.

Jav shook his head, eyes closed. "I have no idea what I'm thinking. Or doing or feeling."

"I think you're feeling the sadness of an ending and excitement of a beginning, like any human being would."

"Am I making it too complicated?"

"A little. But you only just became an amateur lover. You're bound to make mistakes, just like you did when you were learning to be a professional."

"Thing is, I always had you to cover my gaffes."

She laughed. "I can't whisper in your ear through this one."

"I like this guy and I feel like I need to be careful. Careful I'm not digging him just because he's hot and built and the first guy I'm free to pursue."

"Those are perfect reason to dig him."

"Are they?"

Gloria's eyes rolled around the room. "Javier."

"See, I'm an idiot."

"You're scared and playing the idiot card. It's not attractive."

"Fine, I'm smart, but I'm new at this so I'm bound to be a little dumb. I'm only starting to figure out who I am as a non-escort."

"Have you told him about your former career yet?"

"No." He glanced at her. "Is it one of those sooner-rather-than-later things?"

She nodded. "I'd put it on the table while it's early."

"You're right. As usual."

"Often wrong, never in doubt."

"Which is why I love you."

She opened her arms. He rolled his eyes a little, but fell sideways and allowed himself a long, indulgent sigh on her shoulder. She stroked his hair and they sat, quiet and still within their pure, unwavering adoration of each other.

"I owe so much to you," he said. "I don't know what my life would've been like if you hadn't come along."

"I feel the same way. And I still want so much for you."

"I'll find it."

"You will. Let me do the worrying for you, all right? I'm better at it."

"Deal. I won't panic until you do."

"Just be prepared not to find love on the first try," she said. "Love doesn't always play nice. Love plays games you haven't had to deal with before. Love is going to serve up a buffet of emotions you neatly avoided for decades."

"I know," Jav said. "And love isn't going to leave me an envelope on the mantel for my troubles."

That night, Jav prayed. Something he hadn't done formally in years. On his knees at the side of his bed, fingers clasped by his open suitcase and head touching his crossed thumbs. Beseeching the god of his childhood with one simple request.

Let me come home alive.

No plane crashes, no hotel fires, no freak accidents.

The gamut of disasters he envisioned would be laughable if the breathless hope squeezing his heart weren't so damn familiar. Last night, when he looked over his shoulder to see Stef looking back at him, the joyful anticipation that socked him in the gut was both exhilarating and haunting. This was the edge he'd been standing on exactly six years ago, watching Flip Trueblood leave his apartment. Flip looked back from the door, eyes glazed, smile goofy across a mouth swollen from Jav's kisses. Young and sexy and vulnerable, with less than twelve hours left to live.

I'll talk to you later.

Later never came for Flip and Jav.

Later was now.

Please, Jav thought. *If this goes somewhere or if it goes nowhere. If he's cool or if he's an asshole. If I get laid or I get heartbroken. I accept it. Thy will be done. Just let me come home. Give me this chance. Please.*

Let me live to find out who I really am.

Situational Awareness

DR. BLOOM WAS strict with Geno's fitness guidelines, lest he damage what was still healing. "They're the same limitations for post-hernia," she said at the last appointment before he went to school. "If you're more comfortable saying that to strangers."

"For how long?"

"Two months."

"Shit."

Bloom smiled. "If that's what you desire to keep doing naturally for the rest of your life?"

She knew how to get Geno's attention. He could die happy without prepping for her exams with enemas, sitting in one more goddamn sitz bath or sticking one more suppository up his butt. It was no fun being ruled by your rectum.

Truth be told, he needed the slow start. While the worst of his injuries were behind him—har de har har—a host of little aches and pains and discomforts were constant companions. His strained shoulder and back gave him unpredictable grief. His jaw made disturbing clicks when he yawned. His vocal cords recovered, but his voice would always be slightly hoarse and vulnerable to a cold or allergy season.

His wrists had finally healed, though. He could cover the scars on his left wrist with his watch but the battle wounds on the right were out in the open. People stared, no doubt thinking he'd tried to off himself.

If they only knew.

He went to his first session with Wayne, the trainer at the Flatbush YMCA, with his guidelines and a slightly modified medical history, gleaned from a story in the *NY Post*. He told Wayne he was mugged in the subway. Jumped from behind and stabbed in the gut. He had the scar to prove it.

Wayne gave Geno a thorough evaluation and laid out a plan. The walls of his little office were hung with pictures of himself in martial arts moves.

"Taekwondo?" Geno asked.

"Krav Maga," Wayne said. "Israeli self-defense."

Geno looked back. "Are you Jewish?"

"No." Wayne laughed. "It's not a requirement."

"What's it about?"

"The goal of KM is to avoid confrontation," Wayne said. "And if it starts, to end it as quickly as possible. It teaches you a lot about situational awareness."

"Situational awareness," Geno said. The words filled his mouth like some rich, decadent dessert.

"You learn about the psychology of confrontation, and how to see potential threats in your surroundings."

Situational awareness, Geno thought, nearly in a trance. It was what failed him at Anthony's house. He had a gut feeling something was weird but didn't trust it.

Never again.

Situational awareness.

"You train your mind as well as your body," Wayne was saying. "You use your mental strength first to diffuse or avoid a fight. Fists are the last resort." He smiled at Geno. "But first things first, kid. Let's get you back in shape. Man, you got a lot of work to do on your core muscles, otherwise that back of yours is going to bother you the rest of your life."

BEEN WITH

"So," Jav said. "Not to get too personal on the first phone call…"

"Ask me anything," Stef said. "If it gets weird, I'll just hang up."

"You were married?"

"I was. It's not one of my finer moments."

"How did you meet?"

"In grad school," Stef said. "We were young and liberal and had a lot of the same ideas about gender roles and societal roles and free love and open marriage."

"What could possibly go wrong?"

"Everything."

"What was her name?" Jav asked.

"Courtney."

"Was she bisexual as well?"

"No, actually. Strickly dickly, as chicks like to say. Anyway." Stef ran a hand through his hair. "It's hard to condense what happened into a short story. A ton of issues were going on, but the big trouble started when we got into the swing scene."

"Oh shit."

"Yeah, everything just…"

"Blew up?"

"You know, if it blew up it would be sort of noble," Stef said. "It really lay down and died without a fight. I look back now and, man, I'm appalled at how easily we gave up and walked away. Like the whole thing had been a game we got bored with." He sighed, then decided this much was enough. "How about we put a pin in the rest of it," he said.

"No worries," Jav said. "I only want your stories if you're telling them. This one sounds tough."

"It was. Right after I left Courtney, my mother left my dad. Everything fell apart at once. It was a really dark time in my life."

"Leave it," Jav said. "Ask me anything."

"Well, not to get too personal, but when did you know you were bi?"

"That's hard to answer," Jav said. "It's tangled up with the reasons why I got thrown out of my home when I was seventeen. And tangled up with whole lot of denial. I was never out. Not even to myself. Until recently, I've used cutesy expressions like bi-cautious and bi-curious."

"So…" Stef cleared his throat. "Have you actually been with a guy?"

"Two," Jav said. "But *been with* is generous. I haven't done much past kissing."

"Not even a hand job?"

"With both guys, dicks were in hand, but the job was never finished."

"Gotcha."

"So I think the appropriate term is bi-clueless."

"Nice," Stef said. "Who were the dicks? I mean guys. Sorry."

"One was… It ended before it started, and it ended really sadly. I'll put a pin in that one. The other guy was a friend. I guess he still is a friend but it's kind of awkward at the moment. Anyway, he and his wife were the closest friends I'd had in years. Alex, especially. If finding Ari was like finding a little brother, finding Alex was like reuniting with a twin or something. So I took the natural next step of falling in love with him."

"Because, why not?"

"Last thing I expected was for him to feel the same way."

"Plot twist."

Jav laughed. "What was I supposed to do? The right thing?"

"Did you?"

"No. And that's my bisexual resume. Two unfinished jobs and no references. I've always known it was part of me. Two times I tried to do something about it, and both ended disastrously. So besides being clueless, I'm kind of… skittish. Love's really never been a friend of mine. Then again, I didn't give it much of a chance. Hence, this is the new me. Or the old me with not so many parts hidden."

"Have you had any serious relationships?" Stef asked.

"No."

"None? No girlfriend ever?"

"Well." Jav chuckled. "I had a lot of girlfriends."

"I'm shocked."

"Paid girlfriends."

Stef blinked. "Say again?"

"I was an escort for twenty-three years."

A cool, prickling wave passed over Stef's face and his heart felt slightly too big for his chest. "Really?"

"Yeah."

"Twenty-three years."

"Yeah."

"But only for women," Stef said.

"Only for women."

"And on your own? Not like with an agency or a…"

"Pimp? No. On my own."

"What did you make?" Stef asked. "No, don't answer. That was rude. Never mind. Wow."

An uncomfortable pause.

"You texted the other day that it's better to be honest from the get-go," Jav said.

"Definitely. I mean, I appreciate you told me, I'm just…processing."

"I get it."

A lightning-fast slideshow whirred past Stef's closed eyes. A montage of Jav with different women. Out to dinner. In bed. Dressed up. Dressed down. At a party. The opera. Taking women's clothes off. Picking his clothes up from the floor. Collecting his money.

Sex for money.

No doubt the world of a high-end, mouth-wateringly expensive escort was a far cry from a heroin addict turning tricks, or a slave under the control of a domineering madam or sadistic pimp. Still, prostituting yourself for two decades, no matter the wages or perks, had to take a psychological toll. In Stef's experience, voluntarily becoming a sex worker stemmed from a belief you weren't good enough for anything else.

When they were out for beers, Jav said he left home when he was seventeen and had been estranged from his family since. But really he'd been thrown out. Evicted as a high schooler onto the city streets.

Was that when it started? The devaluing of his own currency?

"Did I lose you?" Jav said.

"No, I'm here. Just thinking."

"About?"

"You know I work with survivors of sex trafficking, so my knee-jerk reaction is to make you a victim." *And frankly,* Stef thought, *I don't need another person to save. I save people all day long. If you turn out to have a lot of baggage…*

"Well, I can think of some other ways I was a victim," Jav said. "But the work was a choice, and I was good at it and I liked it."

His tone wasn't defensive or challenging and his self-awareness was downright refreshing. Stef rolled on his side, curling more into the phone. "What made you stop?" he asked.

"I was tired," Jav said slowly. "And lonely. And admitting a lot of things."

"Like?"

"Like admitting that as much as I thought love was my enemy, I wanted it to be my friend. I wanted somebody to love."

Silence ticked by as Stef recalled a couple of male bedfellows who hinted they wanted as much, and how quickly he'd put the kibosh on going to bed again. Fuck buddies were one thing. Boyfriends were something else.

Yet here I am, he thought. *Interested in this guy's thoughts about love and he's been nowhere near my bed. Yet.*

"So do you want me to call you again?" Jav said.

"Hell yeah. I have about five thousand questions now."

Silence again. But softer this time. Almost coy.

"I have to get to a thing." Jav's voice rose up into a more vertical timbre, and Stef realized all this time, Jav had been lying down. His hand reached, closed around the back of an invisible shirt and yanked Jav back.

Don't go, he thought. *Stay. Five more minutes.*

"Go do your thing," he said aloud. "I'll talk to you later."

He let Jav end the call. For five minutes Stef lay on the couch, the phone still pressed to his ear, listening to nothing.

"This is gonna be a long three weeks," he said, sighing.

THE THING

*M*IAMI WAS THE perfect place to kick off the tour. The signing at Barnes & Noble drew a surprisingly large crowd, many of them from the city's Cuban American community. Speaking to readers in Spanish relaxed Jav while the sheer number of them boosted his confidence.

He knew he had an audience, but they'd been faceless until now. Fan letters. Emails. Comments when his fiction was posted on magazine websites. Replies when he thought to put something on Twitter.

Now they were lined up in front of his table. There to see him.

Me?

"I've been following you since you wrote 'Bald,'" a woman said.

"*Gloria* was the best book I ever read."

"*Client Privilege* broke my heart."

He signed new copies of his books as well as old, beat up, tattered ones. They thanked him and he tried to thank them back.

Thank you.

I'm thrilled you enjoyed it.

No, thank you.

Muchas gracias.

The more the grateful words slid out of his mouth, the more they slid out of meaning. He shook hands, hugged, leaned in and out for the innumerable camera clicks. He thanked them more profusely than they thanked him. He fell into bed exhausted, still unable to get his arms around it all. Worried about the venue in Atlanta, where he'd be speaking as well as signing.

His publicist, Donna, was a PR wonder. Brisk, efficient, connected, organized to the most minute detail. She was also supernaturally introverted and, frankly, not too personable. One of those socially cautious people who preferred to be backstage, not centerstage. It made Jav realize it would be nice to have a friend along on this kind of thing. A friend to rehearse with before an event, drink and unwind with afterward. A buddy to stand in the back of the room. One familiar pair of eyes in a sea of strangers. To indicate with a little nod you were doing fine. You had this.

Good luck, Stef texted right before Jav took the floor in Atlanta. **Make sure the barn door's closed.**

Thanks, Jav texted back. He checked his fly, took a last breath and went out smiling.

He'd agonized over this presentation, wanting to come across both prepared and spontaneous.

"They're there to see *you*," Gloria told him. "They know your writing, now they want to know you. Tell them a story. It's what you do."

He couldn't think how to start. Not until he dreamed about Flip Trueblood one night and remembered.

Write it. Write me. Tell the story and don't let it be forgotten.

He started from the beginning in Queens, sharing a bit of the short story he'd submitted to *Cricket* magazine in 1979, winning the $500 grand prize. He left out the part about his uncle beating the shit out of him until he signed the check over.

Save it for date twelve, Jav imagined Stef saying. He glanced over the heads of his audience to the back of the room. His mind placed Stef there, slouched against the wall, arms and ankles crossed. Chin nodding slightly. Eyes encouraging.

You got this.

The room condensed and drew in close when he told them how he met Philip Trueblood in the summer of 2001. How his face had evoked the image of a mariner. The captain of a mythical ship. Inspired, Jav began working on a book, only to abandon it when Flip died on September 11, going down on the ship of Flight 93.

"I stopped writing the story," Jav said, his eyes flicking to Stef's invisible presence. "But in a lot of ways, the story kept writing me. This imaginary ship became a metaphor for my life, with people I met or friends I made becoming crew members. For example, I met my friend Roger Lark last year..."

A murmured buzz went through the audience and Jav looked up, smiling. "Yeah, *that* Roger Lark. The Treehouse Guy."

"Can I get his number?" a woman called out to appreciative laughter.

"You kidding, even *I* don't get his number," Jav said. "But when I… Oh God, now everyone's leaving. He doesn't have Roger Lark's phone number, we're out of here. Thanks. Goodnight."

More laughter and a smatter of applause.

"When I met Roger, I was immediately struck by how simple, unaffected and content he is. He's got this tattoo on his arm, it's a compass rose. So I'm sitting at the Thanksgiving dinner table when along comes The Thing. Anyone here who writes, or draws, paints, composes or creates, you know what I'm talking about. The great, almighty, mysterious creative *Thing* sits in my lap. The fork is hanging in mid-air and I'm adding Roger to my cast of crew members."

He opened his notebook to the marked page where he'd scribbled his thoughts.

"His tastes and emotions were simple," he read. *"The Compass never worried. He patted problems on the head and told them to run along. If he was cold, he put on a sweater. If he broke something, he swept it up. If fear struck, it was a sign he was doing something wrong and he changed direction."*

He talked a little more about his ideas for Trueblood, how they'd been accidentally waylaid by his vision of a book of Latin American folk tales. A woman raised her hand and asked how else 9/11 affected his writing. He took a deep breath and shared how he couldn't get out of bed, let alone write.

It was like taking his clothes off. Then peeling his skin off. He stood up there, bare to the bones, and told them of grief's crippling depression. The audience drew closer. The energy in the room turned heady and exhilarating, full of connection.

Then it was over. He put his skin back on and went to his hotel room. Just another struggling artist on the road. Waiting for Stef to call. Or waiting for the time Stef said he'd be free so Jav could call.

"How's it going?" Stef said.

"It's going amazing."

And still the best part of the day is hearing your voice, Jav thought. *How the hell does that happen?*

"How was your day?" he asked.

"All right," Stef said, and didn't elaborate. Whenever Jav asked questions about his job, the answers were always generalized. Jav wasn't sure if Stef was bound by strict confidentiality rules or if the work itself was so grueling, it was the last thing he wanted to talk about.

Or maybe he thought it wasn't that interesting.

"How do you not come home with your job?" Jav asked, trying a different approach.

"Well, I do," Stef said. "The trick is to leave it outside the door."

"How successful are you?"

"Hmm… I'd say it's a seventy-five-percent success rate. Physical exercise always settles me down, but if I can't get to the gym or go for a run, I have other little rituals to decompress."

"Like what?" Jav asked.

"Yoga sometimes, but the big game-changer was meditation. I do it every morning to set up the day. Then I do it at night to get the day off me. I have this little shrine in a corner of my bedroom. I come home, peel off my skin and put it there."

"How do you handle the unsuccessful twenty-five percent of days?"

"I drink."

Jav laughed.

"I'm kidding," Stef said, laughing too. "Sort of. I mean it has to be a really bad day for me to have to tap out with booze or take a pill. If I can't meditate it away, I'll call some friends. If I'm not in the mood to be social, I'll go see my mother. I've always been close with her. It's not like she fusses over me or babies me or even says a whole hell of a lot. I like to take some art supplies and go up there and draw while she reads or does whatever. Her energy is grounding. She's always been a haven."

"How often do you see your dad?" Jav asked.

"Not often. He lives in Germany."

"What does he do?"

"He builds pianos," Stef said.

"Get out. Really?"

"He comes from a long line of Steinway men, who come from a long line of cabinetmakers."

"That," Jav said, "is fucking cool."

"It's an extremely cool, extremely skilled profession."

"This is the second cool profession I've stumbled across recently," Jav said

"What was the first?"

"Wall dogs. They paint advertising on brick buildings."

"I didn't know they had a name," Stef said.

"Neither did I. I was on the subway and I overheard this guy talking about his grandfather being a wall dog. I went past my stop to keep listening."

"Did you record it?"

"You know," Jav said, laughing. "I almost did, but it seemed like such a dick move. So I just wrote really fast in my notebook."

"Ah," Stef said. "I wondered if you carried one around."

"Never without it," Jav said, thinking, *What else do you wonder about me?*

Lying in bed that night, he prayed again. Not on his knees but on his side, arms wrapped around a pillow. Holding an imaginary body. Then he put the pillow behind him and leaned on it. Wondering what it would be like to be held. To relax inside a circle of strong arms and drift off.

It feels easy, he thought. *Almost too easy.*

If I'm being set up for a sucker punch, I accept it.

If this is going to be a disastrous maiden voyage, I accept it.

Thy will be done.

Just let me come home.

Jav sat up, clicked on the lamp and reached for his notebook, the place marked with his favorite pen. Cap held tight in his teeth, he pinned the thought down before it could find another storyteller.

"Whatever course my voyage may take," Trueblood whispered to receding shore-line, "let me come home again."

BRICKED BOUNDARY

*T*HE SUITES OF Geno's dorm were laid out such that each student had his own hallway entrance. The tiny kitchenette and bath were between the bedrooms and, if he wanted, Geno could keep enough doors closed to feel he had solitary digs.

In a way he identified with the kitchenette, living smack between his desire and his fear of being left alone.

His roommate kept his adjoining doors open and seemed to take Geno's weird quirks in stride. If Geno was the resident recluse, Ben Marino was the mayor. The kind of guy you could abandon in Bangkok Airport and he'd walk out with six business cards and a date. A social chameleon who looked around a room, tasted the air and quickly adapted. Geno had seen him loud and raucous and wild with other guys in the dorm. He could party with the best of them. Yet seemed just as happy to stay in some nights, hanging in the common area watching TV or playing video games. The space had foosball and air hockey but not, thank God, a pool table.

In or out for the night, Ben always made the overture for Geno to come along. Pleased if it were accepted, no hard feelings if declined. He was so preternaturally chill, Geno wondered if anything ever upset him.

Aware he could've ended up rooming with an asshole, Geno made the effort to go with Ben and socialize. One of the dorm's more street-smart residents knew where to get good fake IDs in Chinatown. Geno slipped the astonishingly authentic-looking proof of age into his wallet, then glanced underneath a wad of folded ATM receipts. Checking that Carlos' driver license was still secreted there.

The strange decision to hold onto this piece of his brother infuriated Mos. *He is dead to us.*

I know, but I need it, Geno insisted. *Just in case.*

Out at bars and parties, he was hyper aware of the social dynamics, the ease with which situations turned dicey and how quickly things could get out of hand. Especially for girls. Christ, watching girls negotiate hook-ups and drink themselves into near incapacitation made him a wreck. Their lipstick-printed drinks left unattended made him want to scream. When guys turned backs on their beers with the privileged confidence that came with not being a target, Geno's eyes narrowed in an alarm that was almost contemptuous. Didn't they *know* what could happen? They should know what it was like. It would serve them—

Shame flooded his heart. Not only was he not being kind, he wasn't even being *decent.*

I don't mean it. Not like that.

"Dude," Ben said, leaning in. "That blonde chick in the polka-dots can't take her eyes off you."

Geno looked and the girl turned away with a flip of golden tresses.

"Man, chicks love a wall," Ben said. "You got a bricked boundary and it makes them nuts."

"No, I don't," Geno said.

Ben's eyes circled the ceiling. "You are a guarded man, my friend."

Geno couldn't argue. He was both guarded and guardian. The evening's unpaid bouncer. Staying near exits and keeping eyes on the scene. Practicing his own kind of situational awareness. He talked a lot of girls out of what he thought were bad decisions. He walked a lot of girls home and made sure they locked their bedroom doors behind them.

Sometimes he did the locking.

He'd passionately avoided sex, resolute in not wanting anyone touching him. When getting laid gradually became a more attractive idea, he was convinced he wouldn't be able to get an erection. Oddly though, arousal wasn't the issue. He could sport some respectable wood, but his body didn't know what to *do* with it. He could fuck until he was numb or chafed, but it never went anywhere.

Because you only love it with me, Anthony said at his shoulder. *Right, baby boy? Can't have one twin be gay without the other.*

"I'm sorry," Geno said during one such futile marathon. "This has never happened before."

He was becoming quite a graceful liar.

"It's fine," the girl said.

"Can I... I mean, do you want to come? Show me how."

Laughter as she took his hand and led it between her legs. "Well, aren't you sweet?"

He paid attention and learned how to make girls come hard enough to lose their minds while he faked his own finish. He watched them orgasm with a blend of fascination and apprehension. Such a vulnerable and trusting moment. What if it wasn't him here but some sick asshole? Holding his prey for days and selling it off. Taking pictures as she was raped bloody and broken.

Everything was so fragile. People taking off their clothes for each other, thinking they knew who they were lying down with.

Nobody really knew anyone.

"Are you okay?" she said.

"Yeah."

"Mo, you're crying."

"No, my eyes are just irritated. Allergies."

His eyes burned through other nights, when female hands caressed him in the dark. Running over his defined muscles and lingering on the pictures inked in his skin. He had many of them now.

As his strength built up, he got braver about going to the tattoo parlor. He went nearly every weekend to get a new charm. A reward for surviving the preceding days and motivation to face the days ahead. Hebrew letters, mystical symbols and metaphysical signs crawled along his arms and across his back. Girls sometimes asked what the designs meant and sometimes he told them. Girls always wanted to touch his stoma scar and he always told them not to, because it still hurt.

All of it still hurt so much.

Lying in the dark, a soft, sleeping girl in his inked arms, he blinked through irritated tears and feared it would always hurt.

A TECHNIQUE PERSPECTIVE

"**W**HERE ARE YOU?" Stef said.

"Virginia Beach," Jav said.

"Is it getting tiring?"

"Yes," Jav said. "Living out of a suitcase is getting on my nerves. And I miss Roman."

"Bet he misses you, too."

"Nah, he's getting spoiled up in Guelisten."

"Speaking of which, the exhibition for the women's shelter is coming up this weekend."

"Shit," Jav said. "I'll be bummed to miss it."

"Yeah, me too. But hopefully I'll be doing others."

"I just wish I could be there."

"Me too."

A beat. "What are you doing now?" Jav asked.

"Talking to you. What, you want the visual? I'm just sitting on the couch."

The back of Jav's neck burned. *Quit trying so hard.*

A long silence now. It spilled out of the phone and filled the room. Jav couldn't think of anything to say. He was tired, but he didn't want to hang up. He just wanted to hang.

"I can hear you thinking," Stef said, sounding sleepy.

"Can you?"

"Mm. Unasked questions make a shit-ton of noise."

"When did you know you liked guys?" Jav asked.

"Oh, I think I was about fourteen when I realized looking at men's underwear ads turned me on. You know, it was the era of Calvin Klein boytoy models. Sepia tones, perfect hair, pouting fuck-me expression. And those airbrushed pecs and abs and bulges. My mouth would be watering. Hands wanting to push through the pages and touch it."

"What did you do?"

"Do? Nothing."

"You didn't hook up with anyone in high school?"

"No way," Stef said. "Nineteen eighty-five on blue collar Roosevelt Island? Not an option. Besides, none of my buddies had that effect on me. It was rock stars and celebrities. I saw *Real Genius* eight times just so I could stare at Val Kilmer. Then *About Last Night* came out and I was jerking off to both Demi Moore and Rob Lowe."

"It didn't seem strange to you?"

"Well, you have to understand my background. My mom was a pioneer in the field of gender studies, so I hit puberty already knowing life wasn't binary."

Rory Finch's papers and books on gender fluidity were renowned in the field of human sexuality studies. Stef learned at her knee by virtue of being a late child. He was simply *with* her all the time. Exposed to varied persuasions of people from all walks of life. This was the crux of most of his parents' arguments.

"I'd hear my dad yell, 'He's the best and brightest of our kids, and you're ruining him.' Unfortunately, my brothers heard it, too."

It infuriated Kurt and Nilas on a personal level and enraged Rory on a professional one. And Stef, who crushed on girls and boys with ease, felt the ache of stretched loyalty. He knew he wasn't gay, but knew he wasn't entirely straight either. He had more tools and resources to deal with it than many other teens in his position. He had a font of useful information in Rory, as well as a formidable advocate. She had his back. She was often absent and abstracted by her work, but her love for him was unconditional. And when he asked for her time, she gave it.

"Her opinion had more value than my dad's," Stef said. "Anyway, back to the point. I didn't have any physical interaction with guys until I got to college."

"Where?"

"Skidmore. It was still the eighties, you could count on two hands and a foot the number of people who were openly gay. Still, the world got bigger and the collective consciousness was a whole lot looser. Maybe sexual experimenting wasn't going on openly, but it was definitely going on. You just had to be careful about sussing out who was in the game. First time a player jerked me off, I thought, *That was the greatest hand job I've had in my life."*

Jav laughed.

"I mean, strictly from a *technique* perspective," Stef said. "A guy knows what to do with a dick, end of story. So now I have it all framed out. I like fucking girls. But I like being jerked off by guys sometimes. I stare at shirtless men in magazine ads, and I have a weird compulsion to lick Jon Bon Jovi. This is my life up until I'm twenty-one. Then I met Quinn."

"He's the one?"

"I don't know about The One, but he got all the firsts. First guy to go past hand jobs, first guy I got totally naked with. First guy I gave a blow job to. The first— Sorry, is this too much information?"

"No, keep going. I'm listening." Jav was also getting turned on, but that was beside the point.

"Not much else to tell. We met, we screwed, we parted ways."

"Oh."

"What about you, when did you know?"

Jav lay back on the bed, letting his forearm flop over his face. "Well, when I was seventeen, my cousin Nesto and I stole a bottle of booze out of my kitchen. We got drunk on the roof. And started kissing."

"Out of nowhere? I mean, no context?"

"Pretty much."

"Were you freaked out?"

"No," Jav said. "I was drunk, but I wasn't outraged or shocked. It felt really good, so I kissed back. He put his hand down my jeans and that felt good. So I put my hand down his. And then my uncle caught us."

"Oh shit."

"It went downhill from there. Really fast and really bad."

"And they threw you out because of it?"

"Two months after my father died. It was December when I left home, and I've had a bittersweet relationship with Christmas ever since."

"You left and went where?" Stef asked.

"A teacher's house for a little while. A stockroom for a few months. Then I rented a room in a family's apartment."

"A family you knew?"

"No. They were polite to me, but I wasn't one of them. And I was so terrified of losing my ten square feet of space, I went out of my way to be invisible."

"Jesus," Stef said. "And your own family cut you off completely. To the point where you never knew your sister had a baby?"

"My uncles shadowed me for a while," Jav said. "Shaking me down for money they felt I owed them. Once that debt was cleared, no, I never saw any of them again. I knew nothing of my sister until I learned she was dead. Which was when I found out my mother was dead, too."

"I'm really sorry."

Jav let Stef's words rest on his chest. Burrow in and purr like three little kittens.

"Thanks," he said softly.

INSIDE LOOKING OUT

"*T*HIS IS THE one I keep coming back to," Trelawney Lark said.

"Me too," Stef said.

The tall, vertical piece was called *Inside Looking Out*. Constructed from wood and Plexiglas, it depicted a window frame, complete with curtains. Red and blue LED lights had been coiled in the bottom, set to flash mode to give the effect of police cars "outside."

"How old is he?" Trelawney asked, her finger trailing along the title card.

"Twelve."

"All his idea?"

"He drew out the whole thing," Stef said. "I just had to help with some of the construction and figure out the lights."

"He's going to be someone."

Stef drew a deep breath through his nose. "I hope so."

The Lark Gallery buzzed with a chattering energy. The feel of a wedding reception, although the dress code was casual. Many of the women at the shelter had fled their homes with a single bag or suitcase. They didn't have a second pair of shoes, let alone a nice dress.

Now these women stood by their artwork, holding court and telling their stories. Some pieces were unattended, displayed anonymously or with a false name. On a long, shallow table across a short wall, a dozen cardboard houses marched in a wobbly line, colored and painted by the shelter's youngest residents. Some were visions of what home used to be. Others were of what home became. One, painted in bright rainbow colors, boasted a little doormat reading "Someday."

A sigh rippled out of Stef's chest, part pride, part wistfulness. All night he'd been imagining Jav at the edge of his peripheral. Standing at the top of the steps where Stef had first seen him.

"You seem ever so slightly distracted, Finch," Trelawney said.

"Do I?"

"I'm smugly wondering if you're remembering someone you met here." Her smile danced sideways. "And it's not me."

He felt his own smug smile unfold. "Maybe," he said. "I'm now wondering if you planned the whole thing."

She laughed and took a sip of her wine. "No," she said. "I swear on all my cashmere sweaters, the meeting happened on its own. I detected some interesting chemistry, so I orchestrated the coffee. And when you walked out of the shop, I convinced him to go after you."

Stef leaned back a little. "How much convincing?"

"Not much. A slap upside the head and he was gone. Stool spinning in his wake. Coffee unpaid for."

"How much do I owe you?"

She waved a hand. "No charge for matchmake— *Jesus.*" Trelawney's words were cut off as a rather gorgeous blonde woman slapped her ass. "Bitch, that was low."

"You left it wide open," the woman said.

"Steffen Finch, this is my fucking sister," Trelawney said, licking spilled chardonnay off her fingers.

"Valerie Lark," she said. "Nice to meet you."

"Hi," he said, taking two steps back and putting his ass against a wall.

She laughed. "I don't spank strangers."

"Bullshit," Trelawney said.

Val pulled her in and bit her ear. "I for to eat you."

"Don't touch me. I hate you."

"What's it like when your brother comes around?" Stef asked.

"Like this," Val said. "But with more Tony Orlando and Dawn songs. Enough about us. I wanted to say congratulations and thank you. This exhibit is incredible." Her eyes on Stef were grey-green. They crinkled as she smiled but their gaze was penetrating.

"Thanks," Stef said, thinking this was not a woman to be fucked with.

Val put her hand on her sister's arm, her chin motioning toward the other side of the gallery. "Alex is talking to the shelter's director about animal-assisted therapy." She glanced at Stef. "My husband is a veterinarian."

"Ah," Stef said, followed her gaze to where Adrienne was talking to a tall guy with a goatee. Catching Val's eye, Alex shook Adrienne's hand and came over. Two long dimples framed his smile.

Quite the beautiful crowd in this beautiful town, Stef thought.

Val made introductions but Stef only managed a few words of small talk before Adrienne took to the floor and called for everyone's attention. She made a little speech, thanking the attendees for their enthusiasm and compassion. Thanking Trelawney for hosting the exhibit. And thanking Stef for…

"Everything," she said.

Stef put his palms together and touched his heart. As the crowd broke apart, his phone pinged with the arrow twang he'd assigned to Jav. Because he was dopey that way.

How's it going? Jav wrote.

"Excuse me," Stef said to the Larks. He ducked into a discreet corner to text back. *Really well. Where are you?*

Outside DC.

So why am I looking for you here?

Are you?

Well, it is the scene of the crime, Stef typed. *So to speak.*

And I did live on the other side of the wall. Probably some lingering pheromones.

Trey introduced me to her sister.

Jav replied: *Did she slap your ass?*

Stef really laughed out loud. *Not yet. Keeping my back to the wall.*

Wise. Did you meet Val's husband, too?

Briefly.

I was afraid of that.

Stef's eyebrows furrowed over the keys. *Why?*

Hint: disaster.

Oh? Stef glanced up, looking for Val and Alex, but unable to see them in the crowd.

Then it hit him.

OH, he typed. *I just put two and one together. Alex was the guy?*

That's him. And her. And so on and so forth.

Stef gazed out at the gallery, craning his neck this way and that. Alex and Val stood by *Inside Looking Out,* Alex's arm draped over his wife's shoulder, his hand hidden up under the length of her blonde hair.

They were an attractive couple, no doubt. Smiling wickedly, Stef typed, **You have good taste,** then backspaced it out. The affair had kicked Jav's heart and robbed him of a close friendship. It was probably better to follow his lead on making jokes.

Alex turned his head, pressing his mouth against Val's crown a moment. He said something. She looked up at him, said something. They both laughed then, leaning on each other, heads thrown back.

These were Jav's closest friends. Alex, especially.

So Jav took the natural next step of falling in love with him.

Soon as I get on the train, I'm calling the shit out of you, Stef texted.

Can't wait, Jav replied. **And not that I checked the Metro North timetable or anything, but there's one leaving in 45 minutes.**

"It's not one of my finest moments," Jav said.

"You said that already."

"Plus it's complicated. You may need to take notes. And I'll pause to swear several times that I'm not making this up."

"Get on with it, Landes."

"So, many, many years ago, my sister had a short affair with Trelawney's brother, Roger."

"The Treehouse Guy," Stef said.

"Correct. Nine months later, my nephew was born."

"Ari."

"Yes. The thing is when I got to be friends with Alex and Val and eventually all the Larks, none of us had any idea our families were already connected through Rog and Naroba."

"When you found out, was it before or after the whole…thing with Alex. Affair. Debacle."

"After," Jav said.

"It must've been a mess."

"It gets worse. And I'm not making this up."

"Oh Christ, what?"

"Val and Alex have a daughter, Deane," Jav said. "Who is the same age as Ari."

"Okay."

"Guess who fell in love?"

"She and Ari?"

"Right. I'll let that sink in a moment."

Stef exhaled, trying to work it out. "Val has a daughter, Diane."

"Deane."

"Deane." Stef opened his sketchbook, clicked the end of a mechanical pencil and started roughing out a family tree. "Val…married to Alex…daughter Deane. Val's brother has a son with your sister. That son is Ari." Stef's pencil tapped back and forth between generations. "So Ari would be Deane's… Oh shit, they're first cousins."

"And our little story jumps the shark."

"So when you became Ari's guardian, you had no clue about this?"

"None of us did," Jav said. "Not even Roger."

Stef scrubbed fingers through his hair. "All right, I'm sure I'll have a bunch of questions about this soap opera. Right now, I'm more curious about what happened between you and Alex."

"Well, one night, I went temporarily insane and told him how I felt about him."

"Were you drunk?"

"I had a few chugs of rum in me, but it was mostly an adrenaline high. I committed emotional suicide, left my guts on the ground and drove away, talking to the windshield."

"As one does," Stef said.

"Telling myself I'd lost the battle but won the bigger war in finally coming out and admitting I liked men."

"And then?"

"Alex followed me home."

"Who saw that coming?"

"Not me," Jav said. "I got out of the car and tried to be aloof and cool, but I was dying. Because he was telling me he felt the same."

"I repeat, who saw that coming?"

"Then we were kissing in the parking lot of the Lark Building. Then we went upstairs."

"Hot *damn,*" Stef said. "And what happened up there? Talk slow."

"More kissing and grabbing and touching and clothes coming off. We were rolling around my bed and…"

Stef checked the proximity of fellow passengers and lowered his voice. "And the famous, unfinished hand job?"

"Yeah. Right in the heat of the moment, Ari texts me."

"Ari," Stef said, rubbing his face. "We forgot about him."

"Yeah, he was supposed to be away with his job, but he came home early. Naturally I'd deadbolted the street door so he was out there scratching like a stray cat."

"That'll kill the mood."

"Long story short, Alex went out the fire escape."

Stef laughed. "Who says love in the suburbs is dull?"

"Freakin' Peyton Place."

"Was that the end of it?"

"Oh no, it gets worse. A day goes by and I'm still dying and still insane. So I go over to Alex's house and corner him in the shed."

"The shed?"

"Yeah, like this little garden shed in his backyard."

"Is that where fathers haul you for a beating?"

"Can I tell the story?"

"Continue."

"So it's a repeat grapple among the rakes and hoes," Jav said. "And I…"

The silence was full of chagrin. And full of old longing.

"Hey, we all do dumb things in the shed," Stef said.

Jav sighed. "I knew I was taking what wasn't mine. Alex… It's not that he was weak. But he was tender-hearted and I knew how to play him. No, not play him, that's harsh."

"He was your friend," Stef said. "You knew what made his heart tick."

"Yeah. I'd never felt more like myself but at the same time, I was kind of *outside* myself. Astounded. At one point I was grinding up against him and I said something like, 'I swear I could fuck you right here.' It slid right out of my mouth and I didn't even know what the hell I meant. I was talking from this bizarre pipeline I didn't know I had in me. Luring him back to my place. Begging him to come home with me. Telling what I wanted to do to him in my bed…"

Listening, Stef felt a little outside himself, too, the hair on his arms and nape rising and falling. He wanted to stand in the spray of that bizarre pipeline. Be lured, begged and told exactly what Jav wanted to do to *him*.

"Did he come?" Stef asked. "I mean go. With you. Did you go…get off out of there?" He was laughing by the end. "Could the department of innuendo help me please?"

"None of the above," Jav said. "He freaked out. Which wasn't surprising. Val always said Alex had a moral compass that only pointed one way. I could only interfere with the magnetic field so much before the needle swung around again. He loves her. They belong to each other. It was never up for debate, and it was really no shock he stopped me."

"Unfinished hand job number two," Stef mumbled. "Ouch."

"No, not until we walked out of the shed and Val was right there. *Then* it was ouch."

Stef softly hummed the *Dragnet* theme.

"It was ridiculous," Jav said. "We're both all messed up. Sporting wood. Worst of all, we pulled our shirts on in the dark, so I walk out with mine on inside-out and backward."

"Oh my God."

"I felt like such an asshole."

"Don't," Stef said. "Sure, objectively it wasn't your finest moment, but you're not an asshole. Listen, I'm about to head into the tunnel at Grand Central and I'll lose reception."

"Okay."

"For what it's worth, you tell a good story," Stef said.

Jav laughed. "I should try to get paid for it."

"You should. I'll talk to you tomorrow?"

"You got it. 'Night."

"'Night, man."

Stef ended the call just as the train plunged into darkness. Only a few seconds, then the interior lights flickered on and held. Stef stared at the window, through his own reflection.

I met someone, he mouthed to the window, his breath fogging up the glass.

OCTOBER

CATCH MY BREATH

A THICK, HEAVY NIGHT in the dark of a girl's bedroom. Her skin was smooth as soap, softer than butter. She *gave* under Geno's hands, his fingers pressing and kneading her body beneath him. It felt good. *Normally* good. His hardness sliding into luscious heat and her little moans hitting his ears like notes from a wind chime. He pushed into her, breathing hard enough to break a sweat and…

"Are you okay?" she asked.

"Yeah." He slid off her and rolled to his back, the heels of his hands pressed to his face.

"Mo, what's wrong?"

"Nothing. I'm fine."

"You sure?"

"Yeah. I…" He thought fast. "I was in a boating accident when I was young. I almost drowned." He took his hands away and stared at her through the swirling gold blobs. "Sometimes when I can't catch my breath, I get anxious."

"Oh my God, are you kidding?" She sat up, pulling the sheet tight across her breasts.

"It doesn't happen often." He gave a hearty chuckle. "Usually it waits until the perfect time to embarrass the shit out of me."

"No, don't be embarrassed." Her hand stroked him. "I understand."

"Trust me, I couldn't catch my breath in a good way."

She laughed and lay down, her head on his shoulder.

"I just need a minute," he said.

"Take your time." Her arm tightened around him. "God, Mo, you're so sweet."

Later, when she was asleep, Geno slid from the bed and moved silently into the bathroom. As he did with so many girls on so many nights, he opened the medicine cabinet and searched vanity drawers. Christ, but a lot of chicks had little helpers. Were they all as fucked up as him?

In the glare of fluorescent light, he made judicious and invisible choices, stealing two Valium here. A Clonazepam there. Tablets of Xanax, Ativan and Librium secreted in his pants pockets and taken back to his room to be stashed. He identified athletes in his dorm who had injuries and buddied up to them. He slipped into their bathrooms and pocketed their pain meds, one careful pill at a time.

He was taking inventory of his secret pharmacy when Ben rattled knuckles on the door and leaned on the jamb. "Lauren said you were in a boating accident?"

"Bitch, that was a secret," Geno said, casually sliding his bedside table drawer closed.

"Sorry, it just came up in conversation. Were you?"

"Yeah, I was."

"That's nuts. I'm sorry."

"Thanks. Just don't invite me canoeing, okay?"

Ben rolled his eyes and let it go. That weekend a gang of friends impulsively got on a Circle Line cruise, and Ben seemed surprised Geno was among them.

"Dude, come on," Geno said. "I'm not afraid of a tourist boat."

"What are you afraid of?"

Geno laughed but Ben's gaze was serious. A long staring moment passed.

"Nothing," Geno said, pulling up a hair taller while thinking, *Everything.*

BI-ROMANTIC

"**W**OULD IT BE a dumb question to ask what it is you like about sex with men?"

"Yeah," Stef said. "But for some stupid reason, I like when you ask me dumb questions."

A long pause, through which Jav could hear the distinctive sounds of steel and china, a spoon's handle rapped on the edge of a pot or pan. Lying on his hotel bed in Philadelphia, his imagination constructed a kitchen, followed Stef from stove to fridge to sink. A dishtowel thrown over his shoulder or tucked through a belt loop, the way Jav did when he cooked. Or maybe Stef was a less fastidious chef and just wiped his hands off on himself.

"Wait, what?" Jav said. "Sorry, say that again."

"I was saying I like the physicality of it. It's a different physicality. I mean… Hold on a minute, I can't cook and think about sex at the same time."

"I'm getting the idea eating is a big thing with you."

"I love food so much it's stupid."

"You wouldn't know," Jav said. "I mean, you look like you're in great shape." He sank his face into his palm. *Christ, that sounded idiotic.*

"I have to keep that love on a short leash," Stef said. "Ow." A clanking clatter and some muttered cursing. "Dammit, that's hot. Okay, now I can think." The background noise ceased and Stef exhaled. "So, my attraction to girls was always a soft thing. If I had to draw it, I'd use circles. Overlapping circles. Like I'm red and she's yellow and the attraction is the oval of orange where they merge."

"Venn diagram chemistry," Jav said, doodling two circles on the hotel pad of paper.

"It's nearly always emotion based. Or intellectual. The attraction is soft. Like it...squishes. That's not too sexy, is it?"

"It's not a word I tend to throw around the bedroom."

"Fine, it doesn't squish, it...*gives*. It yields. I sink into her, she sinks into me. But with guys, it's harder. And I don't mean hard like the obvious, or hard like difficult. Hard like... Wow, this is hard to articulate."

"Is it less emotional?"

"Well, not that no emotions are involved, but they're simpler emotions," Stef said. "I keep coming back to the attraction being harder. It's a negative word but I don't mean it like that."

"The attraction is tougher?" Jav said. "More tenacious?"

"*Yes,*" Stef said. "Tenacious. Exactly. It can take my weight. I can push on it hard, be rougher with it. It's not a connection I overlap or fall into. It's something I *lean* on. Hard."

"Are you a..." Jav clicked his teeth closed around the question.

Stef laughed softly. "I do believe the words *top or bottom* are trapped in your mouth right now?"

"Is it bad form to ask?"

"Nah, it was just cute how you cut yourself off. I'm vers. Or a switch, as it's sometimes known. It depends a little on my mood and a lot on my partner."

"Gotcha," Jav said, quelling an urge to take notes.

"So to summarize, I like sex with men the way I like caviar."

"Caviar?"

"Yeah. Caviar's great but I don't keep it around," Stef said. "I don't like it so much that I have a jar stashed in the cabinet. But when it's served to me, I love it. *Oh man, I forgot how good this is, why don't I have this more often, it's fantastic.* Then the plate's empty and I forget again."

"It's a treat."

"But a passive treat. I don't actively seek it out much. I wait until it comes to me. I dig caviar but I don't have a relationship with it. Same with men. I've had some great sexual encounters. When I'm in the moment, I'm stuffing my face and thinking, *Wow, I forgot how much I like this.* But I've never wanted to string together multiple encounters into a relationship."

"I see."

"Yet here I am," Stef said. "Calling you every night. Letting my dinner go cold because I dig talking to you more than eating."

"Whoa," Jav said. "More than eating?"

"I know." Stef's laugh stuttered once, then he cleared his throat. "Anyway. I don't know if I've answered your question. My bisexuality is kind of literal. I have sex with both women and men, but all my serious, long-term relationships have been with women."

"Would you say you ever made love with a guy?"

"No, I can't say I have."

"So basically you're bisexual," Jav said, "but not bi-romantic."

"I'm not bi-romantic, no."

A long, taut pause swelled over the line. Long enough for Jav to get a few things squared away.

He likes me more than eating, he thought. *But it's not bi-romantic. Good. He's a good pick for where I am right now. He only wants to sleep with me. This will just be a sex thing. Fuck buddies. Which is cool. I can figure out if I like it.*

Bisexual but not bi-romantic. Maybe that's me, too. Connect emotionally with women, for the most part. Occasionally leaning up against another man. Because I like it.

If I like it.

"You get one more question," Stef said. "Then I'm eating."

"When was the last time you were with a guy?"

Stef chuckled. "Funny you ask. I could've hooked up the day we met."

Jav blinked. "What?"

"Wait, that came out wrong. I don't mean with you. Not that I didn't… Jesus Christ."

Now Jav was laughing, glad not to be the idiot in the room for once.

"This is my goddamn fault for giving you one more," Stef said. "What I *mean* is later that night, I was out drinking and this guy I know was making the moves. It was there for the taking, but I didn't."

"No?"

"I kind of had a writer on my mind. And on that vulnerable note, I'm off to get my foot out of my mouth and eat my cold dinner. Go think up some more dumb questions."

"Call me later," Jav said, but Stef was gone. No hostility in the empty air, rather it was the sound of shyness.

I had a writer on my mind.

A note stuffed under the door, a doorbell rung and a fast retreat down the block.

Come back, Jav thought, full of heat and questions for later. Stef didn't call him though, and sleep was slow to come. Giving up, Jav stacked the pillows and opened his laptop, but not to write.

The light from the screen splashed on him like milk as he surfed through porn sites. First looking at women. Then, when he was good and bothered and moody, he looked at men. His mood ebbed and flowed as his eyes narrowed and widened. They lingered on one image. Got the swift hell away from another. His finger swept and clicked and scrolled, then stopped to consider before rejecting on the pettiest of grounds.

Too posed. (If he wanted sculpture, he'd go to a museum.)

Too arrogant. (He didn't like porn that broke the fourth wall.)

Too hairy. (*Christ, dude, you look like a rug.*)

A few pictures and clips drew him in, pulled him up erect and curious and made him think, *That's hot. I could do that.* But he found the line was fine between *oh hell, yeah* and *oh hell, no.* He'd be rapt for a rock-hard, breath-held moment, then he scoffed or snorted or winced and, nose wrinkled, he tapped out.

"I'm going to be one picky fuck," he said, horny in the most aggravated way. Well, screw it. After twenty-three years of catering to needs, why not relish being high maintenance? Get laid on his terms for once. Lie back like a king and get instead of give.

Of course, if that were his true goal, he could hire someone. Right now, even. Grab the phone book, turn to the Es and pay to have an escort come service him. Male or female. Or both. Why not?

Because you're worth more.

And like it or not, these are your brothers. You were a sex worker. So are they. All of them making a living with their face and their body and their cock. They're selling the same dream you were.

His eyes swept sculpted muscles, tattooed skin and pouting expressions. Sliding a shirt up to reveal six-pack abs. Peeling undone pants down lean hips to show a hint of what they had for the viewer. Poses he himself had struck when he was throwing down his seduction to the tune of a hundred, five hundred, sometimes a thousand an hour.

My father would've died if he knew what I was doing.

Alone in the dark with strangers, Jav was overcome by a profound and sudden sadness. These beautiful men were hardly more than boys. And he'd been such a beautiful boy once. Ripped out of childhood, hungry and desperate, displaying his merchandise and calculating its worth down to the lick of a bottom lip.

These guys are all somebody's son, he thought. *Abandoned or beloved. Thrown out or cherished. They all belonged to somebody once. Some of them belong to someone right now, and not in a good way.*

He shut the laptop, dismantled the pillows and lay down, not wanting anything anymore.

SO CLOSE

"**J**ESUS, I CAN'T believe the shit I tell you sometimes," Stef said.

"My ears are the round holes for your square thoughts," Jav said from his hotel room in Providence.

"Dude, don't make me like you. And don't make my dinner go cold this time. I'll eat and you can tell me if you ever got hired for a threesome."

"I got hired by married couples twice," Jav said. "First time weirded me out because the husband didn't do anything but sit in the corner and watch. Fully dressed, not touching himself, not directing. Just sitting there glaring. I hated it. Second time was more enjoyable, until the husband started touching me. Then I had an issues attack, freaked out and fled. Never worked with couples again."

"Ever get hired by two women?" Stef asked around a mouthful.

"Yes."

"What was that like?"

"Exhausting."

Stef laughed in the middle of a swallow. It took five minutes to recover from the coughing fit. "You're killing me, Landes."

"Since you're dying, you want to tell me about your marriage?" Jav asked. "I have a backup question if the answer is no."

"I don't really like talking about that," Stef said.

"Why?"

"Everyone has healthy regrets, but my marriage is one that can still make me cringe. And I don't know what your threshold for secondhand embarrassment is."

"It's slightly higher than your average garden shed, but just shy of the Burj Khalifa."

Stef regarded this opened door. It was all well and good sharing your funny stories, telling tales that presented you in a positive light. It was something else to recount one of your more despicable moments.

He could dislike talking about it and talk about it anyway.

He kind of wanted to.

"I was a little dishonest when I summarized it on the phone the other night," he said. "But hey, it was our first phone date."

"I threw my escorting career on the table on that date."

"I didn't want to take away your spotlight."

"Listen, all jokes aside," Jav said, "I only want your story if—"

"If I'm telling it. I know. I dig that about you and I want to tell. I'm just goofing around because it's hard." Stef drained his beer and gathered his thoughts. "Okay. So, I said we were both young. She was actually quite a bit older than me. And she was one of my professors, which is a whole other ethical discussion."

"Yikes," Jav murmured.

"I said we both had the same ideas about marriage and monogamy and so forth. That's not true at all, and it's really the crux of me feeling like such a scumbag. I was… If you want to be kind, you can say my relationship with my wife was unhealthy. If you want to be blunt, it was obsession, not a relationship. I can't honestly say it was abusive. I know abuse. But it was definitely a power imbalance. Definitely manipulative. That woman was…"

Jav gave a soft laugh. "You don't even say her name."

"I know, right? Man, years of therapy and I still can't articulate the hold she had on me."

"It's tempting to round up the usual suspects but from what I've heard so far, this isn't a mommy issue."

"Believe me," Stef said. "I put my relationship with my mother under the microscope and no, it's not. Human connection has an underworld and Courtney was like a Mafia queen. I pretended to be a lot of things I wasn't. I was utterly untrue to myself."

"So when you said, 'We got into the swing scene,' was that really a *we* decision or…"

"She wanted to," Stef said. "And I went along. Acting like monogamy was an elitist social construct when in my deepest heart, soul and guts, I was, *am*, a very devoted and loyal person. I didn't want to share. More importantly, I didn't want to be shared. I knew this about myself. Yet I didn't stand by it and for the life of me, I don't know why."

"I see."

"I had self-awareness out the wazoo and I denied all of it. Because I didn't want to lose her. When I say I was obsessed with her, it was…bad. I got married and I got lost. I was a rotten husband. I don't mean I was rotten to Courtney, I just wasn't a good husband to myself. Wait, that doesn't make sense. I don't know what I… See?" Stef fell back on the couch laughing. "If I had a client with this story, I'd be identifying and labeling the hell out of it. I turn that insight on my case, and I can't put two words together."

"Well," Jav said slowly. "Not to be a nerd, but *husband* is both a noun and a verb. To husband something means to manage it. Conserve it. Use resources wisely so there's enough for a lifetime. So when I hear *I was a rotten husband to myself*, it means you didn't husband your true nature. And when your marriage ended, you had no supplies."

Stef stared. Conscious of moments passing by but unable to speak.

"You there?" Jav said.

"Sorry. My jaw dislocated when it fell on the floor." He sat up. "Hold on, I have to write this down."

"Story of my life."

Stef took a Post-it, scribbled Jav's name and the word *husband*.

Wait, what?

He added *definition* in capital letters. And further clarified, *both noun and verb*.

"Do you still talk to Courtney?" Jav asked.

But Stef was still studying the Post-it. Feeling rather like he did in the moments after he met Jav, which compelled him to add the date to his notes.

Something just happened, he thought. Then aloud, "Hm? No. And that's a milestone I worked hard to achieve. Of course I started out magnanimous and uber-civilized, *Oh yes, we'll still be friends, we'll stay in touch, I wish you nothing but the best…* But my therapist laughed in my face and I snapped out of it. Because no, frankly, I do not want to be friends with her. She was never a friend. She'll never be a stable, healthy, positive influence in my life. She brings nothing to my table. Yes, I wish her well, but I am not staying in casual touch because I have no casual mode with her. Some people you meet are all-or-nothing. You can't be in each other's lives a little because if they're in, they're *in*."

"They get into your warehouses and squander the goods you've husbanded."

"Exactly," Stef said. "So it's unfortunate, but no, I am not in touch with Courtney at all."

"Have you had serious relationships since?"

"Nothing that lasted long. The pendulum swings both ways and I suppose I got hyper-vigilant about my warehouse. There's stockpiling necessities and then there's hoarding. I was so self-actualized I was becoming a dragon. Hence, when I met you and all the hairs stood up on my forearms, I asked for your card, even though I figured you were straight."

"But I wasn't."

"And here we are." Stef crumpled up the Post-it and tossed it on the coffee table.

"Thanks for telling me," Jav said. "I know it's not your favorite subject."

"Yeah. It was a dark time after we divorced. I was just…ashamed of myself. I once had this British co-worker who referred to badly-behaved people as *swine*. Trust me, in his posh accent, it was damning. And man, after all was said and done, I felt like an absolute swine."

"Hold on, we need a dictionary consult here." In the background, Stef could hear pages swiftly turning. "Here we go, swine," Jav said. "Old English Swin… Proto-Germanic… Middle Dutch… No, it's all the same. There's nothing that makes swine anything other than a pig. Sorry."

"You tried."

A long, warm moment.

"I gotta go now," Jav said. "Kind of wish I didn't."

"Same," Stef said. "But go. You're too talented to be a dragon. Go share the wordsmith talent you've husbanded."

"I will," Jav said softly. "Thanks."

Stef sighed darkly after ending the call. It was Sunday. And he fucking hated Sundays. He reached for the crumpled Post-it and smoothed it out.

Jav. Husband. DEFINITION. Both noun and verb.

"You're out of your mind, Finch," he said under his breath, but he took the little square of paper to his shrine, which was a low table in one corner of his bedroom. A string of prayer flags tacked above, a pantheon of small god and goddess figurines in a semi-circle. He lit his candle and drew Guan Yin, bodhisattva of compassion, into the center of the altar. Her Chinese name was Guanshiyin, meaning She Who Perceives the Sounds of the World.

"I am so close to something," he whispered to her, his voice making the flame flicker. "And I want it."

He reached for the brass bell in one corner of the table and rang it once. One single sound of the world holding all his desire.

Please hear me, he thought.

I want this feeling I have with him.

I want to husband this feeling.

When I talk to Jav, I feel honest. I feel authentic. I feel myself and I see so clearly who I want to be and the life I want to lead. And the kind of person I want to have with me on the ride. A curator and sailor.

A person who makes me feel like this.

A GREAT DESTINY

"**Y**OU GOING HOME for Columbus Day weekend?" Ben asked. He and Geno were running side-by-side on the treadmills, their feet and elbows pumping in a steady cadence.

"No," Geno said.

"Just gonna hang around here?"

"Yeah."

Left right left right. Sneakers slapping through the background of clinking, clanking weight machines and rock music.

"What do your parents do?" Ben asked.

"Don't ask. You'll be sorry."

"Come on. What, are they spies?"

Geno counted ten panting steps before answering. "My mother died when I was fifteen. My father and my brother died last July. I'm not going home for break because I don't really have a home." He glanced sideways. "See? Now it's awkward. Magic."

Ben hopped his feet onto the side plates of the mill, letting the tread continue. "You shitting me? I mean… Sorry, that was dumb."

"Yes. it was. And no, I'm not." Geno swiped a forearm over his sweaty brow and shook it out.

"You literally have no home to go to? No family, no nothing?"

"I have a half-sister. She's about twenty years older than me. I lived with her a little while this summer. She's actually cool, I like her. But I had to leave because… Long story. I just had to."

"Where'd you go then?"

"Friend of the family's. He's my father's best friend. Was. And our lawyer. He handled all the estate matters and he's managing my money until I'm twenty-one. I guess technically you could call his place my home. My stuff's there, anyway."

Ben hopped back onto the belt and started running. "No grandparents?"

"No."

"Aunts, uncles?"

Geno didn't answer. His chest burned with exertion and a strange embarrassment. Why didn't he have aunts, uncles or cousins around? How did Nathan and Analisa, two only children, meet and marry and not build a great dynasty to take care of their own? Now, on top of all the other injuries he'd suffered, Geno had to *explain* why he had nobody. It was humiliating.

Where were his people?

"So what will you do for Thanksgiving?" Ben asked. "Or Christmas?"

"I'm Jewish." Even that felt fraudulent. The Caans had been bare minimum Jewish. Geno and Carlos had a bris because their grandparents would've *died* if they hadn't. But that was the extent of the orthodoxy. Neither twin went to Hebrew school or had a bar mitzvah. The Caans lit a menorah and had a big Hanukkah party because Analisa liked to make latkes. They hosted a Seder because Analisa liked to gather with friends and cook and celebrate.

We were socially Jewish, Geno thought. Gazing at the tattooed Hebrew letters and Kabbalah symbols on his arms, he added, *Or superstitiously Jewish.*

"Dude, you know what I mean," Ben said.

"I don't know. I'll go to Vern's, I guess. Or book a flight to the Bahamas or something. Be drunk on the beach for a week. I haven't thought about it yet."

The burn in Geno's chest was reaching fingers into his throat and squeezing. Embarrassment morphed into alarm. The belt beneath his pounding feet unrolled like a long, lonely road into the future.

What will I do? Not just this year but all the years to come?

Where will I sit on Thanksgiving?

Where is my home now?

He was in free-falling panic now. His heart and lungs begged him to stop for air, but his feet kept going. He had to run and keep running until he got somewhere.

I want to go home.

The little red henhouse beckoned from a glade in the woods. Expanded now with a second story and a porch. Triple the number of windows the light could stream out of. Within would be a big table, long-lost loved ones crammed in elbow-to-elbow, waiting for him.

I want to go home.

His feet ran faster. His heart was breaking.

I want to go home…

"Ben, would you fucking stop apologizing and play?" It was later that evening, and Geno and Ben were playing air hockey in the common room. A Xanax and a four-hour power nap put the floor back under Geno's feet. A Valium was keeping it there.

"I just feel bad, man," Ben said.

"A bunch of tragic shit happened to me but it's nobody's fault. Nothing you can do about it."

"Sure there is."

"Like what?"

Ben stopped the puck with the edge of his striker. "You come to my place for Thanksgiving."

Geno straightened up and put his hands on his hips. "For real?"

"Talked to my mom. She wants you to come."

"You didn't tell her the whole poor orphan tale, did you?"

"Not in so many details," Ben said. "I just said my roommate was in a bind for the holidays, had nowhere to go. She was horrified and said, 'Bring him here or I'll kill you.' End of story."

Geno swallowed. "Thanks," he said, the word thick in his mouth. "I'm sorry if I…"

Ben shot the puck over. "Stop apologizing and play."

VAMPIRE

*F*RIDAY OF COLUMBUS Day weekend, Geno and Ben were chilling on the couch, watching the Yankees play the Orioles.

"Look at you guys being all cozy," a girl's voice called. Natasha Kaslov bounded into the common room. Ben's eyes lit up and his face flushed red. He had such a hard-on for this chick, he turned into an amoeba whenever she came around. A lot of guys in the dorm had a thing for Natasha. Geno was undecided. Sweet girl, but she had a loud mouth, pink hair and quite a bit of hardware piercing her face. Ben thought she was gorgeous and he was rabidly curious about feeling her tongue stud on his dick.

"Smile," Natasha said now, leaning over the back of the couch, phone in her extended hands, trying to frame the three of them into a selfie. "C'mon, scooch in, guys."

Ben leaned in but Geno leaned out, pulling the side of his hoodie over his face. He hated being told to smile more than he hated having his picture taken.

"Aw, you're so shy," Natasha said.

"He's afraid you'll take his soul," Ben said.

"I would. For a night. But I'd give it back in the morning." Natasha rubbed knuckles on both their heads and left, a trail of heady perfume in her wake.

"Jesus, I think I'd pay money for one night with that," Ben said.

"No, you wouldn't."

"Can I ask you something?"

"If it's about my family, you won't like the answers."

"You're really sensitive about having your picture taken," Ben said. "Is that a Jewish thing?"

The bout of laughter pouring out of Geno's chest felt good. Normal. It also gave him time to consider the options.

No, Mos said, lurching to life after days of slumber. *We do not talk about it. It is the law.*

"Well?" Ben said, hands spread, laughing along.

"No, dumbass, it's not a Jewish thing."

"You're a vampire. Your image can't be captured on film."

"No," Geno said. "It's kind of the opposite."

This is illegal, Mo said.

"Your image is trademarked?"

"I'll tell you," Geno said, "but you won't like it. And you won't be able to fix it by inviting me home for Christmas."

"Is that a challenge?" Ben said. "Bring it, bitch."

Say it, you little bitch, before I fuck you in two.

"My brother kind of got…"

This was a mistake. His throat was a fist, choking off his voice. Mos wasn't fooling around. Geno had to think fast.

"Got what?" Ben asked.

"He and a girlfriend texted nude pictures to each other." As the lie swiftly formed in Geno's head, his throat eased up, letting it out. "Somehow, someone got hold of them. Texted them to someone else. Who passed them to someone else. Next thing you know…" He spread his hands out.

Ben's eyes widened. "Get the fuck out. For real?"

"Yeah. Then we got an anonymous letter in the mail, showing my brother's image on some porn site."

"Shut. *Up.*"

"Now all these pictures of him are out there on the internet. Strangers looking at him. Perverts jerking off to him. It just made me hyper-aware of how quickly your picture can get out of your hands. Know what I mean?"

"No shit. That is messed up."

"It's a dopey thing, but…"

"No, no, no, I totally get it. Wow. I'm sorry, that's fucking skanky." Ben gave a shiver. "Kind of reminds me of that child porn ring bust in New Jersey last summer."

It was a strange relief to speak the complete, unfortunate truth: "It was exactly like that."

Telling Ben the story, however altered and abbreviated, was tactile. The way it had been when Chris Mudry came out. When he handed over his backpack and Geno felt a bit of the burden settle into his hands. Now Geno had handed over a bit of himself to Ben, who sat still and quiet, a hand running over the top of his head, as if he could still feel Natasha's touch there. Unaware of Geno's trust in his lap.

"So," Geno said, and cleared his throat. "I wanted to say something."

Ben glanced over, eyebrows raised.

"After my mom died, I got a little agoraphobic. A lot, actually. I could leave the house, but it made me really nervous. After the shit went down with my brother, it got worse. I liked being at home, you know?"

"Sure," Ben said, his face soft with a mix of curiosity and concern. "Makes sense."

"It's still hard for me to be out in crowds. So when you ask me to come out and I don't go, it's not you. It's my weird shit. And when I do go out, but I leave early or just disappear to come back here, that's my shit, too. But really what I wanted to say was…I appreciate you always asking."

Ben looked at him a long moment. Geno braced for ridicule, for a shrugged dismissal, for misunderstanding. Finally, Ben unfolded one arm and extended a fist across the couch cushions between them.

"Then I'll keep on always asking."

Geno touched his knuckles to Ben's. "Thanks."

"Thanks for telling me. Honestly, it never bothered me if you didn't come out. But a couple times when you've ghosted, it was weird. I mean, weird like I worried you weren't okay. Now I know the deal. It's all good."

Geno disguised his exhale with a yawn, sinking lower into the couch, heart thumping hard beneath the zipper of his hoodie.

"It's gotta be hard," Ben said. "I can't even…" Then he shrugged, but helplessly, shaking his head a little.

Geno fiddled with his hoodie's drawstrings, wanting to draw the flap of fleece up over his head and pull tight, cinching him in a cocoon. Instead he gathered courage, unzipped and let his heart breathe a little.

SHALOM

"**W**ELCOME HOME," STEF said.

Jav rubbed his face, yawning. "Thank you. Good to be back."

"You must be wiped out."

Nothing some sleep and a good fuck can't cure, Jav thought before he said, "I am."

"When do you go get Roman?" Stef asked.

"Sunday," Jav said through another yawn.

"I won't keep you. Go crash."

"What are you doing tonight?"

"When I'm free on Fridays, I usually have Sabbath dinner with my mom and Lilia."

"You're Jewish?"

"My family, no," Stef said. "But Lilia is. Anyway, I know it's early to meet one mother, let alone two. But you want to come?"

"Oh, I don't know," Jav said. "This is a big step." He leaned back in his chair, tossing a baseball up to the ceiling and catching it one-handed.

"Yeah, once you light the candles it's pretty serious. You don't have to. But I'm telling you, the food's great."

"Then I'm in," Jav said. "I've never been to Sabbath dinner. Should I bring anything?"

"No. I mean, if you hate arriving empty-handed, Mom loves a good cabernet."

"What about Lilia?"

"She loves a good appetite. Bring that."

Jav caught the ball with a satisfying smack in the center of his palm and held it tight. "I will."

"See you around five then."

Jav crashed most of the day, then got up to get a few things from Fairway, make some calls and answer emails. He showered, hit a local liquor store for a bottle of Cabernet, then took the subway downtown. The springs of his heart coiled tighter with every stop, and his stomach danced from one foot to the other like a child who had to pee.

Do we hug? Do we kiss? Tear our clothes off and get to it?

He rang the doorbell of the handsome townhouse, feeling like he should've brought flowers, too.

Stef opened the tall door. A flash of cobalt eyes. A blue button-down shirt, sleeves rolled up to show his tattooed forearms. Open at the collar to show more ink crawling toward his neck. Dimple puncturing one side of a wide smile as he mouthed "Hey" over the phone pressed to his ear. He slapped his right hand against Jav's palm and shook it, drawing him inside with a roll of his eyes.

"Sorry," he mouthed, holding up an index finger like he'd be done soon.

Jav looked around the entryway. He imagined once upon a time, it was an impressive and welcoming foyer, but now converted to suit the comings and goings of both owner and tenants. A staircase on the right went up, one on the left went down. On the landing between was a lone door which, Jav guessed, led to where Stef's mother lived.

"I know," Stef was saying, leaning back on the stair railing. "Edith, I know. You're in analysis paralysis, just step away from the computer tonight."

Jav looked at Stef's hands. He wore quite a few rings, all of them silver. A circlet of wings around one middle finger. Twin bands on both pointers. A single arrow spiraled around a thumb. A ring of overlapping circles covered the bottom joint of one pinky.

Jav stared, wondering how those bits of silver would feel on his skin.

"Tap out and clear your head," Stef was saying. "I know. It's going to be fine. Look, I have to go. No problem, don't worry. I'll see you Monday." He ended the call with a brisk shake of his head. "Co-worker," he said. "She's writing her master's thesis and freaking out."

"Edith," Jav said. "There's a name you don't hear too often."

"She spells it the Old English way with an a-e. Aedith. But enough about her, what's *up*, dude?"

Another handshake with a pull into a hug.

Stef's body was warm and his skin smelled bright and clean. A bit of shaving cream lingered at his ear lobe. Jav checked the urge to smudge it away.

"Hungry?" Stef said.

"Starving," Jav said, now fixated on the ocean wave tattooed along the side of Stef's neck. A single bird at the foaming crest.

"Come on," Stef said. "Meet the mothers."

The parlor floor rooms were railroaded from front to rear. A small study with two desks in front of shelves tight with books. A larger living room with couches and chairs around a fireplace. A dining area beyond, the table set in front of tall windows filled with plants. All the walls were white and crammed floor to ceiling with paintings, classics thrown up next to moderns.

By the window, a woman stood on a stepladder, watering ferns. She was rake-thin in smart wool trousers, a faded and worn oxford and a single strand of pearls. White hair in a bob, dark purple glasses held with a chain around her neck. A man's silver watch. Bare feet with red-polished toenails.

"Don't fall," Stef said.

"Don't nag me," she said, splashing him with the watering can. She looked at Jav then. "Hello, I'm Rory," she said, reaching down.

"Mom, this is Javier. Jav, Mom."

Jav reached up to shake the soft, strong hand, which then held onto his.

"Nice to meet you, dear. I'm coming down, don't let go. Take the can, please." Jav held both the watering can and her hand until her feet were on the floor.

"Something smells good," Jav said.

"Doesn't it?" Rory said. "I hope you brought an appetite. Pony, before dinner, I need you to flip the mattress for me. It's all stripped and ready. Your friend can help."

Stef was folding the stepladder. "Can he?"

"Don't be fresh." She reached and smudged away the bit of shaving cream on Stef's ear. Rubbing her fingertips, her pale blue eyes glanced at the bottle in Jav's hand. "Would that be for me?"

"It would." Jav handed it over.

Rory drew on her glasses. "Alexander Valley," she said. "You know your cabs."

"I know nothing about cabs, I asked the guy at the liquor store for a good one."

"Well then, he knows his cabs. I'll open it now. Go do the mattress." She walked off, still examining the label.

"My mother, ladies and gentlemen," Stef said as he led Jav toward the stairs.

"Flip it side to side *and* head to foot," Rory called after.

"Don't nag me," Stef called back.

Another white-haired woman was coming down the stairs. "Pony," she said. "Shabbat shalom."

"Shabbat shalom." Stef kissed her with European formality, left and right cheek, then turned back to Jav. "This is Lilia Kalo," he said. "My friend, Javier."

"Pleasure to have you, Javier," she said in a throaty accent. She too, wore wool trousers and an oxford shirt, but the shirt was mis-buttoned, one sleeve rolled up and the other rolled down. Her bobbed hair was dandelion fluff. Her string of pearls had a gap. One arm of her glasses was attached to its chain with surgical tape. The band of her watch was cracked, worn leather.

She looked like Rory, if Rory were crumpled up in a ball and shoved in a drawer for a week. Yet something in her bearing made Jav shake her tiny hand and set his other on top a moment. A fragment of a story sliced through his head—a quick picture of aristocrats and balls and military officers on leave. Before he could catch it, the image ran away, embarrassed.

In the upstairs bedroom, the men bumped, shuffled and lugged the mattress, flipping it over and rotating it head to foot.

"How did you get the nickname *Pony*?" Jav asked.

"I was a rather high maintenance baby, not much interested in sleeping. My dad would pace around singing 'Pony Boy' to get me to settle down. So it came from the song, but it stuck around because… Come here, I'll show you."

He led Jav out into the hallway and gestured to one wall, hung with artwork. Most depicting horses and horse figures. All of them signed by Stef, from his full name printed in childish letters, to an adult's bold capital letter dissolving into a scrawl.

"I wasn't interested in real life horses," Stef said. "Only horses in stories. Mythical horses. Pegasus and centaurs. I read Tolkien in school and while my friends wanted to be Aragorn, I only wanted to be Theoden or Eomer. One of the Rohirrim."

"What news from the Mark?" Jav said. One stunning drawing was a twist on the yin-yang symbol. A white Pegasus and a black, circling each other, heads to tails, their spread wings creating a perfect sphere. "This is amazing."

"Won a prize for that one," Stef said, touching the frame. "Wasn't long before it led to all this stuff." He held out his tattooed arm. Jav looked at it a long moment. He watched his own hand rise through the air and rest fingertips on the inked centaurs and winged horses. He traced a path toward the rolled-up cuff of Stef's shirt, lingering on the blue vein in the crook of Stef's elbow.

Their heads were close. The air pressed on Jav's ears as Stef's exhaled breath brushed his face.

"Hi," Jav said.

"Hi." Stef closed his eyes. "If I start kissing you, I won't stop. And if I kiss you outside my mother's bedroom, I'm going to need therapy."

"How about the closet?"

"Shut up." Laughing, Stef shoved Jav away.

His chest tight and his mind foggy, Jav moved toward the opposite wall, this one hung with photographs. New and old. Vivid, modern color mixed with vintage sepia. His eyes widened then narrowed on one black and white shot. A train platform. Open cattle cars. A crowd of people standing with bags and bundles, yellow stars sewed to their coats. At the center, two girls, both blonde, beautiful and luminous, stared curiously at the cameraman.

"That's Lilia and her twin sister," Stef said, pointing to them. "On the platform at Auschwitz."

"Holy shit," Jav said. "How did… Who took this picture?"

"A Nazi documentarian. Wasn't unusual at the camps. Lilia says not thirty seconds after this picture was taken, Josef Mengele came along the platform. Selecting."

"He had a sick, twisted thing for twins," Jav said, remembering newspaper headlines from last July.

"Yeah. Pretty much everyone on this train went to the gas chamber, but Lilia and her sister went off to be little lab rats."

Jav respectfully straightened the frame, lining it up square with its neighbors.

"She's somewhat famous in Holocaust photojournalism." Stef's pointing finger wandered through the maze of pictures and stopped at another black and white. "A portrait of survival. They got her on film arriving at Auschwitz in nineteen forty-four. She was marched out of there in forty-five, when the Russians were moving in. Now here she is being liberated from Bergen-Belsen."

"Holy shit, look at that."

A cluster of emaciated, tattered women in a barracks. Lying on a bunk with two other prisoners, Lilia was barely recognizable in this shot. The eyes gazing at the cameraman were heavy, penetrating. Her expression almost contemptuous as she stared down posterity. *Take a picture,* it seemed to say. *But you will never truly know what happened here.*

Jav searched all the women but found no other with those identical eyes.

"Did her sister survive?"

"No."

"God."

"Check this one out," Stef said. He pointed to a photograph capturing a melée. A handful of gaunt men in striped pajamas surrounded a single man in a flurry of raised fists and kicking feet. Stef's finger rested on one prisoner who stood apart from the mob. Not participating, but his fists were clenched and something in his cold, calculating expression was authoritative. As if the group of avengers moved at his order. His mouth was open as if shouting a command to attack.

"That's Lilia's ex-husband, Micah," Stef said. "They're beating the shit out of one of the kapos."

"Same camp?"

"Bergen-Belsen, yeah. They met there."

"Do they have kids?"

"They adopted a daughter," Stef said. "After Mengele was through with her, Lilia couldn't have kids."

Jav slowly shook his head. "Is this Micah, too?" he asked, finding more and more pictures of the man with the commanding presence. Softening slightly as he got on in years.

"Yeah."

"Interesting Lilia put up so many of him."

Stef leaned against the wall. "I don't pretend to know a tenth of what she and Micah went through or how it shaped their married life. From what I can piece together, it wasn't a particularly romantic relationship, but it was a fiercely loyal one."

"War mates?"

"In a way nobody from our generation could possibly understand. I think when Lilia met my mother, it was like finding her twin and being liberated again. Micah let her go gracefully, I guess because whatever he went through made him understand her better than anyone. They're still close. They'll always be close even if they're not married. Lilia keeps him in the gallery and I'm sure my mother understands." Stef's mouth twisted a little before deciding to smile. "I think love is a big wisdom made of small understandings."

Jav found a picture of Stef in a graduate's black mortarboard and gown, posed between his parents.

"Does your dad know you're bisexual?"

"Yeah."

"How'd he take it?"

"Not well," Stef said. "Basically he felt like my mother ruined me. Corrupted me, so to speak. Same attitude from my brothers. To this day you can feel an invisible line dividing the family. Me and mom on one side and the real men on the other."

"I'm sorry."

"No, don't be. It was rough a while and then it got better. It's not perfect but it's not terrible. They're my father and brothers and I love them. But I think if I were trapped on a desert island with any of them, someone would get eaten."

"Come eat," Rory called.

FANCIFUL DIMENSION

*L*ILIA MADE CHICKEN paprikash, served over egg noodles with a genteel sprinkling of parsley. She herself ate sparingly, while her eyes patrolled up and down the table, making sure everyone else was well-fed.

"This is delicious," Jav said, not just being polite.

"Do have more," Lilia said, passing the platter. Her chambray shirt was now dotted with paprika and grease spots. Jav's eyes snuck under half-lowered lids to Lilia's one rolled up sleeve, looking, unsuccessfully, for tattooed numbers. She caught his eyes and smiled curiously. Slightly ashamed, he took another helping of noodles with the last scrape of gravy. Lilia beamed at him before taking the cleaned platter to the kitchen.

As Rory and Stef sparred and joked, Jav tried to dissect their bond. It was affectionate, but not physical. They caressed each other with wit and laughter.

"Oh, Pony," she said often, the word both endearment and title. Something about her sleek white hair and the proud lift of her neck was equine, Jav thought. He could envision wings spreading on either side of her shoulders, crackling white and majestic, encircling the table and all those seated there.

To be accepted into the White Mare's herd was to be offered a lifetime of protection, he thought. *The Mare would rarely touch you out of love. Her own Pony rarely felt the caress of her feathers. But she'd kill for you with one thunderclap stroke of her mighty wings.*

After the meal, Lilia brought two candlesticks to the table. Everyone stood. Lilia put a napkin on her head and lit each wick. She apologized in advance for her terrible Hebrew.

"No one here knows the difference, dear," Rory said quietly.

"So with this blessing," Lilia said, addressing Jav, "you must make the circles with the hands, like this."

She recited the words while above the flames, her hands pulled the air inward, toward her heart. "Now you cover eyes." Her fingertips lined up along her eyebrows, her palms cupped. "And pray for something you want very much."

All eyes closed. A moment of reverent, hallowed silence crept around the table like a ribbon, gently drawing tight.

Please, Jav said to the dark of his eyelids. *Let me live to find out who I am.*

"Now open eyes." Lilia's hands lowered. "And welcome Sabbath. Shabbat shalom."

"Shabbat shalom," they replied. Rory's hand reached to fold around Lilia's fingers. At the same time, Jav felt a pressing, electric energy tickle the small of his back, then Stef's hand touched him, his palm wide and warm.

As the men readied to leave, Rory handed her son a Tupperware with a cut-up roasted chicken. "To pick at over the weekend."

"Oh, wait," Lilia said, heading back to the kitchen. "Pony, I got you some apples. And the nice Russian rye you like. With the little seeds."

"With the little seeds," Rory and Stef mouthed together, eyebrows high in their identically shaped foreheads. Rory reached up and screwed her fingertip into Stef's dimple. It was a gesture Jav had seen Val Lark do to Alex a hundred times. It filled him with both bittersweet memory and a warm hope.

"Do come again," Lilia said.

Jav smiled. "I will."

"I must," Stef said.

"Don't be fresh," Rory said.

The apartment door clicked shut behind them. Now Jav stood at a cross-roads. He could go down the stairs. Or go home.

Arms laden with chicken, bread and apples, Stef asked, "You want to come down?"

The decision flickered like a candle flame, then held still.

"Okay," Jav said.

Stef tilted his head toward the stairwell. "After you. It's dark, be careful. Just feel for the light switch at the bottom."

Jav went down, his heart thick with each footstep. The stairwell grew dimmer. He stopped, a hand on each rail, and he looked up over his shoulder.

Standing a couple treads up, backlit by the hall chandelier, Stef loomed mighty and mythic. Though his arms cradled things tight to his chest, his shoulders spread out like the broad wings of a Pegasus. A Rohirrim. A centaur drawing back the bowstring and taking aim.

"Can I tell you something?" he said.

"What?"

"When you got here tonight and I was on the phone? I wasn't really on the phone."

Jav wrinkled his brows. "No?"

"I was so excited to see you all day. Counting the minutes. Then I heard the doorbell ring and all at once, it was anticipation overload. I freaked out. I mean, in a good way, but... I just had to create some kind of distance to get my shit together. So I faked a phone call."

"Sounded real to me."

"My heart was pounding. Still is, actually."

Jav was smiling now. Hard enough to stretch.

Stef came down one more step. "Say *pony* in Spanish."

"Pony in Spanish." Jav closed his eyes just as Stef's mouth touched his.

Stef held his leftovers. Jav held the handrails. The kiss was tilted and off-center. Slightly awkward. And so utterly perfect, Jav wished for an instant that the entire rest of his life could be here in the darkened stairwell. No touching, no nakedness, nothing but his head leaning back and twisting up into Stef's mouth. Tongue and teeth and the lingering taste of Sabbath. If he dared free his hands, he'd make circles with them, pulling the air inward toward his heart. Praying for what he wanted. Then he'd cover his eyes and welcome it all within.

"Been waiting a month to kiss you," Stef whispered.

"Same," Jav said, his heartbeat a herd of wild horses on the move.

Come inside, Rohirrim, man of the Mark. Shabbat Shalom.

The kiss leaned on Jav. Hard. Harder. Then all at once, too hard.

"Oh crap," Stef said. "Dude, look out."

"Shit," Jav cried. Laughter filled the stairwell as both men teetered off balance and stumbled down two more steps. Each barely managed to get a shoulder into the wall and slide down to sit. A rolling cascade of thumps as the net bag of apples broke apart and the Tupperware box went end over end.

"No neck breaking on the first date," Jav said.

"Man, that would've been hard to explain."

From over their heads, Rory called down, "Pony, are you all right? What was that?"

"Cockroach," Stef said over his shoulder. "Big one. Close your door."

Still laughing, Jav put his forehead on Stef's bent knee and exhaled a long breath. "Jesus."

"Come on," Stef said. "Come inside."

The last time a door closed behind Jav and another man, they immediately flung each other up against the walls, tearing at their clothes, snarling and grabbing at each other like two rabid dogs. He half-expected the same now, but Stef put the food away in his fridge and popped a couple beers.

"Wander around, feel free," he said, clearing papers and a laptop off the couch. "Fake a phone call. Mi casa es su casa. Pardon my French."

Jav's eyes moved back and forth over the stuffed bookshelves. "You speak any Spanish?"

"I speak White New Yorker Spanish. Clichés and curses with a really bad accent."

One short wall of the living room had been made into a studio, with shelves of supplies and a heavy square table lined with jars of pens, pencils and brushes.

"How much time do you have for your own artwork?" Jav said.

"Not a lot. If I can sit there and make something once a week, it's a good week." Stef glanced at his watch. "I'm going to be a complete nerd and confess it's time for *Planet Earth* on BBC. I don't watch much TV but I'm kind of obsessed with this show."

"Put it on, I love that shit."

"Everyone should have David Attenborough narrate their life for an hour."

Jav used the bathroom, resisting the urge to peek in the medicine cabinet and behind the shower curtain. He took a few shy steps into the bedroom, lit pale gold from a single lamp on the bedside table. Pillows stacked against one side of the headboard, the covers a little dented and wrinkled, as if a nap were taken recently. *Client Privilege* lying open and face-down on the grey comforter.

I'm in his bed.

Smiling, Jav looked at a string of prayer flags tacked wall-to-wall in one corner of the room. Beneath it was a low table spread with a red sari. A round cushion before it. The top neatly and ritualistically arranged. A semi-circle of tiny statues around a single candle. Sticks of incense in a jar. A bell. A small, shallow bowl filled with loose change. A coil of ebony beads and a hunk of quartz crystal. And…

Jav inhaled, a quick sharp hiss. Tucked beneath the base of a happy Buddha was a wrinkled Post-it note. Jav's name was written on it, next to a date. Beneath, Stef had written *husband, DEFINITION, noun AND verb.*

"I thought you were kidding," Jav whispered. "You really did write it down."

Touched, he dug in his pocket and put the coins he found there in the little bowl. Then went out into the living room.

He kicked off his shoes and stretched out along the short end of the L-shaped couch. Stef sat at the other end, socked feet on the coffee table. The *Planet Earth* episode was on the Great Plains, the opening segment showing the grazers inhabiting the Tibetan plateau.

"Wild ass," Attenborough said in his gravelly tones, and both men cracked up.

"Only he could make *wild ass* sound dignified," Stef said.

"Can you imagine the outtakes on this one?" Jav said.

"Bet it was one take," Stef said. "David's the man."

"What's with the fortune cookies?" Jav asked, pointing to a wooden bowl full of them on the coffee table.

"Place I order out from always puts twenty of them in the bag," Stef said. "I don't even like them that much, but they're okay if I'm out of Mallomars and desperately jonesing."

He leaned and took a handful, tossing three cookies into Jav's lap. "Here. Keep two fortunes, chuck one." He cracked a cookie open and read aloud, "'If you have something worth fighting for, then fight for it.'"

Jav broke open his. "'You cannot love life until you live the life you love.'"

Stef cracked and read another. "'You have a flair for adding fanciful dimension to a story.' Wait, I think this is yours."

Jav gaze snagged on Stef's smile a moment. He looked down and read, "'A pleasant experience is ahead: don't pass it by.'"

Their eyes caught again and held. Stef swallowed and looked away, reading: "'The smart thing to do is to begin trusting your intuitions.'"

Jav took a deep breath, breaking open his last cookie. "'Back away from individuals who are impulsive.'"

A long staring moment.

"Are you by nature impulsive?" Jav asked.

Stef nodded.

Jav crumpled the third fortune up and tossed it. "I'm done backing away."

Stef studied his three slips of paper a moment before selecting one and crumpling it. "Fuck it, this story doesn't need any fanciful dimension."

He started crawling along the couch toward Jav. A strange dichotomy of power in his body and vulnerability in his face. He knelt over Jav's outstretched legs, his strong quads enclosing Jav tight. He took Jav's wrists and stretched his arms out along the couch cushions, opening his chest and his heart. He held Jav there, pinned a moment. Then Stef's hands glided back along Jav's forearms, elbows, biceps, shoulders. Back to his head, tilting it up. Thumbs running along Jav's cheekbones, then his eyebrows. Then one across Jav's bottom lip.

When Stef kissed him, Jav dug his fingers into the cushions. His toes curled up tight inside his socks. When a small sigh, almost a moan but not quite, tumbled out of Stef's chest, Jav melted back soft as his body rose up hard and wanting.

From the start, the rhythm of their kiss matched. The instinctive turn of a head, a lean in, a slight pull back and then a press from a different angle.

"God you are something," Stef said. The tip of his tongue brushed Jav's bottom lip, then his teeth closed around it, biting gently. Jav let go of the couch then, slid his hands into Stef's hair and held his head, pulling his mouth in. Nothing should've been sexy about kissing a guy after drinking beer and eating fortune cookies. But it was. Insanely sexy. Crazy delicious.

Jav touched his tongue to Stef's. Opened his mouth a little more. His teeth wanted in on the action now, wanted the roll of Stef's lip between them, to feel the give of that softness. His mouth wanted more, mad and thirsty for this hot, shaking excitement. This heady, thick connection coiling his chest and belly, filling his lap with blood and craving.

Stef's hands glided along Jav's throat, palms pressing to Jav's chest and shoulders. They curled around Jav's T-shirt, drawing it up over his head. Popping free from the neckband, Jav reached for Stef's shirt, hungry for skin. Skin on skin. To put all their inked designs together and find a story.

"Hold still." Mouth watering, Jav ran his fingertips down Stef's sternum. The hair lay short and tight against his chest. It funneled into a thin line, skirting his belly button and dipping beneath the waistband of his jeans. Jav unbuttoned them and ran his hands up Stef's stomach again. He touched the horse head tattooed on Stef's left pectoral. His nipple was pierced with a ring, making the horse look like an old-fashioned hitching post. Jav put his tongue to the hoop, then drew it gently into his mouth.

God, who am I? he thought, unable to remember when he felt more himself.

Stef pulled air in with a sharp hiss and his head fell back. The weight across Jav's thighs shifted, then Stef's hand slid between his legs, finding the pole of his erection. Stroking it, kneading it in rhythm with his kiss which was up around Jav's mouth again.

"Glad I trusted my intuition," Stef said, holding still with his forehead pressed to Jav's.

"I'm kind of loving my life right now."

Stef popped the button on Jav's jeans and unzipped them.

"Fuck," Jav whispered, exhaling as Stef's hand closed around his cock. He eased it up and out and free, a thumb running beneath the ridge. Silver rings gliding on skin. They kissed, hard and open-mouthed, the sigh of one ricocheting off the tongue of the other and rebounding back.

"You all right?" Stef said. "I don't want to make you doubt yourself, it's just... Consent is a very big thing with me."

"I'm more than all right," Jav said. "I just need to ask you something."

"What?"

"You sure you're not married?"

Stef's smile unfolded across Jav's mouth. "Positive," he said.

"There's no one who's going to text or call or break the shed door down?"

"Nobody." Stef straightened up, reaching in his pockets. "Here. My phone's muted. Wallet. Keys." He tossed everything toward the far end of the couch. "No means of escape. No distractions."

"Your watch," Jav said.

Holding Jav's eyes, Stef unbuckled the strap and tossed it with the rest of his effects. He slid a hand around Jav's nape and his kiss went deep. "Do you trust me?"

"Yes."

"Good. Now let a guy finish you off for once."

"Yes." Jav almost growled the word as the hand in his lap moved faster. Freedom coursed in his veins. Permission hot on his tongue. He wasn't a thief or an accessory to adultery. Tonight was a gift. His for the taking.

Or leaving.

I could leave. This isn't a job. This is for me.

For a wild second, he thought about testing the theory. But Stef's weight soon crushed all thoughts to dust. His mouth was soft and lush, a rough-edged sweetness like a burned marshmallow. His hand slid like a bespoke dream, stroking and squeezing as if he'd been born to do nothing else.

"Feel good?" he said.

"So good."

His teeth grazed Jav's bottom lip. "Telling you... Past few weeks, I've been out of my mind wondering how you'd feel in my hand."

It was rising up on Jav, fast and furious. "Yeah?" he whispered.

"Couldn't wait to get you alone."

In Jav's transfixed eyes, Stef blurred into two, then back into one. "Say more."

"I was hard every night thinking about you. About this."

Jav's hips bucked up, fingers digging into the couch cushions and trying to hold on. "Fuck, Stef..."

"God, I hope so," Stef said. "Someday."

"You're making me come." Then Jav was there. Arching, grabbing and exploding as Stef worked him into a frenzy. Hoarse words in Jav's ear pushing him over the edge.

"Come here. Come for me. Been waiting so long, Javi..."

THE BACON BAGEL

STEF WALKED JAV up to the front hall. They lingered there, kissing.

"Still need therapy for necking outside your mother's door?" Jav said.

Stef glanced down the entryway then back. "I've gotten over it."

In the light coming through the fantail window, Jav was stunning. Mouth swollen, hair tousled and eyes a little wicked as they ran up and down Stef's body.

"Holy shit, I finally jerked a guy off," he mumbled behind a smile.

"And vice-versa," Stef murmured. "Big night for you."

"I need to go home and write in my diary."

They kissed again, slow and soft, giving way to a harder grapple and a few inched steps back toward the stairwell. Stef ran a quick mental inventory of his bedside table drawer. He was sure he had at least one condom.

Sort of sure.

Actually, not sure at all.

"All right, I'm going," Jav said. "Delayed gratification. It's a thing."

"Wait. I'm going to say something really un-sexy."

"Good," Jav said. "It'll be easier to leave."

"I know it's early in the game, but I'm a practical guy and you were an escort."

"I'll get tested, don't worry."

"No offense."

"None taken," Jav said. "I've been going to the same clinic for twenty-three years. I got a binder full of blood work if you want it."

"Someday."

Jav smiled. "It's gonna be a hell of a someday."

"What are you doing tomorrow?"

"Hopefully something that involves asking you a lot of questions."

"That can be arranged," Stef said. "In fact, I got a place I want to take you for breakfast. And someone I'd like you to meet."

"I'm open to meeting everyone."

They held gazes, chests and shoulders rising and falling in an inhale and exhale. Fingertips brushing.

"I'm having a good time," Stef said. "I like how this is unfolding."

"Same."

"Good. Now get out of here. Come back tomorrow. Bring your binder."

"For real?

"No. Just bring you."

Jav smiled and Stef's chest turned inside-out. One last kiss on his mouth and Jav was gone, ambling down 20th Street, looking back once to wave.

"Dear diary," Stef said softly. "Holy. Shit."

"So who am I meeting?" Jav said the next morning.

"Lilia's ex-husband."

"The guy from the pictures?"

"Yes. And his daughter. My sort of stepsister. Stavroula."

"Stavroula." Jav's eyes swiveled off to the side, as if he'd heard the name before but couldn't remember where. "That," he said slowly, "is a great name."

"It's Greek."

"It's a queen." Jav blinked through another thoughtful moment, then his gaze cleared and he smiled. "Sorry, I have a thing for names. Where are we meeting up?"

"At the Bake and Bagel. Which they own."

The bakery was often misheard as the Bacon Bagel. Which happened to be the specialty of the house. Their grilled cheese and tomato on the bacon bagel was written up in *New York* magazine, in a feature article of the top ten rainy-day lunches.

Stavroula's eyes bulged when Stef walked into the humming bakery in the company of a Latino hunk, tall and built with laugh lines around his eyes and silver threading through his dark hair. When she made her way over to their table with their sandwiches, Stef was positive her underwear was sitting up and begging.

"Stav, this is Javier," Stef said. "Jav, this is Stav. Which rhymes with Jav."

"Oh, no," Stavroula said, taking a seat. "No, no. This is out of the question."

Stef thought it was hilarious. "It's perfect. Stef plus Jav equals Stav."

"Dude," Jav said into his coffee cup.

"Come on. We should all get married," Stef said. His mouth was ten steps ahead of his brain this morning.

"We should avoid each other entirely." Jav sank teeth into his grilled cheese and closed his eyes. "Christ, that's amazing."

Stavroula put her cheek on a fist. "You like?"

"Call a U-Haul, I'm moving in with this sandwich."

Stef took a bite of his bagel and all the tomato and cheese slid out the other end. He was a hot mess. When he tried to keep from beaming, he blushed. When he tried to fight off the blush, he beamed.

Jav, on the other hand, was perfectly chill. The way he got to his feet when Stavroula's father Micah came over was unconsciously respectful, as if his DNA were coded to rise in the presence of senior citizens. In particular, an eighty-year-old Holocaust survivor who got up at three every morning to make bagels, drove a van for Meals on Wheels, and took a daily five-mile walk. Stef stood as well and let Micah slap floury handprints on his shoulders and back.

Micah shook Jav's hand and set his other on top a moment, sending up another little puff of white dust. He took a chair and accepted what looked like a Dixie cup of coffee from his daughter.

Jav's eyes squinted at the hand-lettered quote on one of the walls. *"El ke alarga la meza, alarga la vida,"* he said. "It looks like Spanish but it's not. Make the table…long? Make life long?"

"The one who extends the table, lengthens their life," Micah said, tearing off the corner of a sugar packet. He tapped about six grains into his coffee and gave the cup a swirl.

"What language is that?"

"Ladino," Stavroula said. "Sephardic Jews speak it."

"And a few goy imposters," Micah said, patting his chest. "It's a real mongrel dialect. Medieval Spanish with bits of Hebrew and Turkish and Greek." The dark eyes under his thick black brows twinkled. "Like Spanish got drunk and had a one-night stand with Yiddish."

"Who makes all the pots?" His hands full, Jav's elbow pointed at the shelves along the exposed brick wall, lined with bowls and jars and jugs and cups.

Stavroula raised a finger.

"You made all of them?"

"Yeah. I got into pottery as post-divorce therapy. Now it's like brain yoga. Sometimes people are nice and buy one."

"They buy them because they're beautiful, habibti," Micah said.

Stavroula shrugged. "Mostly they break them by accident."

Micah crumpled his cup and pushed back his chair. After another round of dusty handshakes, he went back to his dough-making. Jav went up to buy a half-dozen of the bacon bagels. Stavroula collected the paper plates together and spoke out the corner of her mouth. "Oh. My. God."

"Shh," Stef said. "Don't stare."

"Is this the guy you called me about?"

"Yes."

"Dude, does he have a brother? Named Rav?"

"No."

"Where did he come from?"

"The fucking sky. It's really new and really cautious and fragile and..." Stef's eyes darted sideways to the line at the register and then down again. "Please, just behave."

"I'm behaving. You're blushing."

"Shut up and stop looking at him."

"That's like asking me to stop breathing. He's gorgeous." Stavroula smiled wickedly. "And obviously he's not straight."

"He's bi, but he never... It's complicated."

"Well, if it doesn't work out, I get right of first refusal."

"Shut up. And stop looking at me."

"But you're so cute. I've never seen you like this."

Stef glanced up. He imagined his eyes were both tender and wild. "Neither have I," he said.

Jav came back with his paper bag and a small bowl. Or a large, handle-less cup, depending on how you looked at it. A creamy gray on the outside and robin's egg blue inside.

"It's made for coffee," he said, looking ridiculously pleased. "Look how it fits in your hand."

"I love the glaze on that piece," Stavroula said. "Enjoy."

She blushed when Jav kissed her cheek, and she glared sideways at Stef as if daring him to say anything about it.

"Where to now?" Jav said outside the bakery, pulling on his shades.

Stef hesitated. "Today's kind of an anniversary. If you feel like taking a walk, I'll tell you about it."

"I'm in."

"It's a long story."

"I love stories."

JUMP FOR YOU

*T*HEY TOOK A cross-town bus to the East Side, then another north along First Avenue.

"I thought we were walking this story?" Jav said.

"We are. This is the prologue."

"Gotcha."

"So once upon a time," Stef said, turning up his right wrist. Unlike the magnificent sleeve on his left forearm, this tattoo was small and singular. Eight words nestled beneath the heel of his hand:

Alison, I know this world is killing you.

"Elvis Costello," Jav said.

"Also the unofficial launch of my career in counseling," Stef said. "I volunteered at a suicide hotline in college."

Alison was sixteen, home alone with the phone in one hand while the other held a gun to her head. Stef held her on the line three hours. A supervisor sat close by, ready to take over if Stef couldn't handle it anymore. He handled it. He talked and listened. Sympathized. Affirmed. Kept listening. Bit by bit, he got her trust. Gently, Stef got her to say her town. Her school. She whispered the name of a teacher who'd always been kind to her. Stef's supervisor put the pieces together and made the call. The teacher jumped in his car and was at the house in ten minutes. It took Stef another twenty to get Alison to put the gun down and answer the door.

"I love you," she said before she hung up.

"I love you, too," Stef said, his vision beginning to tunnel. "I'm so proud of you."

He disconnected the line and the phone bank burst into applause. Stef stood up and passed out, crashing face first into a row of filing cabinets and slicing open his left eyebrow.

"I take back what I said," Jav said. "This beats the knife fight story."

They stepped off the bus into the cool October afternoon. Jav didn't ask questions about the destination, only followed where Stef led and kept listening.

Stef told how he went to Skidmore, majored in psychology and minored in art. He got a master's degree in social work from NYU and was drawn to the early field of mindfulness-based cognitive therapy. From the start, he showed an aptitude, an instinctive gift for working with trauma victims.

He and Jav reached the entrance to the Queensboro Bridge's pedestrian walkway.

"I've never been on this bridge," Jav said. "Or Roosevelt Island, for that matter."

"Fun fact," Stef said. "You can walk out the front door of Scores East in Manhattan, walk over the bridge and through the front door of Scandals on the Queens side. With a little discretion, you can take your drink with you."

"And how would one come to know this fascinating piece of strip club trivia?"

Stef chuckled. "One may have done it during his bachelor party."

"Sounds like an epic night."

"I don't remember much of it. Anyway. I walked a lot on this bridge after my divorce and my parents' divorce."

A mild depression had gripped him for the better part of a year. He felt lost. Unworthy of love and cynical of its existence. Worse, he felt he wasn't doing what he was supposed to be doing. He was a good therapist, but something wasn't quite right. If his career was a pair of shoes, he had them on the wrong feet.

"I did a lot of walking during that time," Stef said. "A lot of sketching. Trying to pin down some elusive vision and figure out what the hell I was doing with my life. I'm walking across one evening, nine years ago today, to be exact. And I see a woman swing a leg over the railing…"

⌒⟶

Alison? he thought.

Of course not. But she was someone like Alison. She was here and so was he.

He approached on gentle feet. "Hey," he said, just as a car slowed, the passenger window rolling down. "You need help?" a man called.

Stef turned his chin enough to make eye contact. "Nine-one-one," he mouthed, and then gave a flick of his hand to signal the car to move along. Traffic was starting to slow down. He ignored it and stepped closer to the railing.

"My name's Stef," he said. "Is it okay if I stand here?"

The woman stared straight out, brown hair whipping across her face and eyes.

"I'm only going to stand here," Stef said. "You don't have to talk. I'll just keep you company."

He counted the Doppler swoosh of passing cars for a good five minutes.

"He took them this morning," the woman said.

"Who?"

"My ex-husband. He took the kids. They gave the kids to him."

"I see."

"He declared me unfit. I can't see them."

"That's shitty," Stef said.

"He's moving with them to Florida."

"I'm so sorry. What's your name?"

"None of your business."

He backed down. She'd be Alison in his head. He listened as she described a life of addiction and abuse and bad decisions. A life no longer worth living.

When the police arrived, Alison grew agitated, wobbling on her perch. Stef stood completely still, didn't change his voice or manner, didn't break eye contact. Two officers approached and Alison became hysterical, screaming to be left alone.

"Sir?" one cop said quietly. "Come back from the railing."

"No," the woman cried. "He leaves and I'm jumping."

"Sir?" the cop said.

"I'm a clinical psychologist," Stef said quietly. "I have a master's in social work. I run mental health clinics at Bellevue and volunteer with NYC Suicide Prevention."

Alison's wild eyes met Stef's for the first time.

"Stay here," she said.

"You bet. Will you come back on this side?"

"No."

"Can you tell me your name?"

"No. You just stay right there." Alison looked back at the cop. "Get away from me."

"Look at me," Stef said above his pounding heart. "Stay with me. Do you mind if I draw?"

"Draw?"

"I have a sketch pad in my pocket. I draw when I'm upset."

She blinked a few times, wincing as the ends of her hair whipped her eyes. "What are you going to draw?"

"You."

Resting the pad on the railing where she could see, he started to sketch her, with simple horizontal lines indicating the railing. "Tell me more about what's going on," he said.

As she talked to him, he tried to illustrate the pain. Give shape to the despair and dimension to the hopelessness. In the background, he drew the ex-husband. The two young children. The violence. The drugs. He made the paper woman as ugly as the real one believed she was. Then he tore the page out of the book and showed it to her.

"Yes," she said, face crumpling. "Yes. That's me. That's how I feel. That's my life."

"Take it," he said.

She did.

"Now let it go," he said. "Let it fall. Let *her* jump for you."

Alison's fingers unfolded and the paper blew away. Of course it didn't plummet. It floated and wafted. Blown about in the cold gusts from the river and the hot bellows-breath from traffic.

"It can't fall," Stef said, watching. "Most it can do is just fly away. And come down when it's ready to."

But then.

The perfect gust. The perfect updraft and downdraft and side draft. The paper came back. With an almost joyous *thwack* it wrapped around Alison's head. Slowly she peeled it away and her tear-streaked face, full of clarity, was a beautiful thing.

"I think she wants to stay with you," Stef said.

"Maybe," she said. She held the paper to her breast. "Can I… I think I want to get down now."

"All right."

"I'm so tired."

"You must be."

"Help me?"

"You got it."

He never learned her name. Once she was taken away in an ambulance, Stef sat on the deck of the bridge in a cold sweat, fighting off a mean nausea and shaking uncontrollably. Someone brought him water and a blanket. A young paramedic crouched down, hands on Stef's upper arms, breathing with him.

"You did an amazing thing," he said. "You brought her back. Now you have to come back, too. A part of you is on the other side of the railing still. You come back to us now."

"A month later," Stef said, "I was back in grad school. Getting a master's in art therapy. Every October thirteenth, I come back to this bridge. Mostly to mark the occasion of figuring out what I was meant to do in life. But also because I wonder if she marks the day, too. I wonder if maybe one year, I'll see her."

Jav was quiet for a long time. They stood close together, forearms crossed on the railing. Their upper arms and hips touching.

"My cousin," Jav finally said. "The cousin who kissed me on the rooftop. He jumped off the George Washington Bridge. I hadn't seen him since I left home. We grew up like brothers but then I never saw him again and I never knew why he did it. But I always wondered…"

"Wondered what?"

"If he was alone when he jumped. Or if someone came along and tried to stop him. If anyone even saw him. Cars driving by. Another pedestrian. If one person in Morningside Heights glanced out their apartment window and saw him. I mean, it's the freakin' GWB. It's never alone. Someone had to have seen him."

He shook his head, breaking out of the reverie. "I don't mean to make it about me."

"You're not," Stef said, thinking, *This is about us.*

"Thanks for showing me," Jav said. "And telling me. I'm touched."

"I've told people about it, but I've never taken someone with me on the day." He glanced over at Jav. "You're making me do a lot of things differently."

Their eyes held. Slowly their heads inclined until their brows touched. They were still then, breathing together.

"I think I get what you mean about it being something you lean on," Jav said. His finger drew along the ring on Stef's middle finger, shaped from two wings.

Stef laughed under his breath, thinking the moment felt decidedly bi-ro-mantic.

He leaned a little more and the feeling gave way to his weight. His blue and Jav's red overlapping to make a third, dark purple shape.

He kept the thought in his head. Saying it aloud was too big a bridge to jump from. And too long a fall.

SHANKSVILLE

*T*HEY ARRIVED BACK at Cushman Row tired. Stef popped them each a beer and Jav put on ESPN. They watched a little of the EUFA qualifying rounds but soon they were both nodding off.

"And now we're sleeping together," Jav said.

"Funny how it happens."

Jav yawned big. "I didn't sleep much last night," he said. "In a good way."

"Same." Stef clicked off the TV, got up and headed toward his bedroom. "Anyway," he called back. "Isn't siesta some kind of Latin American tradition?"

"It's an institution."

Stef came back out with two pillows. He tossed one to Jav and lay down along the long side of the couch. His feet to Jav, who lay on his stomach with his head in the corner.

A shared inhale and exhale.

Everything in the room exchanged glances.

What's going on?

I don't know.

What do we do now?

Sleep.

Seriously? We're actually taking a nap now?

"Hey," Jav said.

"Mm?"

"Put your head down here."

Stef pivoted around, putting his pillow kitty-corner to Jav's now.

"I'm not usually so boring a date," Jav said. "I'm just really tired."

"I imagine being boring is a refreshing change of pace."

Jav smiled behind closed eyes. "Dig me not working. Not performing. Not feeling like I have to fuck to be interesting. Not cramming an entire love affair into an hour. Just hanging with a guy I like, feeling tired, and saying so."

"I dig it." Propped on an elbow, Stef reached to set his hand on Jav's back. "I'm in no hurry." He glided his palm up Jav's spine and Jav sighed.

"Feels so good."

"Dude, when was the last time you lay back and had it be all about you?"

Jav pulled his hand from beneath the pillow and checked his watch. "Right now."

"Jesus…" Stef's hand moved between shoulder blades and along the topmost bumps of vertebrae, then his fingers dug into Jav's hair. Jav sighed again, then reached behind to grab hold of his T-shirt collar and pull it off. At the base of his neck, the word *Trueblood* was tattooed in black ink, along with a set of coordinates.

"What's Trueblood?" Stef asked, caressing the letters and numbers.

"My sad story. Which I'll tell you someday. Right now, keep rubbing my back like that. Please."

Stef ran his palm down Jav's spine, then up again.

"I like how your rings feel on me," Jav said, the words slurry. "Was thinking about it on the bridge."

"Go to sleep." Stef's mind was blurring at the edges. With his hand on Jav's back, he fell quickly under and didn't dream.

It wasn't a long snooze. He woke and watched Jav sleep, staring at the tattoo. Noiselessly, he reached for his phone and looked up the coordinates on the internet. They were for Shanksville, Pennsylvania.

The name made his eyebrows furrow, a bell of memory ringing from far away. He slid off the couch and pattered on socked feet to the laptop on his desk.

Shanksville is a borough in Somerset County, Pennsylvania, approximately 75 miles southeast from Pittsburgh. Shanksville came to international attention during the September 11 attacks when United Airlines Flight 93 bound for San Francisco crashed in adjacent Stonycreek Township…

"Shit," he said slowly.

Heart thumping, he typed "Flight 93 manifest" into the search box and soon a list of names was before him.

Snyder, Christine Ann, 32, Kailua, HI
Talignani, John, 74, Staten Island, NY
Trueblood, Philip, 31, Bronx, NY

"Holy crap," Jav said, sitting up, his hair mashed flat on one side. "How long was I out?"

"It's twenty forty-two," Stef said. "New York seceded. We're part of Canada now."

Jav smiled, stretching. "What are you doing?"

"Snooping."

"Snooping who?"

"You."

Jav gave a disgusted grunt as he walked over. "It's those damn nudes, isn't it?"

"No. Nothing fun like that."

"What, my rap sheet?" Jav pulled on his T-shirt, then peered over Stef's shoulder. "Ah," he said. "You found my sad story." He leaned his butt against the desk, crossing his bare feet.

"Sorry." Stef felt a little miserable. "I don't know why I did it sneakily instead of just asking you."

"It's fine," Jav said, shrugging. "It's not something I talk about a lot. I don't really know how."

"Were you with him?"

"We were going to talk about it when he got back from California," Jav said. "We'd hung out the entire summer in a weird holding pattern. Me being quasi-closeted and him not being able to get a bead on me or what I was about. But gradually, I opened the door a little and he got a little braver. And we had this one…"

"Night?" Stef asked.

Jav shook his head and his smile was fragile. "Twenty minutes? Maybe? This little pocket of time where we were kissing in my kitchen and I leaned into it. Leaned into myself and into my life and thought, *Yeah, this is it. This is something I am and something I want.* It was everything I wanted. I was right on the edge of my life. And Flip said, 'When I get back, we're having a conversation about this.'"

"Oh, man," Stef murmured, running fingertips along his brow.

"He left to go home and pack. He called me from Newark the next morning. Checking to see if I was all right."

"Were you?"

"I was. Everything about me felt right. Thinking about me with him felt more than right." Jav motioned to the computer screen. "The rest is American history."

Stef slowly nodded, staring at the names on the manifest, all the lives and love stories cut short. "I'm really sorry."

"It was a bad day," Jav said.

They were quiet a while. Quiet, but close.

"I like you so fucking much," Stef said. He'd never in his life said such a thing to a man.

"I like you, too," Jav said, as if the words were bubbles on his tongue. He jerked his head toward the couch. "For what it's worth, that nap was some of the best sleep I've had in a while."

"What do you want to do tonight?"

"Sleep with you."

Stef smiled. Heart thumping hard in his chest, he reached to touch the ship's wheel inked on Jav's forearm. "All right."

ACELA

*J*HEY WENT TO a barbecue joint on Charlton Place. Jav wasn't sure if Stef phoned ahead to friends, asking them to meet up, or if this was one of his regular hangouts and he had the kind of friends who randomly showed up. Either scenario only made him like Stef more.

I like him, he thought. *God, I really fucking like him.*

He met Aedith and Katie, two art therapists Stef worked with. Another co-worker, Beau, a giant man with a giant beard and a diminutive girlfriend. Assorted friends from grad school, other jobs, a lifetime.

They were all cool. Some pulled up stools and grabbed menus, others only hung at the tall table for a drink and a chat, then moved on.

"Good to meet you," they said, shaking Jav's hand when they arrived.

Or "Take care, see you again soon, okay?" with a handshake as they left.

They headed to another Chelsea bar. Dark oak, hip atmosphere, couches and candlelight and cognac. More people Stef knew. Names and stories.

"Jav, this is Kim Bonner."

"Everyone calls me Bunny," she said, shaking Jav's hand.

"We met in the mental hospital," Stef said.

"Literally," Bunny said. "We interned together at Creedmoor Psychiatric." She clinked her lowball glass against Stef's. "Good times, my friend."

I can't think when I had a better time, Jav thought. It was a line he used on clients. It felt good to use it on himself for once. He was wearing one of Stef's button-down shirts, which fit him perfectly. Everything about tonight fit perfectly.

"What do you do?" a woman asked him. "Wait, don't tell me. You're a model."

Jav shook his head, laughing. "I'm a writer."

"Oh?" Her glance over her snifter was skeptical. "Would I know any of your work?"

Her date gave an apologetic eye roll to Jav then looked away.

"Well," Jav said, playing his best card. "The movie *Bald*? With Kristin Scott Thomas?"

The woman's eyebrows slowly raised. "You wrote that?"

"I wrote the short story it was based on."

Now her date was staring at Jav hard. "You're Gil Rafael?"

"It's my pen name, yes."

The man's eyes flicked to the woman, then back to Jav. They held Jav's gaze a confused moment, then returned to his date. "Honey, would you give us a minute?"

The woman's expression trembled, and with a tight smile, she retreated.

"What's your name again?" Jav asked.

"Bryce. Look… This is a little personal, but *The Trade* changed my life."

"How so?"

"My brother died on Nine-Eleven and—"

"I'm sorry," Jav said.

"No, no. I mean, thank you. But I was angry after. Pathologically, irrationally angry. I severed nearly every connection in my life. I broke my parents' hearts. Sabotaged a half-dozen other relationships. I was fucked up."

Jav nodded slowly. As he took a step closer to the moment, the rest of the bar receded into a blurred, buzzing mist.

"It's a miracle anyone is even speaking to me right now," Bryce said. "But a lot of my coming back around has to do with your book. And here's the really fucked-up thing: I didn't buy it. Nobody gave it to me. I found it stuffed in the seat flap on an Acela train to Boston. Just left there with a dry-cleaning receipt as a bookmark. Left behind for me. I'm not even much of a reader. But I started it and it was like a spell, dude. I was sucked in and…" Bryce blinked a few times, cleared his throat. "Shit, this is emotional."

"It's okay."

"It was like you were talking to me." Bryce's voice was a thick bubble. "It broke through, you know? It… I don't know how else to say it, but it helped me stop being angry and let me be sad. I finally had that moment like Glenn Close in *The Big Chill,* curled on the shower floor crying my face off. When I mopped up and toweled off, I felt like I had some kind of hope."

"I hear you," Jav said. "I wrote it to heal myself. I had a buddy on Flight Ninety-Three and—"

"No fucking way."

"Yeah. I lost him and I shut down too. Big time."

The two men regarded each other, an island of connection in the swirling nighttime crowd.

"If you get the chance, I'd love it if you could sign my copy," Bryce said.

"Done. Absolutely." Jav tucked his beer in his elbow and took out a card. "Call me. All right? We'll get together and I'll sign it. And will you tell me more about your brother?"

"I will. Thanks." A hesitating beat, then Bryce hugged him, his fists tapping Jav's shoulder blades. "Man, I can't believe I met you."

"Nothing's an accident."

"Thank you."

"No, thank *you.*"

A slap on Jav's bicep then Bryce walked off, rubbing the hair at the back of his neck.

Stef brought over two shots of rum. "Appleton Estate, right?"

"Right." Jav took one and raised it. "Con muchos abrazos, amor y besos."

Stef tilted his chin. "Cheers?"

"You say, 'pero no pesos.'"

"Pero no pesos," Stef said.

They clinked glasses and threw their heads back.

"What's it mean?" Stef asked.

"Hugs, love and kisses, but no money. It's cute in Spanish because it rhymes, but it doesn't translate."

"Gotcha."

"That guy read my book. Said it changed him."

"Bryce? He was fucked up after Nine-Eleven."

"Weren't we all."

Stef smiled and his dimple flickered. "I wouldn't be surprised if your books changed a lot of people's lives."

"That was really cool," Jav said slowly, taking a long, panoramic look around the new little life he was building. His gaze came back to Stef, who was staring at him.

"What?" Jav said.

"Nothing. Just… What I feel right now is usually what I feel with women."

Jav smiled. "What I feel is nothing I've ever felt with women."

Their eyes held.

"Want to split?" Stef asked.

"And go where?"

Stef regarded his shot glass as if he wished more were in it. "Home? My place, I mean?"

Jav's belly was warm with rum, yet he could've used another shot himself. "All right."

⤜⟶

They were making out as soon as the apartment door closed. Yanking off shirts, ripping open and dropping their jeans.

"Do what you did to me last night," Jav whispered.

"Do me while I'm doing it," Stef said.

It was rough, fast and seamless. Up against the wall, narrowed gazes locked, they grabbed hold of each other, jerking and rubbing until they came, moaning in each other's mouths.

"Jesus," Stef said, his body giving a last twitch.

"Okay then," Jav said, gasping. "I'll just catch a cab. Goodnight."

"Get the fuck in my bed, Landes."

But they were both hungry and wide-awake now. They put their clothes back on, made sandwiches and watched some late-night TV. Slouched side-by-side on the couch, socked feet on the coffee table.

"Wait, where's Roman?" Stef said suddenly.

"He's still up in Guelisten."

"Oh yeah."

"Which means I'm your prisoner."

"That's right." Stef slumped lower, his head by Jav's shoulder and all his warm, solid weight up against Jav's side. He undid the strap of his watch and tossed it on the coffee table. A few minutes later, he took each of his rings off and set them in a little pile. Jav watched, mouth watering and groin tightening into a fist with each clink of metal on wood.

Trueblood regarded the silver rings, he thought. *Piling up in the moonlight coming through the ship's round window. For the Finch to come to him bare-handed was an honor most men wouldn't realize, let alone experience.*

Trueblood wasn't most men.

Stef's bare hand slid along Jav's thigh, kneaded the muscle a little, then held still.

The Finch's palms filled up with light, he thought. *The flesh normally hidden by his rings shone brighter than silver.*

His chest was relaxed. His stomach calm. His expectations gone for the night. He turned his head and ran his mouth along Stef's temple. Stef lifted his chin and his hand slid along Jav's jaw. Slow kisses grew harder and needier until the couch couldn't contain them anymore. Their bodies toppled, twisted and shifted around trying to get purchase. Finally Stef got up, shirtless and tousled, and led Jav by the wrist to his bedroom.

"Now get the fuck in my bed, Landes."

"Which side?"

"All of it."

Jav was thrown down on the mattress hard enough to bounce. Stef came crawling after, stopping with a knee on each side of Jav's hips.

"You sure you're not getting on a plane in the next seventy-two hours?" Jav said.

"No," Stef said, holding Jav's eyes as he unbuttoned his pants. "And I'm not married."

Jav reached to curl his fingers around Stef's jeans and give them a tug down his hips. Stef fell on his hands, pulling his legs free, then slid backward down the bed, dragging Jav's pants with him.

"Another thing I've been thinking about for a month," he said. "Your clothes on my bedroom floor." He glided back up Jav's body. Wings spread and mouth open. Hard against Jav's stomach. One hand tight in Jav's hair and the other reaching for the bedside table drawer.

It was the third time they...

Made love? Jav thought briefly, but then his cock was in Stef's lube-slick hand and all the blood in his head, plus all his uncertainty, headed south to get a piece of the action. His body howled like a wolf in heat. His hands took greedy hold of Stef, yanking him in tight. He couldn't get enough of this kiss, rough on his face and lips but soft and hot in his mouth.

"Come here," Stef said, rolling down on his back and pulling Jav on top of him. "Try this..."

He guided Jav's erection between his thighs. Jav slid between those warm, slick muscles and went a little crazy.

"Oh my God."

"You like that?"

"Oh yeah."

"Lean on me. More." Stef smiled under Jav's kiss. "Tenacious, remember?"

But all at once, Jav was remembering too much. The tiniest, frozen pause as he recalled what he knew about sex, about transactions, about give and take, about value and worth, the price of his time and the price of his body.

An old thought spoke up, soft but insistent: *Dad would've died if he knew what I was doing.*

What I am doing.

"Hey." Stef's hands came up to Jav's head, slid along his jaw. "You just went somewhere."

Jav gave a tight shake of his head and a smile that wasn't exactly loose. "It's nothing. I just…"

He tried to look away and laugh but Stef held both his head and his gaze. "I'm going to say two things, then I'll go back to talking dirty. Okay?"

Now Jav's smile relaxed.

"One," Stef said, "you're no longer for sale. Two, in this bed, it's enthusiastic consent or nothing. Say you need a minute, you get a minute. Say you want to stop and we stop."

Deep in Jav's mind, a sharp, cascading sound, like a violin's strings breaking: *I'm no longer for sale.*

I cannot be bought. Not my body, not my time, not my loyalty.

I give this freely or not at all.

I am free…

He cut ties. He let the long, lonely years go. He flexed his hips and moved along Stef. Between him. *Into* him, overlapping their circles. "I don't want to stop."

Stef squeezed his legs tighter. He bowed up, pushing hard against Jav's stomach, hands fisted in the small of Jav's back, grinding them together. Their bodies writhed and grabbed, arms pushing and legs pulling. Gasping and laughing between kisses, moaning oaths and obscenities in the dark, they ground and slipped and rubbed together, until Jav came between Stef's thighs and Stef came between their stomachs.

"*What* just happened," Jav said, gasping.

"Um," Stef panted. "In snootier circles I think it's called intercrural sex?"

"Intramural sex?"

Stef gave him a weak swat. Then his forearm toppled over his face and his smile spread wide beneath it. "Dude, I cannot deal with how good this feels." His hand ran up and down Jav's back a few times, then he slapped Jav's hip, rolled him aside and sat up carefully. "Yeesh, cleanup on aisle five."

Jav laughed. "I'm tenacious. Not neat."

"What is that, a month's worth?" Laughing, he tossed Jav a towel, then went into the bathroom, where he splashed around a bit. Then he headed out to the living room, coming back in with two lowball glasses and a bottle of Courvoisier.

"Drinking in bed is underrated," he said, pouring them each a nightcap.

"So is drinking in the shower," Jav said.

Stef raised his eyebrows. "Don't threaten me with a good time."

He reached for his phone and put on some music. They lay in the light of a single lamp from Stef's corner shrine, drinking and laughing, talking and touching. Jav's eyes and fingertips wandered over Stef's body, happily stuffing themselves with muscle and ink and stories. "This must've hurt," he said, touching the tattooed horse head and the ring in Stef's nipple.

"The ink wasn't too terrible but the piercing? I *wept* it hurt so bad. I had plans to pierce both, plans which I immediately abandoned. Wouldn't do the other one for a million dollars."

Jav carefully rolled the thin circlet of silver between thumb and forefinger. "Anyone ever hitch you up?"

Stef laughed softly. "Nah. Chains aren't my thing."

He lay back, patient and pliant as Jav's curiosity swept from head to heels, methodically looking at each tattoo. Stef had a lot of ink. Some stories took longer than others. When the canon was exhausted and every tale told, the glasses were empty, the playlist was in its second cycle and they were hard again, reaching for each other.

"What do you want?" Stef asked.

"What we did before. But you do it to me."

Stef slid on top of Jav, warm and strong. His kiss full of cognac. Jav closed his eyes, feeling his hip bones bump against Stef's, feeling the landscape of their bodies line up, settle down, fit together. Stef's quads pressed Jav's legs tight. His hands gathered Jav's wrists and held them down to the mattress. Jav tried to set aside words like *conquered* and *dominated* and *controlled*. To turn them inside out and connect with ideas like *shelter, protection, trust* and *safety*.

"Feels so good," Stef breathed. "I can't *deal*." He let go Jav's hands and burrowed arms beneath Jav's shoulders, holding him tight. Jav's skin was full of nerves and curiosity and electric interest. He was in bed with a man. A man was holding him. On him. Doing him.

I like this. The thought was smooth in his mind. *This feels like* me. *I'm no longer for sale. I can have whatever I want and I want this. I want this...*

"You fuck me up so bad," Stef said against Jav's neck. It would've sounded like a lament, if not for the rough, delighted ferocity of Stef's voice and the quickening of his hips. Jav's chest got all thick and muddy and he could feel it rising up in him. A herd of wild horses thundering in the distance. Stallions of desire and mares of storytelling and colts of overactive imagination.

"Come inside, man of Rohan," he heard himself say, and immediately squeezed his eyes shut, cringing.

Um. Maybe cool it with the thinking out loud thing?

But then…

"No," Stef said. "No, you come out. Let me ride you back to Gondor, and you can tell me what news."

Not a trace of mockery or melodrama was in his voice. The words floated soft and natural, spilling from his own imagination.

And Jav's weird mind ate that shit *up*.

He tossed his head, reared back and kicked at the sky. He came growling and babbling beneath his rider, then softened into wicked laughter when Stef tensed up, cried out and came in his legs.

It was now two in the morning and Jav was slack-limbed, blissed-out and happier than he though possible. Stef stumbled around, checking the locks and turning off lights. They crawled under the covers, pounding pillows and getting themselves situated.

"Confession," Stef said. "I never slept with a guy I just slept with."

"Me neither. I may suck at it."

"I'll never tell."

They lay on their sides, looking at each other, their breathing gently falling in sync.

"I have the fucking best time with you," Stef said.

"Same."

"I can't say I've never felt like this but Jesus, I haven't felt like this in a really… *really* long time."

"How long?"

"Honestly, I can't remember." Stef closed his eyes. "I missed it."

Jav ran a hand over Stef's head. "I missed it, too. Kind of my whole life I've been missing it."

Stef rolled his palm up between them. Jav slid his on it.

So this is what it's like, he thought.

STRONG LIKE BULL

*1*N THE MORNING, Jav woke alone in the double bed. In the corner, Stef sat cross-legged at his little shrine, meditating with his earphones on. He wore only sweats. A feathered wing was tattooed across each shoulder blade. They sheltered a centaur inked dead center on Stef's back, its bow drawn, arrow aimed straight up.

Jav pivoted on the mattress, putting his head at the foot, laying his cheek on his crossed arms. Eye-level with the half-man, half-horse. Beneath the creature's hooves were three lines of print:

> *Man is a centaur,*
> *a tangle of flesh and mind,*
> *divine inspiration and dust.*

Jav started to match his breathing to the rise and fall of Stef's shoulders, trying to connect with the experience. He'd never meditated before. Not easy for someone whose mind was a continuous narrative of thoughts and images and ideas. Quieting the noise was challenging, but he managed to eject most of it as he read the words on Stef's back, over and over.

Flesh and mind.

Divine inspiration and dust.

Finally, Stef leaned and blew out the candle burning on the low table. Reaching up to slide off the headphones, he looked back over his shoulder. Deep blue gaze, a scarred eyebrow, one dimple deepening as his smile stretched open. A curl of smoke around his head.

"Namaste, motherfucker."

He was beautiful.

Jav smiled. "What's up, Buddha?"

Stef scooted over, got a hand around Jav's nape and kissed him. "Tell me you're starving."

"I'm starving."

"Good. I'm gonna make some eggs."

"I need to jump in the shower."

"Towels under the sink," Stef said, heading out of the bedroom. "Make yourself at home."

Jav turned on the water and opened the cabinet under the sink. Pulling out a towel, he upset a small wire basket. He crouched to clean up and his eyebrows wrinkled as he collected two Fleet enemas and a bulb syringe. Plus a bottle of something called Swedish Colt Erotic Anal Douche.

"I'll take 'Words that Aren't Sexy in Combination' for two hundred," he said under his breath. He shut the cabinet and stepped into the shower, not feeling like himself anymore.

You're no longer for sale, Stef said in his mind. *Say you want to stop and we stop.*

Even at this early stage of the game he couldn't imagine Stef trying to force him into anything.

And I'd deck his ass into next week if he did.

The macho thought rolled its eyes. Stef worked with sexual assault victims. *CONSENT* was tattooed on his conscience.

It was a small comfort.

"Find everything you need?" Stef said, as Jav emerged from the bathroom.

"Mm." Jav got a mug and poured some coffee. Stef was dumping an entire bag of baby spinach into a skillet, letting it wilt down and shrink. He took a spatula and made four small holes in the mound of greens, then dropped a sliver of butter into each one. Tip of his tongue held in his teeth, he cracked four eggs on top. A pinch of salt sprinkled, the excess shook over his left shoulder. Four crunching grinds of the pepper mill. The toaster popped up cheerfully.

"Looks good," Jav said, his growling stomach trumping his messy thoughts.

"Lilia taught me this." Stef tilted the skillet this way and that to distribute the egg whites. "I eat it like four times a week." He put on Lilia's accent. "Make you strong like bull."

They took plates to the table, divided the paper and read over breakfast. Beneath the table, their feet touched.

"Something on your mind?" Stef said. He wore Clark Kent glasses to read and they had no business making him look that good.

"No," Jav said. "Why?"

"You're sighing a lot." Stef turned sideways and put his feet on an empty chair. He went back to reading. Jav went on looking at him, finding tiny vulnerabilities juxtaposed against the big, solid frame of Stef's body. Broad in his chest and shoulders, secure in his brazenly inked skin. Yet the fingers curled around his coffee mug were soft, fidgeting a little. Beneath the harsh, stern frames of his glasses, he was biting on a corner of his lower lip.

Unlike the Compass, Jav thought, *the Finch's mind went down fifteen flights of stairs into a warren of secret rooms and passageways. When Trueblood needed direction, he sent for the Compass. When the heart of Trueblood was troubled, he sent for the Finch.*

"Stop staring at me," Stef said.

Jav blinked. "I was writing."

Stef glanced over. "Need a pencil?"

"No."

Stef folded the paper and tossed it on the table. He ran a hand through his hair, then crossed his arms over his chest. "You have fun last night?" he asked.

"Hell yeah."

"Then talk to me. What's in your head this morning?"

"Truth?"

"Please."

"I'm wondering how often you use that stuff under your sink."

Stef's brows came down. Then reversed direction and clarity shot up his face like a window shade. "Oh," he said. "The stuff in the basket. The Swedish shit was a gag gift from a friend with really bad taste. I've never used it, I just keep it under there as a conversation starter." He freed a hand and gestured between them. "You can see it works well."

Jav gathered plates and cups and took them to the sink, both for distraction and distance. "Don't mean to put you on the spot."

"It's a fair question. Fairest answer is I use it if I know in advance I'm going to be on the bottom bunk."

"Gotcha."

"I'm going to go out on a limb and guess you're a hair concerned about what I expect of you in the sack."

"I did invite you into my treehouse," Jav said, putting away the eggs. "I didn't say it was rational there."

"Stop cleaning up."

"Sorry." Jav reached for the wall phone receiver and pretended to dial some numbers. "I'm just going to fake a call here…"

Stef laughed, holding thumb and pinky to his ear. "Pretend I'm on the other end. Hello, what is your expectation?"

"Mine?"

"No, the guy standing behind you. Can you put him on?"

Jav hung up the phone. "So, I watched some gay porn and—"

"Really?"

"Yeah. While I was on the road, I gave it a whirl."

"And?" Stef said. "Doesn't do anything for you?"

"Oh it does, don't get me wrong. But at a certain point it goes from sexy to worrisome."

Stef held up a hand. "Time out. If you're watching the hardcore flicks with men in masks fisting each other, I'll tell you right now, it's not my thing."

"Dude, that shit is a train wreck."

"I know. Horrifying, yet fascinating."

"I saw some guy, I swear to God, his asshole was inside-out."

"Lower that expectation," Stef said. "It's nothing I'm into or even capable of."

"I didn't think it was, but…"

"Can we get away from this visual and talk about what *was* sexy?"

"It's all pretty sexy until one guy starts pounding the other's ass," Jav said. "I mean, riding a guy hard and fast that way? All I can think is *ouch.*"

Stef nodded. "Fair. Did you find any clips that were slow and easy?"

"A few."

"And?"

"Those were okay."

"Only okay?"

Jav exhaled heavily. "Guys look so stupid when they're fucking."

Stef laughed. "Right?"

"I don't know why I don't give it two seconds of thought when it's a guy with a woman, but seeing two guys going at it? It's like a turn-on and hilarious at the same time."

"There's a lot of bits swinging around and flapping. I get it."

"Do you? Am I over-thinking this?"

"Nah," Stef said. "Well, yeah, a little. But it's like a turn-on and hilarious at the same time."

"Great."

"Look, I don't have to tell you porn isn't reality. Those guys are professionals and they're catering to a certain audience. And they look ridiculous fucking because they're playing to a camera angle, not each other."

"I know. I'm just… I don't know."

"This is a good conversation to have," Stef said. "We're having it a little earlier than I expected but okay, sure, if you want to talk about anal expectations, let's talk about anal ex— Stop laughing."

"I'm sorry," Jav said, fighting the most stupid kind of giggles.

"You know, the worst thing about sex with men is you got no good words," Stef muttered, shredding a corner of the newspaper. "Everything is either clinical or crass. Anal. Asshole. Cheeks. *Crack*."

"Taint," Jav said.

"Tweener."

"Balloon knot."

"See? No sexy terminology whatsoever. *Anyway…*" Stef cleared his throat. "I'm not a power bottom by any stretch of the imagination. I need a ton of prep and I don't mean the cleaning supplies under the sink. That stuff is just so I don't feel self-conscious. I mean a guy needs a lot of patience to top me and then I'm only good for about five minutes. I don't know if it's my body's limits, or if it's a partner thing, but I just can't do it for long. Big investment, little return. So I treat it as a closing act, not the main event. I don't like it hard and fast. I definitely don't like it rough or violent or demeaning. I like it to a point and if no one's getting off, I tap out. If my partner doesn't like my approach, he won't be my partner again. And that's the bottom line. Ba-dum *tss*."

"What about when you top?"

The color rose up in Stef's face as his smile unfolded. "I can top about two minutes before I blow my load. Honestly, Landes, I'm a lousy gay lay."

"Shut up."

"Telling you." He exhaled heavily. "Wow, look at my balls on a plate. Attractive. Thanks for sharing, Finch…" Stef scraped the side of his hand on the table, gathered the vulnerability into his other palm and pretended to stuff it in his pants. Still red-faced and smiling, he raked fingers through his hair and barked, "Jesus Christ, say something."

"I know I act like an idiot," Jav said.

You're scared and playing the idiot card, Gloria's voice reminded him. *It's not attractive.*

"The truth is I'm nervous," he said. "More accurately, my ass is nervous."

Stef leaned back on two chair legs. "Remember last night I said in my bed, it's enthusiastic consent or nothing?"

"Everything you said last night was unforgettable."

"You just need to understand… If I found out you did something with me you didn't feel good about, I'd pull back and re-evaluate everything between us. If you don't trust me enough to say *no,* it could be a dealbreaker. It's that big a thing. That important. All right?"

"I understand."

"We're not doing anything that makes you nervous." Stef brought the chair legs down. "And I think I know what you're really asking. The answer is I don't have criteria for what counts as sex and what doesn't. In other words, it's not your ass or nothing. It all counts."

Jav felt his entire body relax. "It's a little scary how perceptive you are."

"As far as I'm concerned, we've had sex a few times now. Once there." Stef pointed to the couch. "Over there." He pointed to the wall by the front door. "And once in there." His thumb flipped over his shoulder to the bedroom.

"It was twice in there," Jav said. "Get it right."

"Which was your favorite?"

"Well…" A fiery blush swept from Jav's neck to his crown as a hundred memories put two hundred hands down his pants.

"Yeah, that was hot," Stef said, grinning. "I even liked the sleeping part, which is kind of a thing. And having breakfast. And contemplating when I can get you back in my bed."

They looked at each other a long moment.

"Come here, Finch," Jav said, reaching a hand.

Stef got up and came to him. His arms went around Jav's neck and squeezed him tight. "I'm a little crazy about you, Landes."

Jav buried his mouth and nose in the curve of Stef's shoulder, slid fingers into his hair.

"You make it so easy," Jav said. "Half the time I don't know what I'm talking about, but it feels safe talking to you."

Stef rubbed his temple against Jav's head. "I am into this like you wouldn't believe. I don't want you to worry about who tops or bottoms. Jesus, we're barely past hand jobs and I'm making no effort to change the pace."

Jav lifted up his head. "None?"

Stef smiled. "I'm taking my cues from you."

"All right then."

"If we do nothing but kiss and rub against each other, I'll be fine."

"You will?"

"I think so." Stef's head tilted toward the bedroom. "We can go test the theory if you want."

NOVEMBER

SHRIMPING

*W*AYNE STARTED TAKING the last ten minutes of training sessions to show Geno basic self-defense. He broke down the moves into logical chunks, demonstrating as both attacker and victim. In these short but effective tutorials, Geno learned to disarm attacks from the front, side and behind.

"Remember, this isn't about being a hero," Wayne said as he drilled. "I'm not showing you how to incapacitate anyone. Once you disarm and get yourself free, what do you do?"

"Run like hell," Geno said.

"What do you *not* do?"

"Look back."

"Good."

Once Geno mastered defense on his feet, Wayne started showing him how to react if he were on the ground. Or, as Wayne called it, a mounted attack.

Then Geno got nervous and Mos completely lost his shit.

Wayne got down on his back in the soft mats. "You come on top of me first so I can show you."

That's not allowed, Mos yelled, his hair on fire.

Geno swallowed. Slowly he lowered himself to the mat and…*mounted* Wayne, a knee on either side of Wayne's hips.

Not allowed not allowed not allowed.

"All right," Wayne said, as if they were shooting the shit over beers. "When you're pinned like this, the most important thing is to get your hips out from under. Your fight-or-flight instinct wants to go *up,* into and against the attack, right?" Wayne made a few half-hearted attempts to sit up, his hands pressing

Geno's chest. Geno nodded, disconcerted by the sheer, muscled mass of Wayne between his legs. How warm and powerful it felt. Like being on a horse.

At this egregious violation of the law, Mos erupted like a volcano, raining down fire and brimstone into Geno's stomach.

Wayne lay down again. "Instead, you go against logic and send your energy *backward* by shrimping. You plant a foot hard in the ground and buck that same hip up. Watch." He demonstrated. "Right foot down, push hard, right hip comes up."

Geno wobbled now on the fulcrum of Wayne's hip, nearly toppling off.

"See how you just went off balance?" Wayne said. "Already you're in less control. Now I'm going to push hard as I can on that foot I planted." He slid straight backward and free, his body folding like a book, elbows to extended knee. "See how my body curls when I slide out? That's why we call it 'shrimping.' From here…"

Smooth as syrup, Wayne rolled onto his feet, crouched in a defensive position. "I'm ready to fight."

His triumphant expression went serious, and one of his fisted hands unfolded to point at Geno's face. "I fight. *You,* when you get back on your feet, will do what?"

"Run like hell," Geno said, his voice shaking. He wondered how much adrenaline the human body could tolerate before it passed out.

Or exploded.

Wayne got down on the floor and motioned for Geno to mount him again. It was easier this time. His heart was still firing cannonballs, but Geno paid closer attention as Wayne demonstrated shrimping. "Ready to try it?"

"I think so," Geno said, not at all ready.

Wayne put a hand on his shoulder. "Is this bringing things back to you?"

"Yeah. A little."

The hand squeezed. "First time's going to be the hardest. Your heart's going to be right behind your teeth. But you're gonna do this. Okay? You trust me?"

Geno nodded tightly, as if a bigger movement would break him in pieces. He got down on his back. Stared up at the ceiling beams as Wayne got on top of him.

Like that one guy was on top of him.

He didn't uncuff Geno's hands when he rolled Geno over. The cuffs clanged along the iron spindles as Geno's wrists crossed over his head, the metal restraints digging even harder into his already-raw skin. The blood ran down his forearms and dripped off his elbows.

We don't think about that, Mos said, sounding utterly defeated behind Geno's eardrums. *It happened to someone else.*

At least now his hands were free, clenched tighter than locked cuffs as Wayne coached him.

"Don't go up. Go backward," Wayne said. "Plant your foot, same hip up. That's it. *Push.*"

The mat squeaked as Geno slid out and away. His body curled like a shrimp. He lay still, listening to his heart pound behind his teeth.

"Here," Wayne said. "Sit up." A bottle of water was pressed into Geno's hand. "Take a sip. You did great. Look at that, huh? You did it. You did *great.*"

Geno took a wobbling sip and wiped his chin on his arm.

"I told you the first time was the hardest." Wayne thumped Geno's back. "Now try again. Before you think about it too much."

They tried again. It was easier. Then again. It was faster.

Wayne checked his watch. "This time, I want you to shrimp out, get on your feet, grab your bag and run like hell. Ready?"

Ten seconds later, Geno was at the door, a crowing accomplishment setting his bones on fire. He looked back to wave at Wayne.

"Jesus, what did I tell you not to do?" Wayne called, laughing.

EASIER THAN BREATHING

*J*AV'S EYES POPPED open with a sharp inhale. It was morning. Stef kneeled by the side of the bed. Forearms crossed on the mattress, chin on top. Jacket zipped, gloves and phone tucked by his elbow.

"I didn't even hear you get up," Jav said.

"Because I'm a trained thief."

Jav smiled. "You leaving?"

"In five minutes. Play me out?"

Stef touched the screen of his phone. As the opening, picked chords of Lyle Lovett's "If I Had a Boat" started playing, Jav slid a little closer to the edge of the bed and put an arm around Stef's head.

> *And if I had a boat*
> *I'd go out on the ocean*
> *And if I had a pony*
> *I'd ride him on my boat…*

So this is what it's like, Jav thought.

Shortly into their little affair, Stef confessed he had a low threshold for the Sunday Blues. "Like the Lyle Lovett song," he said. "I like cream in my coffee, eggs over easy, and I hate to be alone on Sunday."

Jav started staying over through the end of weekends. He discovered Stef wasn't chatty on Monday mornings, but he was ritualistic. He meditated for twenty minutes, then let Roman out into the back garden. Made coffee, showered and dressed. Moving softly. Not speaking. Putting on his armor. For the last five minutes, he liked to kneel by the side of the bed, tuck his head under the wing of Jav's arm, and listen to Lyle Lovett sing about needing nothing but a pony and a boat.

"Eres el más valiente," Jav always said when the song ended.

"See you later." Stef kissed him, then got up, his knees always popping in protest. Jav swatted his butt. Stef pretended it hurt. He left and the front door closed. This was the hardest part of Jav's Monday morning: the door clicking shut and the Finch disappearing into radio silence. His phone muted, sequestered and not checked. His attention laser-focused on his work and his clients. No quick calls or texts during lunch or a break. No flirting, sexting, or carrying on.

"It's not for lack of wanting to," Stef said. "But my attention span is too easily distracted. I can't switch between professional and personal mode during the workday. It has to be one or the other, or I'll end up sucking at both."

Jav understood. He'd exercised the same philosophy while escorting. He still despised the sound of the door closing at Cushman Row. The sinking feeling of abandonment. The eye-rolling self-admonishment: *Good lord, he's just going to work. Get a grip.* The way his fists wanted to pound the pillows, shrieking, *me me me, come back, call in sick, play hooky, stay with me…*

"You are a hot mess, Landes," he said to the ceiling.

He manned up, slid out of bed and sat down at the corner shrine, where he always tried to meditate, but ended up just sloppily praying.

He'd prayed more in the last month than in the entirety of his life. Prayers that started out with the best of grateful intentions, but quickly caved into neuroses.

Thank you, he'd think, present and mindful. *This is going well and I'm grateful. It feels good. It feels easy.*

It feels too easy.

It can't be this easy.

This can't possibly last. I'm just caviar.

He's going to get his fill of this treat and then meet a three-balanced-meal kind of woman and it'll be over.

I guess I'll be all right with that.

No, I won't, actually. I don't want this to end.

God, don't let this end.

"I can hear you thinking, you know," Stef said. From the other end of the couch or across the room or on the other side of the bed, he looked at Jav. Looked up from his sketching or his laptop or his book or his plate. From any direction, any angle, Stef rested on Jav's eyes the way a classic rock song always sounded good to your ears. You knew the words, you sang without thought, you air guitared or drummed on some available surface. Because you couldn't *not*. Your ears heard and your soul obeyed.

Jav looked at Stef and goddammit, his soul started singing. Making up verses about Stef at work and at play. Resting or running. Eating, sleeping, shaving, showering. Anxious, brooding, worked-up, let down, excited, frustrated. Coming and going. And best of all, the bridge before the key change into the chorus—looking right back at Jav.

"Crying out loud, Landes, *what?*" he said.

"What?"

Stef's smile broke apart laughing. "Stop *looking* at me."

"I can't," Jav said, tackling him. Because he couldn't keep his hands off the guy.

So this is what it's like, he thought.

This is what I'm *like.*

This was him, consumed and wrecked. This was his own workday filled with distraction, his attention span wandering off above the keyboard. Torrid moments tapping his shoulder and intense memories sitting in his lap, wanting to be pored over.

This was his self-proclaimed idiocy soothed, learning day by day and night by night, who he was and what he wanted. Hearing words creep from his mouth, clumsy and uncertain at first, then bold and brave. Inhibitions gradually giving way until this was him saying and doing the craziest things in bed, scarcely recognizing his own passion.

"God, I love how you talk," Stef said in the dark.

"What, you mean too much?"

"Not for me. And I love hearing you ask for what you want. Know why?"

"Why?"

"Because you never did it before."

As the days grew shorter and the nights longer, Jav's neurotic gratitude intensified. He'd held his hand out to the world, expecting fiasco. Instead, this magnificent dude, this prince of a guy, this *Finch* flew in and perched in his hand. Custom-made for Jav's body and soul. Someone with a hungry mind and a souped-up imagination. Someone who always had a little story going in their weird head. Someone generous and demonstrative with physical affection.

The way Stef grabbed, pummeled and roughhoused with Jav woke up dormant, childhood memories of horseplay with Ernesto. Only this time, no adult yelled at them to settle down, knock it off or take it outside. Roman was a hopeless chaperone. He pawed at them, wanting to be included. Or he gazed unblinking as the two men wrestled and laughed until they wheezed.

On quieter evenings, Jav lay on the couch with Stef's head on his chest and Roman sprawled on his legs, and happiness would fall on him like a thick blanket. When Stef locked arms around Jav's waist at the stove and leaned on him, Jav had to stop cooking and taste the moment. Close his eyes and hold it tight, unable to remember the last time he felt this content. This complete.

It's so easy with him.

It's too easy…

He spent long moments tallying up Finch knowledge like gold coins. Like how his sneezes always came in threes and fours. How he got weird but tremendous satisfaction from sweeping a floor. His expression turned distant and sad when he talked about his childhood cat, Ping. He kept a stash of Mallomars in the kitchen cabinet and his eyes narrowed when Jav took one. He often laughed in his sleep. He loved to be touched anywhere and everywhere, except the backs of his knees—he'd jump clear out of his skin.

Jav knew things like this now.

He recognized the wistful moodiness whenever Stef got off the phone with his father. He understood why Stef knocked shave-and-a-haircut on Rory's door as he left for work in the mornings. He learned the difference between Stef's creative silence and his exhausted silence. He could judge how bad a workday was by how much Stef put away at dinner. If Stef used the diminutive *Javi*, it meant he was in a vulnerable place. *Landes* meant Stef was looking for action, and when really worked up, he took off his rings and his wristwatch and put them in a little pile. Jav knew the change in Stef's breathing that meant he was falling asleep, and the sounds he made right before he came.

Their lives meshed effortlessly. Stef fit him like a second skin.

This is too easy, Jav thought. *This can't possibly last. It's not supposed to be this perfect with the first guy I find. I didn't even find him. We just met. It was an accident. This can't be The One.*

Or can it?

Desperate for a third-party opinion, he called the one person who probably had zero interest in offering him relationship advice. He sighed as he dialed. Only the idiotic Javier Landes would phone up an almost-ex-friend-slash-lover for counsel. With his wife's counsel as a Plan B.

"¿Qué onda, fucky?" Alex said. "It's been forever."

"I know."

"Are we friends again?"

"I need to ask you something," Jav said, deciding to act as if they were friends and barrel straight in. "When you and Val started dating, was it easy?"

A confused pause. "Easy?"

"Yeah." He could explain further but opted to hold still a moment.

"Dude, it was easier than breathing," Alex said. "I can't even say it was *dating*. Pretty much overnight, we went from being friends to being together. Are you asking me if we fought?"

"Well everyone fights," Jav said. "I'm asking if it ever felt too easy. Like you were waiting for the other shoe to drop?"

"No," Alex said, with a speed and assurance Jav envied. "And if you met someone, and it feels easy and you're waiting for the axe or the shoe or the whatever to drop, it's because you think you don't deserve easy. What did I tell you about that?"

"Yeah, I know," Jav said, exhaling.

"Say it."

"I'm worth more and I deserve it."

"Damn right you do." A few beats of silence passed. "Did you meet someone?"

"Yeah."

"Good," Alex said. "That's great, I'm glad."

"Me, too. It's new. And it's…"

"Easy."

"Yeah."

"Well, maybe I'll meet them someday."

Jav smiled at the safe, gender-neutral pronoun. "Maybe you will," he said. "If I don't fuck this up."

"Oh my God," Alex said. "You're still the same idiot."

"The only one allowed in the room," Jav said, laughing.

HEART BEHIND YOUR TEETH

Between Wayne's incessant drilling and his grueling ab workouts, Geno became the Bubba Gump of shrimping. He could fold and slide by pure reflex now, fast and unconscious.

"Now, this is all easy-peasy in a controlled scenario when I'm being nice to you," Wayne said from the floor, looking up at Geno.

"This is being nice to me?" Geno said, rubbing the sore spots between his ribs.

Wayne grinned. "In a real attack, the guy's not going to be on top of you patiently waiting for you to escape, right?"

"Right."

"So now make like you're choking me, pretend to throw some punches at my head and face."

Geno reached to set his left palm by Wayne's collarbones. He moved his right fist in pretend punches. At the same time concentrating on keeping his thighs completely immobile and keeping a sixteenth-inch space between his groin and Wayne's.

"With your weight pressing down on me, it's hard to shrimp out," Wayne said. "Plus you're whaling on my head. As the victim, what's my knee-jerk reaction now?"

"Push me away?"

"Exactly. Maybe with one arm I'm protecting my face, but this other arm I'm going to be pushing and hitting at your chest, right?"

"Right."

"Wrong," Wayne said. "You have to go against instinct in a fight from above. The attacker is going to expect you to push them away, which is why instead…" In a lightning-fast move, both his hands shot up, grabbed Geno's head and pulled it to his chest. "You pull him in close."

Geno could feel the heat of Wayne's skin through the thin T-shirt. Feel Wayne's heartbeat against his face. Feel his huge, warm hands holding his head. *Don't hold my head. Let go my head. Please let go my head. Stop. Please.*

He closed his eyes and thought about passing out.

"See how my elbows are out?" Wayne said from far away. "Now it's harder for you to throw punches, harder for you to get a chokehold on my neck. Key to an attack from above—pull them in close. Understand?" He let go Geno's head and Geno sat up, trying to disguise his labored breathing.

"Try again," Wayne said. "And really go for it this time."

Geno went for it.

"Come *on,* dude," Wayne said. "Fight me like I just killed your moth—"

Geno went for the jugular. Wayne's eyes bulged, then narrowed. Faster than he demonstrated before, he had Geno's head tight against his chest, his elbows keeping blows at bay. "Okay? Now. I got your head, yeah?"

"Yeah," Geno said, still hoping he'd faint.

"The head is the key." Wayne's hands spread wider, coming around Geno's face. His fingertips pressed into the bridge of Geno's nose, one of them nearly in an eye socket. "You turn the head. Forget about the body. Turn the head and the body follows."

A mighty strain on Geno's neck as his head was turned. His shoulders followed and he began to roll.

"See now," Wayne said. "You just let my hip come up. Now I can shrimp out."

All at once, he was gone, leaving Geno sprawled on his side. He looked up at Wayne, a few feet away, dancing from foot to foot, his dukes up.

"Pull 'em in close and turn the head," he said. "Ready to try?"

Geno stared, his tongue dried to the roof of his mouth.

"First time's the hardest," Wayne said, lowering his voice and his fists. "Heart behind your teeth but you do it anyway, right?"

"Right." Geno's eyeballs prickled as he lay down. He pressed his teeth together when Wayne mounted him.

"So we'll make like I'm fighting you."

One of Wayne's hands curled at Geno's throat. The other raised in a curled fist. His knees squeezed Geno's ribcage and the edges of the gym began to darken.

"Pull close," Wayne said. "Turn the head, shrimp out and run like hell."

The dark swept in from all sides. Blacker than midnight, with no stars to light the way. Within the black, Nos was at war.

Geno pulled against the cuffs, his screaming wrists crossed behind his head, his bloody forearms against his eyes. The man mounting him put a hand on Geno's throat. Then the hand slid around the back of Geno's neck, pulling his head up. The guy's knees weren't at Geno's ribs, they were up around Geno's shoulders. And the guy's other hand wasn't raised high in a fist. It was down low, curled around what he wanted to put in Geno's mouth and—

No, my head, let go my head, no don't, don't, I can't breathe, my head.

Carlito turned his head away.

Turn the head, Mos said.

Look at me, brother mine, look at me look at me look at me.

Mos cried out, making the stars shake. *Turn the head.*

Geno turned his head.

"Holy *shit,* dude," Wayne cried. "That was *amazing.*"

Geno blinked the dark out of his eyes. He was on his feet. Wayne was on the mat, looking at Geno like a kid at a Christmas tree.

"I did it?" Geno said.

"Fuck yeah, you did. Holy crap, you *nailed it.*" He got up and bear-hugged Geno, slapping his back.

"I did it," Geno said. Laughter like sobs hiccupped out of his chest. "I fucking did it."

Mos made a careful note on his clipboard: *We are pleased.*

Tuesday before Thanksgiving, Geno and Ben, along with pink-haired, multi-pierced Natasha Kaslov, took a subway to Grand Central and then boarded a Metro North train. Natasha got off at Port Chester, answering Ben's invitation to come hang out with a vague, "We'll see." But she kissed Ben's cheek before departing, and the new ring in her lower lip sparkled as she smiled at Geno.

"Dude, it's so on," Ben said, craning his neck at the window.

"You've been saying that since September."

Ben's mother was an extremely short, extremely well-put-together woman who hugged both boys indiscriminately at the New Canaan station. She talked nonstop on the way to the house, where she showed Geno to the extra twin bed in Ben's room, pointed out the bathroom and where the towels were. She declared her kitchen was his kitchen but under no circumstances were they to touch the pies. Exhausted by Thanksgiving preparations, she had pizza delivered for dinner and they ate off paper plates in front of the TV.

Geno got no sleep that night. Ben's twin beds had handsome black iron frames. The headboard loomed up over Geno like the grille of an oncoming train, its slim crossbars clanging through the remembered slide of metal cuffs. He'd dealt with the bed issue at school by dismantling the frame entirely and putting the mattress on the floor. Here, he was trapped. Moving to a couch required too much explanation. Moving to the floor only slightly less. Finally he knocked back an extra Ambien and slept with his head at the foot end, then laughed groggily the next morning and said he had no idea how he got turned around.

The grogginess lasted most of the day. Luckily Ben was just as tired. The boys lazed around, decompressing, until Wednesday night, when they drove over to South Salem.

"My buddy Jason's back from California," Ben said. "He graduated two years ahead of me and went straight out to Hollywood to make a movie. Now he's got some part in a Broadway musical opening up this summer. He's the closest thing to a celebrity I know personally. And an amazing cook."

Natasha said she'd come hang out and Ben was so excited, he could barely keep his clothes on. He kept checking his phone and checking his appearance in every reflective surface.

"Jesus, Marino, get a grip," Jason Dahl said from the stove. His clean-cut look was probably trademarked. Sandy blond with bright blue eyes. Scrupulously groomed facial hair. Trim and perfect in track pants and a black T-shirt, he stood barefoot at the stove, sautéing mushrooms, rolling and tossing them in the pan without the aid of a spoon.

"All in the wrist," Ben said.

Another guy in the kitchen, Seth, rolled his eyes. "Dude, I swear if you don't get laid in the next hour, I'm gonna fuck you myself."

The doorbell rang and Ben took off, his vacated stool spinning in his wake.

"Want another beer, Mo?" Seth asked.

"No, thanks."

"Babe, you want one?"

"Yeah," Jason said, grinding the pepper mill over the pan.

Seth cracked open a Blue Moon. Instead of handing it over, he moved up behind Jason and held the bottle in mouth's range. Jason took a swig, winking at Seth over the bottle. Steam from the frying pan floated between them. As Seth chuckled and took a drink, his eyes found Geno's staring gaze and his brows went up. Geno looked down at his phone, heart pounding heavy in his stomach as he wondered, for the first time in a while, how Chris Mudry was doing.

Natasha had new blue and purple streaks in her hair. She accepted a beer, hopped up to sit on a countertop and wrapped the male majority attention around her like a stole. "This is like having a harem," she said. "Four hot studs and yours truly. Come here, guys. Selfie."

"I'll take it," Geno said, holding out a hand for her phone.

"Geno's Amish," Natasha said, slinging arms around the boys. "You can't take his picture."

"For real?" Seth said.

"No," Geno and Ben said together. Jason broke out of the pose, cursing as the pasta water boiled over. Seth went to help him while Ben stayed ensconced between Natasha's knees.

Realizing he was the fifth wheel, Geno shivered. Loneliness put a cold, heavy arm around his shoulders. He bucked it off, determined to have a good time. He had zero to be depressed about. Good company, good food and inclusion. What the hell else did he want?

As they sat around eating big bowls of Jason's pasta, Geno's mouth moved in conversation and his chest released laughter at the right times. All the while he watched Ben caress Natasha's arm or back, or twirl a lock of her hair around his finger. Her normally aloof manner toward him softened and she fed him from her plate. Across the table, Seth and Jason had their chairs close together. Every so often they'd lock eyes or smile like they had a secret.

Was Chris with someone tonight? Or was he back home pretending to be something he wasn't?

Geno moved the last strands of spaghetti around the bottom of his bowl and wondered how it was possible you could crave physical affection even as the thought of it terrified you. His eyes found Seth's fingertips scratching circles between Jason's shoulder blades and he wanted to run crying from the house. He stared at Ben's hand buried in Natasha's cotton candy tresses and he wanted, wanted, wanted…

This is how my life is going to be. Included but excluded. An extra at the table and the one missing from the group photo.

"You okay, Mo?" Natasha asked. Through eating, she now sat tucked in the circle of Ben's arms, practically in his lap. "You look tired."

Geno blinked and found a smile. "I'm good." He got up and started collecting plates.

"You don't have to do that, man," Jason said.

"Sit," Geno said. "You cooked. I serve."

Jason sat back, relaxed and handsome under the drape of Seth's arm, his terrier in his lap.

Geno loaded the dishwasher and ran soapy water into the sink, angry at the world and himself. Hating the two couples. Hating another sleepless night he'd no doubt spend, his head at the foot end of a twin bed and his back pressed tight to the wall. Hating the Thanksgiving meal he'd have to sit through the next day as the odd one out. Hating himself for feeling this way. Analisa would say it wasn't kind. She only wanted him to be kind.

You bitch and cry you have nowhere to go, then you bitch and cry when you get there.

He wiped off his hands and sat at the table again. Jason and Seth on one side, Natasha and Ben on the other

He smiled. He talked. He laughed.

Caught between the desire and the fear of being left alone.

FUN TO BE AROUND

"**D**UDE," JAV SAID. "I think I've officially arrived as an author. I just got a dick pic."

"Look out, coming in hot." Stef hopped over the back of the couch and hustled to the desk to peer over Jav's shoulder.

> From: DDJones0485@hotmail.com
> To: Javierlandes@gmail.com
> Subject: You
>
> Say the word and you'll be in heaven.
> All this for you. Anytime. Anyplace. Anywhere.

A photo of a blond man was attached. Naked save for a pair of gym socks. Sculpted to within an inch of his life and hefting a ten-inch wonder schlong in the palm of one hand.

"Damn," Stef said. "What do you think?"

Jav crossed his arms and leaned back, his head touching Stef's ribs. "What's with the socks?"

"Ugly feet, maybe?"

"I don't know. Leaving socks on suggests a fear of commitment. Plus I don't like porn that breaks the fourth wall."

"What?"

"The way he's looking at the camera," Jav said. "It's arrogant as hell. Don't look at me, dude. I'm a voyeur, not a participant."

The doorbell rang. "Delivery," Stavroula shouted from outside. "Are you decent?"

Jav, extremely indecent, hot-tailed it to the bedroom while Stef got the door.

"What do you think of men who wear socks in bed?" he asked.

"To sleep?" Stavroula said, handing over a paper bag with two bagel sandwiches.

"To fuck."

"God, no. Who fucks with their socks on?"

"No socks," Jav yelled from the bedroom. "If you're getting naked, then *commit.*"

"Stay for breakfast?" Stef said.

"No, I'm taking the moms to brunch. Hi, cookie, you didn't have to dress for me." Stavroula tilted her head up for Jav's kiss on her cheek.

"How do you feel about porn that breaks the fourth wall?" he asked.

"You mean when they're looking right at the camera? Hate it." Stavroula shuddered. "Enjoy breakfast, guys."

"I love her," Jav said, unwrapping his bagel. "She calls me cookie."

"She's good people," Stef said, closing the door. "Her husband was a world-class prick, though."

Jav's eyes narrowed. "How so?" he asked around a mouthful.

"He was a construction manager, worked a huge renovation project at Long Island University, another at C.W. Post. Plus he ran an industrial cleaning company on the side. Long story short, in the midst of this three-ring circus, Robert embezzled a few million dollars. A large portion of which he spent on his…" Stef raised two fingers in the air. "Second wife."

Jav turned his head until only one eye was showing. "While he was married to Stavi?"

Stef nodded. "Which actually turned out to be fortunate. Stavroula didn't know what was going on and never received or benefitted from the stolen funds. But Wife Number Two did, and it made her liable. I think she served four or six months. Bobby's still in Sing-Sing."

"Jesus."

"I guess better heartbroken than heartbroken and in jail. Actually, no, forget it, it was shitty all around."

"I can't imagine…" Both Jav's voice and eyes trailed away. Stef quietly finished his sandwich. The rest of the story wasn't his to tell. Not the physical and emotional abuse. Not the baby Stavroula lost in the bagel shop's kitchen. Not the hole in the dough room's wall Micah made with Robert's head. Not the year it took for Stavroula's smile to come back or the tiny grave in Baron Hirsch cemetery she visited once a year.

"I was talking to Stavroula about her volunteer work at Exodus Project," Jav said. "I'm thinking I want to do something like that, too. Give back."

"Ask her to bring you along one day."

"Wouldn't that be weird, though? Me volunteering where you work?"

"I don't work for Exodus Project." Stef licked ketchup off the crease of his pinky. "I'm employed by the Coalition for Creative Therapy, which happens to be in the same building. If you come two days a week to work in the EP kitchen, I'll just stay away from that side of the house those days."

"You sure?"

"As long as we don't screw in my office, I don't see a problem."

"Forget it, then. Screwing in your office was the point." Jav tilted all the crumbs and bits of egg off the tinfoil into his palm, then offered the handful to Roman. He got up and started washing last night's dinner dishes.

Roman stared up at Stef, licking his chops.

"Help you?" Stef said.

Roman put a paw on Stef's knee and the liquid brown of his eyes deepened into pure adoration.

Stef sighed and fed him a bit of bacon. He loved this damn dog.

He loved everything right now.

He and Jav weren't moved in together but with no discussion, each moved over and made room for the other. A second toothbrush was a no-brainer. T-shirts and socks and sweats and jackets inevitably got left behind, so it made sense to free some space in the closet, clean out a drawer. Getting Roman a second water dish to keep at Cushman Row was no big deal. Stef rarely used his desk, so why not clear it off in case Jav wanted to do a little writing?

Or a lot of writing, as became the case when Jav got back the first draft of *The Chocolate Hour* from his editor, Michael.

"Congrats?" Stef said, not sure if this was good news.

Jav shook his head. "I'm not going to be fun to be around the next few weeks," he said. "Oh, and the talking to myself thing? It's about to get worse."

He wasn't kidding. Jav nattering to himself became a weird background noise in both their apartments. Jav stared into space mumbling. Or paced around muttering. After a while Stef tuned him out, no longer trying to understand the one-sided conversations.

Sometimes Jav would be silent, eyes glued to the monitor, fingers on fire. Then he'd abruptly spin in his chair and point straight at Stef. His eyes lit up wide as if Stef had just cured cancer.

"What?" Stef said.

A slow smile spread across Jav's face. "Yes," he said. The pointing hand retreated and fell flat on his brow. "Yes."

"Yes, what?"

"Nothing. Thank you." And he'd spin back to the computer again.

Stef shook his head. "Glad I could help."

Often Stef came home from work to find Jav in a heated phone discussion with Michael. Almost all of them ended with Jav hanging up and muttering, "Prick."

"Asshole."

"Son of a bitch."

And assorted Spanish epithets Stef was sure weren't flattering.

"Why don't you find another editor?" he asked.

Jav topped up Stef's coffee cup. "Because Mike's good."

"But it sounds like you hate his guts."

"I hate him because he's right, goddammit." Jav put the milk away and slammed the fridge door. He stomped back to his desk, growling like a bear woken early from hibernation, while Stef and Roman exchanged indulgent looks.

Stef was amused by Jav's creative process, but protective of it. He cooked on the rough nights, put plates in front of Jav at the desk and took them away afterward. No matter how engrossed, Jav always said thank you.

Benignly ignored, Stef fell back into his artwork, taking a cue from Jav's fierce discipline and producing something every night. He made a dozen little studies of Jav at his desk. Sometimes he took one of the ubiquitous Post-its with Jav's random scribbling and added an illustration. Jav always stopped to examine the mini collaboration, beam a smile, and pin it to the bulletin board over the desk. Such a board was in both their apartments, each becoming a slapdash collage of two wild imaginations.

Am I falling in love? Stef wondered, as the holiday season crept over Manhattan. It was Jav's haunted time of year, when he had to reconcile "Home for the Holidays" with memories of being homeless. He enjoyed Hanukkah nights in Rory and Lily's apartment, lighting the menorah and devouring enough potato latkes to kill a horse. He looked skeptical when Stef dragged him out to get a Christmas tree, but they decorated it together while putting away half a bottle of

Appleton Estate and watching *The Grinch*. After which Jav went around singing in a deep voice, "You're a mean one…Mr. Finch."

Is this love? Stef wondered, tallying up little, cockle-warming things. Things like Jav, who had an enviable and natty wardrobe, choosing to wear Stef's clothes instead. Ignoring cashmere V-necks or merino pullovers, he slopped around in Stef's old Skidmore hoodie, his scent lingering in the collar and cuffs.

Jav claimed he couldn't meditate to save his life, but any morning he was at Stef's place, he sat at the little corner altar and tried for ten minutes. He lamented he couldn't draw a stick figure, then had an epiphany when Stef showed him the art of Zentangle. This mindful, repetitive doodling technique became Jav's meditation practice, and he presented his little creations to Stef with the unbridled enthusiasm of a kindergartner pinning artwork on the fridge.

Hey, look, I did a thing. You like it?

Stef loved it.

He loved the way they talked in bed, and the running gag of "Wait, am I talking too much in bed?" Sometimes it was playful and teasing banter, sometimes dirty discourse that started wild and got outrageous. Most times, they just…talked. Mumbling and murmuring what they felt in the moment. Square thoughts falling into the safety of round ears. And Stef loved it.

He loved Jav holding his head in the mornings while they listened to Lyle Lovett. He loved Roman trotting up to greet Stef at the door in the evenings, genuinely glad to see him. He loved the women who came by the table at the bagel shop, shyly asking Jav for an autograph. Smiling at Stef as they waited, a little curiosity in their eyes.

Stef smiled back, thinking, *Sometimes I come home from work and Gil Rafael's walking around my apartment in his underwear.*

Don't hate me because it's beautiful.

DECEMBER

PS AND QS

*J*AV WENT THROUGH a background check, attended sensitivity training and started volunteering in the kitchen at Exodus Project. He picked the same days Stavroula worked, because he liked her.

The Bake & Bagel became Jav's downtown office. He kept the cup he bought from Stavroula behind the counter, and sat with it and his work at least three days a week. Word got around Chelsea that Gil Rafael frequented the local bagel store. Business boomed as people, women especially, dropped in for a bite and a glimpse.

Sometimes Jav stepped behind the counter, put on an apron and took orders. Then the line snaked out the door. Stavroula looked on in amazement as all her pottery pieces flew off the shelves and the bacon bagels sold out.

"Not to toot my own horn," Jav said, "but I'm kind of a marketing man's wet dream."

"You *think?*" Stavroula said, closing out the register. "You're walking with me to the bank tonight, cookie." She squared off the pile of receipts, tapping edges on the counter. Looked up to find Jav staring at her.

"What?" she said, sweeping her long bangs out of her face.

"You have the tiniest ears I've ever seen," Jav said.

She laughed, touching one. "I know. Aren't they ridiculous?"

Spending a lot of his daytime hours in Stavroula's company gave Jav some funny feelings to chew on. He wasn't attracted to her. He was pretty sure he wasn't attracted to her, but her tall, Junoesque figure made his hands remember smooth, soft skin and the curved, heavy weight of a breast. When she bent low to pick something from the floor or pull something from a shelf, Jav had to slap his eyes away from her ass. Chiding himself to knock off the reminiscing of a woman bent over the bed like that, back arched and thighs quivering. His fingers curved around the knobs of her hip bones. Giving her the what-for until she screamed.

Recalling sex with women made him horny and defensive, two things that didn't go well together.

I don't want it, he argued to a mental courtroom. *I just remember it. I haven't had that kind of sex in four months.*

Objection, the prosecution cried. Jav was *basking* in sex. He and Stef were at each other all the damn time. Getting each other off in bed, in the shower, on the couch and at the kitchen counter. Pretty much any horizontal or vertical surface that would hold their weight. On the roof of Cushman Row once, which vindicated Jav in all kinds of ways. He came in Stef's hand, in his mouth, between his thighs and all over his body. Then Jav closed his legs tight, or opened hands, mouth and skin to willingly and enthusiastically return the favor. Without a shred of idiocy or an iota of doubt he liked having sex with men.

Well, maybe not all men, he thought. *But I sure as hell like it with Stef. So yes, your Honor, I've had sex in four months. I just haven't had any penetrative sex.*

The court fixed him with a penetrative look. *And?*

Jav averted his gaze. *Never mind.*

A metallic flash before his eyes broke his thoughts apart. Pablo, one of the EP residents, was waving his paring knife through Jav's thousand-yard stare. "Ground Control to Major Tom?"

Jav shook his head hard as laughter went around the large worktable where volunteers and residents were peeling potatoes.

"Hearing voices again?" Stavroula said.

"They're telling him where the mothership is docking," Corley said.

"Hey, don't be dissing my imaginary friends," Jav said. "They always tell me the truth."

"Unlike us," Pablo said, laughing.

Jav could've made any number of smartass replies, but didn't. He minded his Ps and Qs down here, following other jokers' leads instead of instigating his own. He shut down his natural propensity to ask questions, stayed far away from the subject of sex and avoided any and all terms for genitalia. Maybe he was being ridiculous, but better safe than triggered.

The weeks went by and he got to know a few of the men better. He spoke rapid, curse-laden Spanish with Juan and Pablo. Corley was one smart son of a bitch. Jeff could talk books from hell to breakfast. He was deeply offended

Jav had never read any Neil Gaiman and pressed on him a personal, well-worn copy of *American Gods*.

"Read it," he said. "Thank me later."

Jav read it in two days and not only thanked Jeff, but begged forgiveness for his ignorance. In the weeks following, he and Jeff became a two-man book club, discussing reads over prep work and dishes and mopping the floor. Jav made little casual relationships with almost all the residents he met, but he kept it tucked in the back of his mind all of them were here for a reason. When some of them shared bits of that reason, Jav didn't know what to do.

"You just listen," Stef said, as they ran along the High Line, one extraordinarily mild December day.

"I know, I know," Jav said. "I learned that much in training. It's just… Jesus, their stories are fucking horrid and I know I'm only getting a sliver. I don't know how you deal with the whole story."

"Well, I know you can't write a scene unless you're totally immersed in the emotion of it. Which means you're a sympathetic, compassionate guy. And that's all you need to be."

"It's weird, though," Jav said. "Just like you have rules of confidentiality? I feel I'm sort of bound by different ones. Like I shouldn't tell you about the relationships I have with these guys."

"You don't have to," Stef said. "But Christ, if you see a resident testing the edge of a knife against their wrist bone, tell *someone*. It doesn't have to be me."

THE WORST POSITION

"**S**o Wayne, let me ask you something," Geno said. Casually. As if the question had just occurred to him, instead of being mulled over for weeks, waiting for Geno to work up the nerve to ask.

"Shoot," Wayne said.

"How do you get out of a mounted attack when you're facedown?"

Wayne grimaced and blew his breath out pursed lips. "That, my friend, is the worst position to be in. You don't have a hell of a lot of options. Come here, I'll show you."

He lay prone and Geno got on his back, which was a hundred million times easier than straddling his groin, for fuck's sake.

"Turtle on his back has a better advantage than a man on his face," Wayne said. "Your priority is to roll over. How do you do that?"

"Push on your arms?"

"You can use your arms as levers, sure," Wayne said. "But with full weight on top of you already, you risk injuring your back and that does you no good. Key is your hips. To get them free, you have to curl in a ball. That's where all the ab work comes in handy. Don't arch up, curl *in*."

He demonstrated, pulling his elbows in tight, shifting his weight onto this doubled-up platform and jack-knifing his knees in. "Buck like a bronco," he said. "Rock and roll, throw the attack off balance. Anything you can do to get turned around and facing your opponent. Worst position to be in is facedown and pinned."

Wayne grinned then, his eyes twinkling. "But that's not likely to happen to you, pretty boy," he said. "Unless they're trying to get your pants off."

Geno walked out of the gym.

He didn't look back and he never returned.

TERMS OF VENERY

"**G**UESS WHO HAS a signing at the Union Square Barnes & Noble?" Jav said.

"Dude," Stef said. *"Now* you've arrived. And I just came."

At last, Jav didn't have to imagine Stef on the perimeter of one of these events. Tonight, Stef was right next to him. The perfect wingman, always nearby but not hovering. Making small talk and being charming.

As well as a healthy reader turnout, Jav had his professional team. His agent and publicist and his editor, Michael.

"So you're the one Jav's always yelling at," Stef said.

Michael gave a modest bow from the neck. "My day isn't complete until Javier tells me to perform an unnatural act upon myself."

Jav checked his watch. "Oh, God, I'm late. Eat a bag of dicks."

Michael beamed. "Thank you, dear boy."

The hometown crowd was there, too. Gloria came. Rory and Lilia. Stavroula couldn't make it, but Jav was touched to see Stef's co-workers, Aedith, Katie and Beau.

A wave of adrenaline went up the back of Jav's neck when the Lark clan arrived en masse. Alex and Val. Roger. Trelawney. And bringing up the rear…

"Sobrino," Jav said, coming around the table to fold Ari in his arms, noting with alarm he was a hair shorter than his nephew now. "Stop growing."

"I'm trying."

"Try harder."

"Fame makes your ass look fabulous," Ari said.

"My ass is always fabulous."

"Tell me about it," Alex said from behind Jav.

Jav turned around and Alex hugged him.

He thought he'd put some distance between him and the affair. Maybe even forgotten it. But one squeeze of Alex's strong arms, one good inhale of Alex's skin, and…

Holy fuck, I remember.

Everything.

"Let go now," Alex said, slapping Jav's back, then his ass. "Or I won't."

It took less than a minute to pick up where they left off. English gave way to Spanish and then the two of them were flinging open a toy chest of old jokes and lines and holding them up. Laughing. Punching and shoving at each other. Flirting.

Jav got lost in it until Alex's eyes flicked once, twice over Jav's shoulder and his expression turned genial and expectant. Jav turned around.

"Oh, shit. This is Stef." Quickly Jav slammed the toy chest shut, snapped back to English and the present. "This is Alex. Trelawney's brother-in-law. And mine. Sort of."

"Wait, I think we've met," Alex said. "At the Lark Gallery couple months ago, right?"

"We did," Stef said.

As the men shook hands, Ari sidled under Jav's arm.

"This troublemaker," Jav said, getting the boy in a headlock, "Is my nephew."

"And mine," Alex said.

"It's complicated," Jav said.

"It's your average American family," Ari said, shaking Stef's hand and giving him a frank once-over. On Jav's other side, Stef was more subtlely considering Alex.

Oh boy, it got weird in here, Jav thought.

His nerves were jumpy as fuck. Having this cadre of friends *(and my boy-friend)* and relations *(and my ex-boyfriend?)* made him wish he'd done a prac-tice run with his material, instead of relying on cold memory and a couple of index cards. He kept gulping water but couldn't get a dry tickle out of his throat. Finally Stef cut him off.

"Famous authors don't take pee breaks."

"I'm not famous."

"Yet. Your fly's open." Jav looked down and Stef clipped his nose. "Gotcha."

"Fuck you," Jav said.

Stef brushed a bit of something off Jav's lapel and smiled. "Maybe tonight."

"If I don't drop dead first. Wait, what?"

"Good luck." Stef leaned and kissed Jav's mouth then walked away. Trelawney met up with him, graceful as a choreographed passage, and slid her hand around Stef's elbow as they found seats.

I'm having the weirdest night, Jav thought. Then the store manager was introducing him and it was time to go on.

He didn't bumble any of the material, but it felt like an out-of-body experience. After all those events on the road when he longed for Stef's eyes to connect with, Jav found he couldn't look at him, nor focus on any one face in the audience. All the heads blurred together until he got to his story about Roger Lark.

Rog had kept a low profile so far. "It's your night, man," he said quietly when he first hugged Jav. "I'm here but I'll be invisible." He skulked in the stacks, incognito in a full beard and ball cap, then took a seat with Ari in the last row of chairs, slouched low and unobtrusive. He laughed loud at the passage about The Compass, raising a fist above his shoulder a moment, then flicking his index finger toward Jav.

Jav didn't point back, but he held onto Roger's eyes and laughed along. His stomach unwound. The itch went out of his throat and he relaxed for the rest of the talk.

The signing went long. Finally Jav found himself alone, standing on the edge of things and taking a breath. He wandered into the stacks, letting his fingers slide along the spines of books. Inhaling paper and ink and stories. Skimming the Rs in General Fiction to find his babies and ascertain none of this was a dream.

Client Privilege. Gloria in the Highest. The Trade.

"Jodidamente orgulloso de ti, carajo," Alex said, sneaking up from behind again.

So fucking proud of you.

"Thanks."

"I mean it. This is amazing."

"I still can't believe it." Jav's eyes found Stef in the graphic novel section with Ari, their heads bent over a book. Even from afar, Jav could see they were engaged on a creative level. Their talk animated, hands drawing pictures in the air.

"Te estás sonrojando," Alex said.

You're blushing.

Jav glanced at him, heat sweeping his face, mouth open. Then he laughed at his shoes. "Well…"

Alex laughed too, giving Jav a little shove. "I'm happy for you. And jealous. But mostly happy."

"I'm happy and idiotic. Mostly idiotic. But he's extremely patient."

"And it doesn't suck looking at you being idiotic."

Jav smiled. "I miss you."

"I miss you too. But we're where we're supposed to be."

They were quiet a minute as their eyes held and all the teasing drained out of Alex's gaze.

"You and Val all right?" Jav asked.

"We're good." Now Alex looked down at his feet. "I might say we're even better than before."

"Something something, sword through the fire?"

"That which does not make your wife kill you makes you get your shit together?"

Jav laughed and looked off at Stef, who was browsing in the reference section now. Making Jav remember his elementary school days, when he'd spend hours reading the dictionary. The hefty one his father had given him for his twelfth birthday, left behind when Jav left home. Whatever became of it?

"I hope this is good," Alex said slowly. "I really want this to be something good for you."

Jav took a deep breath. "Me too. At least not a disaster."

Alex's smile unfolded, showing his dimples. "After me, you're pre-disastered."

"Right?"

"Excuse me," Val said, appearing in the aisle. "You two aren't allowed to be alone in the fantasy section."

"Excuse me, fucky," Jav said, "but the sign clearly says *ancient history*."

"Hey, only I get to call her fucky," Alex said.

Val whacked Alex. "Quiet, fucky."

Jav hugged them both. "Thanks for coming."

"Wouldn't miss it," Alex said.

"We're your family, dumbass," Val said. "We'd do anything."

"I dig your in-laws," Stef said on the subway uptown that night. "Is that the right term?"

"Close enough," Jav said. "They're easy to dig."

The doors slid open, a shuffle of humanity, an exchange of passengers. The doors slammed closed, the subway chimed and lurched forward.

"I spent some time talking to Alex about animal-assisted therapy," Stef said.

"He's got personal experience. He's had a therapy dog since Nine-Eleven."

"So he said. It's kind of hard to have a conversation with him."

A flutter of indignation across Jav's mind. "How so?"

"Because he can't take his eyes off you."

"You think?"

"Yeah. Quite the interesting dynamic. He watches you, and Val watches him watching you."

Stef's voice was neutral, a little curious. No judgment or jealousy. Jav opened his mouth and closed it, then dropped his hand on Stef's knee, working a corduroy fold between his fingers. He looked around the subway car. No one looked at them. No one's eyes slid away guiltily.

Your average American family.

"I don't know if I'd have her kind of grace in the situation," Stef was saying. "I mean, just chatting away as if you didn't sleep with her husband."

"We didn't sleep together."

Stef snorted. "You weren't bowling."

Jav chuckled through the lower lip he was gnawing on. "I'm glad you finally got to meet Ari."

"He's a great kid. I'm not just saying that. I've met a lot of kids and believe me, he's a great one."

"Weird that I might've gone my whole life not knowing he was in the world. One bad step on a flight of stairs…"

"You were meant to be in his life," Stef said. "And he's lucky to have you, Landes."

Jav picked up Stef's hand and twined their fingers. "I am lucky, Finch."

"How do you say *finch* in Spanish?"

"Pinzón."

"You know what a group of finches is called?"

"Un encanto de pinzones."

"All answers must be in English."

"A charm."

Stef's smile lit up like a surprise party. "Holy shit, I never met anyone who knew that."

"Want to hear a story about it?"

"Sure."

"Alex knows all the group terms for animals. He—"

"In snootier circles they're called terms of venery," Stef said. "Pardon my font of useless trivia. Go on."

Jav leaned in until his head rested on Stef's. "Kiss me first."

Their mouths touched once. Then again.

"Alex and group terms?" Stef said. "Don't try to distract me, Landes."

"We were talking once. This was last fall. Long after we…"

"Went bowling," Stef finished.

"Right. I told him I'd quit escorting and was giving love a chance. After losing Flip nearly destroyed me and loving Alex nearly destroyed him. I said, 'Third time's the charm, right?' And Alex said, 'A group of finches is called a charm.'"

Stef looked him, patient and listening.

"It was September eleventh, actually," Jav said. "Not ten minutes after that conversation, I met you upstairs in Trelawney's gallery. Ten minutes later, you took *Client Privilege* out of your bag and handed me your card. Steffen Finch."

"Jesus," Stef said. "For real?"

Jav nodded. "In a funny way, you gave Nine-Eleven back to me. Now it's the day I found someone instead of the day I lost someone."

Stef touched Jav's chin with a knuckle. "No wonder you came running after me."

"Well, I sat staring for a few seconds. Until Trelawney smacked me upside the head and said, *'Fetch.'* Then I went running."

Stef chuckled. "For the record, I love this story."

Jav slouched so he could put his head on Stef's shoulder. "Me too."

GÉLANG

*S*TEF LAID JAV down with an agenda that night. He supposed jealousy had something to do with it. A need to show the Alexes of the world where Jav's bread was buttered.

He's mine, motherfuckers.

The ferocity of it surprised him. He'd never considered himself a possessive person. Love, loyalty and devotion were things to give, not demand. Nobody could own your heart or stake a claim to your soul. Nobody could ever truly *belong* to you.

Watching and listening to Jav speak tonight, Stef wasn't so sure anymore. As his eyes filled up with Jav's handsomeness and his brain filled up with Jav's talent, Stef broke *belong* apart and played with the dissected syllables, thinking, *be-long to me? Be a long time to me? Long to be with me?*

During the post-signing crush, he slid Merriam-Webster off a shelf and looked up the etymology. *Belong's* origin was Old English, from *gelang,* meaning "at hand" or "together with."

Stef rolled the word from one side of his mind to the other. *Gelang.* He imagined it tattooed in simple letters on the back of his wrist.

At hand, he thought. *Together with.*

He looked over the tops of shelves to see Jav and Alex talking. Both their smiles fragile, both looking more at their feet than each other. As if it were too dangerous to turn up to full wattage in each other's company. Too risky to belong.

Not too risky for me, Stef thought. His eyes and brain were filled. His body wanted it now. He'd take the chance. He'd waited all this time because it was worth the chance.

I want to be at hand.

Be together.

Belong to each other.

In bed now, he seized both their dials and turned them up as high as they would go, throwing everything he had against the wall of Jav's passion. Leaning in a way he couldn't with a woman and never had with a man, he *crushed* Jav into a writhing, sweaty, panting wreck.

"I can't get enough," Jav whispered. "I never felt like this in my life."

"Want to make you feel everything," Stef said hoarsely. "Want to fuck you up so bad, Landes."

Jav groaned and grabbed him. They rolled from one end of the bed to the other, sliding and gripping and rubbing, sucking and fingering and grinding. Until Stef, certain that enough was enough because this wasn't enough, reached long for the bedside table and got a condom.

"That for me?" Jav said, his voice thick and hoarse with arousal.

"Yeah."

Jav's stared as his chest rose and fell twice. "You sure?"

Stef nodded. "You have no idea how sure."

Jav kissed him hard, then sat up. As he moved onto his knees, his eyes shone wild in the dark. Stef couldn't remember being more naked and alive in his life. So turned on and worked up, he felt slightly feverish.

"I'm warning you, I may suck at this," Jav said, tearing the packet open.

"You know what you're doing."

"Yeah, but I don't know if I'll do it well." His shoulders made a sheepish twitch. "I'm scared and playing the idiot card, in case you didn't notice."

"C'mere, baby..." Stef reached to help roll the condom down. "Tell me something you do know."

Jav's hands dropped on his thighs, open and honest. "I know I've been called *baby* a lot, but coming from you, it means something. It sounds...true." He closed his eyes. "I know I love the feel of your hand on me."

"Say more."

"I know there's no one else I want to do this with. I know I'll probably talk too much during it. And I know tonight is one of the best nights of my life."

Stef pulled Jav down, held his head and kissed him. "If you know all that, then there's no way you'll be bad at it."

"Turn over and watch."

Stef glanced up. "See? You do that part great."

Jav slid his palms along Stef's neck and his kiss pulled Stef's mouth apart. Then he whispered through it, "Turn over, Finch."

Feverish gave way to delirium as Stef rolled over and stretched out on his stomach. Jav pulled a couple pillows under Stef's hips, then his big hands slid down Stef's back. His mouth kissed along the spine, between inked wings, stopping at the centaur tattoo.

"I remember the first morning I woke up with you," he murmured. "Staring at the ink on your back while you were meditating. I didn't feel ignored. Something about you was so sexy, but so quiet and easy, too. Like being between divine inspiration and dust." He laughed softly. "Am I talking too much yet?"

"Don't stop."

"I think I knew then we'd be doing this someday. It was so…quietly easy to imagine."

"I've been imagining it since the day I met you."

Jav's palm pressed gently on Stef's nape. Lube dripped cool and slick as his other hand slid between Stef's legs and his finger slipped inside. "I want this to be so good."

Stef sighed and tilted his hips up. "You know what to do with me. Just be yourself. And don't be surprised if I come in ten seconds."

Jav's laugh curled around the dark as another finger joined the first and slid deeper. "I'll probably come in five seconds."

"Mm. Go a little slower…"

Jav was three fingers in now, stretching Stef more than he was used to. Stef exhaled, fighting the urge to clench, making his body release instead of contract.

I want this I want this I want this so bad and want it to be so good please…

"Easy," Jav said, his breath shaking over Stef's skin. "We got all night."

Stef closed his eyes and let himself sink down and open up. He pressed hard against soft sheets, trusting all the heat, anticipation and desire would come back.

After a timeless, slippery time, Jav asked, "Feel ready?"

"Yeah." Stef planted his hands and made to rock back on his knees, but Jav held him down flat.

"No, stay still," he said. He nudged Stef's leg over a hair, hands spreading wide on the small of Stef's back. "I'll go slow. Tell me if it's okay."

The tip of his penis pressed in. Pressed a little harder. He dripped some more lube. Stef reached back to guide him better. Another slick push and Jav breached that anxious ring of muscle with a small grunt and a long exhale.

"*God* that's tight," he said, his fingers curling around Stef's hip bones.

"Mm," Stef breathed. "Stop right there."

"You okay, babe?"

"Yeah."

"Am I hurting you?"

"No, just give me a sec..."

"Easy," Jav whispered. "Take your time. Just breathe …"

It did hurt. Not a violent agony but a checkpoint of discomfort that separated the mildly curious from the intensely committed. Stef breathed slow and deep, remembering the initial pain was part of it. The pain was a thing to get beyond, because on its other side was a pleasure that defied description. A pleasure that couldn't be without the foundation of pain.

"All right?" Jav asked, his voice faint over the heartbeat in Stef's ears. "I'll stop if you need me to."

"No, it's easing up. Here, put a little more lube on… Now come down here. Lean on me."

Jav's palms sank into the mattress on either side of Stef's body. He rested on his elbows, his chest warm on Stef's back, head on Stef's shoulder. Under the pillow their fingers twined.

"God, Finch, you feel so good."

A few tadpoles swimming in his eyes, Stef rubbed his temple along Jav's cheek. "I'm really glad we waited."

"Me too. I love that it's tonight. I loved having you with me at the thing. And now having you with me at…"

"This other thing?"

"Smartass." Jav curled both arms around Stef's body and dug his mouth into Stef's nape. "You smart, tight, hot ass… Jesus, I can't believe we're doing this."

Stef smiled behind closed eyes as he crossed the threshold. "Go ahead," he said. "I'm good now."

Jav leaned off to one side, tilted Stef's head back and kissed him. "You're always good." His fingers tightened and his kiss pulled Stef apart a long dripping, delicious time while his body barely moved. Just his hips slowly canted and nestled, no more than a few careful inches at a time. Stef offered no direction. He was open and utterly relaxed. This was spectacular for a first time. This was enough for tonight. They had tons of opportunity. Plenty of nights.

Possibly the rest of their lives…

Finally, Jav shifted and lay on Stef's back again. "Guess what?"

"What?"

"It's been six minutes."

Stef laughed and curled a hand around the back of Jav's neck. "It's so bad, you're watching the clock?"

"No. You said once you could only do this for five minutes. That you weren't sure if it was a physical limitation thing, or a partner thing."

"Landes, you have this funny habit of listening to me."

Jav's feet wrapped around Stef's shins and his hands slid beneath Stef's body, spreading wide and taking ownership. "I just wanted to get one of your firsts. Have you longer than any other guy has."

Everyone's marking their territory tonight, Stef thought, pushing his erection into Jav's palm.

"It already happened," he said aloud. "That first quiet, easy morning, you'd already had me longer than any other guy."

Jav kept stroking him. "Say more."

"You met my mothers and my stepsister before we even kissed. Because what they thought about you mattered to me and— I'm talking too much."

"I'll tell you when it's too much."

Stef smiled. "I brought you to my bridge, which I never did with anyone before. That night, you borrowed my shirt when we went out and it was like you buttoned yourself inside my skin. You slept with me—I mean you spent the night, sleeping with me in my bed. That was new. So was having breakfast together. Feeling all kinds of bewildered, goofy and lonely when you went back to your apartment. I never felt that way about a guy. It was all new. So don't think you have none of my firsts. A bunch already belong to you. And… God, man, feels so good, I can't even…"

"Don't you stop talking to me," Jav whispered.

"I wanted to wait to do this because it felt like it could be something real. The waiting is another first that belongs to you. And now you're inside me, so…" He teetered on a vulnerable edge before letting go and whispering, "So I guess I belong to you, too."

Jav pulled a sharp breath in. "You do."

"Sorry for the speech."

"No, I'm glad you made it all clear."

"Oh?"

Jav's hips pulled back and then drove forward, bumping a cursed grunt out of Stef's chest. Stef's hands flailed through pillows and sheets, looking for anything to grab onto.

"See, I'm very possessive of things that belong to me," Jav said. "So now that you're mine, I…" He reared back and slid deep. "Am going…" His legs pushed Stef apart. "To fuck your brains out…"

He pulled them back on their knees and moved into Stef like he'd never known how not to. Not too fast. Not too hard. A little more than Stef had ever handled, but not too much. It was perfect. Jav's skilled, patient thrusts hit the sweet spot and a current surged through Stef's soul, conducting through the soaking wet night.

"It was a partner thing," Jav said. "Your body didn't have limits. It was just waiting for me."

"Javi…" Stef's world was aflood. Jav's damp breath on his skin. The mist of sweat rising on both their bodies. The tidal wave of orgasm starting to pull back from the shore.

"Come here…" Jav drew Stef up and back, slowly canting him into Jav's lap.

"God you're all up in me," Stef moaned in a slurry of sound. "I could never take it like this."

Jav moaned too, his arms winding tight around Stef's chest. "Baby," he said into Stef's skin. "You're so beautiful like this."

Tiny yellow pinpricks dotted Stef's vision. He was arched and open like a strung bow. Poised and aimed so tight he couldn't even say he was about to fire.

"Want to see you come," Jav said, breathing hard. "Let me see when I'm filling you up like this…"

He went on murmuring beautifully dirty, obscenely pure things as he pushed deep, stroking Stef up and over and out. Stef let loose a garbled yell as the arrow released. He went rocketing forward, tumbling and rolling, then was sucked back, crashing against Jav's body behind him. Jav's arm under him. Jav's crazy babbling above him. Jav's name, over and over in Stef's mouth, huffing out with every exhale, like a sacred mantra, the password into the next life.

Where have I been all my life?

Where Javi been all my life…

Too soon, the electric pleasure crackled away, leaving the burning ache behind. Jav was still coming, his voice twisting between a laughing roar and a sighed moan.

"Shh," Stef said, his hands sliding along Jav's tight quads, slowing and stilling him. "Stop, stop. Come down now. Come down."

"Holy shit," Jav said through his teeth.

"I know, I know. Just hold still."

"You all right?"

"Yeah, just don't move anymore."

They both fell forward on their faces. After a minute, Jav shuddered, gave one last twitch, and moved back carefully. He pressed his forehead to Stef's nape and whispered, "Christ, Finch."

Stef tried to arrange his mouth around words but gave up and just grunted. Jav took a few raggedy breaths, then got up to chuck the condom.

"Sure you're all right?" he asked, expression worried as he ran a damp wash-cloth along Stef's skin. "Did I hurt you at the end?"

Stef, soaked with endorphins, lolled under the solicitous touch. "Nothing I can't handle."

"I tried not to go hard but holy shit, when you came, I lost it."

"I'm all right. All kinds of right."

"You gonna be sore later?"

"Sore but not regretful. Now quit worrying and get the fuck in my bed, Landes."

Jav got him a couple Advil first. They drained a bottle of water dry, untangled the sheets and covers and collapsed onto each other.

"God, come here," Jav said, turning Stef's head this way and that, kissing his face. "That was unbelievable."

"Nobody ever fucked me like that in my life."

"Jesus."

"I'm serious," Stef said. "This is some of the best sex I've ever had. I don't mean just tonight. I mean everything we do. All of it."

"Same here. I wish I could…say how I…" Jav's squeezed his eyes shut and his fingertips ran along Stef's back. "You don't know… It's… I'm me. I'm making my own love for the first time in my life." He opened his eyes. "On the one hand, I can't believe the time I wasted."

"It wasn't wasted."

"On the other hand, I guess it all meant I was supposed to end up here. With you."

"Dude, you're shaking," Stef said softly.

"I know. Because I'm scared."

"Tell me why."

"Because I know I'm new at the game, and maybe it's too early to say this, or maybe I don't know enough yet to say it, but…I think I'm falling."

Stef shivered now, a warm wave of adrenaline splashing through his chest.

Jav managed a wobbly smile. "See? I just honestly played the scared card instead of the idiot card. I must be learning."

A long staring moment passed. Stef didn't think he was falling. He knew then he'd fallen. Gravity won and the tense was past.

I'm in love with him.

Jav touched Stef's scarred eyebrow. "So this is what it feels like."

"Like falling down the stairs, but softer."

"Mm."

"Remember you asked me once if I ever made love with a guy, and I said no?"

Jav nodded.

"I can't say that anymore."

Jesus Christ, I fucking fell in love with him…

He put his face against Jav's neck, suddenly scared to death.

"Never felt this way about someone in my life," Jav said. "Never felt this way about *me* in my life."

Stef closed his eyes, played his idiot card and said nothing.

A FEMALE NOT HIS WIFE

$\mathcal{G}$ENO SPENT WINTER break with Vern. His house in Berkeley Heights was large and comfortable, Geno could come and go as he pleased. Mostly he stayed put. Vern wasn't married—his acute workaholism had resulted in two ex-wives—but he had a longtime companion named Marsha who came around and cooked. And, ostensibly, slept over, but that was none of Geno's business.

Zoë came one day to handle a difficult task Geno had been dreading. Together they went through their father's clothes, and with Marsha's advice and Vern's input, they put aside suits, ties and shoes. Things Geno wanted to keep. Things Zoë insisted he keep.

"This is a wool-cashmere overcoat," she said. "It will last forever. And when I say forever, I mean you'll give it to your son with plenty of wear left. Keep it or I will kill you."

She held a black, V-neck cashmere sweater against Geno's chest and insisted he acquire it as well. "As Nina Garcia says, I recommend getting the black cashmere version of anything that comes in a black cashmere version."

The sweater was folded and laid aside, along with the coat, a Harris tweed jacket and Nathan's tallis—the prayer shawl he'd worn at his bar mitzvah. In a small box in Nathan's valet, Geno found a handsome gold chain with a star of David. He'd never seen Nathan wear it. He put it around his neck, feeling he had no right to. But Zoë smiled and said it looked good on him. It felt good. Cool on his skin at first, but then warming up, leaving only the sensation of weight. It grounded him. He never wanted to take it off.

Cufflinks and tie clips. A battered pair of moccasin slippers. Nathan's leather shaving bag. His heavy wristwatch and his favorite fountain pen.

"You don't have to decide on everything today," Vern said. "Do a little at a time. However much time it takes."

Zoë came back to Vern's on another day, this time with an appraiser, to go through Analisa's jewelry. Her engagement diamond, gold wedding band and Nathan's wedding band were unquestionably for keeps. But Analisa had a few other pieces that made Allen Goldschmidt smile below the loupe crammed in one eye.

"These are lovely," he said over a pair of diamond earrings. "Two carats each, perfectly matched. Beautiful." His one free eye looked at Geno. "Keep them."

"For your fiancée," Zoë said. "Or a daughter, if you have one someday."

Allen admired a sapphire necklace. Praised the craftsmanship of a brooch shaped like a peacock with emeralds studding its tail. He spent a long time squinting at a gold chain bracelet with a pendant.

"I think you'll want to show this to a numismatic," he said.

"A what?" Geno said.

"Someone who appraises currency," Zoë said, eyes wide and bright.

"The chain alone is high quality," Allen said. "But the pendant appears to be a Mexican coin. An extremely old one." He straightened up and took the loupe out of his eye. "Hold onto it. Get it appraised by a professional. You might have yourself a little treasure there, my friend."

After he left, Geno and Zoë sat in the kitchen, eating ice cream.

"Is there anything of Dad's you're keeping?" he asked. "Or want to keep? Not that I'm the one to give permission. I mean, he's your father, too."

Zoë smiled around her spoon. "When Matthew has his bar mitzvah, I may want the tallis."

"Take it now," Geno said. "I want him to have it."

"Are you sure?"

"Absolutely."

"All right." She pulled figure eights with her spoon through the melting ice cream, her eyes blinking rapidly. "I feel bad I didn't know you all that well," she said. "That it took this to make me… I mean, let me get to know you."

"Same. I sometimes wonder why we didn't see you that much. I thought maybe because of my mom."

Now Zoë's expression turned puzzled. "What do you mean?"

"Well, you know. That she was the other woman."

"The other woman?" Zoë's laughter filled up the kitchen. "Are you serious?"

"Wasn't she?"

She laughed harder. "You dope. My mother left Nathan."

"She did?"

"My stepfather is the other man." Consumed with giggles, Zoë pressed a napkin into her streaming eyes. "Oh my God, where did you get that idea your mother was a homewrecker? Don't tell me that's the story you were told."

"Nobody told me anything, I just thought that's what it was." Shaking his head, Geno pushed his bowl away, feeling both dumb and strangely happy.

His sister planted her hand in his shoulder and gave him a shove. "You funny thing."

"Why didn't we see you more?"

"You saw me a lot, Geno," she said. "I just don't think you *saw* me." The laughter had drained out of her face, leaving a wistfulness. "Then again, for a lot of years, I went out of my way not to be seen."

"Tell me about it," Geno said, staring. Because right at that moment, in that light, from that angle, Zoë looked so much like Nathan, it was as if Nathan were using her as a channel. Borrowing her body to sit with Geno in the kitchen for a minute. Just for one precious minute to look at his son.

"Are you all right?" Nathan asked in Zoë's voice.

Geno's heart tore down the middle. He wanted so much to say no, he wasn't all right. He wanted his father to be at peace and not worry. He drew a long breath through his nose, trying to find something honest that wouldn't kill Nathan one more time.

"Getting there," he said.

Zoë leaned and pressed her lips against his temple, and her hand ran soft over the cropped hair. Geno hesitated, then let his head fall on her shoulder.

Another soul memory, haunting and intense. When he was thirteen and too old to cry, his frustrations and fears either erupted in anger or festered inside. But sometimes things built up, didn't go his way, didn't make sense. It got to be too much. Those times, when Analisa hugged him, he didn't shy away. He didn't fall on her, bawling, either. He just leaned on her. Leaning was acceptable. Staying in her arms a minute and letting the tears quietly dissolve out of him was okay. Letting her presence soothe him was permitted.

Geno didn't cry now. But he exhaled, leaned and let Zoë be both sister and mother.

Just for a minute.

⌐⌐

Geno burned a lot of midnight oil in Vern's study. In the moony light of the computer monitor, he surfed the internet like a legal clerk, looking at laws about sexual assault. Searching for sites that could put the wordy, circular and frustrating language into terms he could understand.

He spent a long time reading article 213 of the Model Penal Code. Developed by the American Law Institute in 1962, the code wasn't law in any jurisdiction in the United States, but it played a significant role in codifying and standardizing the country's penal laws.

Section 1 of Article 213 defined "rape" as a male who had forceful sexual intercourse with a female not his wife.

With a female, Geno thought. *Because men don't get raped.*

Rape was a second-degree felony. According to the next clause, certain circumstances made a man who had forceful sexual intercourse with a female not his wife guilty of "gross sexual imposition," a third-degree felony.

Again, a male with a female.

Because you can't rape the willing.

Sexual imposition. It sounded more like a nuisance than a crime.

I beg your pardon, I didn't mean to rape you. Sorry for the imposition.

Gross sexual imposition sounded like a social blunder made by an up-talking surfer.

Like, gross, I tripped and had forceful sex with you? Like, sorry?

Geno rubbed his eyes, then let the words on the screen come into focus again.

Section 2 was harder to grasp. His tired, sandy eyes kept coming back to the phrase "deviate sexual intercourse." Forceful sexual intercourse between human beings who weren't husband and wife.

"Meaning male and female," Geno said, eyebrows pulling low. "Everything else is…"

Deviate sexual intercourse.

He rubbed his face. "That can't be right."

The code shrugged back at him and pointed to the words that insisted, in black and white, what happened to Geno wasn't rape, but deviate sexual intercourse.

Geno sat back, mouth slightly agape, not sure what to make of this. The open-mouthed bewilderment followed him back to school, where his already hyper-situational awareness started noticing things. Like flyers for women's self-defense courses, one of them hosted at the Flatbush Y by none other than that prick Wayne.

Geno made a point of tearing the flyer off the bulletin board. He stuffed it in his backpack and strode off, muttering under his breath. He went from one end of the campus to the other, but found no such invitations for men to learn to defend themselves. He did find a flyer announcing a coffee hour at the campus center, to discuss date rape in the digital age. Geno parked himself on a couch near the conference room where the meeting was to take place, surreptitiously noting who walked in.

No males attended.

He called a rape crisis hotline, pretending to be a sociology major doing a research paper on rape. Could he ask a few questions, get a few statistics? He was put through to a supervisor who handled the call center data. After a few obvious questions he'd prepared ahead of time, Geno casually asked, "How many calls do you get from men?"

The silence that followed was so familiar.

"I…don't know," the woman said. "Um…"

"If you did get a call from a man, would your staff have the means to help?"

"Well, I'm sure we… Although it might require additional training… It's unusual to the degree that… I'm sorry, I just had someone walk into my office with an emergency, could we continue this another time?"

Geno hung up, already having the answers he sought. He held them in his lap as he stared out at nothing and felt less than nothing. Just as he did on the long-ago day at Zoë's house, when the phone was slammed down on him and his experience.

Nobody knows what to do with you.

What happened has no place in this world.

Which is why we don't talk about it.

From his backpack pocket he drew the crumpled-up flyer for Wayne's self-defense course at the Y. He ought to write on the back, *Men get raped too,* and mail it to Wayne anonymously.

Fat lot of good that would do.

Nobody can help because there's nothing to help.

He wasn't female. So it wasn't rape.

He refused to be the deviant.

So all of this was just a gross imposition.

Like, sorry…?

JANUARY 2008

AN UNATTENDED GLASS

"**H**ANGING AROUND FOR MLK weekend?" Ben asked.

"Don't I always?" Geno said.

"I'm hanging around too. So is Natasha."

"What, it's on?"

Ben grinned like one who was getting spectacularly laid. "Guess where her new piercing is?"

Geno held up a palm. "Pass."

"Anyway, remember my buddy Jason, you met him on Thanksgiving? He's got a new apartment on the Upper East Side. He's having a housewarming thing. Want to come?"

Geno didn't, but he didn't want to sit in the empty dorm on a Saturday night either. He took a Xanax, slipped two Valium into his jeans pocket as backup and went along.

Jason's one-bedroom apartment was crammed tight with Broadway hopefuls. Dancers, chorus boys, musicians. Geno couldn't pick up a hammer to join in the shop talk, so he kept to the perimeter of the open room. Back to the wall, he moved toward the kitchen, where Jason was performing at the little island, plating up appetizer after appetizer.

"Mo, baby, what's going on?" he called over the crush. "Get your ass over here, I need a servant."

Grateful, Geno slipped behind the barrier of stove and sink. Like a surgical nurse, he handed Jason what was needed and cleared away what wasn't, noticing Jason seemed perfectly happy to stay put, provide food and let people come to him.

"Mo, I was kidding about the servant thing," Jason said. "Go mingle if you want."

"I'm not a mingler," Geno said, washing up some pots and pans.

"I hear you. I like a wall between me and the crowd."

Geno looked over his shoulder. "You get up in front of crowds for a living."

Jason looked back as well, grinning. "Ever hear of the fourth wall?"

Lounging on the other side of the island, Seth was telling Ben and Natasha about riding Kingda Ka, the world's tallest roller coaster at Six Flags.

"Four hundred and fifty-six feet," he said. "Straight *down.*"

"Straight up, no thank you," Natasha said, shuddering.

"You must've been shitting your pants at the top," Ben said.

"Worse," Seth said. "I was so scared, I had a fucking erection."

Natasha screeched a laugh and Jason pointed a wooden spoon at his boyfriend. "I don't believe you said that."

"What?"

"I sport wood all the time on roller coasters," Jason said. "I thought it was just me."

"I get a boner at horror movies," Ben said. "And it's not because I'm turned on."

Natasha leaned on her elbow, looking thoughtful. "Maybe fear is a different kind of arousal."

A chill touched the back of Geno's neck.

"Nah," Seth said around a mouthful. "It's fight or flight. All the blood's going to your muscles."

Jason snorted. "Like your dick is useful in a fight."

"Your body's not choosy," Seth said. "It's all hands on deck."

"All hands on dick?"

"You wish."

Geno crossed his arms tight and suppressed a shiver, listening to the blithe, casual banter. Suffused with a weary jealousy. He'd never be able to joke about boners and hands on dicks this way. Sex would always be a *thing* with him. A thing to guard or hide or lie about. Even in seven years time, when his cells replaced themselves and he'd be, in essence, a new man, he wouldn't be a normal one. Ever again.

He pressed his teeth hard, refusing to let them chatter.

I just want to be a regular guy.

Who knew being average could be so enviable?

⌒

They left Jason's apartment around ten and hit a bar on Third Avenue called The Study.

Not a good idea, Mos said as he got a look at the loud crowd within.

It's fine, Geno thought. *I'll practice situational awareness.*

Mos dug in his heels. *Not good.*

It'll be fine.

"You okay, Mo?" Ben said.

Geno nodded and leaned in closer. "Would you mind if we stood near the door?"

"Why?"

"I like it near the door."

"Same here," Jason said. "I don't walk into a place unless I know how I can get out."

"Because you're famous?" Geno asked.

"Because I'm gay."

Geno blinked at him. Jason's smile was wide above an exaggerated shrug of his shoulders. "I mean, come on," he said. "I'm basically wearing a sign that says, *Start some shit with me and prove you're a man.* Believe me, I know where the fucking exits are. Right?"

"Right."

"Come on, Mo, let's carve out some territory." The side of Jason's fist lightly struck Geno's upper arm as he headed toward the bar. He staked out one corner, planted himself on a stool and held court there the entire night. People of all persuasions came to pay homage, while Geno stood by like a bodyguard and nursed a single beer.

"You cool?" Ben asked occasionally.

"Yeah," Geno said each time. It was the truth and it took him by surprise. Standing with his back to the bar, the door within view, nobody touching him, relaxed and situationally aware, Geno did feel cool. His do-not-disturb aura was being respected. Any gazes in his direction were weightlessly curious and without intention. He was a normal, somewhat shy guy out having a beer. Present and invisible at the same time.

"Hey." Jason leaned close to be heard over the music. "What's Mo short for?"

Geno felt so good, he could flirt with the answer. "Take a guess."

"Maurice."

"No."

"Morris," Seth said.

Geno gave him a side eye.

"Mohammed?" Jason said.

Geno pointed the bottle at him. "Yes."

"Really?"

"No."

Jason laughed and socked Geno's shoulder. "Come on, what is it?"

"Geronimo."

"Shut the fuck up."

"Swear to God," Geno said.

"ID, please," Seth said.

Geno tucked his beer into an elbow and got his wallet. He slid out his driver's license, being careful not to dislodge Carlos'.

"Geronimo. That's fucking *awesome,*" Seth said. "So do you, like, jump off shit and yell your name?"

"No," Geno said. "But I've made a lot of girls do it."

A split second and then Jason, Seth and Ben howled with laughter.

"Holy shit, you're human," Ben said.

"What?"

"Dude, I've *never* heard you make a crack about sex."

Warm pleasure flooded Geno's face. Happiness like a nostalgic memory curled around his chest. He was at a bar with friends. He made a joke about sex. He was just a normal guy.

How about that shit? he said to Mos.

Mos crossed his arms, uncommitted.

Oh come on, Geno cajoled, flirting with himself.

Mos sighed over his clipboard, relenting. *We may be having a good time right now.*

"Be right back," Ben said and shouldered through the crowd. It was getting tight in here, but Geno was all right. He could see the door. His back pressed against the bar so nobody could get behind him. Everything was great. He wished he could bottle this feeling up. Compress it into pills he could swallow.

He turned his gaze down the bar, people watching. Mostly young couples. One solitary Asian girl with a martini, looking straight ahead, her expression thoughtful. Maybe even a little lonely. Geno stared, considering going over to say hi. Then his attention was caught by a girl a few stools closer to him. She was pretty.

Soap and water pretty.

"Geronimo," Kelly Hook cried, shoving Geno over the side of the couch. *A long time ago.*

The girl kissed her date and ran her hand through his hair before sliding off the stool. Her date called to her, pointed at the bar, did she want another? From where he stood, Geno could see her mouth shape a reply: just a Coke.

"I'm driving," Geno said, a long time ago. So Fox got him a Coke instead.

Geno's gaze followed the girl through the crowd. Her date leaned back a bit on his stool to track her as well. One hand went into his jacket pocket.

The bartender set down the glass, still bubbling. A bit of froth sliding down the side.

How about a Coke instead?

Geno was suddenly and situationally aware. His focus sharpened into a pin-point beam, the rest of the bar shuttered out and silenced. His tongue pressed the roof of his mouth, remembering the sweet, carbonated taste of betrayal.

The date drew the glass of soda closer, his other hand still in his pocket.

Can we go? Carlito, come on, let's go.

Go.

The guy's hand came out of his pocket and hovered quickly over the glass, fingers moving like a magician's diversionary tactic.

"What's happening?" Geno said, realizing something was in the soda, but now the walls were giggling. Fox's ear was inside out and weird and Geno shouldn't laugh at it but he couldn't help it.

"You should lie down."

Go.

We need to go.

This is against the law.

Geno's eyes flicked up. Another pair of eyes met his gaze. From her stool at the bar, the lone Asian girl looked at him, her eyes wide and hard against Geno's. They stared in a silent commune.

Did he just...?

Did you see...?

Go, Mos yelled and the stars echoed him in a battle cry of rage. *Go go go go go go...*

A shattering of glass as Geno's beer dropped to the floor.

"Mo, what the fuck?" Jason called as Geno strode down the bar, his back undefended and his hands on the offense. He seized two fists of the date's jacket and hauled him back off the stool.

"The hell did you do," he yelled, his voice slicing through the high-pitched cries of girls and the lower shouts of boys. The bar split apart with a crackling energy. Both bartenders whipped around fast as the date's arms windmilled, his feet sliding for purchase on the wet floor.

"What did you put in there?" Geno said, fists tightening as the crowd pulled back from him.

"Crazy son of a bitch" the date yelled. "Get the fuck off me."

"Hey," one of the bartenders shouted.

"He put something in her drink," Geno shouted back.

"I saw it," the Asian girl said. She'd made her way down the bar and slammed her palm on top of the glass of Coke. "I saw him do it. We both saw."

"The fuck is *wrong* with you?" Geno cried. The date was trying to slide his arms from the jacket and get away. Geno quickly got one arm, then the other hooked through the guy's elbows, pinning his arms behind, his whole back against Geno's chest.

"What were you going to do," he said through the wall of his teeth. "Fuck her unconscious? Was that the plan? How about I fuck you, huh? How about I knock you out and get a few buddies to rape your ass into shreds? See how you like it?"

The music stopped and the lights came on. The crowd cringed like vampires at dawn. Two bouncers had shouldered their way into the fray. A short shouting match between the date proclaiming his innocence, and Geno and the Asian girl insisting on what they'd seen. One of the bouncers thrust his hand into the date's jacket pocket and came out with a pair of tiny plastic bags. One crumpled, the other filled with a white powder.

It got surreal after that. The date was pried out of Geno's grip and taken… somewhere. Once he was gone, Geno's tunnel focus turned on the girl returning from the ladies' room, looking bewildered. Geno seized her shoulders. Harder than he should have but he was pissed.

"Your date tried to drug you," he said.

She twisted in his hands, eyes wild. "What?"

"He put something in your soda."

"He…what?"

"How long have you known him?"

Tears sprang to her eyes. She was so lovely. Like a bar of Ivory soap, so pretty and clean and unaware of how close the fox was to her henhouse.

"We just met tonight," she said.

"Oh my God," Geno said, voice tight in his throat. "You can't. You can't *do* that. You can't ever leave your drink with a guy you don't know. You can't." He was shaking her a little. Just a little and he didn't mean to, but he was so *angry*.

"Mo, take it easy." Ben was beside him. Ben, who made Geno tell jokes tonight while a predator was out looking for innocent chicks.

"You have to be careful," Geno cried, getting in the girl's face. "Don't ever leave your drink behind with a guy. I don't care who he is, first date or seventh date, don't *ever* leave your drink alone with him."

"It's all right," Ben said.

"It's *not* all right," Geno said.

"Dude, it's okay. You stopped it."

Jason came to Geno's other side. He slid a protective arm around the girl and put his palm on Geno's arm. "It's okay," he said. "Don't scare her more. Everyone's upset and shook up. Come on, man, it's all right. You did good."

Geno's focus widened and he realized how hard his fingers were clamped in the girl's flesh. He let go, horrified. He'd broken the rules. "I'm sorry. I…"

"Thank you," she said, tears dripping from her eyes. "You saved my life."

Your daddy isn't coming to save you. Your brother waited until Daddy was across the ocean. He brought you to me.

All because Geno hadn't been situationally aware. He drank from an unattended glass.

I think I should take over, Mos said.

You should, Geno thought.

This is all happening to someone else.

Thank you.

"Thank you," the girl said. "I can't thank you enough."

You can go now, Mos said. *I got this.*

GUYS LIKE THAT

*T*HE BARTENDERS AND bouncers shook Geno's hand and said the world needed more guys like him.

Next thing he knew, Geno was throwing up in the alley behind the bar. Like he did when the police rescued him. Because guys like Anthony Fox were in the world.

Ben held Geno's jacket. Natasha offered a stick of gum when the heaving was over. Jason came back with a bottle of water and some napkins, which he wet down and handed to Geno. Hunkered down, a hand braced on the brick wall, Geno wiped his face, breathing hard. "Thanks."

"Damn, man, you brought up food you haven't even eaten yet," Jason said.

Geno tried to smile but could only grimace. "Jesus," he said through chattering teeth.

"Just breathe," Natasha said. "Shake it out."

Geno took a giant, shaking breath and wished he were dead.

"You okay?" Ben asked.

"Yeah." Geno straightened his legs and the world spun. "Shit."

"Whoops, back you go," Jason said. "Put a knee down. Breathe."

"It's okay, Mo."

"Sorry," Geno said to his kneecap.

"Are you kidding me?" Ben said. "That was amazing."

Natasha ran fingers along Geno's short hair. "You're a hero."

"I got two sisters," Seth said. "I worry about this shit all the time."

Then Ben crouched down, balanced on his toes. "Hey."

Geno drank from the water bottle, rinsed and spit. "What?"

"Did it happen to a girl you know?"

Geno looked up, screaming inside, *Why a girl? Why do you assume a girl? Think it can't happen to a guy? Think a guy can't be drugged and raped? Any of you got brothers? Do you worry about them?*

Geno set his teeth and blinked hard and fast, but his eyes were overflowing now. He was about to tell Ben the truth. He was tired. Feeling he was one step closer to ending things for good. Maybe tonight. In which case, what was the fucking point lying anymore?

He opened his mouth to tell them everything, but Mos got there first. "Yeah," he said. "Someone I knew."

I used to know myself.

Ben put a hand on Geno's shoulder. It was a strong, kind brotherly hand and Geno hated how it made him flinch and recoil.

"Let's grab a cab," Jason said. "We'll go back to my place. You need to be somewhere safe where you can chill."

I want to go home, Geno thought.

STR8T DUDE SEEKS SAME

Back at the apartment, Jason made omelets, rolling them onto warmed plates with a practiced roll of the wrist. Geno watched through a hazy, detached curtain. He'd slipped into the bathroom and taken one of his stashed Valium. Then, for good measure, he broke the second pill in half and bit off a quarter. He was floating now. The kitchen light bounced off metal surfaces and twinkled like stars.

"Eggs are soul food," Seth said, squeezing ketchup onto his plate. "I once dated a guy who didn't like eggs. I had to break up with him on principle."

"My ex-girlfriend was allergic to them," Natasha said.

Ben stopped mid-chew. His eyes pressed Geno's a split second. "Your ex-girlfriend?" he said.

Natasha tucked a lock of pink hair behind her ear. "Mm-hm."

"You're bi?"

Natasha raised her pierced eyebrow. "Close your mouth, dear."

"*This* is how he finds out?" Jason said, laughing over the stove.

"Jesus, I dated a girl," Natasha said. "Big deal."

"And ironically, it ended over eggs," Seth said.

"Her eggs were so *small,*" Natasha said, laughing.

"Well, at least you had an adventure," Ben said.

"What makes you think it was only an adventure?"

Ben shrugged now.

"You know," Natasha said, "I am really becoming aware of shit like this."

"Shit like what?"

"The rules and laws of sexual fluidity."

"Here we go," Jason said, rolling another omelet out. He slid the plate in front of Natasha, then did a deft spin and produced two slices of toast for Geno.

"Nibble on that before you try anything else," he said. "You want ginger ale or something? I can make tea."

"No thanks." Geno bit off some toast and chewed slowly.

This is normal.

"Case in point," Natasha was saying. "A straight girl experiments with another girl, and society dismisses it as adventure. The assumption is she'll come back home." Fork tucked under her thumb, Natasha made air quotes around *home*, before finishing, "To being straight. Whereas a straight guy?" The fork pointed around the four males.

"Hey, don't include us in this thesis," Jason said, slinging an arm around Seth's shoulders. Seth tilted his chin up and they kissed.

"Sorry." Natasha's fork flicked between Geno and Ben. "A straight guy experiments with another guy, and it's not adventure. It's the opposite of adventure. It's immediately branded as his true nature, which he's obviously been hiding. And everyone smugly sits back and waits for him to come out as gay."

A moment of reflective chewing around the kitchen island. "Some truth in that," Ben said finally. "A lot of truth. Unfortunately, but yeah, that's kind of how it is."

"Straight guys don't experiment with other guys," Geno said.

Natasha's eyes slid toward him with an aren't-you-adorable expression. "You think?"

"No straight guys I know."

"Jason, can I use your laptop?" Natasha said.

"It's on the bookshelf over there."

"I know hetero guys who mess around," Seth said. "Buddy of mine said nothing beats a hand job from another guy, and he was straighter than Fifth Avenue."

Ben wiped ketchup from the corner of his mouth. "I guess if you're born with a dick, you know what to do with one."

"If you're letting guys jerk you off, you're not straight," Geno said, feeling ganged-up on.

"It's called hetero-flexible," Jason said.

Geno raised his eyebrows.

"I'm straight, but shit happens," Jason and Seth said in unison.

"Or shit gets looked for," Natasha said, returning to the island with the laptop. She had a browser window open to Craigslist and its Casual Encounters section. "Peruse *that*, boys…"

Four male heads crowded around the screen.

Str8 guy wants to try BJ tonight…
Yo, I'm up late. I have a girlfriend but I'm home alone and watching porn. I like watching chicks give head and it's making me think I want to try it too. I'm not attracted to guys. I don't want to look at you or talk to you. Just suck your cock. And just for tonight. Caucasian only.

"Jesus," Ben said, laughing.
"That can't be real," Geno said.
But Natasha kept clicking and scrolling and finding more posts.

Str8 guy looking for friendly sex.
Average white dude looking for not-gay sex with other dude.
Straight dude drunk and horny. Any straights want to rub one out with me?
Seeking straight mates for circle-jerk. Why not?
Str8 dude seeks same: looking to mess around.
Looking to lay back, have some beers and watch some straight porn. Keep our hands to ourselves, just jack together like buds. It's cool.
Looking for Str8 buddy. Come over, watch porn, talk about pussy and stroke bone. No hassle, no feelings, no involvement.
Straight guy wants to whack off with same (no sex, not negotiable)
Str8 guy in a bad way. No girlfriend and dying to get off.

The toast was soggy in Geno's mouth. His legs were perked-up and thrumming. He was starting to vibrate.
Look what we got here, Anthony whispered. *Someone's enjoying this.*
"Mo, you okay?" Jason said. "You gonna puke again?"
"I'm not," Geno said.
I'm not.
He was getting hard.
I'm not.
You love it. You're a whore just like your brother.

"Tash, put that away," Jason said. "It's insensitive. Sorry, Mo. You're already upset."

"I'm not," Geno said.

An awkward silence filled the kitchen. Beneath the counter, Geno's knees knocked together.

I just want to be a normal guy.

Is this what normal guys do?

Say it, you little bitch.

You'll say it. They all do for me.

"Hey," Ben said, putting a hand on Geno's shoulder. "Come back to us."

I can't. I can't go back home to being straight.

Ben's fingers closed around a fold of Geno's shirt and pulled a little. "Mo, come talk to me a sec."

Geno let himself be led into the living room. He stared at the tall bookshelf, looking for another story he could become.

"Look," Ben said. "I don't want to be corny, but… I'm here for you, okay? It kills me you lost your whole family and you don't have a parent or brother you could've called tonight."

"Yeah," Geno said carefully, as if trying not to let the words touch his mouth. "It's hard."

I want to go home.

Was the girl from the bar home now?

She might not have made it. She could've been in a strange apartment by now, limp and helpless under a man's body, being told she loved it.

I rescued her.

I'm the only one around here…

"Hey," Ben said. He touched Geno's forearm, sending off waves of thrumming goodness. "You can tell me."

"It's hard."

And I was hard.

"I know. I'm sorry it has to be like this, Mo. I wish I could do something." His hand slid up Geno's arm and across his shoulders. A heavy warm drape yet still Geno's teeth chattered. Torn apart by longing and fear. Wanting to turn and burrow into this comforting touch. Wanting to turn and run like hell from it. It felt too good. It felt like something he was told he loved.

Don't you, baby boy?

"It's too hard," Geno said. "I need some air." He tugged out of Ben's grasp and went out on the balcony.

The cold air startled him into a gasp. He sucked in breath after breath, hands clenched on the railing. Seven stories below, traffic made diamond and ruby threads across Manhattan.

I want to go home.

Yeah, you do, baby boy. Your daddy's not coming. He's on the other side of the ocean.

He crouched down, hands fisted around the iron bars of the railing, an animal in a cage.

I'm all alone in here.

He stood again, his view free of the bars but still feeling just as caged.

I want to go home.

I want all this to be happening to someone else. Why can't this be someone else?

Mos opened his eyes. *I got this.*

Geno shifted his weight onto one foot. The other leg trembled, getting ready to swing over the railing. *I want to go home,* he thought. *I'm coming back to Nos.*

Stop, Mos said, grabbing a handful of Geno's shirt. *This land isn't safe anymore. The door to the henhouse was left open. Now the laws are broken and everything feels in Nos.*

"I can't stay here," Geno whispered. "I can't."

For the first time, Mos spoke to him in a voice filled with soothing kindness. *I know. It's all right. You rest now. Let me take care of it. I got this.*

Geno's mind pulled apart. Neat and precise as a perforated piece of paper.

It's not safe to be you anymore, Mos insisted. *Let me do the talking, baby boy.*

"Mo," Jason said. "I want you to come inside now. Okay?"

Afraid of Everything

*M*os looked over his shoulder. His eyes slid from Jason's blond hair, ruffling in the wind, down his tight, muscled body to the fashionable shoes. Then up again, taking in Jason's crisp handsomeness and concerned expression.

Is he a whore like me?

"Can you come inside?" Jason said. His superstar smile wobbled. "You're kind of making us nervous."

Ben came out. Tall and strong and authoritative. "Mo, come back now."

You'll say it, then you'll do it.

All my boys are loyal to me.

Mos's fingers slowly loosened on the railing but he didn't let go.

"Let us help you," Ben said.

"You don't have to go in," Jason said. "Just step back from the railing, okay? Can you do that much?"

"Come on, Mo," Ben said. "I won't hurt you. I want to help. Will you let me help?"

He stepped behind Mos and slid hands down his arms to his wrists. "Come on, let go now. That's it. Just step back with me. I'm right here."

The boys lurched backward, like Quasimodo in reverse. Ben bumped against the side of the building and Mos bumped into him. His shoulders to Ben's chest.

Well, look what we got here.

Mos shook hard. Ben held him tighter and the shaking stopped.

The night shifted into a different normal.

We're just two normal straight dudes who want to go home.

Jason stood in front of him now, both hands on Mos's shoulders. "Mo, it's okay."

"No, it's not," Mos said. "I'm not him."

"Not who?"

"I'm not Mo." He fumbled his wallet out of his pocket, shaking fingers digging in the folds for the twin licenses he carried. "See. That's Mo. Geronimo. My twin brother. I'm Carlos. My brother was taken. The porn ring that got busted in New Jersey last summer. My brother knew him. The ringleader. He groomed Mo to trust him and then he took him. They found Mo in the basement, drugged up and handcuffed to a bed. They were selling him. Selling his pictures and then selling *him*. Mo was trapped there two days and they about raped him to death."

"*Jesus*, man," Ben said in a hiss of air, the circle of his arms pressing harder.

"Are you fucking kidding me?" Jason cried.

"Nobody believed him," Mos said, the story jumping the leash and getting away, all the roles mixed up, but it kept spilling. Piling up, lie on top of lie. Bricks to build a wall around Geno and keep him safe.

"Everyone brushed it off," Mos said. "Everyone said guys couldn't get raped. They said Mo was gay. They said he must've brought it on or been asking for it. He even called a rape hotline once. The woman who answered hung up on him. She yelled at him for being a twisted pervert, calling up a hotline to jerk off to a made-up story. Then she hung up. Nobody believed him and he killed himself."

He was fading out, no longer sure who was who, where his truth stopped and the lie began, or who was in control here.

"Nobody believes it," Mos said. "Not even the law. Who knows how many guys are out there in the world, afraid to say what happened to them…"

"Hey," Ben said at his shoulder. "You told me once you weren't afraid of anything. Remember?"

"I'm fucking afraid of everything," Mos said.

"You afraid of me?"

Mos shook his head.

Ben's arms were so strong. "Not everything, then."

"Help me," Mos said.

"Come inside."

Inside, Seth was white and stunned. Natasha was pale and pink, like a bar of soap. She sat on one side of Mos on the couch. Ben sat on the other, warm and strong.

"I'm sorry," they all said.

"I'm so sorry."

"Dude, that's crazy."

"I'm so fucking sorry."

Jason knelt on the floor between Mos's feet, hands on his thighs. "It made what you did tonight even more beautiful. You kind of saved your brother this time. You know?"

"I bet he was watching," Seth said. "I bet he was so fucking proud of you."

No, I'm dead to him.

"You're so brave," Natasha said. "You're amazing."

No, I was a coward. I sold out my own brother. I watched as they raped him. Anthony cuffed me to the bed and made me watch.

I watched.

He remembered the shape of a man's arms behind his back. His shoulders to Anthony's chest.

"Nuh," Geno said, head lolling like his neck was broken. All his body soft and slack except for one part that was rock hard.

"Look what we got here," Anthony said. "Somebody's enjoying this."

Mos remembered. Mo remembered. Geno remembered.

The land of Nos was abandoned now, its laws regarding feeling were suspended and its stars gone dark.

So he went on remembering.

TWO MORE

*H*E WOKE UP.

Am I here?

I'm the only one around here.

Is it still happening?

Wherever here was, it was dark. And quiet.

Am I all right?

He was lying down.

Am I home?

I have no home.

He opened his eyes. Lifted his head.

He was on a couch.

I'm at Jason's place. I stayed here.

He sat up. Parched, nauseous, his head clanging. He felt worn out and raw. He ached all over.

Am I sick?

He got up, breathed through the nausea and stumbled toward the bathroom, digging a shoulder into the wall for support.

He threw up forever. Bringing up food he hadn't even eaten yet.

He'd never catch up to his life.

I told them I was Carlos.

Now I have to be him…or explain why I said I was him.

His head bulged and ached within the web of lies he wove. He couldn't remember what he told to who and why.

I'm too tired.

No one believes. Not even the law.

I told them I was Carlito.

I'm not him.

I'm no one.

He was tired. He hurt all over. He needed something for the pain. Something strong.

He found Vicodin in the medicine cabinet and took two. He dumped the rest of the pills into his palm, pocketed them and put the bottle back in the cabinet.

The apartment was stiller than death. The bedroom door was partly open. Boxes stacked against the walls. A king-sized mattress on the floor. On one side, Seth curled around Jason's back, the clump of their joined hands under Jason's chin.

On the other side, Ben had his arms around Natasha, fingers buried in her fairyland hair.

The spooning couples curved like brackets toward each other. From the door, the odd man stared at the space between.

I want to go home.

He took two more Vicodin.

Say you want it.

He crawled onto the mattress. Eased himself between bodies, like a side thought put in parenthesis.

Say it, you little bitch.

"I want it," he mouthed.

Carlos knew what he was doing when he set the trap. He had an easy target.

I said I was him.

Maybe I am him.

Maybe they were right all along. I'm a whore just like my brother.

Another two Vicodin.

Geno rolled on his side and put his back against Jason.

Can't have one twin be gay without the other. You love it.

Jason made a little sound. A shift of weight, then his hand moved against Geno's arm. Up. Down. It felt good.

Of course it does. And you want it.

He loved it. He got hard for it. He came during it.

But it was all right.

It would be over soon and he wouldn't have to be anyone.

Two by two, he swallowed pills until his pocket was empty. He moved further back against Jason and reached to take Ben's free hand. Then he lay still and waited to die.

The gates of Nos would open and he'd go home. For good.

Ben's fingers curled, squeezed and went still.

Jason's palm slid and rested on Geno's head.

Brother mine.

He could see the little red henhouse, golden light streaming from its tiny windows. His mother would be there. Waiting for him and his common sense.

He smiled.

He was the only one around here.

Not Your Brother

*T*HE BOY WOKE up in Mount Sinai hospital again.

No Vern this time.

No Zoë.

No Mos.

Just a cop, an ER nurse and Dr. Frankenstein.

"How do you feel?" Stein asked.

I don't feel.

"Quite a stunt you pulled there," the nurse said, inclining the bed up a little.

But it didn't work.

"Think you can help us figure out who you are?" the cop said. "Because doc here said he knows you, while the buddies who called nine-one-one think you're someone else."

He had a wallet in his hands, which he opened. He drew out two driver licenses and laid them on the sheets.

Two identical boys gazed out from each card.

Same date of birth. Same height. Same weight. Same hair and eye color. Same face.

CAAN, GERONIMO G.

CAAN, CARLOS N.

"Who are you?" Stein said. "Can you tell me?"

The boy in the hospital bed reached. As his hand touched the license named Carlos, a single tear tracked down his face.

"No," Stein said.

"It didn't happen to me," the boy said. "I just watched it happen."

"Geno."

"I brought the fox a chick," the boy said. "He was a whore just like me. He loved it."

"You are not Carlos Caan," Dr. Stein said. "Carlos Caan was your twin brother. He died. You are Geronimo Caan. You survived."

The boy stared at his lap.

"You are not your brother."

Tears splashed onto Carlos' face, beading up and sliding along the laminated surface of the card.

"But I can understand how it feels easier to be him," Stein said. "It has to be so hard to be you right now, Geno."

The boy looked up. "I don't want to be anyone anymore."

I just want to go home.

He didn't care. They could lock him up, put him away or send him back to the basement. It didn't matter anymore. He watched his own hand reach again, extend an index finger and flick Carlos' license off the bed, between the bars of the railing.

"I think I'm going crazy," he said to the boy who remained in his lap.

"No," Stein said. "No, you aren't. You were brutalized and tortured. It's no wonder you switched places with someone. You're not crazy. You're trying to survive an intolerable situation."

The boy's shoulders gave a tiny shiver as he poured back into himself. Goosebumps like needles swept across his body and his teeth chattered. As he filled back up with Geno, he filled with illegal feeling. His hand curled around his driver's license, the edges digging into his palm.

"I just wanted it to stop," he whispered.

"I know, Geno. You're hurting so bad."

"I wanted to see my mother."

Stein nodded. "You must miss her so much, Geno."

His name finally sticking to him, Geno nodded.

"And your father, too."

"I want to go home. And I don't know where that is."

"I know."

All of Geno chattered now, shaking and twitching and trembling. "I want to die," he said. "And I'm afraid I won't."

Vern came.

The kvater always came.

A meeting was held and decisions made. Geno would be kept in the hospital a week on a suicide watch, then it was recommended he be released to a supervised environment.

"There's an excellent center in Chelsea called the Exodus Project," Dr. Stein said. "I made some calls and they have the space."

"For how long?" Vern said.

"Their rehab program is six months."

Vern's jaw was tight, his eyes flat as the details were hammered out. Geno sensed this was the last time the kvater would take him from one set of arms and hand him to another.

When Stein left the room, Vern walked over to the window. Arms crossed over his impeccable shirt front, he stared out at Central Park. Beneath the cross of his suspenders, his back quivered.

Geno swallowed hard. "I'm sorry."

Vern's head turned a bit. "I miss him too, you know," he said tightly.

"I know," Geno said, and again wished he were dead.

Vern came over to him. He smelled strong and piney, like money and power and aftershave and pipe smoke. His fingers reached for the gold chain at Geno's neck and picked up the star of David. "My parents gave this chain to your father for his bar mitzvah. I loved him like a brother and I mourn him every single day."

"Do you want it?" Geno asked.

"I want you to live." With a tiny thud, the star fell back on Geno's chest. "Look at me," Vern said.

Through blurred wet eyes, Geno looked up.

"I'm not going to let you die," Vern said. "I'll be damned if I stand here and watch Nathan Caan's only son die."

This time, when he put his arms around Geno, Geno let him.

QUIETER THAN USUAL

*R*ONNIE DANVERS TEXTED Stef early in the morning: ***Need to see you
as soon as you get in.***

Hoping it wasn't about Max, Stef headed to her office. In one of the chairs
across from her desk sat Franklin Stein, head of Mount Sinai's adolescent health
center and a frequent consultant with the Coalition for Creative Therapy. If you
looked up "mensch" in the dictionary, you'd find Frank Stein. He was one of
Stef's favorite people on the planet.

"Dr. Frankenstein," Stef said, laughing as Frank hugged him hard.

"Gee, I haven't heard that joke in an hour." Frank slapped Stef's shoulders a
few more times as they took seats again.

"Is this an intervention?" Stef said.

"I wish," Ronnie said. She looked grim. Stef noticed the window was
cracked. The ash tray on the desk was full of butts, which was against the rules.

"I wanted to talk to you about a case," Frank said.

"What kind of case?" Stef said.

"A horrible one."

Stef glanced at Ronnie. "Why do you always do this to me before breakfast?"

The laugh he expected didn't come. His gaze shifted between his colleagues'
unsmiling faces before he put out his palm, motioning for the file folder on
Ronnie's desk. Ronnie put her hand on top of it and shook her head. "Better
Frank explains," she said.

"A young man is coming to the Exodus Project next week," Frank said. "His
name is Geronimo Caan. Goes by Geno. Eighteen years old, grew up in New

Jersey. Had an identical twin brother, no other siblings. His mother died when he was fifteen. Father worked in international law."

Stef noted the past tense but said nothing.

"He's a survivor of the pornography ring busted in New Jersey last summer."

"Also known as the Mengele Ring," Ronnie said.

"Must we?" Stef mumbled, but nodded to indicate he was listening.

"You recall the details of that bust?" Frank asked.

"It was part of the larger ring the Austrians brought down," Stef said. "But this particular cell targeted twins."

"That's right. The Caan brothers were at the house when the police made the raid. They found Carlos Caan hanged from the shower head in a downstairs bathroom. Coroner ruled it a suicide. Allegedly, he had the established relationship with the ringleader, Anthony Fox. The theory is he was financially or emotionally blackmailed into delivering up his twin."

"The details are all in here," Ronnie said, tapping the file folder with her cigarette lighter.

From the top of his crown Stef imagined a smooth molten layer, cascading down like mercury, filling in his pores and making a semi-permeable barrier. A one-way emotional street. Compassion and empathy could go out. But nothing was allowed in.

When confident he was untouchable, Stef spoke. "From what I last read, this guy Fox is still on the run."

"Yes. As for Geno…" Frank lowered his glasses from his head to his nose, picked up the folder and flipped it open. "He suffered close to forty-eight hours of sexual assault. DNA analysis confirmed seven different men, including Fox."

Stef felt a faint vibration as the words bounced off his protective armor, wanting in. He refused them.

I can be sympathetic to your pain. But I do not have to feel it for you.

"Severe internal injuries." Frank said. "Anal fissure, torn perineum, perforated bowel. A close call with peritonitis. He lived on a transverse colostomy for five weeks."

"Lived where?" Stef asked. "With other family?"

"A half-sister for about a month," Ronnie said. "He moved out shortly before he left for his freshman year at Brooklyn College. Reasons unclear."

"I'd seen him regularly while in the hospital," Frank said. "Intermittently in the weeks after he was released. Then not at all by August."

"Toughing it out alone," Stef said.

"I'm not sure it was entirely alone," Frank said. "He was self-medicating with prescription drugs, but he also may have developed a dissociative disorder."

"Conscious depersonalization or a fugue state?"

"I'm thinking conscious. He overdosed on Vicodin at a party on the Upper East Side. Paramedics took him to Mount Sinai and police found two driver's licenses in his wallet, one his, one his brother's. They called me down and of course I knew it was Geno, but the friends who called nine-one-one insisted his name was Carlos."

Stef tapped his teeth together. "So, he switched places?"

"Possibly."

"God," Stef said. He put his elbows on his knees, raked fingers through his hair and held on tight. "Ronnie, you ruined breakfast."

"I'm sorry," she said, and sounded sincere.

Stef pulled in another fortifying breath and let go his hair. "What's his awareness now? I mean, does he know and accept who he is?"

"He does," Frank said. "I don't know what else he's accepted, though."

"All right."

"He's started on Prozac, and he'll be seeing me weekly. But I'd like to be working in tandem with you. Give you the reins, so to speak. Truthfully, I can't see anyone but you handling this boy."

Stef glanced at Ronnie. "Don't call me Obi-Wan."

"I won't," she said. "And you don't have to take him on."

Stef smiled at the floor. "Yes, I do."

Meeting adjourned, Stef walked Franklin down to the lobby.

"How's your dad?" Frank asked, zipping his coat. He was an accomplished pianist, and when Stef's father was still stateside, Stef had arranged a private tour for Frank at the Steinway workshops in Astoria. Frank still talked as if the tour were last week.

"Good," Stef said. "I think he's seeing someone."

"Really?"

"He just got back from a river cruise up the Danube. Usually after one of his jaunts, I have to endure a two-hour recap of his itinerary. This time? He was awful quiet. And a little distracted."

Frank laughed. "Good for him."

A pregnant pause.

"You seeing anyone?" Frank asked.

"Do I seem distracted?"

"I'm inquiring into your current support system. But you are quieter than usual."

I think I'm in love, Stef thought, but aloud only said, "I am. Seeing someone, I mean."

"You trust her? Him?"

"Him. Yes."

"And I'll assume you've got your own therapist on speed dial."

Stef patted the phone in his jacket pocket.

"Good." Frank put a hand on Stef's shoulder. "It's going to be a hard case."

"I know."

"No, you don't know," Frank said, not unkindly. "Look at me. I talked to the Stockton police chief to get some background. He told me about two officers who were at the bust with him. One quit the force within days. The other had to be hospitalized with severe PTSD. Both cops said they couldn't get the Caan boys out of their minds. Chief said he still has nightmares."

Stef nodded, not looking away.

"Part of what makes you so good is your compassion," Frank said. "You've got more empathy radar dishes than that big-ass array out in New Mexico." The hand on Stef's shoulder squeezed. "You're still working with the Springer boy, too, right?"

"Yeah."

"You protect yourself. We work in tandem which means if you need a break, you tell me."

"I will. Always good to see you, Dr. Frankenstein," Stef said.

"Want to hear a better joke than that?"

Frank told terrible jokes. Stef braced himself. "Lay it on me."

"Did you hear about the merger between El Al Israel Airlines and Air Italia?"

Stef shook his head and rolled a palm up to the sky.

Frank grinned. "They're now called Oy, I'll Tell Ya."

Stef closed his eyes. "I haven't had breakfast…"

How Men Make War

O N WORK NIGHTS, Jav knew to give Stef a wide berth for at least an hour after coming home. He didn't hover or chat or ask how the day went. If he could, he took himself out of the equation and went for a run or to pick up food. Or else he went benignly invisible and left Stef alone.

Stef came home tonight and hit the shower straight away. The bedroom door closed and soon Jav could hear music and detect the sweet, cedar smell of incense. Stef was sitting at the corner shrine, prying off his armor.

Jav had sent revisions of *The Chocolate Hour* back to Michael, which meant his time stretched out, empty and luxurious. He'd hit the gym hard this afternoon and now he was drained, not wanting to do anything more strenuous than read. He flopped on the couch's short end, Roman curled at his feet. His nose was sunk deep in Neil Gaiman's *Neverwhere* when Stef finally emerged. He rolled over the back of the couch and fell into the cushions, his head on Jav's chest.

Jav kissed his brow and went back to reading. It was peaceful with just one circle of lamplight falling on them. A quiet evening at home. Roman sighed, his back paw giving a twitch. Jav read, the paperback balanced in one hand while his other fingers combed through the damp hair at the back of Stef's head.

Then all at once, memory pressed him on all sides.

"My cousin used to lie on me like this," Jav said.

"Mm."

"Funny, I never thought anything of it."

Stef turned his face into Jav's shirt. "Those last years of his life, he must've missed you like crazy. I bet he still does."

"You think?"

"I do." A warm yawn against Jav's sternum. "You take a shower and I miss you."

Always a sucker for Stef's mushy side, Jav closed the book and scooched down in the cushions. "I like being missed."

Stef smiled. "I miss you when I close my eyes."

"So open them."

Stef shook his head and slowly the smile faded away. "I'm going to be starting a tough case next week," he said. "I mean really tough. I can't share the details but…"

"Bad?"

"I don't have a word for what it is."

Deprived of mush, Jav tried not to sulk as he replied, "Okay."

"I'm going to do everything I can not to bring it home with me, but some of it's bound to. I tend to pull way, way inside during these kinds of cases. I may act like I don't want you around, but I really do."

"I appreciate the heads up."

"If I'm distracted, or if I'm short with you or pissy, it's not you. It's me trying to hold boundaries in place. Or I might push at ours. Just because I can."

Jav kept a straight face, long knowing Stef was one of those people who liked to label everything. "I got it."

"And since we're on the subject, thank you for being low maintenance."

Now Jav put on his most insulted expression. "I'm low maintenance?"

Stef chuckled as he took the book out of Jav's hand and tossed it aside. He pulled both Jav's arms around his head. Jav held him and held still, staring at nothing, listening to Stef breathe.

"You all right?" Stef finally said.

"Yeah. Why?"

"Your heart is beating really fast. What are you feeling right now?"

"Greedy. Worried."

"Tell me."

"I have so much respect for your work," Jav said. "And I respect the boundaries you set, even when I hate them. Like when you leave in the morning and go into radio silence. I know your phone is turned off and not even in your pocket. Your attention is on your job, where it should be."

"Hey, you know if you ever need—"

"I know who to call if I have an emergency, that's not the point. The point is you're out of my reach during the day. I respect that. *And* I don't like it. The door clicks shut and it's just a bummer. I miss you and wonder if you think about me, and I wish I could insert myself into your day. I don't because greedy boy-friend respects the boundary. But now your work is going to get tougher, and greedy boyfriend has weird, worried questions."

Stef burrowed in closer. "Give me your weird, your worried. Your greedy thoughts yearning to breathe free."

"Do you have a therapist?"

"That's not weird," Stef said. "And yes, I do."

"How often do you see them?"

"Once a month. More if I need to."

"Like if you're taking on a tough case?"

"Yes," Stef said. "And before you ask, I already called Greg and let him know what's going on. I have an appointment next week to establish a baseline."

"A therapist who sees therapists must have a supernatural bullshit detector."

Stef sighed darkly. "You know how you get mad at Michael because he's right about editing? I have the same situation with Greg. He's the worst. I hate him. Next worried question?"

"If a client got…I don't know, out of hand or violent, you know how to handle it?"

"I do," Stef said. "I'm not flexing. I have mandatory training in self-defense and de-escalation, plus a shit ton of protocol and paperwork when and if I have to physically restrain someone."

"Have you ever?"

"Not at my current job. Other facilities where I worked or interned, yeah. Especially with more severe mental illness or substance abuse."

"This next question might offend you."

"I love when you offend me," Stef said. "Fire away."

"Working with male sexual assault victims, has being bisexual ever present-ed a problem?"

"Well, I don't put a lot of personal information on the table anyway. In context, I'll share what I think is appropriate, but my relationship status rarely comes up. Client asks me, 'You married? Got kids?' I'll say, 'No,' and redirect."

"It's not about you," Jav said.

"Right. But I've had occasions in my career when it was discovered and ended up being an issue."

"Like someone actually terminated the therapy?"

"Fired me? Yeah."

Jav affected a professorial tone. "And how did that make you feel?"

Stef smiled. "What can I do? A patient is only going to do well in therapy if they trust the therapist. If their gut is already on high alert and suspicious of my motive, we're not going to get anything done. I can't take it personally. The majority of male sexual predators identify as straight. Not that it's much consolation to survivors. But it's a fact."

"Has a case ever affected you sexually? I mean, after hearing description of ordeals, has it ever turned you off from having sex?"

"Sex with men or with anyone?"

"Both."

"Is this curiosity or anxiety?"

Jav smiled. "Slightly anxious curiosity."

Stef rubbed a fold of Jav's shirt between his fingers, thinking. Jav ran a fingertip over the wrinkled brows, trying to smooth them out.

"Sometimes," Stef said slowly. "I come home with part of a case sticking to me, and I don't want anyone or anything. I don't want to be touched until I deal with it. But other times, the only way I can deal with it is being touched. Sometimes I can only shake off the echo of a sexual abuse story by making love. Like, this is crass, but I need to be fucked back to myself."

"I see." Jav fitted his thumbnail into the scar across Stef's eyebrow. "Is tonight one of those nights?"

"No. I mean, I feel myself. You can fuck me as is."

Laughing, Jav wrapped arms around Stef and squeezed him hard. "Man, I don't know how you do what you do."

"I don't know how you write books."

"I make up bullshit. Your work is so much more important. You know how men make love with each other and you know how men make war on each other. You stand at the middle of this range of male behavior and figure out how to bring the extremes back to center. More toward the making love side, anyway." Jav chuckled. "Or something. There I go making up bullshit again."

Stef nodded against Jav's chest, mouth slightly parted and his gaze going far away, toward some horizon of revelation. "No, you're right," he said slowly. "It's exactly what I do..."

A CLEAN COLOR

*S*TEF TOOK HIS time easing into Geno's line of sight. The kid was following the rules and doing what he was told. His body was present, but his attention was elsewhere. Withdrawing from the prescription pain meds and adjusting to Prozac left him struggling with nausea and complaining of an intermittent buzzing sensation in his head. By the end of the first week, Stef estimated Geno was down about four pounds, mostly in his face.

He had an interesting handsomeness, with cropped dark hair and hazel eyes. Some mix of Italian and German, Stef guessed. He had yet to have an in-depth conversation with Geno. He hadn't seen the boy smile, laugh or even make eye contact. Geno's gaze fixed on some far-away place, contemplating the black hole that used to be called his soul. This wasn't a guy who'd want to draw pictures or practice mindful breathing. He was still in magic wand stage—looking for one lightning bolt fix that would neatly disappear everything that happened to him.

Stef had to handle him carefully. Part of the handling was simply watching, dismissing the academic mind and letting his instincts guide him. Right now, instinct told him Geno was exhausted. Depleted. Not thrilled to be here but not entirely averse to being someplace safe and structured, where other people made decisions for him. He was getting used to the space, the people and the meds.

Let him rest, Stef thought. *Keep watching and keep making it safe for him to exist here.*

Geno was required to come to the group sessions, and while he showed up in terms of attendance, his participation was nil. Usually he sat on the wide windowsills and stared out at the High Line. Sometimes he flopped in one of the beanbag chairs and slept. At Stef's request, the staff included him at the outset, then let him be. Stef covertly watched for any change in demeanor. A whiff of awareness. It could be interested or contemptuous, it didn't matter to Stef. What mattered was the absolute value removed from apathy.

"Well, he made it through the first week," the EP director said, at a meeting she held with all Geno's therapists. "Thoughts? Observations?"

Nolan, who ran EP's group sessions, chimed in. "Minimal participation. Seems to be concentrating on holding himself together during the worst of the withdrawal. He had a couple of severe panic attacks and one episode that looked like a vasovagal syncope."

The facility's young intern looked up. "What's that?"

"It's a loss or near-loss of consciousness when the vagus nerve is triggered."

"Vagus runs from your brain to your gut," Stef said. "Stress triggers nausea, which triggers the nerve. Blood pressure plummets and you either pass out or go into a really weird, surreal plane of *almost* passing out. Feels a lot like insanity."

"Poor kid thought he was losing his mind," Nolan said, sighing. "He's got a kindness. I mean, we've butted heads a couple times but obviously because he's feeling so physically terrible. Short-tempered and irritable. He's snapped at me, but he always apologizes later. I mean he seeks me out to say sorry. So…"

"They didn't get the best of him," Stef said. More to himself than the group, but Nolan glanced over and nodded.

"He seems calm in the kitchen," the EP director said. "He took a shift on Thursday and came back later to prep for four hours. He mentioned he did a lot of the cooking after his mother died."

Which means he's into food, Stef thought, *or he's a caretaker.*

Toward the middle of the second week, the clouds in Geno's eyes parted and he looked around the art room, expression curious. He still had no enthusiasm for the day's activities, but he was interested in the room's materials, their organization and display.

Stef watched him wander. All the supplies were sorted and arranged by function and color, creating a visual inventory of possibility. Geno ran his fingers through the boxes of pens and crayons, or along the edge of paper reams.

Come play, said markers and clay and paints and pencils. *Take us off the shelf. Touch us. Use us.*

The art room had tons to touch. These survivors of sexual violence didn't ever touch each other, but the touching of objects was fair game. They wanted soft, non-human things on their skin. They ran dry paintbrushes along their hands and arms and faces. They drew on themselves with Sharpies. They liked to caress felt, wind pipe cleaners around their fingers, crumple tissue paper and smooth it again. They liked controlling what the art supplies did, as well as knowing things would always perform a certain way. The red marker always drew red, the blue drew blue. Red and blue made purple, always. Glue stuck this to that and didn't let go. Scissors cut and a heart-shaped hole punch made a heart, not a star. An eraser made a mistake go away.

Survivors liked to make a deliberate mess of their projects, and cleanup was as integral to the process as creation. At the end of a session, the muddy paint water could be thrown down the drain. Spills could be wiped up, scraps of paper swept up. It all got rinsed out in the sink and thrown in the garbage.

It could be made to *go away.*

Stef came into the art room one afternoon in the middle of Geno's third week. It was free time, so he sat at one of the long tables with his own sketchpad and a cup of coffee. Geno stood at the tall windows, holding his hands in a puddle of western sunshine. He glanced back at Stef and his mouth twitched in a half-smile.

"Hey," Stef said.

"Hey."

"Are your hands cold?"

"Yeah." Geno stuffed them in his pockets and stared a long time through the glass. He then turned and hitched up to sit on the windowsill. "I like your ink."

Stef glanced down at his tattooed forearms. "Thanks."

"You design it?"

"Yeah."

After a moment, Geno slid down and came closer. Stef held his forearms out, palms to the ceiling. Showing all his horses on one arm, the Elvis Costello lyric on the other.

Alison, I know this world is killing you.

"Who's Alison?" Geno asked.

"A girl who tried to commit suicide. I was working the hotline when she called."

Geno crossed his arms. "She make it?"

"When I hung up she was with people and she was safe. Safer. It was a long time ago."

"Never talked to her again?"

"No. Can't even be sure Alison was her real name. But it sort of marked me as where I was going in life. So I decided to keep her close by."

Geno pushed up the sleeves of his flannel shirt and showed Stef a few of his own tattoos. A lot of Hebrew lettering and mystical-looking symbols. Stef recognized the Kabbalah Tree of Life and the Flower of Life, but none of the others. He praised the work, but asked no questions about the designs themselves.

Geno pushed his sleeves down again and leaned on a chair back. "You know about me? I mean, what happened to me?"

Stef nodded.

The boy pushed his lower jaw out a bit, squinting at the tabletop. "Does all this stuff…" His chin jerked toward the shelves of art supplies. "Does it work?"

"Work is a relative term. Depends on what you want it to do. It helps. I've seen it help."

"How?"

"It helps you say what can't be said in words. Some things are too shitty, too heinous to talk about. But keep them inside and they'll fester and eat away at your guts until you're dead. I try to help people tell their story visually. To tell their story without talking."

Geno's fingers curled around the chair back. He drew a long slow breath in. "How do you do that?"

Stef got up and brought back a box of pastels. "Sit down if you want."

"I'll stand."

Stef sat, tore off a single sheet off his pad and laid it down. "Pick two colors. Any two. One for you, one for them."

Geno's nostrils flared. He leaned one palm on the table and with the other, picked out a blue stick. He made a small smear with the flat side. "Okay, that's me."

His fingers hovered over the colors, then he took black. He turned it on its side and dragged it down, making big, curved lines all around the blue smear. A forest of menacing shadows.

Stef noted the lines stayed far from the edges of the paper. Geno probably wasn't aware, but he was already letting art both express his experience and contain it. The beauty of a sheet of paper was its four edges marking a boundary where pain could not cross.

Geno dropped the crayon and pushed the drawing across to Stef. "There you go. Me versus them. Have at it, Freud."

Stef didn't need to turn the paper around. It was textbook. The victim small, the attackers large.

"Why blue?" Stef asked.

"Why the fuck not?"

"What do you think of when you see blue?"

"The fucking sky, dude. It's blue."

Stef nodded, not expecting more.

"And it's clean," Geno said, looking off over Stef's shoulder. "It's a clean color."

"I think so, too," Stef said. "Blue's dependable."

Geno pressed his lips together tight. "I don't think I want to do anymore."

"Do one thing for me. Just one and I'll let you go." Stef tore off a new sheet of paper. "Draw the exact same thing. Same colors. Same composition. But make one change. Make you big, and them small."

Geno snorted. "Oh, that'll make it all go away?"

"Nothing makes it go away."

Geno picked up the blue pastel. His hand arced over the paper, making one or two practice swipes but not leaving a mark. Finally he let it touch and drew a line.

"Big," Stef said softly.

Geno pressed harder, made the azure mark nearly from top edge to bottom edge. He put the blue down, rubbing his fingertips together. He picked up the black pastel and sniffed hard, pushing the heel of his hand into one eye, the pastel between his fingers like a cigarette.

"It's okay," Stef said.

"Shut up." Geno made small black marks around the base of the blue line. He rubbed his face, leaving a coal smudge like a bruise. He made more marks. Then he shoved the paper away, dropped the pastel and walked toward the window, sniffing and tugging at one ear.

"You can't make it go away," Stef said. "But you can make it smaller."

Geno drew breath in through his nose. It trembled out his jaw and shoulders. "Bullshit."

"You can. And I'd like to work with you. Show you how."

Geno said nothing.

"Think about it." Stef neatly stacked the two sheets of paper and left them on the table. He put his business card on top, then gathered his sketchbook and coffee. "I'll see you tomorrow, okay?"

As he walked away, two tiny words, like chimes on the wind, floated to his ear.

Stef turned back. "What's that?"

Geno looked over his own shoulder, his expression startled. "I said, take care."

The moment folded back on itself in a strange déjà vu. Stef unsure if he'd met Geno before, or if all the ghosts of clients past were looking at Stef through Geno's eyes.

"'Take care' tells me something," Stef said.

"What?"

"They didn't get the best of you."

THE YOUNGEST RESIDENT

"Everyone's nice," Geno told Vern on the phone. "It's a good place." Good in that it could decidedly be worse. He could be locked up in some dingy, gross mental hospital with Nurse Ratched. Exodus Project, he had to admit, was a beautiful facility. Clean and well-maintained and easy on your eyes. The staff was kind and respectful. The food was decent.

Everyone had his own room, because nobody in this joint was keen on roommates. Each room had its own adjoining bath, because residents were even less keen on communal showers. Privacy was held above all else, leading to a stiff politeness on the residence floors. If someone's door was closed, you knocked and took a step back while waiting for an answer. If the door was already open, you still stayed back and asked, "Can I come in?"

Nobody touched.

He was told Exodus Project had no age restrictions but right now, he was the youngest resident. The oldest, Corley, was fifty-six. They were black, white, Latino and Asian. Blue collar, white collar and one had been weeks away from a priest's collar when he was attacked at a seminary retreat. Some residents were gay. Most were straight. All were raped, and Geno learned their stories during group therapy.

Hasan was a former prostitute. One of his tricks stalked and raped him. Chaow was trafficked from Thailand, kept locked up in a shipping container and sold for sex. Juan and Patrick were both raped in prison. It happened to Corley while he was in the navy. To Albie in a college locker room. Pablo's ex-boyfriend brutalized him with a mop handle after they broke up. Jeff was minding his own business, taking a leak at a gas station bathroom, when three guys busted in and raped him at knifepoint.

Story upon story piled up in the center of the circle. A charnel heap, buzzing with flies and oozing blood.

Then it was Geno's turn.

His mouth opened and nothing came out.

"It's okay, man," Corley said on one side.

"No shame," Pablo said from the other.

Geno swallowed and tried again, then shook his head. He couldn't. Mos had a death grip on his throat. Ruby, the woman from the rape crisis hotline, had a fistful of his hair.

We don't talk about this.

I won't let you do this.

"Try a sentence," the group leader, Nolan, said. "It doesn't have to be a story."

"Don't worry about not being believed," Patrick said. "We already believe you."

"Believe me, dude," Jeff said, staring at his hands. "We believe you."

He couldn't do it. Not at that meeting nor the next. By his fourth group session, Geno had descended two levels below rock bottom into some primordial swamp. He sat in the circle, his hoodie cinched tight, his perpetually cold hands fisted in his pockets, letting the discussion stream around him. Albie was talking about his relationship with porn before and after he was assaulted. Patrick said he didn't wish death on anyone, but he'd sit front row at the public execution of a child pornographer. Jeff agreed, because remember that fucked up-shit that went down in New Jersey last summer?

"That was me," Geno said.

All eyes turned. Geno wondered if they could see Mos behind him, furious, ready with a clipboard of lies to cover up this transgression. Geno looked right and left, going around the circle. Counting pairs of feet.

Mos was one. Geno was among many.

Maybe there was another way to rule this land.

"You got this," Corley said quietly.

Geno pulled in a double lungful of air and leaned a little more into the circle.

I, he thought. *I am Mos. I decide what feels.*

"The house the police raided," he said, holding his breath. "I was there. In the basement. I was there almost two days. I got raped by seven guys." He licked his dry lips and added in a faint whisper, "It happened to me."

As one, the heads in the circle nodded. Hands fisted onto knees. Muscles bulged in clenched jaws. Faces pale and eyes wide as the rotting meat of Geno's story plopped onto the pile in the center of the ring.

"Breathe, man," Hasan said.

Nobody touched him, nobody looked away. No averted gazes or hands sliding over mouth and nose to create some kind of shield. His comrades sat still, stony and attentive, like a fence of Easter Island statues.

"Breathe," Nolan said. "You did a great thing today."

Geno waited to feel triumph. Or relief. Or validation.

He only felt sick to his stomach. Nobody followed him into the men's room, but when he came out, Pablo was waiting with a bottle of water and Hasan gave him some peppermint candy.

Geno threw up a lot that first week in therapy. Anxious puking was common in this place, as was gallows humor treatment.

"How you doing, man?" one would ask.

"I only threw up once today," another would answer, to admiring looks.

Weak and dehydrated and riddled with anxiety, Geno had no energy for any of the other activities. Like when they went over to the other side of the building every day for art therapy, whatever that was. Geno had to go, in that he was required to be present in the room. Once there, he sat and looked out the window and felt sick.

Gradually, his mind shook off a bit of the fog and looked around. His eyes picked out more people who were part of his world now, like the therapists on the other side of the old warehouse.

Beau deBrueil looked like Paul Bunyan. Tall enough to block the sun, big as a pile of boulders, with a beard that arrived in the room ten seconds before he did. Aedith Johnson had a gap-toothed smile taller than it was wide, with a Milky Way galaxy of freckles across her broad face. Katie Bernstein was pale as a glass of milk, her plump body always in demure vintage dresses that looked straight out of *Leave it to Beaver.*

Steffen Finch was a built silver fox, with rings on all his fingers and tattoos crawling along his neck and arms. His eyes were deep blue and their direct, quietly confident gaze made Geno feel his atoms were being scrutinized. Like the other day when Geno did Stef's dumb line-drawing exercise. Christ, what a load of pop psychology bullshit. *Make your line bigger, kid, it'll fix everything.* Geno went along, just to get the guy off his back, and for fuck's sake he'd almost started crying. Over *lines.*

"I'd like to work with you," Stef said.

Hell, no. Group therapy was hard enough without turning your ordeal into the Sistine Chapel. *And* with an artistic Jedi master who missed nothing. Fuck that. Geno made a point of keeping his distance from Stef, yet something about the man kept drawing Geno's attention. The energy changed when Stef came into the art room. It didn't ratchet up or fly apart, rather it pulled together and concentrated.

"Day doesn't really start until Stef gets here," Beau said. "Like he's the key that opens the place for business."

"What if he goes on vacation?" Geno asked.

Beau's smile split his big beard apart. "Then I'm in charge."

Stef definitely had a gravitational pull, but it didn't yank on you. It beckoned and soothed. It *attended*. When Stef was in a session, nothing else existed in the universe. A meteor could come through the tall windows and Stef's concentration wouldn't falter. This hyper-attentive force field scared the crap out of Geno, yet it fascinated him. Sometimes he felt a weird envy when Stef was focused on his clients, resurrecting Geno's conflict of wanting to be left alone and fearing being left alone.

I wish he'd look at me like th— Oh fuck, no, dude, do not *look at me like that.*

During free time, Stef sat among residents with his own sketchpad, sometimes chatting about this and that, other times quiet and absorbed. Geno often walked behind to peek, amazed how Stef, using only pencils, could pull something *up* out of the paper. A flick of the point here, a sideways shading there, a smudge of his thumb and you could reach into the pad and gather the thing into your fingers.

He's cool, Geno thought grudgingly, sliding his hand into his pocket where Stef's card was still tucked. *He wants to work with me.*

People in hell wanted ice water.

If work was to be done, Geno would decide when.

INSIDE THE RADIO

*T*HE KITCHEN BECKONED Geno every day. He spent most of his unscheduled time down there, prepping and cleaning and cooking. After two weeks of low-grade nausea, he was nibbling his way back to an appetite. Betty, the head cook, was indulgent with his grazing. A piece of carrot here. A stick of celery there. An apple. A banana. Another banana. An oatmeal cookie. A third banana with some peanut butter on it. He could finally taste things. His stomach wanted to be full again.

The buzzing at the edges of his brain was driving him crazy. It was like being touched with a live wire, making his awareness fade out. Only for a split second, like the vacuum apex of a yawn. Once or twice wasn't anything, but getting zapped all damn day was annoying as fuck. Still, between mini shocks, his head felt a little clearer. A chink of light shone into the gloom and he was noticing things and people. Getting used to the facility and his place in it.

His first month, he'd be strictly monitored. His antidepressants were kept at the infirmary. If he wanted an Ambien, an aspirin or even two lousy Tums, he had to ask the nurses for it. He could only leave the facility to go to appointments with Dr. Bloom and Dr. Stein, and only with a staff member accompanying him. Vern could sign Geno out for an activity or meal, but curfew was nine-thirty and not a minute later.

Everyone at EP had to chip in with the running of the place. To build community, Geno guessed. Besides residents, the kitchen saw a slew of volunteers during the week, each with his or her regular days. Geno looked forward to Mondays and Fridays, when a woman named Stavroula cooked. She was a mature version of his soap and water type. Always looking a little tousled and windblown, like she stepped straight off a sailboat and into the kitchen.

She was a big woman, easily five-ten, with solid shoulders and an impressive butt. Glancing at her, Geno tried to find an appropriate adjective to capture her fleshy presence. She wasn't fat. She had curves but the curves were long and vertical. Geno recalled his grandfather often using the term zaftig. He wondered if it meant women like Stavroula. Stacked and mighty, like the Commodores would say.

She's a brick…house.

A guy named Javier volunteered on Mondays and Fridays, too. He was ridiculously good-looking and should've been an asshole. Instead, he was self-effacing. Quiet, but his silence was abstracted. He always looked occupied with something, brows furrowed as if working out a problem. Sometimes his lips moved like he was talking to himself, to the point where Geno wondered if maybe Jav had a few screws loose upstairs. Staff and residents teased him about talking to imaginary friends and he always laughed along.

"It gets worse as I get older," he said.

Geno and Jav were often assigned to the early-morning prep shift. Jav always shook hands on arriving but didn't speak until he had at least two cups of coffee in him. They worked in companionable and efficient silence, listening to the radio, which was usually tuned to NPR.

"When I was a kid," Jav said, "I thought little people lived inside the radio."

Geno smiled. "My dad convinced me a little man lived inside the refrigerator who turned the light on and off."

The exchange didn't go any further. For some reason, Geno's tongue got tied-up when he was around Jav. Constantly thinking up and rejecting things to say and not sure why he cared how he sounded to Jav's ears.

If Pablo or Juan was working a kitchen shift, Jav spoke Spanish with them. It was half-conversation and half-competition to see who could speak the fastest. Jav always won.

"Dominicans," Pablo said. "You all talk like Death is breathing down your neck."

Jav laughed. "And I'm one of the slower ones."

Juan glanced at Geno. "Sorry," he said in English. "We're being rude."

"No you're not," Geno said in Spanish.

Pablo laughed and fired a carrot across the worktable. It was a typical substitute for physical interaction around here. Instead of punching a guy's shoulder or giving him a shove, you threw something at him.

"How's a nice Jewish boy like you speak Spanish?" Pablo said.

"My mother was from Mexico," Geno said. "Her grandparents immigrated there from Lithuania."

"¿En serio?" Jav said, eyebrows raised. "When?"

"I don't know, in the twenties, maybe? Whenever the U.S. started to make immigration quotas."

"So technically, you're not Latino," Juan said.

"No, I am," Geno said. "My maternal grandmother is Mexican. She converted."

"How'd her family take it?" Jav asked.

Geno shrugged. "I didn't hear that part of the story, but I imagine not too well."

"Every family has their hang-up," Jav said. For a moment, all the muscles in his face tightened like a fist, his eyebrows pulling together. Then he sighed and caught Geno staring. "¿Qué lo qué?" he said, smiling like a big brother. Shyness wrapped around Geno's throat like a scarf and he didn't answer.

Jav always spent his breaks writing by hand in a little notebook. Sometimes like the pen was on fire, sometimes with a lot of heavy, frustrated exhales and staring into space.

"Are you writing a story?" Geno asked one day. "Or is that a journal?"

Jav looked up. "Stream of consciousness journal. Hopefully to be a book someday."

"A book about what?"

"I don't have the elevator pitch yet. Much to my agent's annoyance."

"You have an agent? So, you're like a real writer?"

"Well, I often feel like a fraud," Jav said. "But yeah, I write for a living."

"How many books do you have?"

"Three published. The fourth is being edited." Jav fanned the pages. "This mess will be my fifth."

"Huh. Would I know any of them?"

"I write under a pen name. Gil Rafael." Jav told him the titles and Geno shook his head, not recognizing any.

"How'd you come up with Gil Rafael?" he asked.

Jav ran his palm in circles around the cover of the notebook. "Gil is a family name. Rafael is my dad."

"What's you dad do?"

"He died when I was seventeen, but he owned a restaurant in Queens."

"Oh. I'm sorry." Geno hesitated. "My dad was a lawyer." Another beat. "He died last summer. I was seventeen, too."

"Lo siento."

"Is your mom alive?"

"No," Jav said. "I left home right after my dad passed and was estranged from my mother and sister. They've both passed away. My nephew and I are the last leaves on the family tree."

"Why'd you leave home?"

Jav pushed his lips out a little, brow furrowed. "A cousin and I got into some trouble. And he let me take the fall. Threw me under the bus, if you want to be honest. Everyone turned on me. It got abusive and I left."

Geno's eyes seemed to blink in slow motion. "Do you ever see your cousin?"

"No, he died too," Jav said with a faint smile. "Because the tale wasn't tragic enough."

"Did you ever find out why he turned on you?"

"No. That will be a mystery until I reach the other side." Jav's broad shoulders shrugged. "And I'm not sure I need to know anymore. Somehow I have a feeling he was caught up in a tragedy of his own, and he did what he did to survive. Until he couldn't do it anymore." He picked up the notebook and whacked it lightly against his other palm. "I don't know, man. I spent so many years embittered and angry. You reach a point where letting go and forgiving is easier. Less exhausting, at least. I mean, it still matters. It shaped my life and made me who I am. But all things considered…" His gaze went around the kitchen and came back to Geno. "It's not such a bad little life."

Geno nodded, lost in thought as he touched the edges where his story and Jav's story overlapped. Sharp and keen with betrayal, dull with sadness. The space between where *why* lived.

Why? Why'd you do it? Tell me why.

Your hand poised to knock, to make a fist and bang on the door and demand *why?*

But you didn't.

I'm not sure I need to know anymore.

GOOD MUSIC

Monday mornings, Geno went down to the kitchen at the crack of dawn for prep work. Jav typically stumbled in a little after five. Today, instead of Stavroula, an old man was in the kitchen. The hale kind of old, muscled with years of hard work, his white hair pulled into a little tail at the back of his neck and his thick eyebrows black. Like Martin Scorsese with a mustache.

"Ke haber, habibi?" he said to Jav.

"Miguelito, komo estash?" Jav gave him a hug. "Geno, this is Stavroula's father."

"Micah Kalo," the old man said, shaking Geno's hand.

"Geno. Hi." He couldn't see anything of Stavroula in this man. Stavroula's musculature went up and down while Micah's went sideways. Even his face was broader and wider.

Maybe Stavroula looked like her mother.

"Poor Stavi is sick to her bones," Micah said. "I am here instead."

"Who's making bagels?" Jav asked.

"It's done. I got up at three, made the dough. Now I'm here. I made coffee."

"You kill the average guy." Jav went to pour a cup.

Geno looked at the blackboard where Betty had written instructions for the morning prep. French onion soup was on the lunch menu. Micah was ripping open net bags of onions and spilling them onto the worktable. Fifty pounds of those suckers to be chopped.

"The cooks who cry together, stay together," Micah said, taking up a knife.

Steeling his eyes, Geno tied on an apron, got his own knife and dug in.

It was brutal work. He and Jav kept stepping away to push damp paper towels into their eye sockets, laughing through the streaming tears, blowing their noses and going back. Meanwhile, Micah quietly chopped and chopped, only making the occasional swipe at his eyes.

"All right, old man," Jav said. "What's your secret?"

"Contact lenses," Geno said.

Micah smiled, shaking his head. He made an exaggerated swallow and said, "Spit."

"What?"

"The chemical in onions is attracted to moisture. It loves your tear ducts. So you have to trick it by giving it something else wet to love. You let the spit collect in your mouth and keep your mouth open just a little. Gross, but effective."

Geno tried it. Beside him, Jav went quiet, lips twisting, clearly trying to keep the laughter back as he worked up some spit.

"Don't drool," Micah said, pointing his knife across the table.

"'Sgusting," Jav said through his teeth.

It actually did work. With the gooey puddle behind his bottom teeth, Geno could chop through a good seven or eight onions before his eyes needed a break.

"That's a good trick," he said. "Where'd you learn it?"

"I don't remember. Here or there." Micah corralled his last batch into one of the big silver prep bins and reached for his cup of coffee. A line of blue numbers was tattooed on the inside of his forearm. "When I was a boy starving in Greece, we used to save up our spit for hours. Swallowing it a little at a time to trick our stomach into thinking it was getting soup."

"When was this?" Jav asked, as Geno went on staring. He'd never seen a concentration camp number in person.

"Winter of forty-one, forty-two," Micah said. "Three hundred people a day starving to death. Corpses frozen in the streets." His bushy eyebrows raised over the rim of the mug. "Friend of mine lived through the siege of Leningrad. Each has stories about hunger only the other believes."

"I can't even imagine," Jav said. "How old were you?"

"During the famine? Thirteen." Micah set down the cup and wiped off his hands. "Aora," he said, walking toward the stove. "We've cried enough. Time to light the hearth."

Geno found Jav's sober gaze with his own. Jav slowly shook his head, his red, damp eyes closing a moment, then opening. "Historias de anhelos que solo el otro cree," he said softly.

Stories about hunger only the other believes.

Micah clanged the three big kettles onto the front burners. Into each he glugged copious amounts of olive oil and a half-pound of butter. Soon the smell of frying onions was curling up in Geno's stomach, making it rumble and growl.

"Javier, presiado," Micah said. "Toast up some of that bread there, yeah?"

Presiado, Geno thought, his ears curious. All morning Micah and Jav had used words that sounded like Spanish but weren't. Like *komo etash* instead of *Cómo estás. Presiado* sounded like *precioso.* Precious.

"Do you speak Spanish?" Geno asked.

"Ladino," Micah said, turning the flame down low under the kettles. "Sephardic Jewish dialect."

"It's like drunk Spanish," Jav said.

"Like Spanish got plowed and had a one-night stand with Yiddish." Micah scooped fried onions onto buttered toast and ground black pepper on top. "There. Wrap your bellies around that, habibis."

Geno sank his teeth through caramelized goodness into toasty gold. Jav poured them more coffee and the three men sat eating, mostly silent except for tiny grunts of pleasure.

"Fried onions on toast," Jav said. "So simple, but you never think of it."

"Simple food is best," Micah said, reaching to switch on the radio. He turned the dial through talk, static, classic rock and rap before landing on an oldies station. *Real* oldies. Big band and crooners from the 1940s. Music Analisa Gallinero liked to listen to on Sundays. When Micah warbled along to Dinah Shore's "Shoo Fly Pie," Geno sang a little, too.

> *Shoo fly pie and apple pan dowdy*
> *Makes your eyes light up, your tummy say "Howdy..."*

"See," Micah said to Jav. "This boy knows good music." As his hand reached to ruffle Geno's hair, the blurred, blue numbers fluttered on the skin of his forearm.

Finishing his simple breakfast, Geno thought about stories of hunger nobody would believe. Corpses in the street. A starving teenager with a carefully guarded mouthful of saliva, watching as he became number 157701. The horrors he had witnessed up until that point. All the horrors yet to come. The lengths gone to survive. The will to stay alive, so he could become an octogenarian listening to Glenn Miller and frying up onions on toast.

As Geno ate and thought, a hundred questions piled up in his head.

He asked none. He wasn't sure he'd be one of the others who would believe the answers.

That afternoon, during free time in the art room, he sought out Steffen Finch. Heart behind his teeth, he asked if the offer to work together still stood.

AWARE OF THE STARS

"**M**AX STAYS WITH you," Ronnie said. "Obviously. We won't touch that relationship. Who else do you feel can't be transitioned?"

"Juan," Stef said. "His assailant is out on parole and he's already struggling. And Pablo. He's coming up on another surgery and if this one doesn't work, he'll have that colostomy bag for the rest of his life. It'll be a bitter pill. I don't want to disturb anything around his therapy right now. So it's Max, Juan and Pablo. Those are my three I absolutely need to keep. And now Geno."

"Four tough cases, Obi-Wan," Ronnie said.

"If it gets to be too much, you'll be the first to know." Stef checked his watch. "Geno starts today, I don't want to be late."

"Go. May the force be with you."

Stef didn't make many rules for his clients, but each of them was given a brand-new sketchpad and required to do one drawing a day.

"I can't draw," Geno had said, fanning the heavy, blank pages with his thumb.

"This isn't about talent," Stef said.

"I don't know what to draw."

"Draw anything. Think back to your kindergarten self. What things did you draw at school? What did your mother hang on the fridge?"

Geno came to his first private session and opened the pad to show two boys, dressed alike. Stars filled the two inches of space between their bodies.

"Is this you and your brother?" Stef asked.

"Yeah."

"Can you tell me about the stars?"

Geno got up and walked away to the windows. He stood looking out at the High Line a long time, then came back to sit. "The stars," he said, clearing his throat. "It's called Nos."

Stef was quiet. Geno picked up a yellow marker and started coloring the galaxy between the boys.

"Nos," he said again. "It means *we* or *us* in Spanish. And it rhymes with dos. Two."

"Tell me more."

"It was the bond. The place where two became one. Probably sounds crazy to you."

"Who am I to say what it sounds like? I'm not a twin."

Geno's shoulders relaxed a little. He picked up scissors and cut up the center of the paper, through the starry bond, severing the twins. "Anyway, I don't go there anymore."

"Because your brother died?"

"Because he fucking set me up," Geno said through his teeth. "He lured me into a trap. He… He fucking sold me."

Stef nodded.

"I couldn't believe… How could he just…? My own fucking brother." The chair scraped against the floor and Geno was over by the window again, forehead and palms pressed to the panes.

Inside looking out, Stef thought, remembering the young boy from the domestic violence shelter and his art project with the flashing lights.

Geno came back again. He fitted the two pieces of paper together, lining up the edges. Then he separated them, took one and crumpled it into a ball. He seized the scissors and jammed the points straight down into the wad. They stood majestically for a moment, then toppled over.

"I feel like Michael Corleone in *The Godfather,*" he said. His voice turned husky. "You broke my heart, Fredo…"

"He betrayed you."

Geno smoothed the paper. "I can't take him out in a rowboat and shoot him."

"Would you?"

Tears tracked down Geno's face as he cut his twin into pieces. "Probably not. I wouldn't know what to… I don't know what I'd do if he were alive. I don't know what to do now he's dead."

Stef checked the urge to sigh heavily at the fuck-load of unresolved shit this boy needed to work through. "Do you ever remember a time," he said, "when you and Carlos were… Hold on, I'm not sure what I'm asking." He made a quick sketch on his own pad: two men and the starry bond between. "This is the place of two." He circled the stars.

"Nos. Rhymes with Dos," Geno said. "And we had names in there. Secret names. He was Los and I was Mos. God, I never told this to anyone."

"You'll find we go back and forth between two kinds of secrets in therapy," Stef said. "Nos and your hidden names are private, privileged secrets from the experience of being a twin. Those belong to you, and I don't want you to think I'm pushing you to betray them. They're vastly different than the secrets that were *imposed* on you. The secrets that threaten to hurt you if you reveal them."

"I know, I get it. It's just hard to explain."

"Here's where I'm trying to go," Stef said, circling the stars again. "When you overdosed on Vicodin and your friends called nine-one-one, they told police your name was Carlos. They said *you* told them the abduction and sexual assault happened to your brother, Geronimo."

Geno nodded slowly. "Yeah, I…switched us."

"When did you start being him?"

"It was just the once."

Stef sat back a hair, confused. "The night of your suicide attempt was the first time?"

"The only time." Geno's upper lip curled at the corner. "What, you think I've been pretending to be *him* all this time?"

"It was the impression I got when Dr. Stein first explained the situation."

Geno dragged his hands through his hair, hunched over the table a moment, poised on an edge. "What I did… I know what I did. I had to do it to survive."

Stef sat still and waited.

"I did become someone else. Sort of. Or I split part of my head in two so it could be like…" The boy pressed the heels of his hands to his eyes and spoke behind them. "It was all happening to someone else."

"It's an extremely common defense tactic," Stef said. "Disassociate from the situation to the point where you float up above yourself, looking down."

Geno brought his face out, blinking. "Exactly like that. I was outside my body, watching it happen. It was the only way I could get through it."

Stef's finger touched the paper and circled the stars. "You watched from here?"

"Yeah. As Mos."

A click in Stef's mind as two links of a chain joined. "*Mos* watched what was happening to Geno."

"Yeah."

"So you were split into the two aspects of *yourself.* Not split into you and Carlos."

"No. Shit, I didn't want anything to do with him. When I went into Nos, the first thing I did was kick him out."

"You kicked him out."

"Hell, yeah."

"So for the first time in your life, you were truly alone in the world."

"Mm." Tongue clamped between his teeth, Geno cut the pieces of Carlos into even smaller slivers.

"Are you still aware of the stars?" Stef asked.

"He's dead."

"I know. But I wondered if they were still a presence."

Pieces of paper drifted through Geno's fingers like snowflakes. "We always spoke in we. We're doing this. We went here. We want that. We slept in the same bed until we were six. I mean, we had bunk beds, but we were always in one together. Tangled up tight. That's how we were born. When they did the ultrasound on my mom, the doctor laughed and said, 'Forget it, you'll never deliver them this way. Look at them, they're in a *knot.*' Dad said during the C-section, it took a long time to sort out whose limbs were whose and what cord attached to which kid."

His face was filled with a soft nostalgia, as if he remembered the day well. Stef imagined it was a story told at every Thanksgiving and birthday.

"Anyway," Geno said. "What was I saying?"

"You were talking about bunk beds."

"Eventually we started sleeping apart. When we were ten, we got our own bedrooms. But after my mother died…"

A long pause.

"The night of the funeral, Carlito came in my room. 'Can I crash?' And I wanted him to. I needed him there." He glanced up at Stef. "I mean it's not like we were spooning or cuddling. But in the morning, we woke up and our ankles were stacked up like Lincoln Logs. It just happened."

"It was comforting," Stef said.

"Yeah."

"For nine months of your life, you lived in a little world where it was just the two of you. Floating together. All you needed was each other. Nos sounds like the continuation of that place. I'm not a twin. I can't begin to understand the depth of the bond, but it makes perfect sense to me."

"I've never really talked about it."

"Probably a lot of people ask if you could read each other's minds."

"Oh, God, all the time," Geno said. "It was ridiculous. The most we could exchange was a greeting. Like I'd think *Nos* and throw it out there. Then I'd hear his voice come back saying *Dos*. I couldn't dial into his train of thought. Sometimes I could feel what he was feeling. Extreme emotions. If he was really upset or really scared or really tired. I remember once, I had a shit day. One of those days where everything goes wrong and he said to me, 'Push it over to my side tonight. I'll hold it. Get some sleep.'"

"Did you?"

Geno laughed a little. "I did. Gathered it all up and imagined handing it to him. Not even imagined. It felt real. Throwing it across the stars so he could take it. I went right to sleep."

"Was there ever a situation so intense or upsetting, for both of you, you couldn't pass anything to the other?"

Geno's eyebrows furrowed a moment, then smoothed out. "I don't really get what you're asking."

Stef smiled. "Neither do I, to be honest."

Geno's shoulders rose and fell. "Oh well."

"Doesn't matter. It's the journey, not the destination."

"Oh, that's one I've never heard before, doc."

Stef laughed. "Every cliché was original at one point."

"Are you a doctor?"

"No. At some point I may go for a Ph.D., but no plans at the moment."

"Mm." Geno swept cut-up paper into a pile next to the intact drawing of his severed self. Only a bit of starry border left at his hip. "Are we done today?"

"We're done."

"See ya." Geno pushed back and stood up. Only a few steps away, he turned and pointed at the table. "What do you do with that?"

Stef touched the pile of paper scraps. "This?"

"All the stuff I make in here."

"It gets saved in your folder."

"All of it?"

"All of it."

"When I get out, I take it with me?"

"It belongs to you," Stef said.

Geno rolled his eyes. "What am I supposed to do with it?"

"Whatever you want. Chuck it. Burn it. Wipe your ass with it."

A bubble of laughter made Geno's face into something beautiful. "Good one, Finch. You need more lines like that."

FEBRUARY

A BEAUTIFUL LIFE

*G*ENO TOLD STEF about Nos.

He gave up his secret name.

It ought to have felt like selling his soul. Instead, it felt like he had gifted his greatest treasure to Stef. *Entrusted* it into his hands. A surrender so solemn, it bordered on holy. A vulnerability that left Geno free.

I am letting you hold the most elemental part of my being. If anything happens to me, it's on you.

The broken bond once connecting him with Carlos now regenerated and attached itself to Stef. Not filled with stars, but with winged horses holding strung bows at the ready. Protection instead of sympathy.

I trust him.

Geno felt a weird guilt that he wasn't bonding as intensely with any of the other residents. He supposed he didn't *have* to, but it bothered him.

"If I had to pick anyone I identify with," he said to Stef, "then I guess it's Jeff and Chaow."

"Why?"

"Because all the other guys in my group therapy were raped by someone they knew. Me, Jeff and Chaow, we were raped by strangers. Not that it makes a... See, now I sound like an asshole."

"We're talking about how you *feel,*" Stef said. "Not what is or isn't, not how it sounds. All right? We're identifying emotions. Not labeling them as good, bad, moral, twisted, right, wrong. Emotions don't hold onto adjectives that way."

Geno's eyes flicked toward the ceiling. "If you say so, Finch." The tone was flip but beneath the dismissive snark, he fiercely believed the things Stef said. It gave him courage to try to explain what he meant.

Being in an environment with other men who'd been raped *did* help. It helped in that it didn't hurt him. Their company and affinity didn't shame him. He trusted their compassion and empathy. "I know, man" from the circle of chairs wasn't lip service. They knew. Some of the guys had been humiliated by police and dismissed by doctors. Some had family who denied the rape happened, others had friends who declared it wasn't rape. They *knew* how the personalized shame could become crippling when others carelessly, or even deliberately validated it. Making themselves the victim for having to hear your twisted, made-up story.

Men like you are the reason we need rape hotlines in the first place. You sick piece of shit.

All the residents had a Ruby of some kind. Someone who was supposed to help but didn't. All the men at EP respected Geno's ordeal and his recovery, and he respected theirs. Especially Pablo, who'd been raped with a broken mop handle and still wore a colostomy bag. He probably would the rest of his life. He only talked and laughed about it with Geno. Much like Geno and Chris Mudry had the privilege of making dead mom jokes, he and Pablo could make bag jokes. It was their bond.

But none of it *helped*. It didn't fix anything. It didn't make a tangible difference.

A micro-betrayal on top of all the mini and maxi ones.

"I just want to be a normal guy," Geno said. "Nothing about my life will ever be normal again."

"Normal means ordinary, right?" Stef said. "So what's the opposite of ordinary?"

Geno thought a moment. "I don't know. Special?"

Stef nodded. "Or extraordinary."

"Or bizarre."

"Does bizarre ring true?"

Geno said nothing.

"Think about it," Stef said. "It's true nothing about your life will be quote, unquote, ordinary. But it doesn't mean you've been branded a freak."

"Just a victim," Geno said.

"Or a survivor."

Not for the first time, Geno thought about the numbers on Micah Kalo's arm. The young boy living on the illusion of his own spit. The extraordinary lengths gone to survive. "I guess."

"It also means whomever you choose to love or be with in the future is going to be an extraordinary person as well."

Geno snorted. "To deal with my shit."

"To earn your trust and have the *privilege* of dealing with your legitimate shit."

Geno exhaled heavily. "I can't just… La de da, I was raped but life is beautiful."

"No," Stef said. "You were raped and parts of your beautiful life were taken away from you. You were raped and your life is different now. But it doesn't mean your life is diminished or disqualified. It doesn't make you any less deserving of a beautiful life." Stef leaned forward a little. "Does it?"

Geno's eyes burned and his throat squeezed around the answer.

"It sounds like an obvious question," Stef said. "But it's valid. Do you deserve it?"

The tears dripped down Geno's face.

"Do you deserve a beautiful life?" Stef said.

Geno nodded.

"You didn't deserve what happened to you and you do deserve a beautiful life. You deserve an extraordinary person whom you can trust with your heart and your soul and your body. And trust with everything that hurts and scares you, too. Do you believe it?"

"Yeah," Geno said, thinking, *Right now, that person is you.*

ON THE BEACH

*T*HE ART THERAPISTS at CCT were constantly trying new things, mixing and matching techniques and philosophies. No box could contain their creative thinking as they tried to channel debilitating internal pain into liberating external expression.

You never knew what would wake a client up. One week Stef set Zen gardens on each of the art tables. Large trays with sand, smooth polished rocks, and a small wooden rake. Geno, typically ambivalent to projects, played with it his entire session, raking patterns around the rocks then smoothing the sand out. Rearranging the rocks and starting over, talking the whole while.

"My brother and I got suspended freshman year," he said.

Stef raised his eyebrows.

"We had all the same classes and teachers, but different schedules. One day we had both an English test and a math test." He looked over at Stef. "Can you guess where this is going?"

"I have a pretty good idea."

As he spoke, Geno took all the stones out of the tray and ran a flat palm over the sand, obliterating the squiggled lines. "I was better at math. He was straight As in English. Teachers were constantly mixing us up anyway. So we swapped places. I took the math test for both of us, he took care of the English."

"How'd you get busted?"

Geno's finger flicked every stray grain of sand from the edge of the tray. "Identical tests. Identical mistakes. And when I wrote his name on his test, I put Carlito by mistake. He didn't use that name in school. It was a family thing."

"Oops."

"They called us into the office. Our parents showed up." The memory must have been visceral, because Geno's entire body winced as he placed a single stone in the center of the tray. "God, it *sucked.*"

"Yeah, that's one you eat for a long time."

The rake dragged around the perimeter of the stone. A painstaking effort to match up the lines as the circle closed. Geno made a second ring of lines around the first. He pulled the wooden teeth from the rings out to the edge of the tray, a snaking line.

"I don't have much more to tell," he said. "Just freestyling my feels. As one does."

Stef was pleased with the session. At the next one, he tried Geno at the sand table.

Geno snorted at the setup, but soon he was scooping up a fistful of sand and letting it tumble through his fingers. He poured from one palm to the other. Buried a hand beneath the surface and slowly watched it emerge.

"I always loved the beach," he said, mesmerized by the film of sand on the back of his hand.

"Did you go often?" Stef asked.

"Mm. We had a house in Mantaloking. We spent every summer there, ever since I can remember. Dad always took a picture of me and Carlito at this same place on the boardwalk…"

His body slid sideways, his cheek coming to rest on his knuckles, propped on an elbow while his other hand dug into the past. "The summer I was fifteen was hard. My mom was dying. She died around Halloween and that summer at the beach…we knew it was her last one. I didn't think we'd go the following year but we did. Dad said she'd want us to."

His stillness was magical. "Mom loved to collect sea glass. She loved the blue pieces, the real deep cobalt ones. They were like her holy grail. The first summer after she was gone, Carlito and I must've found twenty pieces. We weren't even trying. We just kept glancing down and seeing bits of blue while we were swimming or surfing. Or we'd be walking along and a piece would be sitting there in the sand. Waiting for us. *Hey, boys. It's me.*"

His chest expanded and contracted in long even breaths. He'd gone somewhere else. Somewhere peaceful, full of wistful memory more sweet than bitter. Stef let him be, knowing such serene moments were few and far between.

"Where are you right now?" he finally asked, softly, not wanting to break the spell.

"On the beach," Geno said.

"Who are you with?"

His mouth poised around unspoken words, Geno's eyes looked around the room, then his head swiveled left and right. "Just me," he said, looking puzzled. "Weird, I was feeling really young, like eight or nine. But I was walking by myself."

"You looked peaceful."

"Yeah." He sounded even more puzzled. He blinked a few times and sat up. He reached for water and poured it into the center of the sand bin, stirring it around with his fingers to make a thin mud.

"So, I was thinking," he said. "Something we talked about last time. My brother and I feeling the same thing together and not able to pass it off?" A muscle quivered in Geno's jaw as both his hands clenched in the wet sand. It oozed through his fingers. "I feel like I'm holding all of it now."

"Tell me." Two words Stef said eighty times a day.

"I think Carlito killed himself because it was too much to hold. Both what he got caught up in, and what he did to me. Some days, I don't give a shit what he had to carry. Other days, I feel like I'm carrying both of us. Like I really believe when a twin loses a twin, they take over everything the dead twin didn't… I mean… I don't know what I mean."

"You're doing great, just keep talking," Stef murmured.

"Like I'm carrying all the unfinished business for both of us. Like it's just *me* in the principal's office, getting chewed out for something stupid we did. But there's no *we* this time. I had nothing to do with… God, some days I hate his fucking guts. Other days I'd…" Geno turned his head to wipe his face on his sleeve. "I'd do anything to see him again. Because he's the only one who understands me. And I need to ask him. I need to *know*…"

Stef's layer of protective armor was cracking a little. He breathed slow, keeping his face and demeanor neutral.

"You need to ask him why," he repeated. "Why he did it?"

"Killed himself?"

"I meant why he brought you into Anthony's house."

"I literally do not want to know that reason," Geno said. "Ever. No reason could make me feel better. The reason is pointless. Useless. No justification exists for what my brother did to me."

He opened his hands and regarded the oblongs of sand, molded and creased to fit his palms. He exhaled a tremendous sigh, slumping in the chair. "I'm really scared that I'm just fucked up for life. Sometimes, I'm even kind of glad my father's dead and he can't see me like this." A tear snaked its way down the boy's face. "It would've killed him."

"You know," Stef said. "I have a dozen ways to explore that statement. But right now I'm going to isolate your concern for your father's well-being and say something I said before."

"What's that?"

"They didn't get the best of you."

Geno's face twisted, his chin dropping toward his chest.

"You still have the best parts of you," Stef said. "I don't think they're lost. I think you put them away somewhere really, really deep inside, where no one can ever touch or hurt or betray them again."

"I don't know where I am," Geno said, fingers moving through the sand.

"The good parts of you are still there. The best parts of you. Your parents are gone but you're still a good son. Your brother betrayed you, betrayed Nos, yet you still feel the weight of his stars. These are signs of a decent, compassionate human being, not a fuck-up."

"Everything hurts so much," Geno said. "I just want it to stop. I can't get away from it. It follows me everywhere and won't leave me alone. All day, every day, all I think is that I want to die, and I'm afraid I won't."

"You're afraid you won't die," Stef said.

"Yeah."

"Can we talk about that?"

The boy's shoulders flicked up and down.

"How often do you think about suicide?"

"Every day."

"Do you have a plan?"

The head shook slowly side to side.

"So it's an ideation of suicide but you don't have any methods lined up."

"No." Now the red-rimmed, blurry eyes found Stef's gaze. "That's good, right?"

Stef nodded. "Suicide is often a metaphor for stopping the pain. You want the pain to die while keeping yourself. You have ideas, but no plans. But when suicidal thoughts are accompanied by stockpiling pills or knowing where you can get your hands on a gun or planning which bridge you'll jump from... That's different."

"I wouldn't know where to get a gun," Geno said. "I'm afraid of heights. I don't have the guts to slit my wrists, stab myself or step in front of a train. I don't want any method that's going to hurt. I hurt enough. So that leaves pills. I tried those. Didn't work. I've listened to like six guys tell their failed overdose stories in group therapy. OD'ing doesn't seem to be a reliable method."

"It isn't."

"I want to die," Geno said slowly. "It's definitely an idea. But I don't think I want to...*kill* myself."

"If your ideas start making plans, do you think you could tell me? Or Dr. Stein? Or anyone you have a shred of trust for?"

The breath Geno drew in trembled. As if this were the scariest thing he could be thinking. "Yeah," he said. "I could tell you."

THE COLOR BENEATH

*D*AYS STACKED UP into weeks, each day following a pattern of sleep, meds, meals, activities, appointments. Group therapy, shifts in the kitchen and time in the art room.

Geno spent about a third of his sessions talking, then Stef came up with some kind of exercise. Sometimes Geno could see the connection to what they'd been discussing, other assignments seemed totally random. Either way, he tried his best. Laughing a little too heartily at his pathetic attempts to be artistic, even as something in his gut blinked at Stef with hopeful eyes, wanting to please.

"You don't suck as bad as you think," Stef said.

"Don't sweet talk me, Finch."

"I'm not. You got a raw talent. Maybe you don't have technique. You don't understand perspective and you shade things bass-ackward. But the way you *see* is special. When you get out of your own way, your subconscious and your imagination come up with some really cool stuff."

Stef's finger ran along the edge of Geno's self-portrait. It was a close-up of his face. The features were all out of proportion and he'd stuck to a safe palette of neutral colors. He spent a lot of time on the eyes, consulting magazine photos and books he found on the art room shelves. In each dilated pupil was the reflection of a twin bed. In the left eye, a figure lay in the bed, hands cuffed to the iron headboard. In the right eye, the bed was empty, the cuffs dangling unused from a rail.

For the assignment of an abstract self-portrait, Geno did little more than lay down a black background, then dump a mess of brown, grey and yellow on the paper, swirling it together in clouds of gloom. Nervousness squeezed him as Stef looked it over.

"No adjectives," Geno said, poking at the damp paper with the tips of scissors, gouging holes in it. "It's just how I feel."

Stef had an ocean wave tattooed on the side of his neck, a single bird flying above its crest. Now, as he nodded, the tendons in his throat flexed, making the bird come alive.

"Yeah," he said. "That's pretty much how I imagine you'd feel." His fingertip moved along a sharp delineation between the black background and the sickly clouds. "This right here is…"

"What?" Geno said.

"I don't know. Something like a sandstorm moving across the desert at night. How it would obscure the stars."

Stef took the paper over to the window. Geno thought he was setting it on the sill to dry. Instead, Stef leaned the paper against the panes, reaching long for a roll of scotch tape to fasten down the corners. He stood back, arms crossed and staring a moment, then looked over his shoulder at Geno.

"Look how the sunlight comes through the holes," he said. "Like the stars are still there."

Geno's next assignment was harder. Another abstract self-expression, but Stef said it had to not only be before the rape, but before his mother died.

"Why then?" Geno asked.

"Because you've often said it was the last time in your life you remember being completely happy."

I say too fucking much in here, Geno thought.

"Try to draw that happiness." Stef said, setting down the blank paper. "Show who you were when you were fourteen. Or even before your mother got sick for the first time. When was that, eleven?"

Eleven, Jesus.

It took Geno a good twenty minutes to work through the frustration of not remembering, then the frustration of not being able to express what he did remember. Then of course, he wanted it to look good, which further frustrated him.

He was fidgeting with the star of David on his chain, cursing under his breath. When all at once the bit of gold took on weight in his fingers. It seemed bigger. *Louder.*

He remembered asking Jav how he came up with ideas for stories. Jav shrugged and called it The Thing. When a portal to some elusive and eternal source of creativity opened inside Jav's head, his fingertips went all itchy, his eyes stared through particles of oxygen and he started mumbling under his breath.

"I have no idea where it comes from," he said. "Maybe The Thing happens to all of us, but only some of us listen to it?"

Lips faintly moving as The Thing whispered in his ear, Geno picked up a pencil and drew a six-pointed star, then drew a circle around it. He frowned. Both shapes were lopsided and off-center. This needed to be perfect. Precise. He got up and prowled along the shelves of supplies, tilting bins and rifling their contents. "I need a compass," he said.

"North is that way," Hasan said, pointing.

"No, no, like a geometry compass."

"Right here," Stef said, striding over and opening a drawer. It was full of drafting tools. "See? The compass never worries."

Geno hesitated, the tool clutched in his hand as the memory of the day Analisa died closed around him. The geometry test. The principal at the classroom door. Geno slamming his fist against the desk and the compass point stabbing his palm. The blood he wiped on his jeans. The little piece of stained denim carried in his wallet all these years.

He looked at Stef and wanted to explain, but he was itching to get started.

"Go chase down that idea," Stef said. "Before it finds another artist."

Armed with compass, straightedge and protractor, Geno started over. Circle first. Then degrees marked. Lines to make the star of David within. Another circle. Curved around the top half, he lettered *Natan ben Heironim*. Beneath, he wrote *Gallinero*. He enclosed the lettering in another circle. Then made another ring and filled it in with music notes.

Completely absorbed, Geno marked and measured, drawing radiating lines in precise, five-degree increments. The circles grew bigger, rippling out from the star of David.

"It's a mandala," Stef said.

A ring of little hens, another of hunchbacked Quasimodos. Hearts. Houses. Kitchen knives. Radios. His own tattoo designs, symbols and signs. When he blanked out, he lettered his name round and round. *Geronimo Gallinero Caan Geronimo Gallinero Caan Geronimo Gallinero Caan…*

With a fine-tipped Sharpie, he inked over all the penciled marks, then took a week adding color. When he was done, a church's stained-glass window filled the paper, dazzling and dizzying.

"Now watch." Stef took the sandstorm-desert self-portrait and laid it on top of the mandala, lining up the edges. *Now* holding *Then* hostage.

"Well, there you have it," Geno said. "I can't find the old me."

"Sure you can," Stef said.

"Can I?"

"Think about it. You've already started."

"You mean therapy?"

"No. Think more literal."

Geno stared at the sickly grey and dun clouds. Slowly he realized Stef meant the holes. He reached and started to widen a few. Tearing them open. Showing the color beneath.

"There you are," Stef said.

EVERY STEP MEANS SOMETHING

*T*HE DAYS BEGAN to orient themselves around Geno's sessions with Stef. More often than not, Geno left them feeling better. Stef could always reach into the junk heap of Geno's soul and extract a tiny piece of gold. One little nugget of truth that sustained him through another day.

Stef began to show up in his dreams. Geno would be climbing a mountain or trekking down a long road. Stef gave a boost, threw a rope or directed the route.

Hold on, let me check first. No, don't go that way. It's not safe. Come this way. Follow me.

In dreams Stef stayed close by. Tough and tattooed and immutable, but soft with compassion. Firm, but gentle. Like a father.

Or a big brother.

Sometimes Geno woke from the dreams alarmed. *Am I crushing on him?*

He reviewed the imagery carefully. *No, I'm just trusting him.*

Everyone trusts him. He's good at what he does.

Geno watched Stef work with Juan one day. Clearly unearthing some painful insight because Juan broke down. Geno could tell it wasn't a clean, cathartic cry but one of those jags that made you feel you were utterly losing your grip on the world. This one would kill you. You were done. Defeated. You couldn't go on anymore.

Stef got Juan to walk. He did this a lot with residents having a breakdown. To attach gross motor movement to the experience. To be present in the moment so you could remember later (if you were alive) you survived. To show that you could carry the fuck on even as you were being shredded into pieces.

"It's all right," Stef said. "Keep moving with me. Every step means something. You're doing great."

Juan leaned on him like a wounded soldier, stumbling and shuffling with a hand over his face. His other hand in a white-knuckled clench on Stef's shirt. Hanging on. Trusting Stef to walk him the hell out the other side.

Another time, Geno arrived in the art room to the sound of sobbing. A pathetic wail that went on and on without a pause for breath. Ebbing and flowing like a siren. Over by the windows, Stef was pacing. His youngest client, six-year-old Max, draped on his broad shoulder, crying and crying.

Geno stared as Stef walked back and forth, backlit by the sunlight pouring through the glass, his hand rubbing between the little boy's shoulder blades as he talked.

"I know he said boys don't cry. That's baloney. I cry all the time, Max. You can cry, too."

Geno's arms itched, remembering his nephew's trusting weight and the press of a wet face in his neck.

"It's all right," Stef said. "You cry as much as you want."

Max moaned and wept harder.

"I'm right here. I got you."

Geno couldn't look away. He could feel that solid mass of muscle and bone under his face. Stef's chest pressed to his. His strong arms carrying Geno away from all of this, like a kvater. The hand between his shoulder blades. The shushing air between his teeth. The beautiful, perfect words that broke apart chains and knocked down prison walls.

I know what he said. He was wrong. He lied to you. I am telling you the truth now. I am here to put it right.

Geno wanted it. He could *taste* that mighty protection. The sweetness of having a champion.

He craved it.

He began to dream about it.

He dreamed of being his grown self in a child's body and Stef was carrying him. Sometimes draped on his shoulder. Sometimes cradling Geno in both arms. This time, being a baby boy was so pure and peaceful and secure.

Hold me, brother mine.

I am one chick in an empty henhouse.

"How have your anxiety levels been?" Dr. Stein asked.

"Better," Geno said. "It doesn't seem as constant as it used to. I still get panic attacks but not every day. I'm getting better at getting through them."

"What do you do?"

"Visualize safe places. Or places I remember being happy. I remembered the other day how much I liked being at the beach. Stef found this app I could download that plays different kinds of white noise. One setting is ocean waves. It helps get me into that place in my head."

"Ah," Stein said, nodding. "Excellent."

"Stef's got a lot of good ideas."

"I'm glad you're working with him. He's extremely insightful as well as creative. He comes at a problem from all directions."

"Yeah, he's good. They're all good there. Even some of the people who aren't therapists are good. I mean, I feel like I made a few friends."

In fact, he had to build an addition onto his little henhouse. Stef already had a room. Now Javier and Stavroula had moved in.

Geno watched them all the time in the kitchen, studying their interactions like a map. Putting down pins when Jav's gaze went far away into the zone where his ideas lived, then came abruptly back when Stavroula walked by.

Gotcha, Geno thought. Pin after pin making a route when he caught Jav looking at Stavroula. Quick little glances, like he was taking careful spoonfuls of some delicious dessert. Stavroula's eyes on Jav weren't as intense, but she called him cookie sometimes. Like he was something she wouldn't mind nibbling on. The guys gave him a ton of shit about it, helping themselves to his new nickname.

"Hey," Jav said, a finger pointing around. "Only Stavroula calls me cookie. Everyone else, it's Mr. Cookie."

He totally likes her, Geno thought.

Stavroula was easy to like. And goddamn, she had that *look.* The clean, simple beauty that came out of Geno's past like a long-forgotten memory. It was older on Stavroula, mature and solid and a little weathered. Still, it rested easy on his eyes, while the age difference kept it safely at a distance.

Her hair was brown, with pretty blonde highlights and a few faint streaks of silver. She had a way—as most women did—of gathering her hair up in a sloppy fist, winding an elastic around the whole mess and ending up with a bun that looked on the verge of falling apart, yet never moved. The shorter pieces of hair fell down around her temples. Over and over, she'd brush them to the side and tuck them behind one ear.

"Geno, look at her ears," Jav said. "They're the tiniest ears I've ever seen."

Stavroula laughed. "I'm like the opposite of an elf."

Her ears weren't pierced, either. Small, pink, perfect ears. Just like her fingernails: short, pink, unpolished and perfect. The veins and tendons of her hands lay close to the skin's surface. Swift, competent hands that chopped and sliced and stirred. When she leaned over a pot or bowl, her short hairs fell in her face and she pushed them back with the sleeve bunched around her elbow. The crook of her arm soft and secret, a single blue vein flickering. If you kissed that spot, would you feel her pulse?

Jav looked at her. Geno looked at him looking and it filled him with a warm, luscious pleasure. His eyes followed the path of Jav's finger, through the air to catch the tendril of Stavroula's silver-and-gold hair, drawing it back behind the pretty pink seashell of her ear.

"Oh, thank you," she said, laughing.

Are they together? Geno wondered. *Or getting there?*

His imagination sawed and hammered at the henhouse, assembling a master bedroom. Busting out a back wall to expand the kitchen. He hauled bricks and built a fireplace, dragging furniture around it. A comfy couch for Jav and Stavroula. Mismatched armchairs for himself and Stef. The door latched tight against foxes. Feet stretched toward the flames. Stavroula's hair tucked behind her little ears. Companionable silence within and the sound of ocean waves outside.

XAVIER

*T*OWARD THE END of February, Jav got Stavroula pregnant.

He didn't mean to. It was The Thing's fault. In the kitchen one day, Stavroula took her hands out of soapy dishwater and stretched. Back arched with one hand pressing into the small, kneading the muscles there. The other hand, thick with woven bracelets, brushed her bangs back, water droplets sliding down her forearm.

And shazam, she was pregnant.

Pregnant with the world, Jav thought, his fingertips itching. *Pregnant with the sun. The son or the sun?*

Little Ears was drawn out of the water. Bracelets of rope at her wrists. Her hair never dried. She was always pregnant.

She was on the ship a year before anyone thought to mention she hadn't had her baby yet.

That's when everyone knew she was pregnant with the world.

She was the one they'd waited for.

"What?" Stavroula said.

Jav blinked. "What?"

"Stop *staring* at me," she said, laughing.

"I'm not staring at you, I'm staring through you. An idea is on the other side. Hold still and let me get it."

She rolled her eyes but her face went rosy pink. "You're really making up a story right now?"

"A character. She might tell me a story."

"What will you name her?"

"I love Stav," he said. "And not just because it rhymes with Jav."

"It's a strong name," Geno said, who'd been quiet up until now. "What does it mean?"

"Stavroula? It's Greek for cross." Stavroula tucked her hair behind her ear. "My birth mother's last name was Cross."

"You're adopted?" Geno said.

"Mm-hm."

"Cross," Jav said. "That's a good name, too."

His shift was over and just in time. His head was starting to overflow. He had to get some of this down. He got a little lunch and sat at a table with his notebook, scribbling away. He'd filled two pages when his phone pinged an incoming text from Roger Lark.

Brother from another mother, Rog typed. *Got some news. Can I call you in about ten minutes?*

Sure, Jav typed back. *Good news or you-better-sit-down news?*

Good news. Bad news I send by registered mail. Talk in a few.

"This seat taken?" Geno said, appearing with a plate of ziti and meatballs.

"No, no," Jav said, putting down his phone and pushing a chair out with his foot. "Siéntate."

Geno plopped down with a long exhale. His dark hair, cropped short when Jav first met him, had grown in enough to start waving a little. His light brown eyes were smudged with fatigue.

"Qué lo qué," Jav said.

"Nothing."

"Feel all right?"

"Didn't sleep much last night."

Jav nodded sympathetically, capped his pen and let it roll into the notebook's spine.

"You're almost done with that notebook," Geno said.

"I know. And I still can't figure out what story I'm telling."

"What were you writing about Stavi?"

Now the circled eyes had the tiniest sparkle of curiosity, and Jav wanted to coax it bigger. "Oh, I'd tell you," he said. "But the voices in my head would say I had to kill you."

"Come on."

"No, I'm serious, they get really angry when I share the— Shh, wait." Jav put up a finger and tilted his head toward the ceiling. "Did you hear that?"

"You're ridiculous," Geno said, and right then, with the rolling eyes and the snort, he was Ari. Young, full of sass and bemoaning the tragic unhip-ness of the adult population. Jav's brain swelled with questions begging to be asked.

Where are you from? Where are your parents? How long will you be here? What happened to you?

Instead he asked, "Is Geno short for something?"

Geno looked up from his plate, brow furrowed.

"Sorry," Jav said quickly. "That's personal. I'm a writer. I like names. I read the newspaper just to collect them and sometimes—"

"It's short for Geronimo."

Jav sat back a little. "Shut up."

"Swear to God."

Geronimo, Jav thought. You couldn't think it quietly. It begged to be yelled. Preferably as you were jumping off a diving board.

Geno laughed now. "Dude, you're looking at me like I gave you a million dollars."

"That's the greatest name ever."

"My dad's father was Jerome. My mother wanted the Spanish version. Doesn't exactly go with Caan, but…"

"Caan. Like James Caan?"

"Yeah."

"Huh," Jav said, thinking, *Geronimo Caan.*

Yes, he Caan.

Jav chuckled then. *Wrath of Caan.*

"What?" Geno said.

"Nothing. It's a great name."

"So, what comes first when you're writing? The character or the name?"

"Usually the name." Jav tapped the cover of the notebook. "I have a ton of them in here. Like the other day I came across the name Ike. You don't hear many guys called Ike these days. It feels cool to say. A character named Ike would definitely be badass."

"Ike Turner?"

"Well, he was an asshole. I guess that theory's ruined. But I still think names with X or K sounds have a lot of strength." Jav was babbling a little now, his mouth jumping off the diving board. "Rex is Latin for king. Rex is a badass name. Javier in French is Xavier. If my parents changed one letter of my name, I could've had a whole different life. This is the kind of shit I think about."

"No, you're right," Geno said. "A lot of great leaders or legendary kings had those sounds. Constantine."

"Tutankhamen."

"Alexander."

"Lex Luther."

Geno laughed. "Christopher Columbus."

Jav pointed. "Carlos Quiñones Velázquez," he said, exaggerating all the hard syllables. "Not a king. Relief pitcher for the Milwaukee Brewers. Before your time."

Geno's expression trembled a little. He looked down and with his fork, drew lines through the tomato sauce on his plate. "My brother was Carlos. Carlos Caan."

"Oh."

"He died last summer."

Jav blinked, adding this death to Geno's father, also last summer. "Lo siento," he said. The obvious next question being, *What happened?* But he didn't ask.

"It's kind of similar to your situation," Geno said. "The thing you told me about with your cousin. How he turned on you and died before you could find out why? Something like that happened with my brother. Left me with a shit-load of unanswered questions and unfinished business."

"I see," Jav said. He switched to Spanish, drawing a bit more privacy around them. "Man, I'm sorry. You got my heart on that one. It's so hard not knowing why."

"Yeah." Geno made a vague gesture around. "One of the many pleasant things I'm working out in this place."

Jav tried not to laugh too heartily. "Was he older than you? Younger?"

"We were twins."

Jav's phone rang. He twitched at the sound, having forgotten about Roger. "Shit, that's my buddy. I have to take this."

"And I gotta go get my head shrunk." Geno took his half-empty plate and left.

"What's up, ugly," Rog said, voice booming over the line.

"Hey," Jav said, thrown by the abrupt end of one conversation and the quick-change into a different language and dynamic. "Where are you?"

"Hibernating in Vermont. But guess where the show's coming next?"

Jav hummed, eyes circling an imaginary globe, looking for locales Rog would be calling him about. "The Dominican Republic?"

"Close enough. Randall's Island."

"Get out," Jav said. "You're building a treehouse in Manhattan?"

"This is a first," Rog said. "I'll be in town maybe second week in March to scout the site with my team. Hopefully start building in April. Wrap-up end of June, budget willing."

As Jav took in the timeline, a germ of an idea took root in his mind. "Where will you live?"

"I'm crashing on your couch for three months. That okay?"

Jav opened his mouth, closed it. Managed a weak laugh. "Really?"

"No, dumbass. They find me a long-term hotel or a studio apartment."

"I see," Jav said. "Well, this'll be great. Let me know as it gets closer."

"Will do. How's your boyfriend, when you getting married?"

"Jesus," Jav said, laughing. "He's fine and not anytime soon."

"Tell him I said hi. Gotta run. Adiós, amigo."

Jav collected his things together, pulling the pen from the pages of the notebook and giving a broad glance at what he'd written. He'd had more but it was gone now. Flounced out in a jealous huff to find another writer.

Walking home, his head was a mess. Loose threads of ideas snarled in a knot. Women pregnant with the sun (or the son). Kings with X and K names. Names you had to yell rather than speak. The wrath of Caan (really, he needed to write that down). Last summer. How hard it was to not know. But hey, good news, Rog was coming to town. And needed a place to stay.

I could sublet him my place, Jav thought.

April to June. The lease is up in July.

Let Roger live at my place and I move downtown with Stef.

Three months. See how we feel.

Why not?

Is this too soon?

It's too soon. You're out of your mind.

It's just for the spring. See how it feels come summer.

His swirling mind pulled and tugged at the tangle of thoughts. Last summer. The high sun of summer. Pregnant with the summer sun. Or was it the summer sons?

The sun god, he thought. *The sun god is two sons. Sun sons. Twin gods born in the sun.*

Twin gods…

He stopped walking. *Last summer.*

He turned around, looked down Eleventh Avenue. He could just make out the facade of the brick warehouse where a boy Ari's age lived, got his head shrunk and worked out unpleasant things.

"Something like that happened with my brother," Geno said. "Unanswered questions and unfinished business."

We were twins.

"Twins last summer," Jav said under his breath, remembering newspaper headlines three inches tall. Remembering the effort it took to say *prostitution*. The worst-case what-if-ing on what might have happened to Ari if Jav hadn't been around. The luck that allowed Jav to survive and be there for his nephew. The there-but-for-the-grace fortune of not bouncing off the streets of Queens into the hands of…

"Oh my God," he whispered.

THE LAST CHAPTER

"A TREEHOUSE ON RANDALL'S Island?" Stef said.

Jav turned in his desk chair, taking off his glasses. "That's what Rog said."

"That'll be wild. How long will he be in town?"

"About three months. April to June, budget willing"

"Huh." Stef opened the fridge, got a beer and took a greedy chug. It had been a bitch of a day. During his session, Geno had a panic attack and threw up ziti and meatballs in the art room sink. The residents on custodial duty this week weren't too happy. The windows would be cracked open for hours, which gave the security guards extra agita. Incidental reports had to be filed in triplicate. And of course, Geno felt like a world-class loser. It added up to hours of damage control and little to show for it. Stef rarely went straight for the booze when the whistle blew, but today, he'd earned an ice-cold St. Ambroise and its 9.1% ABV.

Come to papa, sweet elixir of life…

He crouched down to let Roman say hello, which involved much sniffing and licking of ears. Also beer bottles, if they were within reach. "Easy, you lush," Stef said. "You're underage."

Jav clicked off the desk lamp and stood up. "So, I was thinking…"

"What about?"

"I could sublet my apartment to Roger."

Stef took another long pull and swallowed slowly. "And where would you live?"

Jav crossed his arms and shrugged. "Here?"

A long staring moment.

"I think that's a great idea," Stef said.

Jav groaned.

"What?" Stef said. "Was that the wrong answer?"

"Yes," Jav said. "You're supposed to say it's too soon."

"I am?"

"This is too goddamn easy."

"It is?"

Jav's eyes flashed almost angrily. "Jesus Christ, why are you *like* this?"

"Whoa, whoa, wait," Stef said, putting up his hands. "If you want to freak out, then freak out and own it. But don't make *me* the freak."

"I'm not."

"You are." Stef chugged the last of the beer. "Fucking talk to me and tell me what's wrong."

"Nothing's wrong."

Stef felt a ripple of annoyance. "Don't give lazy answers and *please* do not bullshit the shrink."

Jav gave a ragged exhale. "Here's what was supposed to happen. This is the way I wrote the story. Prologue, I finally come out and open my mind to meeting a guy. Just a cool, decent guy I could have sex with. Pop my homosexual cherry and figure out if it was something I liked. Not a big love affair, not an unhealthy obsession. A fuck buddy. Training wheels. My transitional person."

Stef's body temperature dropped. Veins and arteries stiffening, making the tips of his fingers prickle.

So I'm a transitional person, he thought. *Wait, is he breaking up with me? No, he just offered to move in. The hell is going on?*

"Either I wouldn't like having sex with a guy," Jav was saying, "and I'd think, *Cool, good to know, check that off, I'll go pursue a woman.* Or I would like it."

"Okay," Stef said, thinking about where Jav's mouth had been last night. You didn't do that if you hated it. "And?"

"Next chapter, I'd try to find a…starter relationship. I'd put myself out there. Go on Grindr or Manhunt or whatever. I'd date. Some guys wouldn't work out. I figured a lot of guys wouldn't work out. The point is I was prepared to be out there a long time. I was prepared to be dumped, to dump someone, deal with some bullshit, get my heart broken and my feelings hurt. I was prepared for it to take a while to get used to, physically and mentally. I thought it was going to suck for a while before it got better. Before the last chapter when I finally, hopefully met someone to…love." Jav exhaled, his hands falling limply to his sides. "That's the story I wrote. Instead I got this."

"This," Stef said.

"The last chapter."

Stef blinked. "You lost me."

"You're the last chapter," Jav said. "I went from the prologue to you. I skipped everything in the middle. I got sensational instead of suck. I got a best friend instead of the bullshit. Now I'm in love with you and it's everything I wanted, it's everything I'm terrified of losing, I'm scared to death and I don't know what the hell I'm doing. This is not what I *wrote*."

Stef felt an intense rush as his entire circulation system dilated back to normal, which let the strong beer clobber him. "Wow," he said, rubbing his numb lips. "We have a lot going on here."

Jav's voice rose. "I said I'm in love with you."

"I heard what you said. I've been in love with you since December."

"Since De—…" Jav's eyes narrowed as he crossed his arms. "How come you never told me?"

Stef opened his mouth, then shut it. "I don't know."

"Don't give lazy answers," Jav said quietly. A little coldly.

"I'm sorry. I think because… I was scared, too. Scared of how you've become everything. How this is nothing I've ever felt with a man before. Shit, I didn't even feel this way with my wife. And maybe I didn't know how long this feeling was going to last so I shut my mouth and…husbanded it. Hoarded it."

Jav nodded. "So we've both been a couple of dragons."

"Yeah."

As they stared at each other through anxious silence, Roman came over and sat precisely halfway between their trembling gazes. His own sober eyes looking back and forth.

"I didn't think I was going to fall in love," Jav said. "I didn't hope for that. I didn't prepare for it. And I've never been in love. Ever. I have zero skills here. I'm a complete virgin. I'm still getting my head wrapped around the sex, meanwhile my heart is… Jesus."

Stef walked toward him. "Come on," he said through a deep breath. "It's all right." His heart was pounding, his head buzzing, but someone had to keep the rig on the rails.

"I thought I was going to be caviar," Jav said.

"Caviar? The fuck are you talking about, caviar?"

"You said once that you liked having sex with men the way you liked caviar."

"Oh," Stef said slowly. "That. Right."

"I know I'm being an idiot. I'm just trying to…"

"Hey, come here." Stef tried to get his arms around him, but Jav was like a slippery baby after the bath. "You are the stuff in the fridge that I need all the time. All right? You're eggs. You're my Mallomar stash. You're coffee. You're fucking *beer*. My relationships with other men were caviar because none of them were you. I didn't know someone like you was out there and I didn't know meeting someone like you would change me."

"I'm sorry," Jav said, sighing. "A whole bunch of weird stuff happened today and then Roger's phone call. I don't know…"

"Javi, you're the best—"

"Look, I—"

Stef squeezed his arms like a python. "Listen. You're the best thing that ever happened to me. And you are, I shit you not, the best lover I've ever had in my life."

Jav's chin dropped. "Stop."

"*And* you make me a better man. A better son, a better friend, a better thera-pist. I work better because of you. I move through the world differently during the day because at night I'm with you. You're not fucking up here, Jav. You're making miracles."

"Let me go, dammit," Jav said, his voice keen with frustration. Stef released his arms and Jav sat down on the windowsill, rubbing a palm on his sternum. "Feels like my chest is gonna explode."

"Because you got a big heart." Feeling desperate, this emotional train not responding to the brakes, Stef stepped between Jav's feet and put his hands on the bowed shoulders. "I don't know anyone with a bigger heart."

Jav said nothing.

Something's still wrong here, Stef thought. Each had confessed to being in love, but this exchange kept on feeling like an argument.

"Javi, you never fucked love up," he said. "The few times it came to you, you didn't… You didn't fuck up with Nesto. You *got* fucked up afterward. You didn't fuck up with Flip. That plane going down was nothing you could've prevent-ed. If Flip came back from California, I wouldn't be standing here right now."

Jav looked up, but only met Stef's eyes a second before glancing away again.

"Alex?" Stef said. "You didn't fuck up with Alex. Yeah, fine, you were a bit of an obsessed jackass. We've all been there. You got your jackass stripe, welcome to the club."

Jav's crown pressed against Stef's chest. He was shaking all over as his fingers closed around the hem of Stef's shirt and he whispered, "I love you."

"Look at you and Ari," Stef said. "That's your greatest love story. Jesus, Jav, if anyone deserves to skip straight to the happy ending, it's y—"

"Stop," Jav said, louder. Now when he looked up, his gaze was almost anguished. "I know you just got home from work, I know your armor is still on, but for fuck's sake, stop *analyzing* this."

Stef shut his mouth so fast, his teeth clicked. A prickling sensation swept along his skin. His mercury layer moving in reverse, drawing up toward his head.

"Querido," Jav said softly. "I know you like to label everything but right now, I just want the *I love you* part."

Stef seized Jav's head and kissed him hard. "I love you."

Jav's hands closed around his wrists as Stef flung himself into the moment, kissing Jav's face all over. "I love you. You could've moved in yesterday. I hate coming home when you're not here. This place isn't home unless you're here."

Now Jav's arms coiled around Stef's waist like vines and his exhale was like a small windstorm. "Since *December?*" he half laughed, half groaned.

"I'm sorry. I didn't… I should've…"

"Finch, I am going to kill you," Jav mumbled against Stef's chest. "I love you so much I'm going to *kill* you."

"Do it. I'm an idiot. God, I love you like nothing I've ever known. Longer than December. You have been on my mind all day, every day, ever since the minute we met. And I want you here all the time."

He pushed his face into Jav's hair and held him tight. "All the time. I love you and I want you here all the time."

Roman came close and leaned against their legs, tail thumping on the floor.

Finally, Jav lifted his chin, looked up through the circle of Stef's arms. "I'm sorry I sprung this on you the minute you walked in. I usually know to give you an hour to unwind."

"It was important. And it's not always about me."

Jav turned his cheek against Stef's heart again and gave a big sigh.

"Three things I need you to remember," Stef said. "You're the best thing that ever happened to me. You're the best lover I ever had in my life. And you make me a better man."

"I'm good on one and three." Jav stood up and his grip on Stef's clothes tightened. "*You* obviously need a refresher course on the second thing…"

"What was the weird shit that happened today?" Stef asked.

"Hm?" Jav grunted from under closed eyes.

Stef was worn out and ached pleasantly all over, but he managed to lift his head an inch from the pillow. "You said a bunch of weird shit happened before Roger called you. Then a bunch of weirder stuff happened when I got home. I think we had an argument about being in love. Then you distracted me with make up sex. Twice."

Jav's hand rose and dropped down, forearm heavy on Stef's chest, his index finger brushing Stef's mouth. "Soon to be three times because I'm still mad at you about December."

Stef turned his head free. "Stop distracting me. What happened?"

"I was talking with one of the residents. Young kid. Geno." His finger stroked Stef's jaw and then he took his arm away.

"Ah," Stef said. They lay still a moment, poised on the boundary. Stef's professional confidentiality on one side, Jav's self-imposed, comrade confidentiality on the other.

Geno in the middle.

"Not surprised you met him," Stef said. "Or were talking with him, rather. Probably in Spanish, right?"

"Yeah. Did you know Lithuanian Jews immigrated to Mexico City?"

"Was that the weird conversation?"

"No. He wasn't testing a knife edge on his wrist, either. He just dropped a couple of things that I fitted together. I mean, I figured out who he was." Now Jav's eyes opened and stared hard into Stef's. "I know you can't tell me. But if a teenager from New Jersey lost a twin brother last summer and he's now in a facility for survivors of sexual assault, my mind thinks Mengele Ring. Am I wrong?"

Stef drew in a long breath through his nose. He closed his teeth around the tip of his tongue and kept his lips pressed tight together as he moved his head left, then right.

Jav's eyes closed. "Don't tell me anymore."

Stef was already regretting he had.

MARCH

BRAIN CHEMISTRY

*A*FTER SIX WEEKS on Prozac, Geno had enough of what he called "the brain zaps." Mild nausea seemed to be a constant sidekick and he felt like he'd been fighting off a cold for a month.

"Get me off this shit," he said to Dr. Stein. "I know I need to be on something but this isn't it."

Stein warned him switching meds could mean toughing out another six weeks. His body would be confused coming off the Prozac while accumulating citalopram, the next choice.

"You need to check in with me," Stein said. "If your thoughts start turning violent or suicidal, I need to know. Any blacking out or severe dizziness. If Mos starts speaking up or you have any disassociation episodes."

"I will."

"No Ambien. Not when you got two antidepressants in your system. I'm sorry, it'll be another thing to tough out, but…"

"It's fine. I'll catch up on my reading."

Stein smiled. "You'll probably feel worse before you feel better."

"I can handle it."

Stein's expression turned stern. "And you'll call me every morning while you're handling it."

Something fatherly was in his tone. A hint, just a hint of *your ass will be grass and I will be the lawn mower.* Instead of resenting it, Geno leaned on it, with a strange urge to tack a *sir* onto his, "I will."

He started transitioning the meds the next day and felt fine for a week. Almost smugly fine.

"Brain chemistry is one of the most delicate things in the world," Stef said. "Sometimes it's more art than science. Finding the right combination and dosage that levels out your brain without making you numb and decimating your sex drive."

"The latter isn't exactly an issue for me lately," Geno said.

"Have you had sex with anyone since the ordeal?"

Geno's smug peace flickered like a light bulb on the fritz. "Kind of."

Stef didn't say anything and in the silence, Geno heard Mos' dry impartial voice: *This isn't allowed.*

Geno flicked his head away from the warning. "Few times at college," he said. "But I'd… It made me feel sick."

We don't talk about this, Mos said.

Shut up, Geno thought, feeling the disturbing pull of divided loyalty.

"Tell me about the sick feeling," Stef said.

"I mean, I'd be doing all right, getting worked up and everything. But sometimes not being able to catch my breath would trigger bad memories and then I'd be in full-blown panic attack mode."

"Being out of breath triggered anxiety," Stef said.

We don't talk about it.

This time, Mos got a hand around Geno's neck and squeezed, making his voice waver. He cleared his throat hard. "I know I haven't shared a lot of the details of the whole…thing. But I… My face was pressed into a pillow for a lot of it. Not being able to breathe puts me right back there."

Stef nodded, his eyes heavy and serious. "Are you seeing the link between those two things in hindsight? Or were you aware of that trigger in the moment?"

"No, I could see it," Geno said.

"What did you tell your partner?"

We don't speak of it, Mos said.

Geno's face grew warm and he shifted in his chair. "I lied and said I'd been in a boating accident. Almost drowned. So not being able to catch my breath made me anxious. Blah blah."

Stef smiled. "That works."

"I got really good at lying."

"You were protecting yourself. Thing about lies, though, they're tiring."

Geno nodded. "Remembering who you told what and when. Weaving the tangled web."

"Did you ever have sex and not feel anxious?"

"Sure," Geno said. "It would be all right, but I couldn't…"

Say it, baby boy.

Geno pegged his paintbrush away. "It's hard to come." His heart beat thick in his chest and he swallowed against the pounding. "Really hard. I can't…let go."

"How about when you masturbate?"

"Jesus, could you be any more clinical?" Geno made a show of rolling his eyes but beneath the table, his knees were knocking.

"Sorry," Stef said. "Professional habit."

"I get we can't do this over beers but, Christ, you can talk like a normal guy while you're shrinking my head."

Stef held up his palms and their ringed fingers. "Fair."

"Anyway." Geno exhaled heavily. "Yes, even *then*. I can get hard, no problem, but my body just doesn't know what to do." He was shaking all over now. Panic began to rumble in the distance like an approaching storm. "Oh God, here we go," he said.

"You just lost all your color."

"Holy fuck," Geno said through his chattering jaws. "This is a bad one."

"It's okay," Stef said, pushing back his chair. "Come on. Can you stand up? Let's walk it out."

Geno got to his feet, trembling within his pant legs. He could feel the fabric swishing against his skin. Stef came around the corner of the table and, for a bizarre instant, Geno thought about taking his hand. He stuffed his fists into his pockets. "Where are we going?"

"My office. I have something I want you to try."

All was surreal and shouting inside Geno's head. Putting one foot in front of the other gave him something to focus on. When they reached his office, Stef picked up a Chock Full o' Nuts coffee can. He gave it a clanking shake before handing it to Geno. The weight of it surprised him.

"What's in here?"

"Dump it out," Stef said, sitting on the floor. Geno put a shaky knee down, peeled off the plastic cover and dumped out a mess of nuts, bolts, screws and washers.

"Now sort it all out," Stef said. "Organize it."

"For real?"

"I read about it in a journal. It gives your left brain something to do and helps you get out of the right brain free-fall."

Geno reached with sweaty, trembling fingers and started moving things around, making piles.

"Keep breathing," Stef said, elbows on his knees, chin on his folded hands. "I'm going to ask questions while you're sorting."

"All right," Geno said, thinking, *Please don't. Don't ask me anything about sex anymore. No more. Don't ask me. We don't speak of it, it isn't allowed, it didn't happen to us. Don't ask. You're not allowed to ask.*

"What's your father's name?"

Geno looked up. "Nathan?"

Stef's eyes crinkled. "Are you sure?"

"Nathan. Nathan Benjamin Caan."

"What's his father's name?"

"Jerome."

"Who's Jerome's father?" Stef asked.

"Um, I don't know. I think Benjamin?"

"Keep sorting."

As pieces of hardware were moved into neat groups, Stef kept up a running demand for factual information. Birthdays. Middle names. Hair color. Eye color. Teachers from elementary school. Front men for bands. The nine times table. The capital of South Dakota. The more Geno had to think about the answers, the more the knot in his chest and stomach loosened.

"This is working," he said, scooting backward to make more room on the rug for his piles.

Stef looked ridiculously pleased as he rolled the empty coffee can around on its rim. "I'll make you one of your own," he said. "In the meantime, I'll keep this one there." He pointed to the credenza. "You need it, you come get it. You don't have to ask first."

"What if it's the middle of the night?"

Stef gave a laughing shrug. "Between you and me, the lock on the door doesn't work." His gaze around the room was thoughtful, as if noticing for the first time its bare walls, the desk piled with papers and magazines. No personal touches or artwork. "I take my laptop home at night," he said. "Everything in here's pretty boring. Really I think of the art room as my office. This is just a glorified coat closet."

Geno pulled in a deep breath to the bottom of his stomach.

"There you go," Stef said, looking even more pleased. "Now you're back."

"Yeah," Geno said. "So was Mos. For a minute."

"Was he?"

"Yeah. I'm supposed to say when he comes around. So. I'm saying." He looked away. "I feel so stupid talking about my imaginary friend."

Stef moved a screw into its proper pile. "Did he say something?"

Geno shrugged. "Usual shit. Don't talk about it. Don't say anything. This isn't allowed."

"As far as friends go, he's pretty protective of you."

"Dude, I don't know how to handle someone talking about Mos like he's a real person."

"I'll rephrase. As far as super-egos go, it's pretty protective of you." Stef began to stack washers. "And it showed up when we started talking about sex."

Stef made a rectangular frame with his thumbs and fingers and looked at Geno through it. "Right now," he said. "Right this second, you're being forbidden on a deep, deep level. Aren't you?"

Geno had to consciously separate his lips and unclench his teeth. "I obviously have…things to talk about," he said. "I don't know if I can yet."

"I understand." Stef dropped his hands. "And I give you my word, I won't push you."

"All right."

"All I want you to know is you are allowed."

Geno nodded but said nothing. Stef reached on his desk for a pad and a pen. He wrote something down and handed it to Geno. "Take this. It's my home number. You shouldn't have to use it, but I want you to have it."

"Why?"

Stef flipped the pen in his fingers. "A lot of this work is instinct. I've learned to listen to hunches. Right now, one is telling me we're getting close to some really tough, really traumatizing shit. Another hunch wants you to have another option of getting hold of me if you need me."

Putting the square of paper in his pocket, Geno felt he owed something in return. "Right now," he said, "my hunch is saying if I tell anyone what happened in the basement, I'll tell you."

As they cleaned up screws and washers and nuts, fatigue wrapped around Geno's bones. He went to his room and slept for three hours. Groggy and hungry, he went down to the kitchen and made a peanut butter and banana sandwich. He ate it with the radio tuned to NPR.

He missed his mother.

He wanted his father.

And because he was alone, he slid his back down the stainless-steel fridge, sat on the floor and felt sorry for himself.

"I'm allowed," he said to the quiet, dark stove.

He sat a long time. Staring. Eyes in and out of focus. Gazing a long time at a book underneath one of the work counters before realizing it was an odd thing to be under there. He scooted over, fished it out and knew immediately what it was. He'd seen it so many times before, this notebook with the brown leather cover. Pages held open under Jav's fist as his pen flowed back and forth. To see it alone was strange. Like it was a dismembered hand.

The leather cover had been cool when he first picked it up, but quickly warmed in his palms. His thumb ran along the edges of the pages. They were interrupted by folded pieces of paper. Newspaper and magazine clippings. Bits of this and that. All of Jav's ideas.

Did Jav know he lost it?

He must. He always had it. He said everything in his weird mind went onto the pages. He must be freaking out. Tearing apart his apartment, retracing his steps through the day. Growing frantic. His life was in there. His weird mind was in there. His *heart* was in there.

Geno wondered where he lived. He hesitated, then peeked at the flyleaf to see if any identifying information were there. *If found, please return to…*

Nothing. Geno didn't even know Jav's last name, let alone have his number. He could text and be a hero. He could fix something for once, instead of being the broken loser around here.

He imagined how Jav's face would light up. *Dude,* he'd cry, swooping in for his lost treasure. He'd look it over, then hook an arm around Geno's neck and pull him in. *Gracias. Eres increíble.*

His mind embellished the scene, re-setting it on the porch of a little red house. *Thank you so much,* Jav would say, and then he'd open the door wider. *Come in. Come sit down. Stay awhile.*

Geno took the book up to his room and put it carefully, almost reverently in the center of his little desk. He'd give it back Friday when Jav came in. He'd be so glad.

Gracias, hermanito, he'd say, patting Geno's head.

Thanks, little brother.

STORIES OF HUNGER

> The air in New York City has no dimension, Jav wrote.
> The air is so sullen in this city. (Ugh, too much alliteration)
> The summer air sulks over bags of garbage on New York City streets.
> The air in Guelisten had depth. I remember in winter, nights so cold and clear and the scent of wood smoke coming out a dozen chimneys. Even the smoke had depth. Sometimes it smelled like licorice. Cold, black winter night like licorice.
> Cold clear winter night with a licorice scent. Like a glass of Sambuca with a coffee bean…

Geno lifted his head from the notebook and sniffed, thinking about winter nights in the suburbs.

> The air of summer nights was soft and luscious.
> The first late spring evening when the neighborhood fired up the grill for the first time. Maybe the same day the lawn mowers were fired up. The meaty smell of burgers on top of the bright green scent of cut grass. Heady perfume floating across the streets, like hands reaching to shake.

Geno's stomach growled as he turned a page. He could go for a cheeseburger right now. Eaten outside on the deck with the smell of fresh-cut grass. It was two in the morning, and whatever guilt he'd felt when he cracked open Jav's notebook had long been replaced by fascinated curiosity.

> His tastes and emotions were simple. The Compass never worried. He patted problems on the head and told them to run

along. If he was cold, he put on a sweater. If he broke something, he swept it up. If fear struck, it was a sign he was doing something wrong and he changed direction.

"The compass never worried," Geno murmured. The words were tantalizingly familiar. Where had he heard that before? Had Jav said it once, down in the kitchens? Probably. He went on reading.

The scar was the price for bedding the Queen. Trueblood didn't take the cut personally. She kept his eyebrows in a locket around her neck—how many men could say that?

The pages turned over and over. Lists of names, lines of dialogue. Paragraphs. Images. Thoughts. Questions. Documented details of the world going by. Returning over and over to a ship called Trueblood. Or maybe Trueblood was the captain of the ship.

"Trueblood," Geno said softly. It didn't have any Xs or Ks but it sounded kingly.

Once we had a brother moon and a sister moon and the skies never went dark.
Brother and Sister joined by a beltway of stars.

Geno blinked and read it again. *A beltway of stars.*

A belt broken by a ship sailing through the night sky.
The ship sailing above and below, round and round, lost and landless. Her holds full of nothing but stories.
Stories of hunger from when the spice trees died and love was a famine.
Each sailor had stories of hunger only the other believed.

The last sentence was underlined several times and Geno smiled, as if reuniting with an old friend.

Micah said that, he thought. *I was there.*

He turned a page. A square of drawing paper was tucked in the spine. A sketch of two men lying in a circle, each nose to the other's knees. Both were winged, like angels. One was dressed in black, the other in white. Like a yin-yang. Beneath the sketch was written *Namaste, motherfucker.*

Geno tucked the picture back into the spine, yawned, and looked at the clock. Two-thirty now. He'd read one more page.

Just one.

He turned the leaf and a piece of graph paper fell in his lap. He unfolded a handwritten note.

Crazy how I've never wanted something so bad. Crazier how I've never been so patient for something in my life.

You asked the other night, "What if it takes months?"

Then it takes months. I don't care. It takes as long as it takes until you're ready for me. And then…God then…

The things I want to do to you shock me.

Geno's face grew warm and his eyes widened. This was a love note.

I'm going to kiss you until you're limp. Lick you in places you didn't know you wanted my tongue to touch. Then I'll roll you over and get my mouth on you and my fingers in you. Get you begging for me to fill you up because you need to be close to me. I want to hear you say you need me in you.

Your trust means the world to me. It's heavy in my hands and I'm aware of it all the time. It's so bound up in everything else I want.

God, I want this and I'll wait for it. Until you say it's time and not a second before. But I think about it. I can taste it. Makes me feel like fucking dying sometimes.

We'll go slow. Slow as you want. I'll get you so ready and slowly, never taking my eyes off yours, I'll slide into you. Christ, I can't wait to feel you. Can't wait to see you come harder than you ever came in your life. Can't wait to hear you say you want more, say you want me to fuck you again. And I will. Anytime you want. Anytime you ask me. Anytime you tell me.

And each time, I'll be wondering if you have any idea how crazy about you I am. If you know I've never wanted anyone the way I want you. That I'm just as shocked as you to hear this kind of stuff coming out of my mouth or falling onto pieces of paper. I've never talked like this to anyone. I've never wanted to say these kinds of things to anyone. Never felt this way with anyone else.

*Every time I fuck you, I'll be wondering if you know what all
of this means to me.*

Jesus. Did Jav write this to Stavroula? Whoever it was for, Jav was fucking
nuts about her.

Geno's eyes skimmed again. This was hot. This was almost…lewd. Reading
it, he pushed back into the pillows, distancing himself from the bald, raw
strength of an adult man's passion. It should've scared him. It didn't. Maybe
because, between the lines, it was so solicitous and patient. The desire was clear,
but so was the promise.

Until you say it's time and not a second before.

Was Jav in love with someone who was abused?

Geno looked up, brow furrowed, wondering for the first time exactly why
Jav volunteered at EP.

For that matter, why did Stavroula?

Since he was on the subject, how did Stef get into this line of work?

Did it happen to them? All of them?

The edges of the universe slammed together in beautiful understanding.
It had to be. They were all survivors. Even Stavroula, and Jav was being so, so
gentle. So patient and thoughtful.

The sexual imagery in this note might be too much.

No wonder Jav couldn't send it yet.

Geno folded the graph paper and put it exactly back as he found it. He put
the notebook under his pillow and turned out the light.

Your trust is heavy in my hands.

The sentence rang in his heart like a great bell. He remembered Chris Mudry
handing over a backpack, weighted down with a secret. The heft of that confidence.

Geno put his second name and his citizenship of Nos into Stef's hands.
Sacred mysteries that were heavy as gold bars and just as unforgettable.

I'm aware of it all the time. It means the world to me.

"Trust is heavy," he mouthed to the darkness, his palms open and ready to
receive. After a minute, one hand crept under the waistband of his sweats. He
squeezed and stroked, thinking about trust and mouths and fingers and loving
and dying. It didn't go anywhere, but he was hard and it felt good in his hand.

You're allowed, he thought. *It takes as long as it takes.*

When you say it's time and not a minute before.

He fell into deep sleep, where he dreamed of his henhouse, the heavy secrets
inside and the people he trusted with them.

BROUGHT HERE FOR DRINKING

"**H**E TOLD ME Mos showed up yesterday," Frank Stein said on the phone.

"He had a pretty bad anxiety attack," Stef said.

"I heard. Good call with the nuts and bolts. I told my wife to save the next empty coffee can."

"Did Geno tell you about the trigger?"

"No," Frank said, "he was in one of his more reticent moods."

"We were talking about his sexual experience since the rape and it hit. My gut is telling me we're approaching the deep jungle."

"He's talked nothing about it so far?"

"Yesterday was the first time I got any kind of detail about the ordeal."

Frank let out a slow exhale. "If he's getting ready to talk about it, I'd rather he weren't transitioning meds. Either Mos will show up to put the kibosh on telling, or he won't be in a good place to deal with what he does talk about."

"It's never the perfect time," Stef said. "Rape trauma doesn't play nice."

"At least he's communicating with both of us. We'll just…do our jobs."

Stef hesitated. "This is a hard one, doc."

"You protecting yourself?"

"Always. But it's still hard. Got a joke for me?"

"A drunk was in front of a judge," Frank said. "The judge says, 'You've been brought here for drinking.' The drunk says 'Okay, let's get started.'"

"Good advice," Stef said. "Goodnight, Dr. Frankenstein."

"Goodnight, Igor."

Leaning back in his chair, Stef pulled his hands back through his hair. Long day followed by a long staff meeting. Now the skies had gone dark and the harsh, fluorescent light inside made a mirror of the window. He had a ton of paperwork he'd been avoiding for weeks, his office was a sty and Jav was in a foul mood after losing his notebook.

"I hate Tuesdays," he said to his haggard reflection.

He picked up the phone again and called Jav's cell. "Find it?"

"No," Jav said. "Goddammit."

"I'm sorry."

Jav gave a growled grunt of frustration. "It's not the end of the world," he said, as if witnessing the end of the world. "It's not cancer. I wrote that shit once, I can write it again. I'm just *pissed.*"

"You retraced your steps? Everywhere you went yesterday?"

"Yeah. The apartment. The Bake and Bagel. The gym. The bank. The kitchens. The Bake and Bagel again. The apartment. Linen closet. Dryer. Under Roman's water dish. The fridge."

"Tank of the toilet?"

"Covered."

"Fuse box?"

"Checked."

"Oven?"

"Twice."

Stef laughed. "I'm sorry, man. That sucks."

A tornado sigh. "I'll live."

"Well, listen. I'm gonna plow through some shit here and then I'll buy you a steak."

"You don't have to," Jav said.

"I want to. You need solace and distraction and I need motivation to clean my office. The solution is steak-frites at Estelle's. Creamed spinach. Mucho beers."

The beat of silence at the other end was thoughtful. "What's for dessert?"

"Me."

Another big sigh. "Fine. I guess I can cheer up for that."

"Meet me here in an hour," Stef said. "You know, I've never given you a tour of this place."

"An after-hours tour of your office?" Jav said. "What could possibly go wrong?"

"I'll tell the security guard you're coming."

"I'm not even touching that."

"I mean you're *arriving.*"

"Yeah, yeah, we both know what you meant, Finch."

THE WRATH OF CAAN

*G*ENO TURNED A page of Jav's notebook and saw his own name.

Geronimo Caan.
Geronimo! The crowd yelled as he went up for one of his signature dunk shots.
Genghis Caan, the wrestling star of PS 194.
The bleachers were dotted with hand-lettered signs:
Genghis Caan!
Wrath of Caan!
Anything you can do, he Caan do better!
"Honey, I can't," the girl said, limp and spent.
"Honey, you Caan," he said against her neck.
"Geronimo," the girl cried in the dark, as she came for the third time.

The pages shook in Geno's hands, a thousand emotions rippling through his chest as his head spun in both directions at once.

This is me.

He's writing about me. I don't play sports. Genghis Caan, what does that mean? Who's this girl? Why's he writing about me?

He read the lines over and over, his chest now filling up with a warm, flattered curiosity.

He's writing about me.

"Genghis Caan," he said. Softly, then louder. It never occurred to him his surname sounded like the title *Khan*. It was a word you didn't fuck with. King was light and noble but Khan was a hammer on an anvil.

Khan.
A strike on a gong. Name and title. Caan and Khan.
Beware the wrath of Caan.
"Damn," he said, turning the page.

> The sun is not one but two. Two in one. Two gods burning within.
> Sun sons.
> Sacred twins.
> Twins whose bond is magical.
> Gemini.
> The bond is the place where two become one.

Geno felt his eyes bulge and his last inhale wouldn't release.
Holy fuck, he thought. *This is like Nos.*

> Is the bond literal: skin, actual flesh that joins them? Conjoined twins are magic?
> (Christ, I can't write conjoined twins, that's too many people in a bed.)
> So the bond is metaphysical. Like an aura, maybe.
> "Our power is in what joins us," one twin said.
> "Our combined power is in the space between us," the other finished.
> So if it's magic, can you steal it? Magic things are meant to be stolen, right?
> Like, "So-and-so gained his power by stealing the bond from the Gemini."

Geno's fingers trembled as he turned a page.

> It's an ancient saying in these lands, my child:
> "Break the bond, the Gemini cries.
> Take the bond, and the Gemini..."
> Lies?
> Flies?

"Dies," Geno said. "Take the bond and the Gemini dies."
He stared across his little room. His throat now tightening up for some stupid reason. His heart revving beneath his ribs, dissolving all the warmth that had just been there. The awful *rolling* sensation of impending anxiety, coming over the horizon like storm clouds. Like a herd of wild horses. Coming for him.

He stood up. Sat again.

Calm down, he thought. *C'mon, let's walk it out.*

He stood up. His room wasn't conducive to pacing. He had eight steps up and back, tops.

The leather notebook was warm in his hands. Tactile like dough. Like skin.

He put his nose to the covers. His hands squeezed, trying to wring a presence out of the pages.

I need somebody.

He wished Jav were here.

He wanted him.

The thought made his stomach twist in fresh panic.

Easy, easy, he told himself. *I don't* want *him. I just…want him.*

He tried to pretend. He turned on his white noise machine to waves. Imagined a long stretch of sandy beach and the red house in the distance. Up higher on stilts now, to keep from flooding at high tide.

I'm going home. I'll just go home and bring him back what was lost.

The lost bond.

His teeth chattered above his footsteps. Round and round in the carpet, believing he was walking a straight line in sand.

Hey, you dropped your notebook in the kitchen.

Want to go for a walk?

Jesus, that sounded gay. What the fuck was he doing?

He sank onto the bed, head in his hands.

My head, my head, what is happening in this fucking weird, fucked up head *of* mine?

I just want to be a normal guy.

Str8 dude seeks same.

His fingers shook as he fanned the pages of the notebook. The piece of graph paper with its fiery, loving sentiments slipped out and settled in his lap.

"Trust is heavy," he whispered from memory. "Your trust is heavy in my hands."

His secrets were safe with Stef. They were in Stef's big, strong hands. Their weight couldn't be forgotten. Geno's palms turned up to the ceiling, needing to feel them. His fingers itched to sort through and measure them.

Trust is heavy.

It's heavy…

Then he remembered the coffee can.

MESSY WORK

"So this is where the curating happens," Jav said, walking along one of the long tables of the art room, fingers trailing. "Funny, I envisioned it messier."

"Clean environment. Messy work. Plus we like things in their place."

Jav smiled, lined in silvery streetlight from the tall windows. "Now I'll be able to put you in this place. I mean, when I think about you during the day."

Stef stared back, suspended in the thick moment. "You think about me during the day?"

"You know I do."

"Pretend I forgot."

Jav leaned back against the sill, hands in his pockets. "I just wonder what you're doing. Who you're sailing with."

Stef walked toward him. "I feel bad I can't share much about the voyages."

Jav shrugged. "Now that I have the setting, my imagination can fill in the blanks." One hand came out of its pocket and slowly moved along the side of Stef's leg. "Mostly I wonder if you think about me."

"You know I do."

"Pretend I forgot."

Stef ran the backs of his fingers along Jav's neck. "When I'm not thinking about the ship, I'm thinking about you."

Jav wet his lips, teeth shining in the dark. "Same. Pretty much all I fucking do is think about you."

They kissed, Stef sliding his thumb along Jav's throat, over his Adam's apple, around his chin and across his bottom lip.

Jav closed his teeth around the caress. "Show me your office?"

Stef put his face against Jav's neck, breathing in. "It's nothing to show."

"I want to see where else you spend the day."

"It's nothing," Stef said, as his soul whispered, *God, you are everything, every-thing to me.*

Jav pushed him back. "Go."

SCREWS AND BOLTS

*G*ENO'S SNEAKERS SQUEAKED across the cool marble of the lobby. Streetlight sliced through the front doors and made silvery grey rectangles on the floor, while the security booth was bathed in warm gold from a single lamp. Kandice was on duty. The light picked up the bronze strands in her black hair as she yawned over her books. Geno knew she worked two different night jobs after attending nursing school in the day. Her eyes were ringed with smudged circles but her smile was broad.

"Child, what are you up to," she said. "Signing out?"

"I left something in the art room."

She raised her ballpoint pen to the ceiling. "You know the way."

Geno took the steps two at a time. His quads burned after only a few treads and he had to stop on the first landing to catch his breath. He was so out of shape. So slack and weak.

Aren't you, baby boy?

"Knock it off," he said behind his teeth. He sat on a tread, breathing through the dizziness. His cold, clammy hands shook, craving the feel of bits of metal. Screws and bolts to push into piles as he recited multiplication tables.

I'll sort it out, he thought. *And if that doesn't work, I'll call Stef.*

I'll try to handle it myself, and if I can't, I'll get help.

I can do this.

I'm allowed to do this.

SAY YOU WANT ME

WALKING ALONG THE upper hall, Jav slid his hand into Stef's. Fingers folded, palm to palm, their feet in step on the carpet. Stef all at once wishing the corridor were twice as long. Wishing they were on the High Line. A beach. The Appalachian Trail. Somewhere they could walk forever, holding hands.

He hit the wall switch in his office. The bleaching overheads lit up the small room. Neater now, but still as inspiring as an empty cardboard box.

"This is terrible," Jav said.

Stef turned the light off.

"Better," Jav said.

"Come here, you moron." Stef yanked him in and around, nudging the door closed with his foot. Hands on Jav's shoulders, he walked him backward toward the window. Laughing and kissing but wrestling at the same time.

"I was told there'd be steak," Jav said.

"Fuck steak."

"You can't lure me out of my spectacular sulk with dinner and not deliver."

"I'm delivering on dessert." Stef whipped Jav around and pressed him up tight to the wall by the window, threading his arms through Jav's elbows and pinning him.

"No fucking at the office," Jav said, his smile a beautiful thing.

"Believe me, Landes. When you're ready for me to fuck you, it'll be in my bed."

"Our bed," Jav said against Stef's lips. His tongue brushed, his mouth opened and a rash of prickling goose bumps swept over Stef's skin. He needed to get them out of here. It was a highly inappropriate place to be screwing around.

And the door didn't lock, either.

In a minute, he thought, his thoughts sticking together.

"I still want my steak," Jav said.

"Say you want me."

"No."

"Say it." He pulled up on Jav's arms a little more.

"Make me."

Stef threaded a hand in Jav's hair and turned his head back. "Say it," he whispered, and kissed him. A kiss for the ages. A kiss to tear Jav slowly in half, until his chest rose up and he moaned into Stef's mouth.

"You're killing me."

"You love it." Stef pulled Jav's head back more, showing his throat to the streetlight. His soul was down on its knees, first banging fists on the ground in a terrible need, then throwing hands to the skies in rapture.

"Finch," Jav said, his voice like ice cream melting on Stef's skin, hoarse with desire.

Stef's arm tightened through the tunnel of Jav's elbows, pulling him in. "Say you want me." He slid his lips along the curve of Jav's neck, toward his shoulder. He dragged back with his teeth, slowly let them press into the skin. "Say it, baby—"

Then something exploded.

Guys Like Him

STEF'S OFFICE DOOR was closed, but Geno knew the lock didn't work. Stef had trusted him with that information.

And trust is heavy.

He pushed the door open.

Two men in Stef's office. One up against the wall. The other pinning him.

"Say you want me."

A back to a chest. A head yanked by the hair.

"You love it."

A twist. A moan. A silhouetted struggle.

"Say it, baby…"

This is not allowed, Mos said. *This is against the law.*

Fear seized Geno by all four limbs, then let go just as quickly and anger filled him. Guys like that were in the world but the world also had guys like him.

The world would be wise to beware the wrath of Caan.

He grabbed the coffee can full of nuts and bolts and threw it.

RAINSTORM

A CLANGING CRASH AND Jav let out a yell as Stef's teeth bit into his shoulder. The air was filled with flying pieces of metal, pouring on him like a weighted rainstorm.

A pipe bomb? he thought. Then Stef made a garbled moan and his slumped weight was pulling Jav down, dragging at his neck.

"Stef," he said, turning in the choking grip. *"Stef…"*

Stef let go and went stumbling backward.

Someone else was in the room.

TALONS

*S*TEF'S BRAIN SLOSHED from one side of his skull to the other before settling into a dull, aching throb. Bits of cold metal were in his hair and tumbling down the back of his shirt collar.

Something in the ceiling…?

He grabbed and clutched the solid mass that was Jav, still in his arms. Time and memory doubled back on themselves. He and Jav were falling down the stairs, bumping and rolling like apples tumbling into the dark.

No neck breaking on the first date.

He was falling.

Something sank talons into his shoulders, grabbed big folds of his shirt and then he was *flying…*

TURN THE HEAD

*G*ENO DIDN'T KNOW he could be so strong. He was mighty and terrible, flinging the man down to the floor, sending the wastepaper basket skittering.

Not in my house, he thought. *Not in my land, not on my watch.*

"Stef," a voice cried.

Stef?

"You?" Geno said, dropping to his knees on top of his beloved big brother, *mounting* him. Hands flew up, inked patterns on his forearms. Horses and archers and wings. Bows and arrows.

"You son of a bitch," Geno said, his hands reaching toward Stef's throat.

"Geno," It was the same voice as before. "Qué mierdas pasa. Basta..."

The hell I'll stop. Not this time. Not in my house.

"Ya basta," the voice behind him cried. "Suéltalo."

Hands were pulling at him but Geno had the power of two in his body, the fiery strength of twin sun-sons in his bones. And he had the weight of trust in his hands. Weight that became immeasurable when it was betrayed.

Take the bond and the Gemini dies, motherfucker.

His fingers squeezed Stef's neck but then the winged horses reared up and grabbed his head.

"Get *back,*" Stef shouted. "Jav, get off him. Move."

Jav?

The name and the Spanish smashed together, tearing a hole in Geno's mind. His head was yanked down, pulled tight into Stef's chest, two big hands spreading wide on Geno's face. Fingers hooked against the bridge of his nose.

Hey, Mos said, almost happily. *He knows the move. In an attack from above, they'll expect to be pushed away. Instead, you pull them in close.*

"Off me now," Stef said, starting to turn Geno's head. Hard. Then harder. "Geno, stop."

Turn the head, the body follows.

Geno writhed against the force but the strain on his neck was pulling into pain.

"Stop right now," Stef said. "I don't want to hurt you." He writhed too, but with a smooth, liquid purpose. He was shrimping out, throwing Geno off balance. Now Stef's hip was free. One hand kept turning Geno's head, the other started pushing at his shoulder. A foot pressed Geno's hip bone and he was beaten. Rolled off and over and down. Onto his back in the musty carpet, nuts and bolts and screws digging in his skin.

Stef didn't run like hell. He stayed put, hands on the balls of Geno's shoulders, pushing him straight into the floor.

Trust is heavy.

"You're done," Stef said. "This is over now. Look at me."

The room lit up harsh and white then. Stef loomed over him, pale beneath five o'clock shadow. His eyes were coal black. They were supposed to be blue.

You're not Stef.

What did you do with Stef?

A winged horse took him by the jaw, moved his head this way and that. "Geno, look at me. Are you on something? What did you take?"

This isn't happening to us, Mos said.

Geno stared over Stef's shoulder, looking at the window, searching for the stars and the portal into Nos. He made himself small. Made himself disappear.

Made it happen to someone else.

VASOVAGAL SYNCOPE

"**W**HAT THE FUCK," Jav said, down on his knees in the shrapnel on the floor. The room was getting crowded. The security guard came on the run, along with Juan and Corley, who'd been passing through the lobby when they heard the commotion. Their grim expressions stared at Jav, but if they wondered what he was doing here, they didn't show it. Juan was especially pale, crossing himself and fiddling with the gold crucifix around his neck.

"Nurses are on the way," Kandice said. "Is he breathing all right? Was it a seizure?"

"He's breathing," Stef said. "I'm not sure."

He turned his head then, and Jav saw the gash along his cheekbone and the blood starting to run.

"You're cut," Jav said, reaching to catch the drops. Stef shied away and touched his face himself, then shrugged.

"You all right?" Jav said, wiping his fingertips on his legs.

Stef grunted, his jaw set hard, muscles twitching beneath his eyes.

"The hell is all over the floor?" Corley said, crouching down and picking up screws.

Geno made a choked, gagging noise.

"Jav take his head," Stef said. "Let's roll him on his side."

Jav, right by Geno's mouth, shuffled his knees back a little, braced for a projectile. The boy twitched, gave a weak, uneventful heave, then went still again. Another twitch. His eyes fluttered and opened. He blinked a few times at Jav's kneecap, then slowly reached to touch the bloodstain there. He whispered something, and Jav swore it sounded like, "The compass never worries."

How in the hell would he...

Jav shook the thought off and took Geno's hand. "It's all right, mi pana. Just lie still."

"Corley," Stef said quietly. "I need you and Juan to go, okay? Give him some space."

Corley left. Juan lingered, eyes wide. "Javi," he said. "¿Cuidarás a mi hermanito?"

Take care of my little brother?

Jav looked up. "Sí, por supuesto."

Juan crossed himself, gave one last, worried look at Geno's outstretched body on the rug, then left as well.

"Jav." His eyes on Geno, Stef put his palm against Jav's shoulder and pushed. "Move back for me now."

Jav got up and moved toward the window. Shock wrapped around his nervous system and his eyes couldn't leave Stef's bloody cheek, but he grasped it was best to let Stef do his job.

"Hey, bud," Stef said. "You feel sick?"

"No," Geno said.

"Think you can sit up?"

"Yeah."

Stef took Geno's arm and helped him up. "How's that."

Geno pulled his arm free and slid away, putting his back against the desk. His gaze moved around the room. From Stef, to the security guard, to the field of hardware sprinkled across the floor. To Jav. Back to Stef for a moment. Then his eyes went far away.

"Stay here," Stef said. "Stay with me. Look at me."

"I thought..."

The room went still as a painting. Jav held his breath and willed himself invisible.

"I thought you were..." Geno's head swung back and forth, mouth parted in confusion. "It was dark. And you were..." He looked at Jav and his index finger lifted. "He was... It looked like..."

Kandice broke the spell with a forced, hearty laugh. "No, child, it was just the lovebirds."

Stef winced and Jav clenched his teeth as Geno's eyes made another circuit around the room, wide and bewildered.

"Lovebirds?" he said.

"Jav's my partner," Stef said. "We live together."

Geno glanced at Jav.

Jav raised a palm. *Hi, nice to meet you.* Then, like the idiot he was, he blurted, "We were just fooling around."

Stef's eyes swiveled, looking daggers at him. Kandice gave a nervous laugh and Jav thought about exiting quietly out the window. Thank God the nurses arrived, their energy taking further control of the situation.

One knelt by Geno's legs, taking his wrist in her fingers and looking at her watch, counting. "He lost consciousness?" she asked Stef.

"All of thirty seconds maybe."

"Convulsions?"

"No. Looked like a vasovagal syncope, which I've seen with him before."

She looked at Geno. "Honey, did you take something tonight?"

Geno shrunk away from her eyes as he answered, "No." His whole face trembled, as if he might cry.

"It's all right," she said. "I'm not angry, you're not in trouble. I just need to know."

"I didn't take anything. I don't *have* anything to take."

"All right. I don't mean to accuse, it's my job to ask. You're going to come down to the infirmary so we can look you over a little more. Think you can stand up?"

Geno got up, his expression inside-out with confusion, his gaze going between Jav and Stef and then far away again.

"Come on now," the nurse said. "You come with me. It's all right."

Once he was gone, Stef gave a tremendous exhale and came off his knees. He rolled onto his butt and slumped back against the wall. The other nurse crouched by him.

"Now let's look at you," she said. "How'd you get that cut?"

"He threw something at my head," Stef said. "Coffee can full of this shit." He flicked a washer aside. "A screw or something must've nicked my face."

"I don't think it'll need to be stitched, but it's a little more than a nick." The nurse took his jaw in her hands, thumbs beneath his eyes. "Plus you are dilated to kingdom come, Finch."

Jav moved a little closer and saw indeed, Stef's pupils had eclipsed all the blue of his irises. The nurse drew Stef's head toward her and palpated at the base of his neck, moving up into his hair.

"Shit," Stef said. "Yeah, that's where it hit."

She examined his scalp. "No blood. I'm surprised."

"Fuck, stop touching it."

"I'll get you some ice packs. Then you're going to want to get checked out by a doctor."

Stef made a non-committal noise as he got up, neither yes nor no. The nurse looked at Jav with raised eyebrows. Her mouth shaped a word. *Hospital.*

Jav nodded.

"Jesus, I hate Mondays," Stef said.

"It's Tuesday," Jav said.

"Monday, Tuesday, whatever. C'mon. Let's get that fucking steak I promised you."

POTENTIAL HAZARDS

*O*UTSIDE THE WAREHOUSE, Jav stepped into the street, arm raised to hail a cab.

"Where are we going?" Stef said. "Estelle's is—"

"We're going to St. Vincent's."

"I'm fine."

"You didn't know what day it was. Get in."

"Jav."

Jav's eyes pressed him hard. "If you ever want to get laid by me again, get in the fucking cab."

Stef rolled his eyes but he got in. Jav slammed the door, gave the destination and they both slumped against the seat, arms crossed, staring straight ahead.

Finally Jav spoke. "My alternate threat was 'Get in the cab or I'm moving out tonight.'"

Stef glanced at him. "You'd go back and sleep with Roger?"

"No. So I went with the getting laid thing."

"You know my weakness."

Jav unfolded an arm and dropped his hand on the seat between them, palm up. Stef blinked at it a few moments, then laid his on top. He drew a deep breath and sank a little lower into the leather. Fatigue swept over him, the kind that came at the end of an adrenaline rush. He realized his head ached bad. His cheekbone throbbed and the vision in that eye was beginning to narrow. A faint nausea touched the back of his throat and he swallowed hard, took another breath to tamp it down.

"All right?" Jav said.

"It's hitting me." He folded his fingers around Jav's and squeezed. "I gotta call Ronnie."

"It can wait."

"Javi, I could get fired for this."

"Don't," Jav said. "One thing at a time. Getting you checked out is first and foremost. Then damage control." His thumb ran across Stef's knuckles. Once. Twice. Then was still. "We're almost there."

Date night in the ER was seriously overrated. After a ninety-minute wait, the cheekbone was glued shut and butterfly-bandaged. The concussion assessment was satisfactory and they went home with some guidelines. "Rest. Fluids. Eat light. Severe headache or nausea, or any vomiting, come back in."

Stef was exhausted now. And hungry. Two things that made him impossible. Jav made a call to Lilia and when the men returned home, a pot of plain chicken broth and noodles was on their stove. Stef had a cup, took a hot shower and then called Ronnie Danvers.

He told her everything that happened. He omitted no detail, made no excuses. His apology was heartfelt. "I feel terrible," he ended. "I fucked up."

"You never fuck up," Ronnie said. A whirring click from her cigarette lighter, followed by a long exhale. "Is this really Steffen Finch?"

"Unfortunately," he said, face in his palm. "I'm so sorry."

"All right. Look. This is extremely unlike you. In all the years we've been working together, I've never written you up. Jesus, I'm usually consulting you when there's an incident."

"I know. I let you down and I feel like shit."

"Let me down? Stef, while I'm aghast at your behavior, it isn't anything close to a pattern. I confess I often wondered when and if you would finally exercise some bad judgment."

"I fucked up," Stef said insistently. "Javi had no business being in my office. I know better."

"He picked you up at your place of employ," Ronnie said. "It was well after hours. You signed him in with security and showed him around. No rules broken. The indiscretion was making out in your office, especially knowing the lock didn't work. An egregiously rotten decision and yes, you do know better. And unfortunately, your toughest client walked in and totally misconstrued what he was seeing. There's our liability."

"Fuck," Stef muttered. "Ronnie, it's my liability. This is on me. I'm sorry."

"I know you are. I have to write this up, I have no choice. We'll put the facts on record and let it pan out. If Geno wants to lodge a complaint, we'll handle it. Let's not catastrophize."

"I need to apologize to him."

"No spontaneous and melodramatic amends," Ronnie said, with authority. "I need to know what you intend to do and say before you do and say it. But nothing more tonight. You need to rest. And take tomorrow off."

"Max—"

"I will reschedule Max."

"I'm sorry."

"I know you are. Thank you for your honesty and transparency. We will prevail. Look, Frank Stein is calling on the other line, let me take this."

"Tell him to call me after."

"I will tell him to call you tomorrow. Go rest. That's an executive order."

Stef hung up, wishing she'd given him more of a harangue. Sighing viciously, he flopped on the couch in front of *Planet Earth*.

"You want more of this soup?" Jav called from the kitchen.

Stef's stomach seemed amenable to the idea so he grunted. Jav sat down and held out the mug. Stef didn't take it. Just opened his mouth to be fed.

"Dude, no," Jav said.

Stef waited, arms crossed, eyes on the TV and mouth open. Being stubbornly pathetic and rather enjoying it.

"Seriously," Jav said, taking up a spoonful and feeding it to him.

"You're so my bitch."

"Shut up." But he spooned Stef the whole cup without further comment, then settled back and reached out an arm. "Come here, you moron."

Stef pivoted on the couch and put his head in Jav's lap. Jav scooched down low in the cushions, pulling Stef more on his chest. His hand ran slow through Stef's hair. His heart beat slow in Stef's ear.

"Cold?" he said.

"Little," Stef said.

Jav pulled the blanket down and spread it over Stef's legs.

"Sorry you didn't get your steak," Stef said.

"Shh. Just rest."

Stef pressed his head closer, curling in the circle of Jav's arms.

"Don't be stupid tonight," Jav said. "You start to feel bad, you tell me. You wake me up."

"I will."

"Promise."

"I'll wake you up and tell you."

Jav stroked his head. David Attenborough narrated. The room pulsed with a quiet energy.

"I love you," Stef said.

"I love you too." Jav pressed his mouth on Stef's crown. Inhaled and exhaled. "And you scare me sometimes."

"Tell me what scares you."

"You're tired."

"Tell me," Stef said, raising his voice.

"I'm not afraid of us breaking up," Jav said. "I'm not afraid if we grow apart or come to an amicable but sad end. I can probably even deal with coming to a bitter end if it's by choice. What I'm afraid of is something happening to you. Something beyond my control where all of a sudden, you're gone and I had *no* choice in the matter."

"I'm not going—" The words cut off as Jav's thumb pinned his mouth shut.

"I know. Look, I know I'm jumping to worst-case scenarios. I know you can take care of yourself. I know you have a thousand professional skills to stay in control of that kind of situation. It was actually fucking amazing watching you work tonight. Amazing and terrifying." He released his hold on Stef's mouth and his hand turned soft again. "You're good at what you do. But now that I've seen some of the potential hazards, I need you to be careful doing it. All right?"

Stef nodded, inhaling against the bright, clean smell of Jav's shirt, and the dimmer, richer scent of his skin.

"Geno needs you," Jav said. "But so do I."

"I know. I love my work, but coming home to you is now the most important job I have."

Jav's arms squeezed, held tight a moment, then relaxed. "I'm thinking it might be better if I didn't volunteer in the kitchen while you're getting this sorted out."

"Yeah. I can see Geno needing distance from both of us. God, this week sucks and it's only Tuesday."

Jav's palm fell soft on Stef's face, rasping against beard growth. "Right now's not so bad."

LOVEBIRDS

"**I**'M FINE," GENO kept saying to the infirmary staff. "I'm *fine,* I just got upset. I was already anxious and seeing those guys triggered me."

Useful word, trigger. Both nurses and the doctor and even Frank Stein—who left the dinner table to call in—agreed that was what happened. They also agreed Geno should spend the night in the infirmary and be restricted to the facility for another forty-eight hours.

"Great, so I'm being punished for something I couldn't help," Geno said.

It's for your safety, the consensus replied.

Bullshit, he thought. He sat on the narrow bed in the tiny, sterile infirmary and hated everything. He wished he could head to EP's fitness room, jump on a treadmill and run until his head exploded.

I want to die, he thought. *I mean it this time.*

What he really wanted was that coffee can full of hardware to sort out. But with it came the memory of the sound it made when it collided with Stef's head.

I could've killed him.

What if he had? He'd be in fucking *jail* right now.

That is, if Jav didn't kill him first.

Holy fuck, Jav and Stef.

Crazy how I've never wanted something so bad.

Groaning, Geno fell back and closed his eyes. He tried turning his head away, but the handwritten words of that fucking love note were etched on the insides of his eyelids. Because, like an idiot, he'd read them not once, but about twenty times.

I'm going to kiss you until you're limp. Lick you in places you didn't know you wanted my tongue to touch.

Geno pressed the heels of his hands to his burning face. He was an idiot. He'd memorized the words but it never occurred to him the handwriting didn't match the other notebook entries. It wasn't a note Jav wrote. It was a note he *got*. From Stef.

"Jee-zus," he said through his teeth. He'd *touched* himself to that shit. Fine, he didn't get off on it because he was fucking defective in that regard. But he'd gotten hard and had a grand old time stroking himself to all those lewd, racy, intensely passionate and, now, undeniably *gay* words.

Watching your face the whole time, I'll slide into you.

Geno's head turned this way and that, trying to get away from *into*. He clenched up, remembering all the pain, all the indignity, all the mortifying exams. His own shit funneled to a bag strapped to his body because his asshole had been reamed for two days. Every enema. Every suppository. Every fucking gloved and lubed finger that had probed up his works.

You need me in you.

Don't you, baby boy?

He threw the thin pillow against the wall and sat up, violated to his core. His henhouse ransacked and pillaged. Furniture overturned, feathers floating from slashed pillows and ashes raked out from the hearth. Dirty footprints trampling on everything he'd worked so hard to build. Worst of all, the sleeping arrangements rearranged. Stavroula kicked out of the bedroom to sleep on the couch.

Gurl, sorry. This house craves dick.

"Son of a bitch," he said. "How could you fucking do this to me?"

What was he even talking about? What the hell was this *jealousy* flooding his guts as he stared at the closed door of the master suite. Wondering what they did in there. Wondering how they felt in there. Closed up together, alone and naked with all those words.

Never wanted anyone the way I want you. Never felt this way with anyone else.

The room swam wet. Geno ran the back of his hand roughly over his eyes, remembering crumpled notes he'd pulled out of Carlito's jeans. Corny lines he thought were written by a girl. Rolling his eyes at the sappy sentiments while tasting the new and bitter knowledge he no longer had exclusive rights to his twin's love.

You're the only one who knows me, Carlito wrote back to the A who wasn't an Amy or Amanda or Andrea. *You're the only one who sees me.*

The words joined hands with Stef's note and sidled up next to Anthony's voice. Geno hunched over, fingers clenched in his hair, pulling a silent scream out of his follicles.

Crazy how I never wanted something so bad.

Yeah, you want it. Can't have only one twin be gay.

You're a whore just like your brother.

Geno sniffed hard, swallowed harder through the swamp in his throat. Trust was heavy, but it was so fragile. When it slipped out of your hands, it shattered into delicate, sharp pieces that cut hard and deep.

"It's nothing to fucking *cry* about," he said.

Cry all you want, baby boy.

He stood up and started pacing up and down the short length of the room. The anxiety was coming over the horizon and nothing could stop it.

Except the wrath of Caan.

His fists clenched as he mindfully ripped circuits out of anxiety and plugged them into anger.

"Sick fucking faggots," he said, his feet smashing his raging emotions into the linoleum, grinding them down until they were nothing he owned, but every-one else's character flaw.

He couldn't *believe* he didn't know Stef and Jav were gay.

He stopped walking. Did anyone else know? Did Stavroula know?

Did *everyone* know except him?

"Child, it was just the lovebirds," Kandice said, while Corley and Juan stared. Not at the lovebirds but at Geno. Like, *What kind of clueless schmuck is this kid? Thinking Stef was trying to rape Jav? Stef of all people? What a moron. It was just the lovebirds.*

The Finches. Perched on the roof of the henhouse like they owned the place. Rubbing beaks, chortling and laughing because they loved each other more than they loved Geno.

In his mind, he seized a rock and pegged it. A flurry of wings and feathers and they were gone.

Good.

He didn't need them. He'd find another set of hands to hold his trust and the homo lovebirds could find somewhere else to butt-fuck each other to death.

Not in my house.

Not in this land.

SLY DOGS

*S*TEF STAYED HOME two days. The first voluntarily, the second under duress.

Friday he went in. Max was making up Wednesday's lost session and Stef needed to project normalcy before the rumor-mill got a foothold.

Fat chance.

The staff had him for breakfast, the story embellished to the point where he and Jav were boning on one of the art room tables. But the ribbing was affectionate, punctuated by a lot of hugging, examination of his wounds, fussing and clucking and an unspoken, *Whew, that was a close one.*

Corley and Juan's lips were sealed tight around Geno's involvement, but they didn't waste the opportunity to throw a little shade at Stef.

"You and Javi," Juan said with relish, elbowing Stef's side. "Check out the secret work romance."

"Couple of sly dogs," Corley said. "Christ, each of you is more handsome than the other. How do you even leave the house?"

Stef took it in stride, pulled at his collar and looked appropriately sheepish, but made no comment. He hoped least said, soonest mended.

By late morning, he was tired. A grudging admission he wasn't a hundred percent. A slow realization he didn't feel so hot. He was slightly off-kilter. Slightly nauseous. Not enough of either to be debilitating, but enough to make it feel like the world wouldn't hold still. His instincts and his knowledge kept wandering off and getting lost.

Worst of all, as the morning progressed, he felt more and more teary. His throat anxious and lumpy, his emotions poised on a precarious edge. The blow to the head had upset some sensory applecart and everything was in a jumbled mess on the floor of his stomach. Every twenty minutes he considered holing up somewhere, having an ugly cry and getting it over with.

A cry over what?

He finally retreated to his office, but he chose to meditate instead of cry. He sat cross-legged on the floor, breathing slow and deep, regarding the spots of dried blood and the stray screws and bolts still scattered on the carpet. He came to a rather swift conclusion that he was mortally embarrassed by his unprofessional behavior. He upset Geno. He scared Juan and Corley. He let Ronnie down, and even if she hadn't issued an official reprimand or taken disciplinary action, either was warranted. He deserved to be rattled right now. Ronnie put a profound amount of trust in Stef, and he violated it. His clients' trust in him was paramount, and he violated that, too. Geno was blameless: he reacted precisely the way you'd expect a traumatized kid to react. Stef was the adult in the room, and he knew better than to make out with his boyfriend at the office. After hours or no after hours. Closed door or no closed door.

He swallowed hard and shook his shoulders into line. *What you're feeling is called healthy guilt,* he reminded himself. *You regret your poor behavior. Good. It serves as a reminder for the future. It tastes like shit, but you'll remember the taste next time you want to bend Jav over your desk.*

He glanced at said desk, considering the idea, then squeezed his eyes shut. "Fucking unbelievable," he muttered. He took a few more deep breaths, even managed an ironic chuckle. "Go eat something, you dumb horndog."

He managed a little lunch, then he wanted nothing more than to lie down and sleep. But now Max was running the length of the art room and flinging arms around Stef's legs. "Where were you? What happened to your face? Did you fall down? Did you bleed? Can I see? Did you cry?"

He climbed Stef like a tree, digging feet into Stef's quads and sides. Stef heaved him up on a hip and kept his head back from the inquisitive pawing. "Easy, easy. Don't touch."

"Does it hurt?"

"Yeah, but I'm okay. What do you want to do today?"

Max pointed to the sand table, then fearlessly leaned out of Stef's arms, following his pointing finger. Stef had to scramble not to drop him. He stumbled as Max's feet hit the floor and pattered off, dragging Stef behind by the hand.

The whole goddamn time, Geno watched. Like a vulture, the kid perched on one of the wide windowsills, regressed to the sullen silence from when he'd first arrived at EP. But instead of a checked-out, thousand-yard stare, his eyes followed Stef everywhere, narrowed and calculating.

Stef did his best to ignore him, but his mind was all over the place, wondering if maybe he *should've* made it known he was in a relationship with a man.

What the hell does that have to do with how I do my fucking job?

"I have to poop," Max said to the room at large.

Deadpan, Stef flipped a thumb toward the door and settled back to wait. Max's bathroom breaks took at least fifteen minutes, ten of which were spent playing with the door. Like most survivors of sexual assault, Max adored a lock. Both the predictable mechanics—the comforting turn and shift and click—and the autonomous act of creating instant, inviolate privacy. He'd go in and out of the john a half-dozen times, testing the knob over and over. Extra inspection to make sure it worked from the outside and no one could come in. One last flip of the lock, just to hear the comforting, solid *click* and the rattle of a handle that couldn't be turned. Then he'd take care of business.

Leaning back on two chair legs, Stef rubbed vigorously at the unwounded side of his head. The other side ached. He could use a couple Tylenol.

He looked up to see Geno glaring at him.

Jesus Christ, what do I do?

This was still Max's session. Stef didn't dare start something he couldn't finish and end up caught between two clients. But he had to say something. Praying he had enough time, he held Geno's gaze and said, "I apologize for the other night."

He almost added, *it was inexcusable,* but bit it off. He promised Ronnie no dramatics.

Geno was winding a pipe cleaner around his index finger, cutting off the circulation and watching the tip turn purple before unwinding and letting the blood flow back in. "No biggie," he said in an icy voice. "I just thought you were raping the guy."

Stef kept his face immobile even as he felt the blood drain out of it.

I don't have the skills for this today.

"I truly regret you got that impression," he said evenly. "I mean it. I'm sorry."

"Can't believe I didn't figure out you were gay," Geno said.

Stef hesitated, then decided being bisexual was beside the point. "Is it going to be a problem?"

The boy shrugged. "I don't have a problem. Just hope Jav lubes you up good. It's the considerate thing to do."

Stef bit his tongue hard. It was such an effort to keep his game face on, his cheekbones were going numb.

Geno tossed the pipe cleaner aside, slid off the windowsill and approached the sand table. "I mean, I assume you're the bottom."

"I can see you're upset," Stef said.

"You think? Why didn't you fucking tell me?"

"My private life doesn't come into play here."

"Yeah, well, your private life disgusts me."

"I can understand that," Stef said. "At the same time, it has nothing to do with—"

"Nothing to *do* with? I had seven guys rape me."

"I understand."

"You understand you fucking make me sick?"

"I'll be happy to talk about this when—"

"I don't want the details of how you crave dick."

"—but right now I'm with another client."

"Yeah, a six-year-old boy," Geno said. "That's just great."

"Hey." Stef clenched his fist to keep from pointing a finger. "You're out of line."

"I trusted you," Geno said. "But you only hold people's trust in your hands when you're trying to get in their pants. Telling them how *heavy* it is and how you're so aware of it all the time. Bet men just line up to fuck you after they hear that shit, huh?"

The blood that had drained out of Stef's face now drained out of his gut. "What?"

Looming above him, Geno had gone pale as well. "Nothing."

In a simple chain, Stef linked up the boy's stunned expression to the kitchen, to Jav, to the lost notebook, to words Stef had shyly written on a piece of graph paper. Shocked by his own ardor. Embarrassed at his lack of eloquence.

"Nobody ever wrote me a love note before," Jav said after reading it, his voice a little gruff. He then folded the graph paper and tucked it precisely between the pages of his little leather tome. Putting it among his most private thoughts like loving Stef was one of his best ideas.

"How do you know?" Stef said quietly.

Geno swallowed. "Know what?" But all his bravado was gone and his voice trembled at the end.

"How do you know what I told Jav about trust?"

Geno looked at his shoes, lips pressed tight.

"You took his notebook," Stef said.

"I found it. I didn't take it, I found it."

The blood returned to Stef's stomach, angry and boiling. That notebook was off limits. Stef didn't know what was in there. He *wanted* to know, but hell if he'd ask. It wasn't something to ask for. It was a privilege earned and double hell if he'd fucking *snoop* before he earned it.

This burgling punk snooped. Read every page, and the things tucked between pages. Now he knew things Stef didn't. He had information Stef didn't believe himself worthy of yet.

"Look, I didn't read anything but that note," Geno said. "And only because it fell out of the pages."

"You read it without his consent." Stef said.

At *consent,* Geno, merely pale before, went white. Stef's anger melted into a profound sadness as he saw the deed's ramifications sink in. He watched this boy realize how reading the notebook and the letter was an act of spiritual assault. He fucked Jav's mind without permission. That fragile, weird, complex, curious, passionate, beautiful mind. Parts of which were still such a mystery to Stef.

Geno's eyes blinked rapidly. He was close to tears and now Max was coming back.

"You still have it?" Stef asked, pleased that his voice didn't betray how much he felt like crying, too.

Geno nodded.

"Please get it and put it on my desk," Stef said. "I want to see you in Ronnie's office at three o'clock. We have some things to talk about."

"Finch, I—"

"Go now, please. This is Max's time."

FOR GIVE

1N A WAY, Geno wished Stef had simply beat the shit out of him, rather than his cool and professional handling of things.

Sitting in Ronnie's office with Stef and the EP director, Geno couldn't have constructed a more perfect reenactment of his high school fuck-up with Carlito, when their parents were called in after they took tests for each other. It sucked then and it sucked now.

Floating in a surreal bubble of anger and guilt and shame, his mouth mumbled apologies until he shut down, shut up and nodded like a robot as Stef declared their working relationship could use a breather. No time limits set, just a vague interval until everyone's emotions had calmed down.

The theft and snooping of Jav's notebook weren't mentioned, for which Geno had to be grateful, but it pissed him off he had to be grateful. He was high on emotion and short on humility right now, with an overwhelming desire to cut his losses and get the hell out of this place. But he couldn't. He was barely two months into a six-month sentence and he had nowhere else to go.

And I like it here.

Which only made him feel worse, like he'd deliberately pissed his own bed. Once the torturous meeting was over, he hid out in his room the rest of the day. Sulking, sure, but he wasn't hurting anyone, so the world could kiss his ass and leave him alone.

I fucked up.

"Yeah," Stef said about the high school debacle. "That's one you eat for a long time."

Geno resisted an urge to spit on the floor, his mouth coated with such a sour and shamed flavor, he might never eat again.

He disappointed Stef and it tasted like shit.

Now Stef would tell Jav that Geno took his book and *that* was going to suck.

Jav probably wouldn't work in the kitchen anymore, or he would and it would be awkward as fuck. Which would make Stavroula pissed at Geno, too.

He sucked.

Everything *sucked.*

A soft knock at the door. Not a soul existed on the planet Geno wanted to see. He'd prefer a proctology exam to visitors right now. Still, his feet were moving, his hand was turning the knob and he was opening it.

It was Chaow. The young Thai man stood at the threshold, cupping a bowl in his palms. In it, three plump yellow matzo balls in golden broth. Tiny chives sprinkled on top.

"I for give," Chaow said, holding it out.

Geno stared into the bowl, then at Chaow, who didn't meet his eyes.

"I for give," Chaow said.

"You forgive me?"

"I give. For you."

Slowly Geno took the bowl, then the spoon Chaow offered. "Thank you."

"Eat," Chaow said. "It's good. You feel good."

Geno's fingers pressed into the bowl's smooth sides.

Eat. It's good.

A remembered echo as Geno, now master of the henhouse, offered food to the tired, grieving rooster that was Nathan.

Here, Dad. I made you this.

Eat something.

Is it good? Do you like it?

Do you like me?

His eyes filled with tears. "Thanks," he said, every cell in his hungry body wanting his father back. Wanting his life back.

"I for give," Chaow said, and slipped away.

Geno sat at his desk and ate the soup. He felt better.

Not good, but better.

He put his shoulders into line and made a few decisions.

He'd work with Beau and not be a dick about it. If he saw Jav in the kitchen, he'd apologize. He'd own his shit and not jeopardize his chances of getting out of here.

In the meantime, he might be able to get out a little bit. He knew some of the other residents, after hitting the two-month milestone, had been allowed to volunteer outside EP or even get part-time jobs. Juan worked at a barber shop. Patrick had a little gig at an animal shelter. Jeff shelved books at the Muhlenberg Library. Everything had to be vetted and the hours were limited. But it could be done.

He'd ask.

He was allowed to.

HOUSE BOY

"**H**ONEY, I'M HOME," Stef said.

From the couch, Roman shook his head, dog tags jingling, then hopped off Jav's legs. Jav shook his own head and sat up. He'd slept so hard he drooled.

"What year is it?" he said.

"Twenty sixty-four. We cured cancer but have a new super herpes virus." Stef sat on the couch, letting the dog come up between his knees. "Yes, I missed you too." His hands scratched Roman's coppery ruff and ears. "Was it hard to be here with Javi all day? Was he depressed?"

"Depressed, but productive," Jav said, stretching. "We ran three miles this morning, did laundry, cleaned the bathroom and food shopped."

"Roman did laundry?"

"Then he walked the whole High Line with me this afternoon. Dinner's in the oven. Beer's on ice. Maybe I'll leave this whole writing gig and just be your house boy."

Stef reached for his messenger bag. "I brought you a present."

Jav touched his chest. "You wish to give me a present?"

Stef drew out a small book and held it up. "Yours, I believe?"

Jav blinked at the brown leather cover. Once. Twice.

My notebook.

"Dude," he cried, falling off the couch.

Stef stretched his arm long, holding the book out of reach as Jav went crawling up his chest. "How bad do you want me right now?"

"Where the fuck did you find it?"

Stef switched the book from one hand to the other. "I don't feel the right amount of gratitude here."

"Give me that. Jesus Christ, I don't believe it." Jav wrestled the notebook out of Stef's teasing grasp and sat back in the couch cushions, fanning the pages against his thumb. His chest caved in with relief, sending up a cloud of happiness that nearly choked him.

Thank God. Oh thank fucking God.

"Where'd you find it?"

Stef got up and headed toward the kitchen. "Told you the day we met. I'm not an art therapist, I'm a professional thief."

"What? Come on."

Stef popped a beer and drained nearly half of it. "Let's say it was in the wrong hands." He leaned on the counter with a rough exhale and rubbed at the back of his head.

"Feel all right?" Jav asked.

"Yeah. Just one of those nights." He cracked open the oven door and peered inside. "You're roasting a chicken?"

"Pigeon. Roman found it in the park. I figured we should start eating on a budget if we lose my income. Of course, circumstances have changed dramatically since then." Notebook still in hand, he hopped over the back of the couch and went to get his arms around Stef.

"Thank you," he said. "I loved you before but now I worship you."

"I know."

"Where was it? Tell me."

Stef wiggled out of the embrace and took a pull of his beer. "I can confirm you lost it in the kitchen at EP and it was found by a young, mutual friend of ours."

"Geno?"

"I can neither confirm nor deny."

Jav's eyes widened. "That little punk," he said. "Think he read it?"

"Can neither confirm nor deny," Stef said. "Though I can say it's odd to hear a little punk quote an extremely private, embarrassingly klutzy note you wrote to your lover."

Jav's entire body cringed. "Oh Jesus, really? No."

"Yeah."

"Dude, that ain't cool." Jav found the pages where the piece of graph paper was stuck. It was awfully close to that ridiculous little passage with Geno's name. Did he read that?

Fuck. Oh well, it wasn't making fun of him. It wasn't insulting, it was just stupid. And Jesus Christ, it was private…

"Good thing I won't be in the kitchens anymore," he said.

"I'm taking a break from him myself."

"Really?"

Stef killed his beer and turned to get another one. "Had a little meeting with Ronnie and it's for the best. I'm annoyed with him on a personal level now and until I get over it, I won't be effective on a professional level. I'll be bringing my shit into it." He made an apologetic gesture with his bottle. "I can't say much more than that."

"No, no, it's fine. I mean, not fine, but I got this back." He hugged Stef. "You got it back for me."

"It's what I do."

Stef's body felt stiff in his arms. His tone was slightly edgy. A clever Stef impersonation with something essential left out, enough to make him weirdly not himself.

"You feel all right?" Jav asked again.

"Mostly right. I want to eat. Possibly I'll want to get laid later."

"Get plates," Jav said, heading for the oven.

A long beat where Stef didn't move from the counter or say anything.

"What?" Jav said, catching Stef's penetrating look.

"You going to carry that around all night?"

"What? Oh."

Jav looked at the notebook, still in his hand. He had to admit a reluctance to put it down. But he did, and served up dinner.

He resisted the pull as long as it took to eat. Then he took the notebook to his desk, a man on a mission. Determined never again to keep all his creative eggs in one easily lost basket. What the hell was he thinking?

He put on his porkpie hat and glasses and started transcribing all his hand-written scribbles into a new document. He'd still use a notebook. It was more portable and his flow was more liquid from his mind to a pen. He liked the physicality of writing by hand. But he'd move it to electric copy once a week from now on, if not more. With double backups.

"Leave that," he said, when he heard Stef scraping dishes and tearing off sheets of tin foil for leftovers. "Stef, leave it. I'll clean up."

"I got it. You cooked."

Page after page after page. Grimacing at old, dopey things he'd jotted down. Re-reading others with raised eyebrows. *That's not bad.* Sometimes an old idea collided with something new he'd been kicking around, in an immaculate conception that busted up a problem or gave a fresh perspective. Then he had to grab a Post-it and scribble it down, making even more to transcribe.

Behind him, Stef changed channels between this and that. Sometimes Roman trotted over and put his muzzle or a paw on Jav's knee. Jav petted or scratched with one hand, typing with the other.

"Dude, he wants to go out," Stef said.

Impatient, Jav hustled Roman around the block, which naturally made the mutt take his sweet-ass time with business. Jav couldn't get back to his desk fast enough to pick up where he left off.

Page after page after page. Another empty beer bottle.

"I'm hitting the sack," Stef said at eleven. "I'm not myself."

"'Kay," Jav said, head swiveling between the notebook and the screen. Notebook. Screen. Notebook. He looked up and over his shoulder when the bathroom door clicked. The kitchen was cleaned up, the dishwasher humming. The lights were all off except for Jav's desk lamp. Roman curled in his bed by the French doors.

He went back to work, the apartment still and silent except for his fingers on the keypad and the occasional mutter under his breath. The scratch of pen on pad. A line of Post-its now stretching across the bottom of the screen.

"Hey."

Jav blinked back into reality. It was one-thirty in the morning. Stef stood in sweats and T-shirt, arms crossed and a shoulder in the doorframe. "It's time to stop," he said.

"I need to do a few more pages, then I—"

"I need you to come to bed now, okay?"

Jav took off his glasses. "Are you all right?"

Stef's chin lifted. "I'm your lover and your partner and I want you to stop working and get in bed."

The whole room crossed its arms now, staring Jav down. Without a word, he hit Ctrl+S, turned off the lamp and went to brush his teeth. He slid into bed a few minutes later. Punched his pillows into place. Moved up against Stef's back and slid his arm around him. "Sorry."

"For what?"

"For how I lose track of time."

"I'm not expecting that to change. If I want you, I have to be a big boy, walk out there and say so. So I did."

Jav pressed his nose against Stef's nape and twined their fingers. "You feel all right?"

"Yeah." Stef drew a long breath, his shoulders expanding against Jav's chest. "No. Maybe. I don't know. I took a Klonopin. Let's just go to sleep."

Jav lay awake. In his arms, Stef's body was relaxed, but a precise, measured cadence in his exhales showed his mind was busy. A long breathing silence. The air between them prickled.

Something's wrong.

In all their time together, Jav had never seen Stef play passive-aggressive games. He always said what was on his mind. Putting a label on every thought and feeling and problem.

Something is so wrong, even he doesn't know what it is.

Is it me?

Jav backtracked through the night with a growing concern he'd missed something. As he went through everything said and done, lights began to turn on.

Just one of those nights.

Possibly I'll want to get laid later.

Jav squeezed his eyes shut, now remembering the night Stef said he'd be taking on a difficult case. He said, "Sometimes I can only shake off the echo of a sexual abuse story by making love. Like I need to be fucked back to myself."

I'm not myself.

Stef leaning against the doorframe tonight, arms crossed tight. The slight lift of his chin under the unwavering gaze.

I need you to come to bed now.

I'm your lover and your partner and I want you to stop working…

Jav's vision blurred and focused, coming to rest finally on Stef's bedside table. A glinting pile of all his rings and his watch. Stef only stripped off his hardware when he was in a mood. A signal he was worked up and capable of grabbing hard enough to leave marks. Or sometimes he did it because he wanted nothing between his hands and Jav's skin.

Jav knew these things.

He was careful not to let a sigh out with his next exhale. He sucked it back, sucked it up and faced a fact.

He was trying to tell me something and I missed it. He wanted me and I didn't notice.

A bit of bristling defense tried to elbow its way into the conversation. *Well, why didn't he just say so?*

Jav pushed the excuses aside. Most of the time, Stef voiced his needs. Sometimes he wanted Jav to *know*.

Stef tested him tonight and Jav blew it.

I need to be better at this.

He slid his hand under Stef's shirt and rubbed his back, knowing from the sound of his breathing he was drifting away. Floating back to himself with Klonopin's help, not Jav's. Jav was too late.

"I'm sorry." He mouthed the words to the dark and meant them.

I can do more than this. I can be a better lover and partner.

Stef loves his work but he said coming home is his most important job.

It needs to be mine, too. And it will.

He drew another breath to say so, but then Stef gave a little snore and his limbs twitched.

"Shh," Jav whispered to both of them.

Don't announce it. Talk is cheap. Just do it. Take your rings off and be better.

APRIL

HÁBLAME

*G*ENO HAD EXACTLY two sessions with Beau before a spring virus of some kind swept through Chelsea. Beau went down for the count, then Aedith. Half of EP was walking around sneezing and hacking, the other half trying to keep the infected at a distance.

With a reduced staff, CCT had fewer one-on-one sessions and more general free time. Geno showed up and worked quietly, staying far from Stef and Max. He took his shifts in the kitchen where, as predicted, Jav wasn't volunteering anymore. His presence was sorely missed, with much speculation as to why he left.

"He didn't *leave*," Stavroula said. "He just needs to work on his book."

"Yeah, well, he didn't even say goodbye," Pablo said.

"Story of my life," Hasan said.

Geno kept his head down, telling himself no one was looking at him, when of course it felt like everyone was.

He killed time in the fitness room and taking walks around Chelsea. He dismissed how much he missed Jav. Ignored the hole left in his daily life where Stef used to be.

He stopped in the middle of the sidewalk and squinted at a steakhouse on the corner of 15th and Ninth. *Help Wanted: Busboy,* read a little sign in the window. Geno went in, talked with the manager, Ed Shaughnessy, and filled out an application. Ed talked with the EP Director and Geno started working weekend brunch shifts for peanuts, but it wasn't about the money.

One Saturday, Ed said he was short a head for the dinner shift. Could Geno come back and work that night? EP extended his curfew to midnight, Geno grabbed a catnap and went back in time for Happy Hour.

The restaurant's vibe changed dramatically after sundown, going from respectable to desperate. The crowd from the bar spilled into the dining area, raucous and noisy. Waitresses maneuvered through the needy crush with trays held high. Everywhere the eyes, looking, considering what they had, what they might have, what they could've had. Women staring up at men who glanced sideways at other women who were oblivious to men staring at them.

I really do not like bars, Geno thought, clearing and wiping tables as fast as he could, invisible in his all-black clothes. It was hot in this meat market. He paused, a knee on the seat of a chair, running a forearm across his brow. He cracked his neck to the right, then turned his head to the left and saw Anthony Fox sitting in a booth.

Oh look, he thought. *It's him.*

His hands loaded two more glasses into his bus tub before it hit home.

It's him.

He didn't exactly piss himself. Not a full flood. But he definitely dribbled as his stomach screamed and went fleeing for the exits. For a surreal moment of abject terror, he gripped the edges of the tub, sure he was about to vomit into it. He went immobile, poised on the edge of a heave and not daring to move.

A cool, measured voice spoke in his head, but it wasn't Mos this time.

All right, Stef said. *Listen to me carefully. Move out of sight. Calmly. Pick up the tub and move. Don't run. Walk like hell. Don't look back.*

Now.

His head floating miles above his body, Geno shouldered the tub, walked toward the kitchen doors, then abruptly ducked into the alcove of the waitresses' station. A scrolled lattice partition separated it from the dining area, offering a bare minimum of cover.

Now look, Stef's voice said. *Carefully. Make damn sure about this.*

Geno peered through the criss-crossed strips of wood.

Anthony wore a ball cap pulled low. When he took it off to scratch his head, his hair was cropped close and bleached to white.

But the ear.

The cauliflower ear from his wrestling days.

The fuck is he doing here? Out in the open where anyone could see him?

For a wild moment, the fear in Geno's belly turned to white-hot anger. The nerve of this fucker, strolling into a Manhattan bar like a fine, upstanding citizen of the world. Thinking a cap and a dye job would make him invisible. What, was he fucking *stupid?* Or just…

Geno inhaled sharply, remembering what Detective Mackin said all those months ago.

Often a case gets cracked because a criminal is dumb or greedy. Or both.

Geno's chest squeezed tight around his held breath. The dumb, greedy fox was in the henhouse and only Geno knew it.

What do I do?

His hand crept into his pocket, fingering his phone.

Call Stef.

But Stef was pissed at him.

Call Vern.

Vern was too far away.

Call the cops.

And say what?

He couldn't do nothing. Anthony wasn't alone in the booth. Across from him was a guy who looked no older than Geno. A baby chick prime for plucking. Possibly one with a twin back in the nest.

You can't let this happen.

The fox is in the henhouse and you're the only one around here with a lick of common sense.

"The hell are you doing?" Ed Shaughnessy appeared, clapping a hand on Geno's shoulder and making him jump in his shoes. "Hey, hey. Easy. What's going on?"

His heart pounding, Geno stared up at his boss.

"Dude, you're like, *green,*" Ed said. "You feel okay?"

"I need help," Geno said.

"And I need tables bussed."

"Listen to me. Please just listen. See that guy in the last booth? Plaid shirt and a ball cap?"

Ed leaned and looked through the lattice. "What about him?"

"He's an FBI fugitive."

"What?"

"Do you remember the Mengele Ring? The porn bust in New Jersey last year?"

Ed looked at him sharply now, but said nothing.

"His name is Anthony Fox," Geno said. "The ringleader. He's wanted by the FBI. Ed, I swear to God it's him. He's right there."

Ed's gaze rested on Geno a long, deliberating moment.

He doesn't believe me.

Just like Ruby, the woman from the rape crisis hotline.

I won't let you do this.

"How do you know?" Ed said.

You're not the first sick pervert to make up a twisted story. Get a life.

Geno swallowed. "Because I was there. I was one of his victims. That's why I'm at Exodus Project. Me and my twin brother were at the house the night it was busted."

A long staring moment, during which Geno thought about dying. Maybe tonight. Then Ed put a hand on his shoulder again. Gentle this time. "I am not doubting your experience," he said, low and even. "But before I make a call, let me ask: *are you sure?*"

"Yes."

"Did he see you?"

"No."

"Would he recognize you?"

Fear splashed up like acid in Geno's chest. "Yes."

Ed looked back over his shoulder and called to a waitress passing by. "Erin? Get Andre for me? Quick." His fingers tightened into Geno's collarbones and he walked them a few steps backward, further into the alcove, cutting off the dining room from their line of sight. "You stay right here with me."

Geno swayed on his legs and leaned back against the wall. "I need to get out of here. Before he sees me."

"It's okay," Ed said. "Deep breaths. I'm not going to leave you alone."

"You need me, Ed?" Andre, the bouncer, came around the corner into the alcove. Short and burly with bad skin and a nose that had been broken more than once. Ed explained the situation quickly.

"You're positive about this?" Andre said to Geno.

Geno nodded a little crazily.

"Deep breath," Ed said.

"His name's Anthony Fox," Geno said.

"I remember," Andre said.

"But he's probably moving under another name now."

"All right, all right," Ed said. "You're going green again. Take it easy, let me think."

"This has to be quiet and quick," Andre said. "If we start drawing attention, this fucker might bolt."

"We'll go in back and make a call. Andre, tell the hostess no more reservations. Whoever's waiting gets seated upstairs. Then figure out a way with the cooks to delay the order on that table. Burn it, drop it on the floor, do something. Then buy him a free round. Geno, come with me."

Off the kitchen was a small office, just enough room for a desk and a couple of folding chairs. Geno sat, shaking, his stomach a wreck, teeth chattering.

"Kathy," Ed called out the door to one of the bartenders. "Get a ginger ale for me please?"

Just a Coke, Geno thought.

Ed called 911. "We have a positive identification of a known federal fugitive in my restaurant."

They won't come. They'll take too long to come and he'll be gone again. He'll take that guy with him and…

"Anthony Fox… Positive identification… One of the victims… That's right… He's absolutely sure…"

They won't believe me. Nobody will believe me.

Geno felt a debilitating rush of dizziness. He slumped, put his forehead on his knees and concentrated on not throwing up.

Somebody help me, he thought.

Mos came. But a calm, kind Mos. He didn't shout. Didn't lecture or forbid. He just gently drew Geno away.

You're too close, he said. *It's not safe. Move back a little so you don't feel so much.*

Geno retreated a single step into the land of Nos. The walls of the tiny office blurred, sparkling like stars at his peripheral. Ed's voice grew faint, only every few words reaching Geno's ears.

That's perfect, Mos said. *Don't go away. Just make some distance. Put a few stars between you and what's happening to you.*

Ed hung up the phone, glanced at the waitress who came in. "Thanks, Kathy, just set it down."

Geno looked at the highball of bubbling ginger ale. He did not drink from unattended glasses.

You don't have to, Mos said. *When you say it's time and not a moment before.*

"You all right, G?" Ed said.

Geno nodded. His limbs were still fiery with adrenaline, but the dizziness was clearing. He was here. But not *completely* here.

Good, Mos said. *This is good. Many interesting things are happening. Let's watch.*

The phone on Ed's desk rang. Another conversation, more urgent this time. Ed raised eyebrows at Geno and mouthed, "FBI."

Stay back, Mos said. *A little longer.*

Ed held the phone away from his ear. "Shit just got real…" He listened more than he talked for the rest of the call, and hung up wide-eyed, a mist of sweat along his hairline. He picked up the ginger ale and drained half of it himself. "Holy hell."

"What do we do now?" Geno asked.

"We sit tight. Cavalry's coming. You're staying right here until he's gone, okay? Bastard will have to get through Andre, over the bar and past me first."

Geno nodded, breathing deep as he came closer to the situation again. He trusted the glass now, and he took a small sip.

You may feel this, Mos said. *But not too much.*

"Is there someone you can call at EP?" Ed asked. "Your folks? A friend?"

"Yeah." Geno turned his phone over and over in his hand. He brought up Stef's contact entry. His thumb quivered over the call button.

Just call him. He's a professional. It's his job. He'll help or send someone who can.

He swallowed hard, closed his eyes and let his thumb touch down.

Two rings. A third.

"Hello?"

Geno's eyes opened. It wasn't Stef's voice, and Stef always answered by saying his full name.

Did I dial right?

"Hello?"

"Stef?"

"No, it's Jav."

I called the home phone. Shit, Jav's the last person who wants to talk to me.

"Hello?"

He clenched his free fist. "Jav, it's Geno."

A beat. "What's up?"

"¿Stef está en casa?" He hoped Spanish would help pave the way.

"No, he's up at a thing in New Rochelle," Jav said in English, his voice cool and dry.

"Oh." Geno pulled in a trembling breath. "Okay."

"What's going on?" The tone, while not warm and friendly, wasn't angry either.

"Um…"

"Where are you?"

"I'm at work. There's kind of a situation and…"

"Are you all right?" Now Jav's voice leaned on Geno like an arm around his shoulders.

"Yeah, I'm okay, but—"

"Do you need help?"

Geno's throat seized up hard. "I need…"

"Háblame, mi pana."

Talk to me, buddy.

"Something's happening right now," Geno said in Spanish. "It's hard to explain."

"Do you want me to come get you?"

Yes, come get me, Geno thought. *Come find me, Dad. Find me. Save me. Come get me, Dad, please come get me out of here.*

"Geno," Jav said, with a little edge of alarm.

"Please come here," Geno said. "I need… I need someone…"

"Here, give it." Ed took the phone and had a short talk, telling Jav to come to the back door where one of the bouncers, Billy, would be. "Show him some ID and he'll let you in. Right. Okay. Hold on." He handed the phone back to Geno. "He needs to ask you something."

"Do you want me to call Stef for you?" Jav said.

"Yeah," Geno said, clearing his sludgy throat. "Tell him Anthony Fox is sitting in this bar. He's here. Stef will know what it means."

A beat of silence that felt like a gamble, then Jav said, "I know what it means. I'm on my way."

"Jav, I'm sorry," Geno said. "About—"

"It's all right," Jav said. "None of that matters. Let's just get you the hell out of there. You stay with Ed. I'm coming."

I'LL TAKE YOU HOME

"**1**'M UP IN New Rochelle," Stef said on the phone. "I'm about to give a lecture but I know what's going on and I'm getting on a train right afterward."

"Okay," Geno said.

"You do whatever the police say, understand?"

"I will."

"Do not go back to EP alone. Not even in a cab. I want someone to walk you through the doors and I want a call from the security desk when you get there."

"Can I go with Jav?"

Stef didn't answer.

"Please let me go with Jav," Geno blurted. "I know you're mad and I don't know if it's allowed but I swear… Stef, I was an asshole to him and he didn't have to come for me but he did. I called and he said he'd come right away. He's… I trust him. Please, let me stay with Jav."

"You can stay with him," Stef said. His voice was tight and it made Geno feel desperate.

"I'm sorry," Geno said. "About the notebook and what I said—"

"It's okay," Stef said, sounding like himself now. "Geno, listen, I am not mad. I'm not even thinking about the notebook. I'm frustrated because I'm far away from you. I'm nervous because this is a serious, possibly dangerous situation. I only want you to be protected while the shit is going down, then get to a safe place. Now promise me: you listen to the police, you do what they say. Then you go with whoever you feel comfortable with but do not go alone."

"I'll go with Jav." Geno swallowed. "And I promise. All those things. I'm scared, too."

"The police will not let Anthony see you," Stef said. "He will not see you, talk to you, threaten you or touch you. Ever again."

The words were fierce. This was Stef, the big brother of dreams, scouting the path ahead, sensing the danger and directing the way. Tears sprang to Geno's eyes.

"I need to go now but I'm coming back in a few hours," Stef said. "Don't be afraid. They're going to get him. It's almost over. I'm really proud of you and I'll see you soon."

"All right," Geno whispered. "Thanks."

Despite ID and Ed's vouching, police wouldn't let Jav into the restaurant. They had the bar in a quiet lockdown. Nobody was allowed in or out. Jav went to a Starbucks across the street to wait.

Sequestered with Ed in the tiny office with the door closed and an FBI agent posted outside, Geno floated in an anxious and isolated bubble. How would police make the arrest without causing panic? Would Anthony bolt? Was he packing heat? Would there be a shootout?

Will he see me?

Jav texted from across the street, sending short bursts of support.

Vern called. He was standing by, ready and waiting for anything Geno needed.

I'm OK, Geno texted Stef, even though he knew Stef couldn't answer.

Ed leaned back in his chair, hands laced behind his head. "Buddy of mine from college lives a couple towns over from Stockton," he said to the ceiling. "He's got twin boys. Man, he was out of his mind last summer, reading about the story. I remember talking to him and…" He rubbed his face hard, then sat forward with a sardonic half-smile. "I don't give a damn what the cops do. If they have to shoot the place up or firebomb it apart to get that motherfucker, so be it. I'm insured."

"Thank you," Geno whispered, clutching his phone.

Nothing was happening.

And then it was over.

He didn't see a thing. The cops and agents wouldn't let him out of the office until Anthony was gone, so Geno didn't get the satisfaction of witnessing the proverbial perp walk. No chance to lock eyes with the Fox and call, "Have fun being someone's bitch in prison, asshole."

It was over so invisibly, Geno couldn't take in that the world was a profoundly different place now. The cops finally let Jav in through the kitchen. He stood quietly in the narrow hall outside the office while Geno gave police his statement.

"Geronimo." One of the FBI agents was holding out his cell phone. "Call for you."

"Me?" Geno said, taking it. "Hello?"

"Mr. Caan, this is Captain Hook."

The Irish accented voice hit Geno square in the chest and melted all up and down his limbs. "Hey," he said, exhaling to the bottom of his lungs

"Congratulations."

The new and different world teetered on its axis as the single word threw arms around Geno and squeezed. He sniffed hard, pressing a hand into his eyes. "Thanks."

"I couldn't be more relieved or happier," Hook said. "Or prouder."

"I… Yeah. Thanks. It was…really scary for a minute, but…"

"You got somewhere safe to go?"

Geno glanced at Jav. "Yeah. I'm with a friend."

"Good. You put your head down tonight and rest easy. Son of a bitch won't hurt anyone ever again."

All at once, Geno was exhausted. "It's really over, isn't it?"

"It's over. Will you give me a ring tomorrow? Let me know you're all right?"

"Sure. Thanks."

"No, thank *you*. Goodnight, son."

The commendation piled up until it was dizzying. Every agent and cop shook Geno's hand. Ed hugged him hard, then went on patting his back and squeezing his shoulders.

"Come on," Jav finally said. "I'll take you home."

Geno sat in the back of a cab in a trance, not realizing Jav meant *his* home until the cab pulled up in front of a row of brick townhouses in the west twenties.

"I have a curfew," Geno said. "I have to sign back in by midnight."

"Stef took care of it with EP. They know you're with me."

Geno didn't question it. He was too tired. His feet shuffled as he followed Jav down a flight of stairs. The apartment was warm and snug and a dog came to greet them at the door. A copper-colored retriever who barked a few times, then sniffed Geno thoroughly from the knees down.

"This is Roman," Jav said. "He's my nephew's dog."

"Where's your nephew?"

"At college. New Paltz." Jav went into the little kitchen. The sound of cabinets opening and mugs rattling. "You want a hot drink? Tea or something?"

"No, thanks."

"Tell me what I can do. Do you want to eat something? Collapse? I feel kind of stupid and helpless here so please…" His hand made a broad sweeping gesture around. "Mi casa es su casa. ¿Vale?"

"Can I look out there?" Geno pointed toward the French doors.

"Sure."

Roman followed Geno out into the tiny garden, a little green box inside Manhattan, strung with Christmas lights. Twinkling like a hundred stars. The way Nos used to be.

Maybe it can be that way again.

A different Nos.

Roman sat on his haunches and tilted his head as Geno crouched down and let go of the night. It was a harsh, painful cry that left him raw and empty. The violent release of tears took all his body heat as well. He shivered as he dragged his face along his sleeve. From up between his thighs rose the faint smell of urine. His pits stank with dried, nervous sweat. He needed to get out of these clothes.

He went back in, the dog on his heels.

Jav was washing a few dishes. "Hey. The kettle's on the stove if you want that drink."

Geno took a deep breath. "If I told you I needed to borrow a pair of sweats and put these clothes in the wash, would you not ask me any questions?"

Jav turned off the water immediately. "My nephew keeps some clothes here," he said, walking toward the bedroom. "The washer-dryer is in the bathroom. You'll see the detergent on the floor. Take whatever you need, use the shower. I'll get you a towel."

Geno threw his clothes in, then took a quick shower and put on sweats, socks and a long-sleeved grey shirt with New Paltz across the chest.

"Thanks," he said, coming out into the living room. "That's better."

"Mugs are in the cabinet over the microwave," Jav said from the couch. "Help yourself."

Geno wasn't a tea man, but he found Sleepytime in the cabinet, which was supposed to be calming. He walked around, sipping and looking at things. A desk with a computer circulating scenic photos as a screen saver. Next to it was a wooden stand with a black hat, a little white feather in its band. Tall shelves were stuffed with books and artwork hung everywhere.

"You can turn on the TV if you want," Jav said.

"No. It might be on the news. I don't want to see anymore tonight."

"Good call."

"You said you knew?"

Jav's eyebrows wrinkled over the rim of his mug.

"When I said Anthony Fox was in the restaurant, you said you knew what it meant. Did you know who he was in general, or who he was to me in particular?"

"I knew *of* him," Jav said, setting his tea down. "And I had a hunch based on things you'd told me. That you were a twin and your father and brother died last summer. The pieces kind of fit together but I didn't know for sure until you said his name tonight. And I wanted to be wrong. Goddamn, I never wished so hard to be wrong."

Geno resumed pacing the room, looking at the same things two and three times. Jav read his book, but Roman followed Geno's circuitous path with a worried expression.

"Sorry I'm making the dog nervous," Geno said. "Walking in circles helps me settle down."

"You don't have to explain. I pace the shit out of this place when I'm writing."

Geno stopped to inspect the bookshelves beside the desk again.

"See anything you like?" Jav said.

"Not really," Geno said. "I don't need a story right now. I just need something to look at."

Jav's hand pointed over the back of the couch. "Try the bottom shelf on the left there. That's the fun stuff."

The tomes down here were larger. Art books and photographic essays on space, Mount Everest and Africa. A big volume of the artwork of Walt Disney. Another on Pixar. Titles like *A Map of the World. The Atlas of Cursed Places. The Encyclopedia of Myths & Legends. The Birthday Book. The Book of Names.*

Geno eased out a mid-sized blue tome. *"Planet Earth,"* he said. "Isn't that the show on National Geographic or something?"

"BBC," Jav said. "Have you seen it?"

"No. I heard it's pretty cool though."

He sat down with the book and turned a few pages. Jav had his feet on the coffee table, so Geno put his up, too, sliding them between stacked magazines and a big bowl of Chinese fortune cookies. Roman jumped on the couch and turned three times on a neighboring cushion, pushing into Geno's side. The warm, panting weight pressed in tight. First one paw on Geno's leg. Then the other. Then his muzzle laid on top with a big sigh.

"Is he always like this?" Geno asked, scratching the domed forehead.

"I think you remind him of my nephew. You're the same age."

The room was quiet, but not oppressive. Geno could hear the tiny tick of Jav's watch through the soft scrape of turned pages. The edges of his mind began to soften. The blocks of text swarmed in and out of focus and the photographs blurred together. Geno put the planet down on his chest and closed his eyes.

He woke with a start. Jav and Roman were gone. The apartment was dark except for a little light in the kitchen. It backlit Stef, who crouched by the side of the couch.

"Hey," he said. "I'm home."

"Hey," Geno said, taking his feet off the table.

"You all right?"

"Yeah. They got him."

Stef nodded, his mouth a tight, hard line. "They got him."

His eyes shone in the dimness. He put a hand on the armrest. His body gave a little start, then stilled. "I'm so proud of you."

"Holy shit, Finch." Geno slid off the couch, onto the floor and into Stef's arms.

Stef caught him up tight, a hand on Geno's head. "You helped bring him in. If not for you, he'd still be out there."

"He had a boy with him. Like my age. He could've…"

"I know. That boy is safe now. So are you."

"I was so fucking scared."

"I know. But they got him." Stef rocked their bodies side to side. "All because of you. Tonight's a victory. You did a great thing."

Geno willed his fists to let go of Stef's shirt but they were locked in tight. He kept waiting for Stef's grip to loosen, signaling he was letting go, but he didn't. Geno held on and Stef held still. His heart beat in a steady cadence beneath Geno's face. His tattooed forearm looked like a piece of marble sculpture. Winged horses and centaurs at his command, all gathered around to shelter this moment. Time stretched out long. Then longer.

I'm home, Geno thought. *And I'm so tired.* "Can I stay here tonight?"

"If you want. You can sleep on the couch or sleep upstairs in my mother's guest room."

"I want to stay here. If that's okay."

"Not a problem," Stef said.

"I'm sorry about everything I said. Jav's such a good guy."

Now Stef leaned back from him, smiling. "I know."

He got Geno a pillow and blanket and a bottle of water. Then he said good-night. "Yell if you need me."

Geno woke again, a little before two. He got up and took a leak. He glanced at the short hallway and the half-open door at its end. The apartment was wreathed in silence. The floorboards made no noise under his feet as he peered into the bedroom.

Stef slept on his back, one forearm flung up next to his head. Beside him, Jav lay on his side. Bottom arm crossed over his chest, the other hand on Stef's heart.

Geno stared a long time at the sleeping men and their strange, strong beauty.

The space between their bodies almost seemed to twinkle.

"Dos," he whispered.

THE ONLY ONE LEFT

*T*HE NEXT MORNING brought a ring of the doorbell and a call from the other side. "Everyone decent?"

Weird, it sounded like Stavroula. But it couldn't be.

It was her.

"You live here too?" Geno said.

"My mother does," she said. "And she has summoned you to breakfast."

"Me?"

"All of you. Lilia made matzo brei. Hi, cookie." She hugged Jav as Stef tapped Geno's shoulder and handed him a new toothbrush. Geno retrieved his black jeans and shirt from the dryer, ran wet hands through his hair and used a few swipes of the Right Guard he found in the medicine cabinet. They went upstairs to a gorgeous apartment, inhabited by two white-haired ladies.

"This is my mother, Rory" Stef said, indicating the neater dressed of the pair.

"And this is my mother, Lilia," Stavroula said, an arm around the other.

Geno looked at the two women. He looked at Jav and Stef, then back.

"It's nice to meet you," he said, deciding nothing was going to surprise him for the rest of the day.

Two matzo breis graced the dining room table. Circles of crisp, unleavened bread fried with beaten eggs and cinnamon, each bigger than a steering wheel.

"Wow, I haven't had this in years," Geno said, pulling his chair in.

"You're Jewish?" Lilia said, leaning on his chair to pour coffee. "Who made it for you?"

"My mother. We called it matzo surprise."

"Did she make savory or sweet?"

"Sweet. Sprinkled with sugar."

"I make both," Lilia said. "Help yourself. Please." As her hand made an encompassing gesture to the food, Geno caught the tattooed numbers on her forearm.

Maybe nothing would surprise him for the rest of his life.

He ate a big triangle of the sweet brei, piled high with fresh peaches, strawberries and blueberries and sprinkled with coarse sugar. Then he managed a small piece of the savory, topped with a poached egg.

"Ugh." Jav put his napkin down, groaning. "I ate too much."

"Wimp," Stef said, stabbing the last pieces off Jav's plate.

"You're a garbage disposal."

"He used to be the pickiest eater," Rory said, setting her silverware across her plate. "Drove me demented."

"What's everyone up to today?" Stavroula said, checking her phone.

"I have to finish my taxes," Stef said morosely, picking up brei crumbs with a fingertip.

"I have editing," Jav said, looking even more morose.

"Lilia and I have tickets to Avery Fisher Hall," Rory said, glancing at her watch.

Stavroula set her elbows on the table and her chin on her fists. Her eyes met Geno's. "Feel like being of service?"

Stavroula opened the door of The Bake & Bagel on Horatio Street and ushered Geno in. The shop was humming. A din of conversation and shouted orders mixed with heady, crisp smells of dough, coffee and bacon. Like a couple of goodfellas, Stavroula and Geno went behind the counter and into the back room. It was hotter in here, the yeasty, baked smell stronger. Stavroula walked around a half-dozen shelved rolling carts and big wire baskets. Two huge industrial ovens took up the back wall, and two men were loading them with long planks, each plank lined with plump, boiled bagels.

"Baking is done up here," Stavroula said. "Dough is made downstairs." She stopped and looked back at Geno. "You did want the tour, yes?"

"Oh hell, yeah," he said.

She took him through a door and down a flight of wooden stairs. They emerged into the cool, low-ceilinged dough room. Everything was clean, white and silver. Two big mixers, each coming up to the middle of Geno's thigh. More rolling carts with white shelves. White five-gallon buckets. White sacks of flour. Two metal doors leading, Geno guessed, to walk-in coolers. Dean

Martin warbled from a radio and Micah Kalo sang along as he tidied up the work surfaces.

"Dad, this is Geno," Stavroula said.

"I remember you," Micah said. "You know good music." His handshake was dry and dusty, leaving Geno's palm coated with flour.

"He's agreed to be your sidekick for the afternoon."

Micah drove a van for Meals on Wheels. His regular partner was sick, so Geno rode shotgun through the route in Brooklyn. The spring day was beautiful. Clear blue skies over the Big Apple. Cool enough for a jacket, bright enough for shades and frequent pauses to let the sun shine on your face. The afternoon also carried the odd sensation of a blind date. Geno was sure Stavroula hadn't teamed him up with Micah out of need. She wanted them to spend the day together for a reason.

Whatever the ulterior motive, Geno enjoyed the work. They delivered the pre-made meals mostly to homebound senior citizens. At some stops, they carried in milk crates of pantry items as well. Lots of boxes of matzo, bottles of wine and grape juice, kosher salt and horseradish.

"Getting ready for Passover," Micah said. "This is nothing, though. Week before, when we're running around delivering fifty shank bones and a hundred dozen eggs? It's crazy. Then some of the real orthodox ones box up and sell me all their leavened items." He made air quotes around *sell*. "I hold the boxes a week and then they buy it all back. It's a charade but it makes the rabbis happy."

As they moved in and out of apartments and duplexes and houses, Geno noticed Micah could converse in several languages.

"It's what I did after the war," Micah said.

"What?"

"Translate for the British."

"Where?"

"Bergen-Belsen."

"Oh," Geno said, but asked no more.

The day passed quickly. Geno relished long, deep breaths into the bottom of his stomach and the wide-open tunnel of his chest. How for once, his thoughts didn't rest in a snarly tangle in his head, but moved aside to let other people's problems take priority. Or even let absolutely nothing have a turn.

"Volunteering is like soul food," Micah said. "Sometimes you need to do selfless things for a selfish reason. But everyone wins, so no harm, no foul."

Back in Manhattan, Micah checked the van in and took Geno to the Bake & Bagel for a late lunch.

"House special," Stavroula said, setting down two paper plates. "Grilled cheese and tomato on the bacon bagel."

"Holy crap," Geno said.

"Reward for a job well done," Micah said, taking an enormous bite with a grunt of pleasure.

"You don't keep kosher?" Geno asked.

"I'm not Jewish," Micah said behind his fist.

"Oh. I thought because you were in the camps…"

Still shielded behind his hand, Micah shook his head. "My father was a top gun in the Greek Resistance. Nazis arrested me and my mother and my siblings trying to flush him out."

"No shit."

"We wore green triangles. Not yellow stars."

"And they sent you to Belsen?"

"Haidari first. Mean little camp outside Athens. My mother died there. Then we were sent to Auschwitz. When the Reds were advancing, the Germans evacuated the camp and marched us west. The British liberated us from Belsen."

"Oh."

"Oh?"

Geno smiled weakly. "My mother died too but it doesn't really compare."

"Why not?"

"Well, she didn't die in a concentration camp."

"How did she die?"

"Cancer. When I was fifteen."

"Same age as me, then," Micah said. "Your mother is your mother. Whether she's snatched away from you by disease or violence, you're never the same."

"It's kind of like the end of the world."

Micah nodded and wiped off his mustache. "For me, though, the world had already ended. When the Nazis came and then the famine, the world I knew was over. When my mother and older brother died at Haidari, I was already numb. I was sad, but the sadness was detached. It wasn't a priority. It required too much energy."

"Like your brain noted it on a clipboard," Geno said. "*The human is sad. This is unfortunate. We will address it later.*"

Micah's finger raised off his coffee cup. "Exactly."

"Like you made all the feeling and emotion happen to someone else."

The old man's eyes were steady on him, the chin continuing to nod. "You speak like one who knows."

"Did anyone from your family survive?"

"No."

"You're the only one left?"

"Yes."

"Same with me."

But that wasn't quite true. And later that night, he called Zoë.

"Oh my God," she said. "I was just about to call you. Tom and I read the news in the paper. The FBI arrested Anthony Fox. Geno, they got him."

"They got him."

"It was *right* in Manhattan." Her voice was raised, shaking a little. "I mean he was right there, close to where you're living."

"I know," Geno said, and told her what happened at the bar.

"Oh my God," she cried. "Geno, thank God. Holy shit, you must've been terrified."

"I was but it was so surreal at the time, and now it feels like a dream."

"Still, the relief…"

"I'm still taking it in."

"I'm so happy for you," Zoë said. "Does happy sound weird? Should I be saying something else?"

"No," Geno said, laughing. "Happy works fine. But actually, I wanted to ask you something else. Totally unrelated."

"Fire away."

"Do you know where Dad's relatives lived in Europe?"

"Oh God, no," Zoë said. "Dad was third generation. His great-grandparents came here in the eighteen-nineties. From somewhere in Germany. Why?"

"I was talking to a man today who was in the camps. I wondered if we had family who were caught up in that whole thing."

"Well, I don't doubt some Caan ancestors and relations were caught up in it, but I couldn't say who."

"I was just wondering."

"It might be an interesting project," Zoë said. "I'm always seeing commercials for ancestry websites and it gets me thinking about my roots."

"Yeah. Well. How is everyone?"

"Good. Matthew still misses you."

"I miss him too," Geno said. "Anyway, I wanted to say hi."

"I'm so glad you called," Zoë said, sounding exactly like Nathan. "And I'm so weirdly happy for you about everything."

He laughed. "Me too."

Something to Someone

*S*PRING, WHEN A young man's fancy turned to thoughts of...

"Go away," Jav mumbled.

"Rise and shine, Landes," Stef said, looking for some action.

"I'm sleeping."

"You're hard."

"This is morning wood, it doesn't count."

Stef got out of bed and pressed his palm to the cold window. Held it a count of twenty and then burrowed under the covers again. "The hand of death is coming for the Gil deSoto family jewels."

"Dude, I will kill you if— *Jesus.*" Jav let out a laughing yell. "You bastard."

"Shh," Stef said. "Don't struggle."

"Goddammit, Finch," Jav said, shivering, but not moving out of Stef's icy grip.

Stef bit the back of Jav's neck. "You're so my bitch."

"Get off me. You suck."

"I fucking love you."

"I know and I want to *sleep.*"

He didn't put up too big a fight. Stef made it up to him by taking the long trek up to Inwood for breakfast, to a joint Jav insisted had the best Dominican food on the island. It was a tiny, homey place, where all the old waitresses knew Jav on sight and fussed over him. They spoke lightning-fast Spanish, laughing and teasing. It all went over Stef's head, but he was too busy eating to feel left out.

"Hola, Javi."

Both men looked up. A woman in her late sixties, maybe early seventies. A tiny thing, silver-haired but traces of what was once a great beauty.

Stef glanced at Jav, expecting an introduction.

None came.

The woman's face was expressionless as she looked down at Jav. He stared back, jaw tight and eyes narrowed. His hands had gone to fists on the table. Stef's gaze volleyed between like a tennis spectator before he decided to go invisible. Under the table, he gathered Jav's ankles between his own.

Finally, Jav spoke: "Tía, este es mi novio. Stef, this is my Aunt Mercedes."

"Hi," Stef said. Even with his limited White New Yorker Spanish, he knew *novio* meant boyfriend. He also knew what a giant gauntlet it was to throw in front of Jav's Dominican aunt. The woman's eyes turned to him, blinked once, then crinkled at the corners. Her hand extended. "It's nice to meet you."

Stef nodded, shaking her hand.

"You're looking well, Javito," Mercedes said.

"Thanks, so are you."

"I'm older."

"We all are."

She smiled. The silence shuffled its feet on the floor.

"How's Kiko?" Jav asked.

"He passed away two years ago."

"I see."

Stef noted the un-extended condolences and resisted the urge to clear his throat.

"I recognized you as I was leaving," Mercedes said, a slight tremor in her voice now. "I wanted to say hello. It's been a long time."

Jav nodded. "Twenty-eight years."

"Well," she said, drawing a deep breath. "It's good to see you. And so nice to meet you, Stef."

"Likewise," Stef said, smiling up and pressing down with his feet.

"Vale. Adiós, sobrino."

Head held high, purse clutched tight, Mercedes walked away.

Jav's eyes followed her out of the restaurant, then he exhaled like a hurricane. "I did not see that coming."

"That was Nesto's mother?"

"Mm."

"You okay?"

"Yeah." Jav rubbed the back of his hand between his eyebrows. "Just thrown off." His feet were still tucked between Stef's and one of them was shaking.

"What was your relationship with her like?" Stef asked. "Before everything went down, I mean."

"Like a second mother, combination of love and nagging. But she was my aunt, and my aunt by marriage. So more love than nagging."

"I see."

Jav sighed and roughly shook his head. "Sorry. I'll snap out of this in a bit."

"Take your time. It was a shock."

"I love you," Jav said, looking out the window.

"I love you too." Stef wiped his mouth and crumpled his napkin. "What do you want to do today?"

"Truth?"

"Yeah."

"I went to your bridge once," Jav said. "Will you come to mine?"

The sun threw handfuls of diamonds on the Hudson River. Boats cut precise wakes through the water as the wind buffeted through the geometric girders of the George Washington Bridge.

"I almost asked her if Nesto left a note," Jav said, leaning on the railing. "I always wondered."

"Why didn't you?"

"I'm not sure what I want the answer to be. I mean, really I'm asking if he left a note for *me*. If he didn't, that's heartbreaking. If he did, what happened to it? If it's around somewhere, do I want to see it?"

"Do you?"

"Jesus, I don't know," Jav said. He ran fingers through his hair. "I should warn you, I'm gonna be in a really weird mood the rest of the day."

Stef laughed. "Uh, yeah, I figured."

"Thanks for coming."

"Thanks for asking me to come."

Jav slid a hand around the back of Stef's neck, bringing their foreheads together. "You're my best friend."

Stef smiled, giving Jav's wrist a squeeze.

"I mean it," Jav said. "When I die, I want to be buried next to you."

"Oh my God, man, stop," Stef said, laughing again.

True to his word, Jav was moody and distracted the rest of the day. A thousand-yard stare into the past. A lot of sighing and restless pacing around the apartment. Gazing out the window for long stretches. He wasn't hungry. He went for a run late in the afternoon, by himself. Came back and showered and dressed, but he didn't seem transformed or less troubled. Wearing Stef's Skidmore hoodie, he sat sideways on the wide windowsill and stared outside.

"I keep coming back to me and Ari being the only ones left," he said.

Stef looked up from his sketchpad and nodded. "Yeah, that's a tough one."

"God, I…" Jav let his breath out and seemed to deflate. "See, I had this crazy idea he was alive all this time."

"Nesto?"

"Yeah. Like him jumping was just a story Kiko told me to be a dick. A story to cover up their own estrangement. I had this nugget of hope in the back of my mind that maybe Nesto was out there somewhere. We'd meet again and we could talk about it. Tell our stories. I could find out why."

Stef put his pad aside and got up. "This really haunted you."

"I didn't know it did." Jav ran fingertips along his temple. "He was…" His shoulders rose and fell with a few chuckles. "Shit, man, I don't even know what I'm saying. I don't know what any of this is."

He was laughing. When Stef put hands on his shoulders, Jav was still laughing.

"I didn't know and I don't know," he said. "I'll never know."

He laughed as Stef slid arms around him.

"He was a Trueblood," Stef said. "Your cousin and your best friend. Your shadow. You told me if he wasn't following you somewhere, it felt like you were missing a sock."

God, I feel like I'm talking to Geno, he thought. *It's the same betrayal. Why didn't I see it before?*

"I don't understand," Jav said. "I never will."

"I know."

"Everyone just leaves," Jav said. "I don't get to say goodbye to anyone. I don't get a say at all. They leave and I just sit around making up stories to explain why. They pass me on the street and say nothing. Did I ever tell you that? I passed her and Kiko on the street once and they wouldn't even look at me. Now she sidles up to my fucking table like it's no big deal. 'Oh Javito, so nice to see you, you look so well.' Really? As opposed to the way I looked when your brother- and sister-in-law were beating the shit out of me over a five-hundred-dollar check? You didn't recognize *that*, now did you? Christ, you were a bigger doormat than Naroba. At least she tried to defend me. You just fucking disappeared."

Stef held still. He'd never seen Jav like this.

"Where were you when my mother shut me out and cut me off?" Jav said. "When your son ambushed me at school? Where were you when I couldn't walk from here to there without getting beat up? When I was getting kicked to death in bathrooms and locker rooms and my own fucking kitchen? Class fag.

The neighborhood punching bag. The family disgrace. Where the fuck were you when I was living in one room with my life savings in a coffee can? When my uncle staked out my apartment and took a day's work out of my pocket, saying I should suck enough dick to make the next payment? When your own husband told me to pay him back or he'd leave a hole in my ass so big, I could fuck two men at once?"

He wasn't laughing anymore.

"Oh sure, you recognize me in a restaurant now. You got no problem approaching me now. But not back then. You didn't recognize what all of them were doing to me back then. You didn't know I'd end up fucking for a living. Making me waste twenty years of my life when I could've *been* something to somebody…"

Then he was crying.

Stef pulled him in tight and stood still against the storm, his hand running in slow circles between Jav's trembling shoulders. "You're something to me," he said. "You're everything to me."

"They can't just throw me away and expect…"

"No," Stef said. "They can't. Not anymore. Not while I'm here."

He set his teeth together, electric with rage.

"Sorry," Jav said, wiping his eyes on his sleeve. "Probably overreacted but every last encounter with my family involved getting beat up or robbed. Or both. I saw her and…I guess something inside me panicked."

"You fucking *under*-reacted," Stef said, still crackling. "She did nothing while you were being abused by her husband? If I'd known that this morning, I would've… Jesus fuck, none of them ever deserved you."

Jav took Stef's hand, then leaned his head against the windowpanes. The light turned his dark gaze to amber and reflected off the bits of silver in his beard growth.

I've got one of the last Gil deSotos, Stef thought. *I'm not throwing him away. I'll never leave without saying goodbye. If this comes to an end, I'll give him a reason. He'll get a goodbye. He won't sit around and make up a story to explain.*

His fingers tightened on Jav's. *But I don't want to leave. I want to stay and watch you write our story. I want to go to all your bridges. Because I recognize what they did to you then. And I recognize who you are now.*

"I love you," Stef said.

Jav's lips shaped *I love you too,* but no sound emerged. He looked so small, like the kid he'd been when his tribe turned against him.

"I wish I'd known," Stef said. "I wish I knew you when you were seventeen. From school or the neighborhood. I would've been your friend. I would've brought you home with me."

"You were twelve," Jav said softly, half his mouth smiling.

"Hey, I was a force to be reckoned with at twelve. Just ask my mother. And my old man could do terrifying things with piano wire. One visit from him and his Steinway buddies, and your uncles would've given back your money. With interest."

"I could've had a whole different life."

"Yeah, well… Fuck your family. And I think you're with me on that because you looked Mercedes in the eye and introduced me as your novio. You didn't crawl, you didn't eat shit, you didn't apologize. It took guts. But guess what— I'm more than a boyfriend. I'm your curator. I can't change your past but I sure as hell can collect, catalog and label the shit out of it. And you know what else I am?"

Now Jav looked at him, blinking. "What?"

"Your guardian," Stef said. "I keep watch over your life story. Everything that made you who you are is a gallery. And I guard it."

Jav swiped his face against his sleeve. "You're killing me, Finch."

"I mean it," Stef said. "Everything that happened to you is mine to protect. Because it all happened so you could be with me. I need to be worth it. And I will. I'm your lover, your partner, your curator *and* your guardian. Any tiger that comes looking for a piece of you is going to get their ass kicked by a winged horse."

Jav's gaze melted again as he swung his legs off the sill. Stef moved between his knees. He held Jav's weeping head to his heart and stood tall, gazing around the room as if assessing a threat.

"Fuck all of them, man. They'll have to come through me to get to you this time."

TANGLE OF FLESH AND MIND

NEW YORK CITY was never completely silent. Nor completely dark. When Jav woke in the middle of that tender night, the city outside the window breathed with a quiet, nocturnal rhythm. Enough streetlight filtered through the curtains that he could see the silhouette of Stef's body. Sprawled on his side like a mountain range, hulking and majestic. Sound asleep. Quieter than the city.

Are you there?

Jav's fingertips gently touched the center of Stef's back, where the Sagittarius was inked between his shoulder blades.

> *Man is a centaur,*
> *a tangle of flesh and mind,*
> *divine inspiration and dust.*

Jav rolled more on his side, wincing a little. He was still sore. Stef said it would be fine in the morning and Jav believed him. He believed everything Stef told him now.

Tonight their bedroom overflowed with magnificent sex. Death by sex. Grandiose, over-the-top sex. They were making love like architects of the universe. Fucking like mathematicians. Multiplying, dividing, canceling each other out and starting from zero.

Jav couldn't get enough.

They ripped apart the bed, going at each other like knights in single combat. A grab became a caress before turning into a seize before melting into a kiss before fingers clenched and teeth sank and the weight of one crushed the other.

"It all happened so you could be with me," Stef whispered. "Don't ever forget it."

A crocodile death roll in the sheets, then Stef was pinning Jav's wrists to the bed, kissing his way into Jav's mouth and sliding hard along Jav's stomach, rubbing the two of them together the way Jav loved.

But it wasn't enough.

Stef sucked on Jav's throat, marking him. He slid his tongue along the hollow between Jav's collarbones, tasting him. Then he glided down Jav's body and wrapped his mouth around the aching need, sliding his slick fingers deep, the way Jav loved.

But it wasn't enough. Not after what Stef told him.

Everything happened so you could be with me.

Now it's mine to protect.

Stef leaned on him like a tower. "I love making love with you. God, I've never known anything like it in my life."

"You don't know the half of it," Jav whispered, as he made up his mind. It came to him with the same quiet resolution as the decision to stop escorting last summer. No lightning bolt revelation. No fed-up fist shaking at the sky. The same, almost laughably easy decision: *This isn't enough.*

I'm more than this.

He'd been Stef's lover for six months now. Half a year of intense, sexual exploration, negotiating his boundaries and setting his limits. "I don't really see myself as a bottom," Jav said. And Stef, who wanted enthusiastic consent or nothing, took it at face value. He said it didn't matter and Jav believed him.

But it did matter. Because Jav could see it just fine. The idea of Stef taking him appealed. It enticed and beckoned. Sometimes it begged. But Jav pretended not to hear. Because he was afraid to try. He topped because it was what he'd always done. Not just in bed but in life. He'd made a career of topping. An identity. A suit of armor. On top was his place. It kept him in control. It kept a hundred thousand women who fucked him from touching him. It was how he got *this* without ever having to give *that*. He topped because he didn't want anyone inside. He didn't want anyone walking in his weird head and laughing at what they found. He certainly didn't want anyone treading in his heart and deciding what was there could be abandoned.

I top because I play it safe, Jav thought. *Stef knows this. He knows me like nobody else. I trust him like nobody else. I've let him closer to me than anyone, but I still haven't let him inside. Because I still think everything that happened to me is shit. My life is ruins. Nothing of value in all that rubble and ash. It's worthy of being left behind. Passed by on the street without a shred of acknowledgment. Or the kind of acknowledgment that comes with a punch in the head, a kick in the side, and taking all my hard-earned money before walking away, laughing.*

It's not worthless. It all happened so I could be with Stef.

I held out my hand to the world, expecting fiasco. Instead, a finch flew in. Perched on my palm, looked around at the rubble and started sorting it out. Labeling it. Arranging it.

Everything that happened is a gallery.

I am a gallery.

Stef is my curator and guardian but how good a job can he do if he's outside my heart's museum, his back to a door I still keep locked? How can he curate and guard me unless I let him in?

I want to let him in.

This time, when the bedside drawer opened, Jav took the condom and rolled it on Stef.

"Wait," Stef whispered. "What's happening?"

"It's now," Jav said, shaking all over. "I mean, it's time. I want to try."

"You sure?" Stef said.

"Positive. I'm done playing it safe."

Stef fell on his hands and his mouth sank into Jav's. "Oh my God, you don't know," he whispered.

Jav shivered, tasting sweat and juice and need. The rattle of teeth against teeth, Stef kissing like he was trying to eat Jav alive. All the while something in Jav screamed for more. His body peeled open, layer after layer of desire. A mountainside fallen away to show centuries of strata. The love Jav thought himself incapable of. It was here, within him. Cataloged and documented, arranged and organized and beautifully on display.

Stef was careful. He'd been waiting and wanting a long time and his body was primed with raging excitement. A stallion rearing up and pawing at the night. Jav could feel him rein it in and gentle it down. Make his hands patient and slow.

"The second this doesn't feel good, we stop," he said.

Jav trusted him implicitly, still his faith faltered on the edge. A split second of denial when Stef pushed into him.

It won't. I can't.

Then it did.

And he could.

"Don't move," Stef said. "Just breathe."

"Holy shit."

"Let your breath out." Stef reached and his hand ran slow over Jav's face. "Look at me. Open your hands. Just breathe, Javi."

Jav drew a long slow breath in and let go his fists. He was wide open. Stretched to the limit of his physical and mental being.

"All right?" Stef whispered.

"Mm."

"Burn?"

"A little. Yeah. Getting used to it."

Stef put his brow against Jav's. "Just breathe with me. I don't need any more than this."

"Querido…" The seconds dripped by, pink and anxious, as Jav concentrated on opening more. Reaching out to the strangeness instead of shying from it. His right hand clasped Stef's, palm to palm, fingers wrapped around and thumbs crossed. His voice floated above the bed: "I feel so…here."

Jav had never been able to completely shut his mind off. He lived in his head. The most he'd ever been able to do was muffle the constant inner monologue to a dull roar. But right now, with Stef inside him, his mind was *silenced*.

"Am I hurting you," Stef whispered.

"I…don't know."

"You do." Stef drew back a little. "Tell me, or I will stop."

"No don't stop," Jav said. "I do. I mean… I'm okay, I just… it feels…" In this clear, bright, timeless bubble of *here,* he could barely put words together. "I can't say how it feels…"

It hurt, but it wasn't an agony that debilitated you. It was a complex ache that *captivated* you. Took your attention hostage. Demanded your full presence. *You are here and nowhere else. Nothing else exists. No other thought. No other feeling. No other moment in any other time but now. No other man but him. No other love but his.*

"This is intense," Jav said, with an effort.

"I know."

"I never let someone this close in my life."

Stef drew a slow, sharp breath in. "I *know…"*

"I feel so *here.*" A groan spilled out of Jav's throat as Stef's hand closed around his cock and started to stroke. Jav leaned into the familiar grip, let it link up with the foreign pressure spreading him open. Letting Stef be both the squeeze inward and the pull apart. Letting Stef be everything.

"I'm so in love with you," Stef said.

"Come in more." The words were barely audible while within his soul's gallery, Jav was throwing open doors, yanking curtains apart, flinging up windows, unlocking display cases.

Come inside. Come in. Come into me.

Stef moved into him, finally hitting the pleasure on the other side of pain. It revved like gas to an idling engine and Jav thought he would do anything to never let it stop.

"I'm finally here," he said, running hands up Stef's tight arms. His fingers pressed in, nails digging. He could've torn the world apart, laughing and screaming. Then curled up small in Stef's palm, be tucked in a pocket where he could stay forever.

"God, when I hold still, I can feel your pulse." Stef's fingers tapped a beat on Jav's arm. "I can feel you living."

Carefully he dropped onto one elbow, then the other. "Makes me think about all you had to do to keep yourself alive. Go on living." His warm, hard body pressed tight, pushed deep. "You survived so I could find you." He hit the sweet spot and the world wrapped around Jav twice. He began to babble, his fingers clenched tight in Stef's hair.

"Come," Stef said. "Just let it come."

Both Jav's body and his kiss opened wide as he took tight hold of himself and came. Pinwheeling through the dark. Plummeting through the colors behind his squeezed eyelids. All of him unfolded and unwrapped and undone.

Afterward, Stef ran a towel along Jav's body. Brought him water. Tucked the covers tight and pulled Jav close, guarding this newly curated treasure. The room drew in, rocking them in its dark arms. A heart beat in Jav's ears. The sound of living. Jav touched the fine white line bisecting Stef's eyebrow, then the healing seam along his cheekbone. Each scar a tribute to a life changed.

The scar was the price he paid.

The Finch wore his finest hours on his face and Trueblood never tired of looking at him.

"I love you," Jav said. The words tried to wrap around the emotion and felt inadequate. But when Jav wrapped arms around Stef's body, it felt like prayer.

Mine. My most treasured friend and mate and lover and partner and…man. Man.

I am a man and you are my man.

He felt it in his core. In his bones and marrow and cells.

This is how I was born to love.

My family can think what they want. The tigers can call me whatever they need. I know who I am now.

I am here. And I am Stef's.

Still sore, wide-awake in the middle of a New York night, Jav reached through the tangle of flesh and mind, through divine inspiration and dust, and touched the sleeping centaur's wings.

"Finch," he whispered

The silence stretched wide.

"Stef."

"Mm?"

Jav smiled and closed his eyes. "Never mind."

A rustle of skin against cotton as Stef looked back. "Whasrong?"

"Nothing. Just seeing if you were there."

Through his eyelids, he could feel Stef's sleepy confusion. He could taste it as the confusion turned to a soft amusement. Hear when amusement melted into understanding as Stef rolled over to face him.

"I'm right here," he said against Jav's head.

"Sometimes I need to check."

"I know."

"I'm an idiot." Jav's hand crept around and curled in the small of Stef's back. "Go to sleep."

"You're scared and playing the idiot card," Stef said, his voice slurred and drowsy. His thumb tilted up Jav's chin. "I'm right here. And you can wake me up to check anytime you want."

Six

"So," Geno said. "Do we just pick up where we left off? Pretend I wasn't an asshole?"

Stef waved a hand. "Bygones," he said. "But it'll probably be weird a little while. You slept on my couch and had breakfast with my mothers. The usual boundaries are…"

"Erased?"

"Smudged." Stef's dark blue gaze was piercing, but he smiled below it. "Then again, nothing about what happened to you played by the rules. Makes sense that our working relationship wouldn't either."

Through the residual guilt he was still carrying around, Geno exhaled in relief.

"How have you been feeling since the arrest?" Stef asked.

"Vengeful."

Eyebrows raised, Stef pointed a finger. "Good word."

"Weird emotion."

"Tell me."

"I've been having these…fantasies, I guess. Revenge fantasies."

"Completely normal," Stef said.

"You think?"

"Can you tell me one?"

Geno rubbed his forehead. "I don't know. They're pretty twisted."

"Sideways question," Stef said. "Before now, before the arrest, did you entertain thoughts of revenge on Anthony? Tame or twisted?"

"You know, I didn't think much about him at all. Other than the generalized, nauseating awareness of him being out there in the world still, I didn't imagine him dead or getting killed or anything. But now?"

"Now?"

"Dude, it's all I fucking think about." Geno's eyes blinked rapidly, his heart galloped like a wild horse.

"Why do you think that is?"

"Because he's behind bars?"

Stef nodded. "The beast has been caged. He's in chains and on display. You can get up close and taunt and jeer. Throw garbage. Spit on him. Scream for justice."

"Yeah," Geno said. "It's, like, obsessive."

"You're entitled to it," Stef said. "Correct me if I'm wrong, but I don't think you have the means or connections to order a hit on him inside prison walls."

A tiny smile broke through the tremble of Geno's jaw.

"I don't condone violence of any kind." Stef looked around the room and cupped his hands around his mouth. "For the record," he said loudly, "I don't condone violence." He dropped his hands. "But it's a brutal fact of the penal system that life for sex offenders is not pleasant on the inside. Your visions of revenge have a high chance of coming to fruition."

Geno nodded, licking his dry lips.

"I imagine they're pretty elaborate," Stef said quietly.

More nodding.

"Have you been drawing them?"

"I try." Geno took out his pad and flipped to the last used page. He turned it to show Stef the hands gripped around prison bars. "By the way, hands are fucking hard to draw."

"I know," Stef said. "That's why I draw hooves instead." He turned the page. The next leaf was torn out at the spine, only a little fringe of paper left clinging.

"I had to rip it out," Geno said. "It was so bad."

"I've seen bad," Stef said. "If you trust me, I'm a pretty good litmus test of what's normal and what's psychotic. If you show me, I give you my word I won't judge you as good or bad. I already know you're good. You have zero chance of horrifying me because you drew your ordeal flipped on the one who deserves it."

"It's in my room."

Stef smiled. "I'll wait."

Geno went and got it. "Jesus, my heart's pounding," he said, putting the folded sheet of paper in front of Stef. Stef opened it briskly and his eyes flicked top to bottom, side to side.

"You're normal," he said.

"Don't bullshit me," Geno said. "Scale of one to ten, one being apathy and ten being psychotic. Where am I?"

"Where are *you* or where is this drawing?"

Geno flicked the paper with his index finger.

"Four," Stef said.

"*Four?*"

"Under the circumstances, this is on the lenient side. None of them are raping him with objects."

Geno stared. "I didn't think of that."

"Take a deep breath," Stef said.

Geno inhaled deep and let it go, slouching in his chair a little.

"Take another one."

Geno did.

"Now pretend for a minute I don't know you personally or any details of your experience. I'm Joe Shrink and this drawing is an exam question. All I know is one, you were gang-raped by seven men, and two, you're drawing a revenge scene. That's it. Okay?"

"All right."

"First thing, like I said, no objects are involved. I've seen pictures like this with mops, brooms, pool cues, broken bottles and baseball bats. You haven't drawn any blood, literally and figuratively. Next, and forgive the crassness, but I don't see any double penetration. It's not a free-for-all or an attempt to inflict the greatest amount of damage at once. This guy's going at it, and everyone else is lined up over here, waiting their turn. They still have clothes on. Nobody's even reaching for their fly or touching themselves. It's civilized for revenge."

Before Geno could interject, Stef held up an index finger. "Remember, I don't know *you*. I'm just looking with my master's degree and objectively saying what I see."

Unasked, Geno took a big breath.

"Last," Stef said, "and most significant, is the number of men here."

"What do you mean?"

Stef turned the drawing around to face Geno. His finger circled the man on his hands and knees. "This is Anthony?"

"Yeah."

His finger moved to the man mounting. "Count with me. One." He pointed to the lineup. "Two. Three. Four. Five. Six." His fingertip held on the last man and his eyes pressed Geno hard. "Not seven. Six."

Geno stared back, not understanding.

"You're not in here," Stef said. "You're not one of them."

Geno's eyes swam. Warm wet trickled down one side of his face and into his mouth.

"I keep telling you, man, they didn't get the best of you."

"I'll be right back." Geno went to his room and got the others. He'd drawn dozens of scenes, each worse than the last. Disturbing and grotesque tableaux. Exaggerated dimensions. Graphic depictions of oral and anal sex.

"I have so much fucking hate in my heart," he said, looking at the gallery of violence spread across the art room table. "So much hate and anger and… My mother always said she only wanted me and my brother to be kind."

"Your mother would've killed these men with her bare hands," Stef said, the words thin and tight between his teeth.

"Man, I'd watch that," Geno said. "I feel like my heart would fucking love it. That's one way I changed that really scares me. Like my heart's different now."

Stef was quiet a long time, his eyes resting on the drawings. "Did you ever read your medical file?" he finally asked.

"No."

"None of it? None of the reports from the hospital?"

"No. Why, did you?"

Stef nodded. "Did you know you almost died?"

"Well. It felt like it. But—"

"Do you know what Ketamine is?"

"No."

"It's an anesthetic primarily used by veterinarians. Street name is Special K. It's a date rape drug. A roofie. Know what Rohypnol is?"

"It's like a roofie too?"

"Yes. Know what a Trimix injection is?"

Geno shook his head.

"It's a mix of three drugs. Phentolamine, Papaverine and Alprostadil. PDE5 inhibitors. You probably know them by their brand names. Viagra, Levitra and Cialis." Stef crossed his arms and leaned back in his chair. "Overdosing on Ketamine *or* Rohypnol *or* PDE5s can put you into respiratory failure. ER doctors found all three in your bloodstream."

"I don't…remember much from the hospital," Geno said.

"Considering your blood pressure was seventy over forty-five when you got to the ER, I'm not surprised. You were bleeding internally, in the early states of peritonitis and you needed immediate surgery. But with the Trimix and the sedatives in your bloodstream, plus your system in shock and fighting an infection, surgeons knew they had a significant chance of losing you on the table. Let me tell you something, Geno. The only reason you're alive today is because you have a strong heart. A *really* strong heart."

Geno stared.

"You had one of the top surgeons in Manhattan putting you back together. Still, Dr. Bloom gave you only a thirty percent chance of recovering normal bowel function. That means you had a seventy percent chance of going the rest of your life with a colostomy bag. *Seventy* percent. I know it doesn't sound as romantic to say you have a strong gut to go with your strong heart, but I'll say it anyway. What I won't say is it was a miracle. You didn't have divine help getting better. You did it all yourself. Somehow, in spite of everything that could've killed you, your heart found a way to live, and your body found a way to beat the odds and heal."

Stef leaned forward, his right hand extended, elbow planted as if inviting Geno to arm wrestle. "Let me tell you something else."

Geno hesitated, then put his palm against Stef's and their fingers folded down. The gesture felt ancient. Medieval. Rooted in the chivalric mysteries of brotherhood and bravery.

"I think you're the strongest, most resilient person I ever fucking met in my life," Stef said.

Power radiated through their clasped hands, making the air shimmer and press.

"Thanks," Geno said, barely able to make a sound.

"Your heart is bigger than hate," Stef said. "You tell the story. Words or pictures, nothing's going to push me away, all right? If you can live it, I can listen to it. If your heart can survive it, mine can too."

Geno's palm thrummed. The blood sang in his veins and his strong heart thudded like military drums. Banners unfurled and flags fluttered in Nos, even the stars were crowing with joy.

Beware the wrath of Caan, for his heart is strong and will not be vanquished.

He was vindicated. Affirmed and validated. He was good. He was kind and courageous. He wasn't a monster.

He would never understand why he did what he did next.

WHAT LOVE LOOKS LIKE

*T*HE ROOM JUMPED in its shoes as Geno erupted, heaving over the table, sending chairs, markers, pencils and sketchbooks flying. Heads turned, residents and staff on their feet as Geno spun around, howling like a ghost.

Without taking his eyes off Geno, Stef stood up, his hand raised to the crowd behind him, signaling he was in control. He stood still. When Geno fell on his knees, Stef crouched at a careful distance, his mercury layer swiftly falling from the crown of his head and cloaking him. His heart wanted to break. He couldn't let it. Now more than ever, he had to stand apart from the pain.

My most important job is going home.

He squatted on his heels, silent and motionless. Without judgment. Watching the boy weep into his hands and gradually go quiet again.

"Sorry," Geno said.

Stef got a sheet of paper and the pastels. He put them on the floor.

"Go back to day one," he said. "Draw you and draw them. Do it right now."

Red faced and swollen-eyed, Geno made the big blue mark and the small black ones. He didn't shove the paper away this time. He held still, a pastel in each open palm. Head bowed. As if waiting instructions.

"Pick another color," Stef said. "For you. The most powerful color you can think of. Add it on."

Geno picked red and drew around his blue line. A thin border. Then he held the paper steady with fingertips and made the red border thicker. The line gained weight, becoming a skinny rectangle.

Without prompting, Geno reached for orange next and made a second outline. A perimeter of fire. He hesitated, then drew lines radiating outward. Flames. He took the red again and made scarlet fire in between the orange. He found yellow and made flame tips at the end of each line.

He pushed the paper away then, but gently. Without anger. He put the pastels back into their slots and rubbed his fingers together.

"I'm sorry," he said. "I'll clean up."

"It's not important," Stef said. He tapped the paper. "This is."

Elbows on knees, hands steepled over his mouth and nose, Geno looked at himself. Clean, dependable blue encased in fire, looming over the black shadows.

"It hurt so bad," he said softly.

"God, it must have."

"And it just went on, and on, and on. I stopped counting after a while."

Stef rolled onto his butt, sitting cross-legged. His fists clenched tight but he kept his demeanor soft and neutral. "Can you tell me more?"

Geno's fingers reached and started blurring some of the orange and red together. "I was afraid I would die. And then I was afraid I wouldn't die." His hand lifted to touch his face, leaving marks of red and orange, black and blue.

"I don't think words exist to describe that kind of terror."

Geno's head bowed, his fingers clenched in his hair. "I never had sex before that night," he said. "That's what it was like the first time."

"That night wasn't sex," Stef said. "It was rape. Rape is about power and nothing else. It's the opposite of sex."

"God, I want to go home." Geno sniffed and drew his colored face across his sleeve. He turned the piece of paper over, picked out the red pastel and began to draw a house. The architecture was odd—it seemed to be a shack on miniature stilts. A row of square windows by the roofline and the door smack in the middle of the front wall.

Stef held the paper steady as Geno took green and made rolling hills, nestling the house within them. Dark brown made a tree, its branches a curved shelter above. Then he took yellow and made light spilling out of the square windows.

"What is it?" Stef asked.

"Home," Geno said.

"Tell me."

"My mother kept her maiden name. Gallinero. It means henhouse. She called me and my brother her little chicks." Geno drew a long ramp from the high door to the ground.

"I see it now," Stef said, fascinated.

Orange was in Geno's fingers again, drawing a four-legged figure in the distance. Like a dog with a long, pointed snout. A wolf?

No. Of course not.

"Fox," Stef said.

Geno exhaled and the orange crayon fell from his fingers back into the box.

"The fox in the henhouse," Stef said.

A little snort made Geno's chest hitch. "My life as a metaphor, ladies and gentlemen."

"Do you feel like he'll always be in the picture, no matter what?"

Geno reached and tore the bit with the fox out, crumpling it up. His finger tapped the little coop. "This is one of my safe places. Like the beach. In my dreams, I see this house in the distance. Far away with the light spilling out of the windows."

"Who's inside?"

"Sometimes my mother." He swallowed hard. "Sometimes you. Or Jav and Stavroula. Sometimes, though, it's empty. Or I can't reach it. It's up there ahead, calling me and I want to go home so bad. But I can't get there. Because nobody's there. Nobody's left. The road keeps going on and on and I don't know what I'm going to do. I don't know who's going to love me."

A tremendous sigh, like a tree toppling. Stef let it crash to the earth, at an utter professional loss.

"Does he love you?" Geno asked.

Stef blinked. "Who?"

"Jav."

"Yeah."

Geno pulled the pad of paper close and tore off a sheet. He pushed it toward Stef. "Draw you guys."

"Me and Jav?"

"Draw love."

Stef thought about it. His fingers picked out a couple of pastels. He made simple, broad strokes. A thick, curved ribbon of gold and brown that with a little imagination, could be a man sleeping. He took green and slate blue and drew a second curve around the first.

"Which one's Jav?" Geno asked.

"The brown."

"You're the dominant one?"

The question would be tactless, if not for Geno's earnest expression. No guile or contempt was in his eyes, just a desperate need for understanding. The boundaries were already smudged.

And nothing about this case ever played by the rules, Stef thought.

"That's personal," he said slowly.

Geno looked away. "You're right I'm sor—"

"Let me finish. It's personal, and the word *dominant* doesn't apply, but I understand what you're asking and why. I drew it this way because the dynamic shifts, depending on what's going on in our lives. Something kicked Jav down recently, so right now it feels like I'm sheltering him. Other times, it's the opposite."

A single, exhaled chuckle through Geno's nose. "Like when a can of nuts and bolts gets thrown at your head?"

Stef laughed too. "Yeah, like then. But anyway. That's what love looks like to me."

"I'm really tired," Geno said. Just like a woman not named Alison said when she stood on the railing of the Queensboro Bridge.

"You must be," Stef said. "Go on upstairs if you want. I'll clean up."

"Sorry."

"Don't be. Take that with you."

Geno took his paper and got up as if he had broken glass in his bones. "Thanks," he said.

"You call me. Anytime. Any hour of the day, I'll be there. I'll listen to whatever you want to tell me."

A chime on the wind, soft and faint. "Okay."

MAY

THE RIGHT WORK

*G*ENO CAME DOWN to work the Monday morning prep shift. Stavroula was in the kitchen, so was Micah.

"What are you doing here?" Geno asked, shaking hands.

"Seeing if you wanted a new job," Micah said.

"Me?"

"My dough assistant is moving on to other ventures. Stavi says I'm too old to do the work alone."

"That is *not* what I said," Stavroula called. "Don't listen to him, Geno. I made a high recommendation for you."

"Why me?"

"Because it's a good job for insomniacs," she said, winking. Then her expression turned serious. "In my limited opinion, G, I don't think working in bars is the best thing for you right now."

"It isn't," Geno said.

"So, you want to give bagel-making a try?" Micah said.

"Sure."

"Stavi's right. It's early morning work. I start at four."

"Stavi's right," Geno said. "I don't sleep much."

He was a little concerned about handling dough, but hell, that whole weird episode was practically a year ago. He'd be in the company of an old man, not a baby boy. Worst case, if he popped a boner, he could cool off in one of the walk-ins and tell Micah the work wasn't for him, thanks anyway.

As it turned out, he took to the task immediately, but adjusting his clock to the new schedule nearly killed him the first week. Up at three-thirty and at the shop by four. Micah was wide-awake, showered and shaved, hair slicked back into its tail. Coffee made and the radio tuned to oldies.

"You kill the average guy," Geno said, borrowing Jav's line.

Using the five-gallon buckets and a scale, they measured flour, yeast and warm water into the big mixer bowls. Micah added a brown syrupy substance he said was sourdough starter, honey and canola oil. The wire guards of the mixers were lowered and the barber shop spiral hook went into action, pulling liquid into solid, activating the gluten.

"How'd you learn to do this?" Geno asked, amazed how Micah rarely needed to add an extra dollop of water or scoop of flour to get the correct consistency.

"My friend Samouel Franco opened this place," Micah said, adding salt from a small silver bowl. "He came from a long line of bakers. He was the brains of the operation. I just lifted the heavy stuff."

"Where did you meet him?"

"We were childhood friends in Athens. His was an old Sephardic family. He spent the war hidden in a monastery."

"So you learned Ladino from him?"

"Yes. It's all his family spoke. And I loved it."

"How did you find each other after the war?"

"Oh, one of those post-war reunions that's so serendipitous, it's divine. Six months after my wife and I get to New York, I bumped into Sam on the street. We wept, we wailed, we clutched each other and we opened a bagel shop." He winked. "We may have gotten drunk somewhere in there."

"I know I would," Geno said.

Micah turned off the mixer and lifted the guard, indicating Geno should do the same on his batch. History lesson over, he returned to Geno's education in the art of dough. He was a patient and thorough teacher, giving the why for every how. Putting a dusty white hand over Geno's to guide him in the rhythm of kneading or shaping a bagel.

"Don't be so angry at the dough, habibi," Micah said. "Knead with kindness or it won't be kind to you."

Micah peppered his speech with Ladino endearments. Besides habibi—an all-purpose word for brother or friend or companion—he called Geno *presia-do*, precious one. *Mi corasón.* My heart. *Querido.* Dear boy.

Geno put kind, tentative hands on the dough. It was tactile and pleasant. Nothing more. No thrumming or weird arousal. He exhaled and relaxed into the work.

Plain bagels and bagels that were coated—sesame seed, poppy seed, salt, onion—could all go through the machine to be shaped into the iconic rings. These were put on white trays, slid onto the rolling racks and put into the cooler to rise for eighteen hours. Then another batch of dough was made for the bacon bagels. Those could go through the machine, too, but dough that had fruit or nuts had to be shaped by hand.

"You don't want to clean raisins out of the machine, corasón," Micah said. "Sam and I learned that the hard way."

To Dean Martin and Rosemary Clooney and Glenn Miller, the men portioned off dough. Rolled it into short snakes, then folded each snake around a hand to make the ring, rolling the edges smooth. Micah could shape bagels two-handed, each identical to the next. Geno's came out lopsided at first, but he soon got the knack. He enjoyed it. Five hours passed quickly, and when the mixers and machine were immaculate and every surface wiped down, Micah praised him. Stavroula sent him on his way with a cup of coffee and an egg-and-cheese on a bacon bagel. It was nine in the morning and the rest of the world was just getting to business.

Slackers.

By two in the afternoon, Geno was dying. Too tired to chew his lunch. Nodding off in group therapy and then stumbling to the art room. Looking at Stef with a thousand-yard stare when asked something. Sinking his head onto his hand and then nearly breaking his chin when his elbow slid off the table. "Dude, go back to bed," Stef said, laughing.

Within a few days, Geno was hitting the sack by eight-thirty—something he hadn't done since fourth grade—and he was *sleeping*. Deep, honest and dreamless sleep with only the occasional Ambien to help him settle down.

"When it's the right work, you sleep well," Micah said.

Down in the clean, white dough room, Geno asked Micah many questions. And Micah told him many things.

ARSCHFICKER

ICAH SHOWED GENO a picture of his mother, a dark-haired woman with intense, intelligent eyes. The same prominent brows as her son, but scrupulously groomed. She sat at a desk, hands poised on a typewriter, as she smiled for the camera. The smile was distracted though, as if the work couldn't wait.

"She's beautiful," Geno said. "Was she a writer?"

"She taught English, French and German at a high school," Micah said. "She had an ear for languages. So do I, to a lesser extent. It came in handy."

At Haidari, the concentration camp outside Athens, the Nazis tortured Eva Kalo for information on her husband's whereabouts. They flogged her eldest son Nicolaus in front of her to get her to talk. When that failed, they flogged her to death in front of the camp inmates, making Micah and his younger brother, Christos, watch. Then the Kalo brothers were thrown onto the cattle cars heading to Poland. It was February of 1944. Micah was fifteen, Christos eleven.

When the boys fell out onto the platform at Auschwitz, Christos was near death. Micah, on the other hand, looked strangely full of life. A Jewish woman on the train had bitten her own lips until the blood ran, then rubbed the blood on her cheeks as a makeshift rouge, adding false vigor to her skin. She took some of the excess and rubbed it on Micah's face, pinching him into a portrait of health.

"You can't save your brother," she said in Ladino. "Stand up straight. Look strong. They want workers." She pushed Micah's filthy hair into place. "You're handsome. Use it to your advantage and look like a man."

Cramped for weeks in a square foot of space, Micah didn't think he could crawl, let alone stand. Somehow, he locked his knees and threw what chest he had out. When German officers came along, shouting orders to the confused crowd, he translated to those closest to him.

"You speak German?" one of the SS said.

"Ja," Micah said, not making eye contact but not relaxing his posture.

The officer fingered the green triangle on Micah's shirt. He took Micah's jaw in his hand and turned it this way and that. "Schönling," he said. One of his lower teeth was gold.

"What does that mean?" Geno asked.

"Pretty boy," Micah said.

Christos Kalo went straight to the gas chambers. Micah marched off to be deloused, have his head shaved and his arm tattooed with number 157701. He was given striped shirt and pants with his number and the green triangle, then marched to a zugangblock, a barracks for new prisoners, where they'd wait until assigned to a work team.

"Were you fucking terrified?" Geno asked.

"I felt nothing," Micah said. "Because feeling wasn't—"

"Allowed," Geno said. "Feeling was illegal."

Micah nodded as lowered the spiral hook into the mixing bowl, dropped the wire guard and turned the switch on. "You make your own laws in times of war, habibi."

The SS officer with the gold tooth came to the zugangblock the next day, looking for the griechischen Schönling who spoke German.

"I was made a Lagerschreiber," Micah said. "A clerk, if you will. At roll call at dawn and dusk, when prisoners lined up for hours to be counted, I was the one counting. During selections on the platform, when some were sent to the left and some to the right, I counted. That was my day job."

He was quiet a long time, rolling rings of dough around his hands. Then he said, "By night I was a pipel."

"What's that?" Geno said.

"It doesn't translate literally. It's a good-looking boy who gets special privileges. Because he's the property of a kapo. Or, occasionally, he's the property of a commander."

The SS officer was called Heinrich Schultze. He was tall and stern and authoritative, but seemed to lack the streak of brutal sadism so rampant in the Nazi ranks and the kapo underlings. When he smiled, and he often did at Micah, the kindness of the smile seemed genuine.

"Don't trust that grinning Arschficker," one inmate muttered under his breath. "Trust no one in here."

That Schultze might be homosexual was a piece of information Micah wasn't sure what to do with. At fifteen, he already knew some Greek men bedded other men and he knew the rules about such things. The one getting fucked was the object of derision. The one doing the fucking was merely tending to his manly needs.

Being revolted or squeamish or worried people would think he was a *poústis*—these were luxuries left far behind in Greece. Micah had aged a decade in a few short months and thrown all useless things like ego away.

During the horrible days in the camp, in between the roll calls and the beatings and the executions. Through the smell of burning flesh and the smoke always lingering in the air. Through the delousings and the inspections and the constant abuse. Through the weak tea, moldy bread or the warm water with rotted vegetable peels floating through like sewage. Through it all, Micah's new cunning mind, wired for survival, turned the matter of Schultze over and over.

As a piece of blackmail, it seemed useless. Homosexuality was a grave offense in the Nazi ranks, but the value of this secret was dependent on Schultze's nature as a human being. If he was spoiled by power, brainwashed by ideology and no longer in possession of a soul, then…

I'd just be a hole to him, Micah thought. *I'm good for nothing else. He'd fuck me and kill me and no one would know the difference.*

But if Schultze's golden smile were true. If he had a heart beneath that uniform, a scrap of conscience or decency. If he'd led a lonely life of lying and hiding. If he'd seen his kind shunned and jailed and killed. If he identified, just the slightest bit, with the camp inmates because it could just as easily be him. And if he were willing to risk his life for human connection…

Micah turned the problem over and over.

Does he want a hole? Or a heart?

Does he want to fuck me or know me?

His survival goals had shrunk to hours. He never thought about tomorrow. Next week ceased to exist as a concept, as did the words "one day."

I only have here and now.

I have no power here or anywhere.

Die now or die later, that's the one choice I can make. Death is inevitable in this place. I'd rather march to the gas chamber knowing I tried everything I could. Rather than trudge along wondering if I'd let Schultze fuck me, could he have done something for me? But it'll be too late to un-ring that bell.

Bribery was a way of life in the camps, yet it remained a dangerous business. In just a short amount of time, Micah learned it was best not to give up the goods until you had what you wanted. These goods could get both him and Schultze killed.

And what do you want anyway? he asked himself.

The answer was simple: *A chance.*

The word was luscious in his thoughts, like honey dripping between layers of phyllo in a slice of baklava.

I want a chance to survive. When I march off to the gas or stand on the stool or look at the gun, I want to be able to say I did everything I could to survive.

Schultze took him to the kitchen the first time. Micah went willingly. He wasn't afraid of shame or pain. Only that Schultze would kill him afterward. Bent over some boxes and slicked up with lard, he thought about nothing and waited for either the fucking or his life to be over.

"This is unfortunate," Geno said, pretending to write on a clipboard. "But it's not our concern."

Schultze zipped up, handed Micah a rag and allowed him to live. A fortnight later, he took Micah back to the kitchen. The third time, they were interrupted by one of the cooks. Possibly coming down to steal provisions. Schultze kept one hand on Micah's hip. The other drew his service revolver and shot the cook dead between the eyes. He resumed fucking Micah and afterward they tossed the body into the furnace. Schultze gave Micah a brick of margarine and two salamis to take back to the barracks.

Micah knew the game by now. He turned over the margarine and one of the salamis to the Blockältester, Lazar Nadelman, the kapo in charge of the barracks.

"Mean little prick of a Jew," Micah said to Geno. "Drunk on power for lack of anything to eat."

Micah gave the other salami to his block mates, taking only a slice for himself. If letting Schultze fuck him came with privileges, he'd take enough to survive and share the rest, because getting drunk on his own meager power would get him killed when that power was taken away.

And it's when, not if.

This could end tomorrow.

"Did it?" Geno asked. "How long did it go on?"

"Eight months," Micah said. He looked at Geno a moment, then down at the work surface. "Don't knead the dough so angry, habibi."

HOME, HEARTH AND FAMILY

*T*HE MORNING WAS chill and rainy. Geno cinched his hood up and aimed for awnings and overhangs as he walked back to the warehouse. He had a breakfast sandwich, but he didn't feel hungry. Micah's story sat in his gut and he didn't know how to digest it. Other than the knee-jerk *Holy fucking shit.* Under the surface horror, though, he was sure a deeper message was lurking. But what?

He speaks as one who knows, Geno thought, crossing Jane Street.

Micah let an SS officer fuck him in return for a chance. Little privileges that let him live another day.

He did it willingly, because things like ego didn't matter anymore. Only survival.

Analisa died when Geno was fifteen but the world had already ended for Micah Kalo by that age.

He did it willingly.

So does he really speak as one who knows?

Is he gay?

His eyes squeezed shut and he flicked the thought off hard. *Shut up. Shut your mouth because you have no fucking idea. None. You, baby boy, would've been dead five minutes after getting to Auschwitz. You speak as one who knows jack shit, so shut up.*

He arrived at the art room in a confused state of self-recrimination. Stef sat at one of the long tables, sketching his empty coffee cup. This was usually the time he worked with Max. Max, however, was sitting under the table, scowling like he'd been told he couldn't have a rocket ship.

Respecting that Stef was technically on duty, Geno took a seat at a neighboring table.

"How was work?" Stef said.

"All right. You want this?" Geno held out the sandwich.

"Don't offer the beast food if you don't mean it."

"You can have it, I'm not hungry." Geno unzipped his jacket and peeled it off. It was muggy in here. The rainy morning leaned on him like it was exhausted, smothering him with complaint. Meanwhile, Max hadn't moved a muscle.

"Gee, Stef," Geno said loudly. "Max sure looks mad at you."

"What an astute observation, Geno," Stef said in the same tone.

"Why is he mad at you, Stef?"

"I'm afraid that's confidential, Geno, but you could ask him."

Geno leaned out of his chair to look under the table. "Max, why are you mad at Stef?"

"He won't marry my mother."

Geno straightened up and raised his eyebrows at Stef. "Now I'm mad at you too."

"I'm the worst."

The minutes passed in silent attrition. Stef sat eating and drawing. Max sat doing nothing. Geno got some pastels and newsprint and tried to freestyle some of the shit in his head. Finally, Max came out and made a show of leaning on Geno's shoulder, showing Stef who the new best friend was.

"Dude, breathe through your nose," Geno said as he blended grey and black with his fingertip, making long rectangles in a row. Like cattle cars, he guessed.

Max closed his mouth and moved closer. Then closer. Until he was sitting in Geno's lap. Thumb in his mouth, head tilted against Geno's chest. Warm, solid, trusting weight.

"Is this allowed?" Geno said.

Stef looked up. "He came to you. You're the one who says if it's allowed."

"I know, but..."

"Is it making you uncomfortable?"

"No."

A little, Geno thought. *Yes. Because it feels so good.*

Unconsciously his head lowered, his nose skimming Max's head. It wasn't the baby smell he remembered from Matthew. It was dirtier. No, not dirtier. *Earthier.*

"He's asleep," Stef said.

"Sorry," Geno said. "He's supposed to be working with you."

"He is."

"What do you mean?"

"I'm not at liberty to say," Stef said mildly. "But you make astute observations. What did you see here?"

"Max is mad at you."

Stef's hand circled in the air.

"He's mad at you and…" Geno trailed off, lost. And then he got it. "He's mad at you and he said so."

Stef touched his finger to the side of his nose.

"He showed anger," Geno said. "He said *no,* and he removed himself from your unwanted company. Because he's the one who says if it's allowed."

"I can neither confirm nor deny that today is a success story," Stef said. "Suffice it to say I am pleased with the turn of events."

Dude, you sound like Mos, Geno thought. He shifted the sleeping boy a little more comfortably. Muscle memory from long-ago days when he could deftly hold Matthew on his hip while cleaning house or cooking. The thrum in his limbs. Warm serenity in his chest.

It feels so good. Why does it feel so good?

Is this how it starts?

Anxiety wasn't yet coming over the horizon, but Geno could hear the rumble of it in the distance. His arm around Max tightened a little.

Great, I'm using him as a shield.

"You're good with kids," Stef said.

"My half-sister had three. They were sweet. Two girls and a boy. The boy was eleven months, just starting to walk. He was my buddy."

"Are you a Cancer?"

"Yeah. How'd you know?"

"Wild guess," Stef said. "I read once that Cancers were all home, hearth and family. Not that I believe any of that stuff, but interestingly, every Cancer I've ever met has been that way. Loves to be at home. Loves to be in the kitchen. Loves to be a haven." He sighed. "Please note this study has not been peer reviewed."

Stef's attention and tone were so different out of sessions. As they kept company and drew, he answered Geno's questions, talking about his own relationship to kitchens and houses and food. How the idea of having his own family was an appealing, but not driving force in his life.

"And I'm getting on in years, of course," he said.

"How old are you?"

"Forty-one last December."

Geno shrugged the shoulder Max wasn't leaning against. "Both my parents said they had no idea what they were doing until they were forty."

"I know I'm not far in, but it feels different somehow. It's like you corral the energy of your twenties and the learning of your thirties, throw all the bullshit over the side and what's left is…" Stef smiled, shrugging his own shoulders. "Pretty great."

The hour was up and Max's mother arrived. Max gave Geno a dramatic hug and walked off without a word to Stef. Mrs. Springer caught Stef's eye and smacked her palm against her face. Smiling, Stef put his palms together and shook them a little.

"You ruined his life, Finch," Geno said.

"All in a day's work."

"He wants you to be his dad. That's kind of awesome."

"Mm."

"It's called transference, right?"

"I see we took Psychology One-oh-One." Stef turned a page of his pad, then slid one of his rings off and set it on the table, like he was going to draw it next. He got up to sharpen his pencil and Geno picked up the ring. It was made of heavy silver. A pair of feathered wings crafted to wrap around the wearer's finger. He hefted it in his palm a few times, liking the weight, then put it down again. When Stef came back to sit, Geno hesitated, not sure if they were in a session now or still hanging out as buddies.

"So, I kind of did some transferring to you."

Stef smiled. "I guess I am old enough to be your dad."

"It was more like a brother thing."

"Ah." Stef nodded over his sketching.

"Like you and Jav were brothers," Geno said, getting it out before he could change his mind. "And Stavroula was a sister. We all lived together in that little house of mine. Actually I thought Jav had a thing for Stavroula so they were sharing the bedroom before I figured out what the real arrangements were."

"You were making a home."

Geno's throat grew warm. As usual, Stef knew how to bypass the bullshit and find the nugget of gold. "Yeah," he said. "Just… Yeah. I guess."

Stef looked up now, his blue eyes gentle. "Are you waiting for the ceiling to collapse?"

"Kind of."

"Dude, if what happened to you happened to me, I wouldn't build a little house. I'd build the freaking Taj Mahal and fill it with everyone who was minimally nice. I'd be making the window washer my brother if he waved at me."

Geno's heart kicked up a few beats as a small chill went through him. "Can I ask you a question?"

"Sure."

"Have you ever slept with a woman?"

Stef laughed. "I was married to a woman for three years."

"Oh. But you're gay now?"

"I identify as bisexual."

"Oh. When did you come out?"

"In college." Stef glanced at his watch. "Not that I'm not enjoying this conversation but I think you have group therapy in five minutes?"

"Oh crap." Geno pushed back and started putting pastels back in their slots.

"I'll take care of those," Stef said. "Go on."

The rest of the day didn't sit well with Geno. He couldn't put a finger on what was wrong, only that something was not entirely right. Around eight o'clock, he went up to Stef's office to get the coffee can. Oddly, the light was on. As Geno walked down the hall, the light turned off and Stef came out.

"You're still here?" Geno said.

"I forgot my power cord, I had to come back. What's up?"

Why was it so much easier to say "nothing"? The word formed itself on Geno's tongue, ready to jump out and not be a bother.

"What's wrong?" Stef said.

"I'm not sure."

"You feel okay?"

"No. Not all day. I can't figure out why. I was coming up here to get the can and try to sort it out."

"You want to talk?"

"I don't want to keep you. It's late."

Stef reached back into his office, got the Chock Full o' Nuts can and gave it a shake. "Let's go in the art room."

Before they even reached the stairs, Geno was letting it out. "You know, the night I got…taken. I was at a party at this girl's house. A girl I really liked a lot. It was her birthday, a bunch of people were over and I was trying to figure a way to kiss her. But my best friend Chris was there, too, and he came out to me. Told me he was gay."

"I see," Stef said. "What was that like?"

"On its own, it would've been blindsiding, but he accidentally outed my brother, too."

"He was dating your brother?"

"No, no no. He said he saw Carlito with a guy, around the side of Target, making out. So he knew. He said if he told anyone about himself being gay, it would be me, because he figured I'd understand. Instead I was totally knocked out again."

Stef snapped on a couple lights in the art room. "Have you been thinking about your friend today?"

Geno sat at one of the tables. "I was thinking about not knowing many gay or bisexual people. Which made me think of Chris. Which made me think of the party. And Kelly. God, I wanted her so bad but I can barely remember what she looks like. I remember the wanting, but it seems so long ago. Not just another person, but another lifetime that doesn't even belong to me. I don't know who I am anymore. I don't know who I like or who I want or how to be with…"

Across the table, Stef tilted his head. "How to be with girls?"

"I don't even know how to be with *guys.*" Geno dropped his head in his hands. "I don't know how I feel about guys. I don't know how to act with guys anymore. I'm suspicious all the time. I want…I just want…" He lifted up his head and exhaled hard. "When I build that little red house and fill it with people, I'm filling it with more men than I am with girls."

"You lost your father and your twin brother," Stef said. "One or the other would be shattering. Both together is life altering. And the loss of your twin, with all the unanswered questions and unresolved pain? Geno, that kind of trauma can carve new neural pathways in your brain and say, *Hey, this is the new normal.* Your experience is objectively comparable to that of a combat veteran. It's left you with a huge void anyone in your shoes would be desperate to fill."

"But when I try to fill it, I don't know what… I don't know how to be friends with men anymore. When I found out you and Jav were together, I wanted to… I was so fucking pissed. I don't know why. All that stuff I said about your lifestyle making me sick, that was bullshit. That was me trying to cover up how confused and…and…jealous. Jesus Christ, I don't know what I'm saying."

"Keep going," Stef said. "It doesn't have to make sense, I just want you to talk."

Geno put his burning face back in his hands. "I feel fucking ridiculous telling you this."

"It's not about me."

"I forgot what I was saying."

"You were confused when you found out Jav and I were together," Stef said. "You felt jealous. You felt angry."

A beat of frustration as Geno flailed around for whatever the hell was bothering him right now. He wanted to talk about how it felt to hold Max, instead it came out as, "When did you know you liked guys?"

"Middle school."

It was either the wrong answer or the wrong question. Geno let his elbow slide sideways until he was sprawled on an arm. "I don't know who I am anymore."

"In terms of being straight or gay, you mean?"

Geno nodded, wanting to hide, at the same time grateful it was out there.

A scrape of chair legs on the floor as Stef hitched a little closer to the table. "Listen. You would not be the first straight male rape survivor I've worked with who is questioning everything he thought he knew about his sexuality. Wondering if you were asking for it. If you put out a gay vibe. If it now makes you gay. None of those thoughts are shocking to me. All those feelings are real and valid reactions. They can be confusing on a good day, terrifying on a bad day."

"It's a bad day."

"I can tell," Stef said. "But hear me out. Every rule has its exception, true, but I'm ninety-nine-point-nine percent confident if there existed the *slightest* inkling you might not be straight, you would've had it by now. You would've known long ago, Geno. It would be something you *knew*, something inherently and intrinsically part of your identity. Sexual persuasion is not like addiction or disease. Nobody and nothing can *make* you gay."

"Yeah, but…" Geno pulled a long, deep breath in and said, "I think I need to tell you something."

"All right," Stef said, but then his phone pinged.

"It can wait until morning," Geno said. "I know you need to go home."

Stef looked at him a long beat. A second chime came from his pocket. Then quietly, politely, he said, "Excuse me." He took out his phone. His thumbs moved over the keyboard. He clicked the side switch that put the device on mute, then slid it a foot down the table. He folded his hands and said, "It can't wait. And I'm not going anywhere."

Geno peeled the lid from the coffee can and spilled it onto the table.

MY LAST JOB OF THE DAY

*A*TIME COMES IN a man's professional life when he knows he's done some of his best work. Looking back later, much later, Stef knew he'd surpassed his finest hour. In the thick of it, though, he felt he barely got both of them out alive.

He was prepared for one single bombshell revelation. Instead it was a firestorm. Geno opened the coffee can and spilled pieces of hardware onto the table. At the same time, he opened the bomb bay doors and unleashed his private hells. It all spilled out in a mess, sloshing and dripping over the table and onto the floor.

Geno talked about his attachment to his little nephew. Then something about pizza dough, the feel of it in his hands. A call to a rape crisis hotline that went badly. Needing to leave his sister's house because it wasn't safe. He recited parts of the Model Penal Code. He talked about his roommate Ben. Someone named Jason, whose boyfriend was Seth. He talked about the girls he slept with in school and never being able to come. A night at a bar and seeing a girl come close to being drugged.

"They asked if it happened to a girl I knew," he said, the color up high in his face like he was running a fever. "A girl. It's always a girl. Even the law says it's a girl."

Stef tried to interject. "Whoa, hold on, wait a—"

He couldn't even correct the erroneous statement. The sky was burning now, Geno's desperate confession strafing the air. Something about a girl named Natasha and Craigslist ads. "Straight dude seeks same," he said over and over. The desperate decision to become Carlos because the alternative was jumping off Jason's balcony. One more lie in the tangled web. Finding the Vicodin and getting into bed with his friends. Lying in Jason's arms, holding Ben's hand and waiting to die.

When Geno finally stopped talking, nuts and bolts and screws and washers were sorted in neat piles. He breathed hard over them, but not with the exertion of a mission accomplished. He looked like the sole survivor of war.

Slowly, Stef picked through what the strainer of his instincts had kept back. "The dough felt really good in your hands."

"Yeah," Geno said hoarsely, hands slightly cupped on the table, remembering.

"It's similar to human flesh," Stef said. "You know from working with Micah that because of the yeast, dough is technically alive. It's an extremely tactile thing to hold and it can evoke deep emotions and deep sense memories. The same thing happens with sand. You put your hands in the sand table and you go somewhere else. It's why we work with it, and other things like clay. Because it allows survivors to be touched without being touched."

Stef's mind turned over another piece. "You got aroused working with dough at the same time your nephew was hanging onto your leg. You were attached to him. It sounds like he trusted and adored you, and he was the one thing that made you feel good."

Face in his palms, Geno nodded.

"Matthew may have even triggered extremely deep memories of being young with Carlos, but...no, put that aside. You said you left your sister's house because it wasn't safe."

"Yes."

"Not because it wasn't safe for you," Stef said, "but because it wasn't safe for Matthew."

Another nod, eyes squeezed shut.

"The woman on the hotline said you were the threat. *You* were the reason we needed rape hotlines in the first place."

A stab of anger for this insensitive and poorly trained stranger, which Stef quickly parried. *It's something to address later. Not now.*

"You thought you were a threat to Matthew," he said.

"Yes," Geno whispered.

"Why?"

"Because I got hard for him." The last word got gulped into the back of Geno's throat and his skin went grey-green.

"What just happened?" Stef said, already halfway out of his seat.

Now the boy's ghostly face was slick with sweat. "I feel so sick."

"Come sit by the window."

Stef cracked it open, then wet a hand towel at the sink, getting it as cold as he could. "Put this on the back of your neck." He wet another towel and had Geno hold it between his wrists. He held a third against Geno's forehead. "Turn toward the window, let the cold air blow on your face. That's it. Deep breaths. This is going to stop."

Geno's teeth chattered as he pulled a breath through his nose. "I'm so dizzy. I feel like I'm…not even here."

"It's your vagus nerve reacting under stress," Stef said. "It's happened before. A sudden drop in blood pressure. It feels horrible and surreal, like you're losing your mind. You're not. It has a name. Do you remember?"

"Vasovagal syncope," Geno said.

"That's right. It's temporary. It will pass."

"Promise?"

"I promise," Stef said. "You're doing great." He filled a paper cup with water and brought it back to the windowsill. "Do you know what it is that triggered you? Just say yes or no."

Geno pulled his knees to his forehead, shaking as he wrapped arms around his shins. "Yes."

"All right. Take a drink. Don't gulp. Nice and easy."

Geno took a wobbling sip, then put his head down on his knees again. "You're the only person I trust right now," he said, muffled.

"I will not mess around with that trust. You are being incredibly courageous and I'm really proud of you."

Geno nodded but didn't speak. He took the damp cloth off his forehead and twisted it tight, pulling in ragged breaths.

After a minute, Stef said, "You lost all your color when you said you got hard for him."

"Yeah."

"Got hard for Matthew?"

"Yeah."

Be careful here, Stef thought, then asked, "Or was it someone else?"

"Fuck…" Geno yanked the towel open and buried his mouth in it.

Stef ran to wet another towel at the sink. "It's okay," he said. "Let it go. Sick it up. Get it out of you."

"I can't…" Geno's chest bucked again. He was only dry heaving, but it was relentless. The kind of paralyzing nausea that dehumanized you.

Stef held out the dripping towel. "Put this down the neck of your shirt. Get it right over your chest. Good. I'm going to put my hands on you." He waited two beats before he pressed one flat, neutral palm between Geno's shoulder blades and the other over the cold, wet cloth on his sternum. Between his hands, the planes of Geno's body quaked like tectonic plates. A rolling, cataclysmic event ready to break out of this boy.

"I'm going to squeeze you a little," Stef said. "Tell me if it's too much." He pressed his hands in, equal force front and back. Sometimes pressure could break up anxiety. He made a quick mental note to get Geno a weighted blanket if this worked for him.

"Too much?" he asked.

"No, it's helping."

The spasms stopped. With a last shiver, Geno leaned his head back, breathing hard. Stef wet down the towels again for him. Brought more water to drink. Geno breathed slow behind closed eyes. His color was back and the inhales and exhales seemed calmer.

"You're doing great," Stef said.

Geno opened his eyes. "It happened with Anthony."

"All right."

"While I was... While he was...raping me, I... Jesus." He was breaking apart.

"Tell me." Stef held perfectly still, face soft but his teeth closed around the tip of his tongue almost to the point of pain.

"He was behind me and..." Geno's fists clenched and his face twisted into a contorted mask of shame. "He was holding up all my weight. I didn't have anything left. No strength, no fight, no nothing. I... I caved in. I gave up. I couldn't fight anymore so I just took it. And that's when he... His hand reached around and..." Geno pressed his forehead into his palms, fingertips digging into his scalp. "He found it."

"You had an erection."

Geno was weeping too hard to answer but he nodded.

"It's not unusual," Stef said, keeping his voice controlled and firm. "Listen to me, it's not. I've seen and heard this a hundred times. It *happens.*"

"He *made* it happen." Geno's voice was like melted tar under the sun, bubbling up and bursting open. "He saw and he fucking laughed, said I was a whore just like my brother. Said one twin couldn't be gay without the other. He fucking broke me then. That's when it happened. He told me to say shit to him and I said it. He told me to come in his hand and I did. He fucking made me *come* and he smeared it all over my face and in my mouth and said I loved it. It's all I can hear. His voice in my ear saying, 'Yeah, you love it, baby boy…'"

Geno's shaking hand pointed over his shoulder. "He's right there. On my back, breathing on my neck, talking in my ear, reaching for my dick. Anytime I lie down with a girl or anytime I get friendly with a guy, it's his fucking voice in my ear telling me what I really love, who I really am. That's why Carlito brought me in there. He knew I was an easy target. He knew. They all knew."

Stef let him cry it out hard and gradually come down, shuddering and sniffing.

Be careful, he thought. *This isn't over yet.*

"We have a lot to talk about here," he said. "I'll start by saying what happened to you would drive anyone to the brink. But not everyone would come back from that kind of edge. Don't dismiss how strong you are, Geno."

"Strong, shit. I'm fucking weak."

"You're not weak. You didn't get hard for Anthony and you didn't *come* from being raped. It was an involuntary response of ejaculation which had nothing to do with pleasure. It had nothing to do with *you.* You were loaded up with enough Viagra to stop your heart—"

"So *what,*" Geno cried. "It shouldn't have made a fucking difference."

"You had no control over the situation. Not the circumstances and not your body's reaction. I can pick up the phone and get eight doctors to confirm that some men get an erection when they're under stress or even terrified. They'll all tell you a penis does what it's made to do regardless of context. It doesn't know the difference. It has one job and sometimes it does it when the circumstances aren't even *close* to sexual."

"You don't understand." Geno twisted and writhed. His palm spread wide across one of the windowpanes, fingers digging into the smooth glass. "That fucking son of a bitch destroyed my family and I got hard for him. He upset my mother, he preyed on my brother and I came for it. He was raping the shit out of me, he made me come and it *killed* my father."

The fist reared back and Stef lunged to grab Geno's wrist before it could plunge toward and through the window. He hauled the energy in the other direction, but Geno was already uncurling off the window ledge and flinging himself toward Stef's arms. The combined momentum was nearly enough to barrel Stef over and send them both sprawling. He managed to pivot and get his back against the wall as his arms closed around Geno.

"I got you," he said.

"Anthony killed him," Geno cried.

"I know," Stef said, holding him tight. "Stay here and tell me."

"He took my brother and he broke him and he *killed* him."

"Hold onto me. Keep telling me. I got you."

"He killed my father."

"I know," Stef whispered. "And it nearly killed you. Day after day it goes on. Almost killing you. But never finishing the job."

Geno convulsed with weeping. Stef kept the embrace as strong as he could while liquid mercury dribbled down from his head, filling in his pores.

I can be sympathetic to your pain, but I do not have to feel it for you.

"I miss him," Geno said, like a knife slicing through the air. "Carlito served me up. He sold me. But he was mine and I *miss* him."

"I know."

"I miss him so bad." The cry didn't even sound human anymore.

"I know," Stef said, a hand at the back of Geno's head. "I know you do. Your heart is broken."

A machine gun rattle of wet sobs against Stef's chest and Geno's hands clutched harder. "I want him back…"

Stef's heart fractured into pieces. Slivers and shards that pierced clean through his protective armor. It was no use now. He was feeling all of it.

"He was your twin," he said, rocking both of them. "You're cut in half. You've been severed in two."

Geno's head nodded furiously against Stef's collarbone. His weight was growing heavier, deader, starting to drag downward. Still holding tight, Stef helped both of them get to the floor, on their knees. They stayed there a long time, long after Geno stopped crying. Finally his white-knuckled grip on Stef's shirt sleeves relaxed, and he rolled down to sit with his back up against the wall. Stef sat as well, both of them with knees drawn up and arms wrapped around. Geno's head was pressed to his kneecaps while Stef's was turned to the boy, only touching Geno with his eyes.

"I couldn't get away from it," Geno said. "It followed me everywhere. I tried to have sex with someone and all I could hear was Anthony telling me I loved it. Like he controlled everything. And only he could make me come."

"On top of everything you endured, you feel sold out by your own body."

"He told me I loved it."

"He lied."

Geno buried his head again, shoulders shaking.

"It's hard not to equate your physical reaction with the emotional reaction," Stef said. "But your body's response during the rape had nothing, *zero* to do with arousal. Zero to do with your sexuality. Rape is about power and nothing else."

"I feel so fucking ruined."

"You're not."

"Shut up," Geno cried. "You don't know anything. You have *no* fucking idea what it's like to be me. To be cuffed in a bed, getting a strange man's dick shoved up your ass or down your throat. Lying there smelling your own blood and shit and jiz and being told you love it. You don't know anything, so shut the fuck up."

The words bounced harmlessly off Stef's skin. Often the greatest display of trust a client showed his therapist was lashing out in anger. It took more confidence than allowing tears.

"Sorry," Geno said.

"Don't apologize," Stef said, astounded by this boy's heart. "Your job isn't making *me* feel comfortable with your ordeal. Your job isn't worrying if it's too much for me to hear or worrying I'll take your anger personally. Your job is to talk about whatever you need to talk about."

Geno exhaled roughly and looked around the room. "How do you not bring all this home with you at the end of the day?"

"That's my problem," Stef said. "Not yours."

"I'm just asking you a question. Come on."

"I do bring it home with me. My last job of the day is peeling my job off my skin and leaving it outside my house. And I don't always do that last job well."

"Do you talk about your day with Jav?"

"Sometimes."

"Do you talk about me?"

Stef hesitated. "I think what you're really asking is do I forget about you when I leave here at night. The answer is no. I don't."

Geno said nothing, but his chin gave the tiniest of nods and the last bit of tension sank out of his shoulders. He took another sip of water, looking like an athlete who'd played the game of his life. "I think I want to go lie down."

"All right."

Geno's teeth worried at his bottom lip. His head half-turned to Stef and stopped. "I'm a little…afraid of being alone though."

Afraid of being forgotten, Stef thought. "You want me to sit with you a while?"

"Just until I fall asleep. Is that allowed?"

"You're the one who says if it's allowed."

The EP bedrooms had the same wide windowsills as the art room. Stef sat here, looking out on the street. Through the ocean waves of the white noise machine, he heard Geno's breathing getting longer and softer. Once or twice, the boy twitched, moaning each time.

"I'm here," Stef said, turning his muted phone over and over in his hands.

I'll be back soon, he texted Jav. *Everything's fine. Don't worry.*

He wasn't fine and Jav would worry. It was how things were supposed to be.

His eyes fell on the pastel drawing tacked to the bulletin board. The little red henhouse nestled in the hills. A bit of the background torn out, where a fox once prowled. A hole through which other horrors might come creeping.

Stef stared until he fell into the picture. He raised up the ramp of the henhouse, cutting off access to the door. He shouldered a rifle and put his back to the rough, red walls.

I'm on guard, little brother.

You fought hard and brave. Rest your heart now. Don't be afraid.

I'm here.

They'll have to come through me to get to you this time.

A MAN'S DESIRE

STEF WENT HOME and shook his head at Jav. "Pretend I'm not back yet."

He peeled off his clothes as if they were contaminated and went straight into the shower. He washed his hair twice and wore the soap down to a wafer. Emerged boiled red and still feeling dirty. Bound up in frustrated shame because he was the one pretending. Acting like he wasn't dying for Jav to step into the tub and take possession. Take control. Take all decisions out of Stef's hands. Pin his empty palms to the tiles and fuck him hard, until this job, this day, and this case conceded defeat, slid off Stef's skin and disappeared down the drain.

He'd do it if I asked, he thought.

He won't unless I ask.

And I don't know how to ask.

Stef toweled his head vigorously. Didn't know how to ask. Horseshit. It wasn't even a question. *Babe, if you love me, take me to bed and make me forget my name.* Simple. Yet the words always jammed up in a gooey, guilty blob in Stef's throat. He didn't like knowing how rough sex could break a tough case's hold. It galled him that brutal intimacy was the best bar of soap after crawling through a client's cesspool of rape and sexual abuse. Especially tonight, when he'd brought home the image of Geno asleep in his bed, relaxed beneath a weighted blanket of trust. Still raw and bleeding after he'd courageously ripped the demons out of his soul, but secure that Stef wouldn't forget him. Peel him off like a jacket, drop him in a heap outside a closed door, then go get laid like nothing happened. Like Stef were utterly unfazed by the secrets he'd been entrusted with.

You are one sick fuck.

He flicked his head away from the self-incrimination. *All right, none of that,* he told himself sternly. *This is hard, intense work and how you get it off you is nobody's business. Especially not your mental peanut gallery, so knock it off.*

Screw this, he was tapping out. In the medicine cabinet was a Klonopin with his name on it. He'd call his therapist in the morning and tell him what happened. Again. Over and over, a skilled professional had tried to help Stef chart a course through this weird psychological minefield. Stef was armed to the teeth with maps and strategies, yet when the time came to use them, he chose to step on a tripwire and blow himself up.

Because it's easier and I'm too damn tired, he thought. *I'm good at what I do because I have great instincts and more empathy radar dishes than that big-ass array in New Mexico. I don't want to be my own savior tonight. I want a satellite to turn in my direction and pick up on my pain for once. Just once...*

"You back now?" Jav said, coming into the bedroom.

Stef grunted and shrugged.

"Hungry?"

"I don't know. Maybe later." Stef dug in one side of the drawer, then the other, looking for his favorite sweats.

Tell him, he pleaded with himself. *Stop suffering.*

He swallowed hard. He needed it so goddamn bad, but the context seemed so appallingly inappropriate. Disrespectful and tasteless and...*wrong.*

Jav leaned a shoulder against the door jamb, watching. Dark and worried. Solid and strong. "What can I do?" he said gently. "How can I be a good partner right now?"

The irony made Stef's shoulders twitch: he'd taught Jav that particular phrase, to use down in the EP kitchens when a resident unloaded their story or their pain or their need for validation. Rather than blindly guess what to say, Jav could turn the need around and tactfully but compassionately put it back in the guy's control. Saying, *How can I be a good friend right now?*

"Sound good?"

"What?" Stef said.

"I said, we could order out," Jav said. "A new Thai place opened around the corner."

"That's fine."

"Or I can throw something together if you want."

"I want you to stop talking." Stef yanked open another drawer. "I don't know what else I want."

"Bullshit."

The word was calm and conversational. When Stef looked up, Jav's stance hadn't changed, but the worry had vanished from his face, replaced by a great wisdom made of small understandings.

"You're a shipwrecked sailor," he said. "Foundering at that far end of the spectrum where men make war on each other. Is that it?"

The edges of the room blurred hot and wet, and Stef couldn't answer.

"Yeah, I think that's it." Jav hit the light switch, took a step and put his hands around Stef's head. He gave a pull and his mouth crushed down hard. Stef dropped the clothes he was holding and wrapped arms around Jav's neck. A stumbling turn and Stef's shoulders hit the wall.

Jav's thumbs smudged the tear tracks on Stef's face. "Is it one of those nights when you need to be fucked back to yourself?"

Stef nodded.

Jav tugged the bath towel off. "I'm on the way."

"I want to come home," Stef whispered. "Get me out of here."

"I know." He took hold of Stef's head again. "I'll find you…"

His tongue slid deep, and his clothed body crushed Stef's nude one against the wall. Stef pulled the kiss closer, sucking and biting. Leaning all his weight into it. Flinging the day onto Jav, pushing him to be harder and rougher until Jav seized his wrists, squeezing tight and halting the violent manhandling.

"Take your rings off."

Out of his mind, Stef stripped his hands bare and let the pieces of silver fall to the floor. Jav took him off the wall and down to the bed. Stef turned on his stomach, but Jav turned him back over.

"Hold still." He pulled off his clothes and came crawling along Stef's body. Fierce and commanding, ignoring Stef's pleas to just fuck him already.

"Hurting you won't help," Jav said, reaching for the lube in the bedside table drawer.

"I got this. Javi, come on, I'm good."

Jav slid slick fingers inside Stef with a tiny, knowing smile. "Not yet."

"I can—"

"Shh. We're doing this my way. Lie still now."

He took the time to get Stef open, then rolled on a condom. "No, lay back," he said, batting away Stef's impatient, guiding hands.

"Hurry *up*," Stef said through his teeth. "Jesus Christ, please."

Jav didn't hurry. His slippery fist took hold of Stef's hardness and squeezed tight as he moved slowly inside.

"God, man," Stef cried, as Jav pressed from within and without, breaking up the day.

"Found you," Jav whispered, pushing in more. "Look at me."

Stef lay still in Jav's gaze. He rested his heels on Jav's hip bones, breathing into the burn, feeling himself adjust and accept. When the ache was satisfied it had his full attention, when it had all Stef could give, it smiled. It rolled over, rose up and melted through his bones like warm gold.

"You did all you could," Jav said. "Now I'm taking you home."

His palms settled into the mattress on either side of Stef's head. His triceps pulled long and taut. A dragonfly fluttered. A ship's wheel spun lazily. Muscles winked in and out of definition as Jav's hips rocked back and then pushed forward. With every push came a pull. With every glide out, he reeled Stef in.

"Come back to yourself," he said. "Come back here where I can love you."

Flashes of light dotted Stef's peripheral. The soles of his feet prickled. He set his teeth against the rising heat, writhing in a fever. Full of hard blood and hot ache and lit-up want. Full of Jav.

"I love you," Jav said. "Stay with me."

"Feel so lost," Stef said, his voice tiny against the immensity of Jav's body over him.

"There's nowhere you can go that I can't find you." Jav freed a hand and held Stef's face. "When I'm inside you, you are *home*. Nobody and nothing else can take you away. Come with me now…"

A fine mist of sweat rose to the surface of Jav's skin. The scent of a man's desire filled Stef's nose and eyes and throat. Dark and earthy, like a forest floor. Smoky and syrupy.

"Stay with me." Jav's damp head dipped, his teeth closed around the ring in Stef's nipple and pulled. A twisting bite of pain which his tongue then soothed.

"Want to come home," Stef whispered, his chest bowing into Jav's warm, wet mouth. "Don't stop."

Jav rose up, his hands bracing beneath Stef's knees. He rocked Stef back and pushed deep. Long, gorgeous, painless strokes in and out, rubbing against the fulcrum where making love and making war balanced.

"Javi…"

"I know. Come here and let me love you."

Jav flexed his hips and moved faster. Forward. Backward. *Homeward.* The scales tipped. Stef felt a rippling jolt down the axis of his body. A golden zipper gliding open, allowing his skin to peel apart, fold around and turn him right side out. As he spilled over, white crackled in his peripheral like a lightning strike.

Then he went dark. The master switch shut down for a pinprick of blackened silence. Then the circuit panel flicked back on and Stef let out a yell as the world poured in. He came together and came apart, his voice dissolving into a stream of singsong babble. Above him, Jav was bucking and cracking like a whip. Head thrown back, the long tender line of his throat tensing and relaxing. With a last shudder, he collapsed down, wrapping Stef up in a tangle of sweaty limbs, rolling their bodies into a tight ball.

"Shh," Jav said, breathing hard against Stef's head. "I got you, Finch. Stay here with me."

Stef went limp and blank, reset to zero. Little keening noises huffed out of his throat: not quite crying, more the exhilarated gasps of a narrow escape. He pushed his face against Jav's shoulder, heartbeat thudding in his ears.

"It's all right," Jav said. "Everything's all right. Shh…"

The day was gone. It had been a close one, but Stef was home. Jav's embrace opened like a palm and caressed his soul.

"You here now?" Jav said.

"I'm here."

"You with me?"

"I'm with you."

"You belong to me?"

"I'm yours."

"The next time it's one of these nights, all you have to say is, 'It's one of those nights.' I know what it means now. Can you do that?"

Stef closed his soaked eyes. "Yes."

"You promise?"

"I promise."

Jav kissed Stef's mouth. "And I promise no more questions."

"Thank you…"

Jav slid off the bed, picked up all the silver rings and tenderly put them back on Stef's fingers. He took the ringed hands and led Stef into the bathroom. He turned on the shower and nudged Stef under the spray, stepping into the tub with him.

"Hold still," he said, his voice filled with care. "Just rest now."

Stef closed his eyes and turned his body in Jav's soaped-up hands, finally feeling clean. He let himself be rinsed, wrung out, dried off and dressed in Jav's clothes. Let himself be led to the kitchen, where he ate what Jav put in front of him.

"And I am *not* feeding you this time," Jav said.

Stef ate in silence, knowing Jav would damn well feed him if asked.

Because it's one of those nights. That's all I have to say...

Back in bed, they lay on their sides, kneecaps touching.

"Te amo, pinzón," Jav said.

Stef smiled. Perfectly relaxed, perfectly content. Drifting away. Tucking his head beneath a wing and giving a last flutter of feathers.

"You're the best thing that ever happened to me," he said.

Jav's fingertip drew across Stef's eyebrows. "Loving you is the best thing I do."

Their eyes blinked in unison, their shoulders and chests rising and falling together.

"You make me a better man," Stef said.

Jav's eyes closed, then opened. "I couldn't find a better man." His fingers raked through Stef's hair.

"You're the best lover I ever had," Stef said.

Jav's eyes shone in the dark. He pressed his lips tight a moment before his voice wobbled out like a baby taking first steps.

"You're the only lover I ever had."

Stef was exhausted. His hands trembled as he pulled off the ring shaped like a pair of wings. He slid it onto Jav's index finger. "Gelang."

"What's that?"

"Old English for *belong*. Means at hand. Or together with."

Jav's palm slid warm on Stef's face, the ring cool and sleek. "Gelang," he said slowly, nodding a little. "We are gelang."

Then Stef was asleep.

THE BREAD BASKET

*T*HE BAKE & Bagel was closed up tight, dark within except for the lights in the bakery case. Geno went down the service alley and around the back of the building. The basement transom windows were lit up, the light slicing through the last hours before dawn. A beacon to a safe place, a warm cave of flour, water and yeast. Geno used the keys Stavroula gave him to open the back door.

"Micah?" he called, with an undertone of *Dad?*

"Down here, corasón," Micah called back, like a father.

Geno went down the rough wooden steps into the heart of the shop. The belly and soul.

The breadbasket, Geno thought.

Big and floury, Micah smiled at him, but said nothing. Geno sat on a flour sack, watching the rotating dance of the mixer's wire hook. The shifting patterns of looped dough, like taffy, separating and combining. Stretching and condensing.

The Andrews' Sisters sang *Apple Blossom Time.*

"What happened after eight months?" Geno asked.

"Schultze left," Micah said. "He must've been transferred. Who knows. But once he was gone, I became Lazar Nadelman's pipel."

"The mean prick? The kapo?"

Micah nodded. "But I didn't take the role willingly."

"He raped you."

The old man went on nodding. "Either him or his underlings. I think he got more pleasure handing me out like a little reward."

Like a present, Geno thought.

"Never in private though," Micah said, shaking salt from the stainless-steel bowl. "Whether him or one of his henchmen, it was always a show. He'd beat my ass bloody in front of the barracks or watch someone else do it. Then he'd have his way. Or make a spectacle of picking whose turn it was. Even saying what could or couldn't be done to me. That's what really got him off. Controlling the whole business. Keeping it unpredictable. No one would touch me for a week, then I'd get beaten up and fucked four nights in a row. Afterward, Nadelman would feed me butter and give me an extra blanket. Let me sleep through roll call. Two or three days of peace, relatively speaking. Then he'd haul me into the latrine block and make me blow all his buddies. And that would be all I had to eat until his mood changed again."

Wincing, Geno looked away, swallowing hard against a remembered taste. "How did you endure it?"

"You tell me."

For a long moment, the boy and the man looked in one another's eyes.

"You made it happen to someone else," Geno said.

"You speak as one who knows, habibi."

To the rhythmic whine and chug of the mixers and the slower melodies of wartime, Geno told his story. He spared no detail, telling things he hadn't even told Stef.

Micah listened. His black eyebrows pulled low. A muscle flickered in his jaw as his chin gave a single nod. A grunt of agreement in his chest. A hum of understanding. When Geno was done, Micah snapped off the mixer. He crouched at a low cabinet and brought out a liquor bottle and two shot glasses.

"You know ouzo?" he asked.

"I know what it is. I've never had it."

Micah poured two shots and handed one over. Geno sniffed at it. Clear licorice. Like a winter night in the suburbs.

"Na ziseis," Micah said. "May you live."

"L'chaim," Geno said, and they threw back the shots. The ouzo burned like sweet fire down Geno's throat and sank fingers into his tired muscles. Micah poured them another then capped the bottle and put it away.

"When did you get moved to Belsen?" Geno asked.

"January of forty-five. The Reds were advancing and the Nazis started blowing up the crematoria and the barracks. Evacuating the camp and force-marching us west. The march killed thousands but in a way, it freed me. All the ranks and hierarchies broke down. I was able to get far away from Nadelman and blend into another section of the walking dead. That's where I met my wife. She'd been in Mengele's special compound. Her and her twin sister. He was fascinated with twins. But I don't have to tell you this."

"Did her sister make it out?" Geno asked, sipping slower this time.

"No. I didn't think Lilia was long for the world, either. We got to Belsen and I lost track of her. I was sure she'd never make it. But, as you said, it was unfortunate and not my concern. My only concern was survival."

"I don't know how anyone survived. I can't get my mind wrapped around it."

"Habibi," Micah said, "in the camp, we were treated as less than human. Sub-human. When you're in that situation, you have two means to survive. By enhancing your humanity or suppressing it. Neither is good, nor bad. Neither guarantees survival. You make a choice and take your chance. I chose to suppress humanity. During the time at Auschwitz and then at Belsen, I was Pipel Schönling. I made it my name. Everything happened to him, not Micah."

"What happened to Nadelman?"

"When the British army came in April, they kept a certain degree of order. But they also turned a blind eye to a certain degree of justice." Micah kicked back the last of his ouzo. "We beat the shit out of the guards and the kapos."

"No way," Geno said, a little bit of relish in the words.

"We threw them out windows. Strung them up on the barbed wire. Pulled their boots on our bare feet to kick them in the face. One day, someone called me into the yard. They had Lazar Nadelman stripped naked and tied to a post. I was handed a knife and told to cut off his cock and we'd eat it for dinner.

"I looked him in the eye while I tested the edge of my knife in front of him. I was drunk on revenge and power. I was *hard* with it, habibi. I relished it like a lover. I said to him, 'I'd cut it off if only I could find it, Lazar. It won't be enough for a meal. Maybe it will suit as garnish.'

"I got right up in his face, beating his balls around with the flat of the blade. 'Think it bothered me when you fucked me, Lazar?' I said. 'I couldn't even feel it. I shit bigger than your cock.'"

"Then what?" Geno said, barely breathing.

Micah's gaze went far away. "I wanted to do it," he said. "My blood was up, my anger was high, I could've done it and gotten away with it. I could've cut off his cock and carried it around with me as a trophy the rest of my days. But maybe the little bit of food I had in my belly brought my old self back to me. Something in me was wiser and knew it was time to become human again. Become Micah Kalo again."

"You did nothing to him?"

"Well." Micah's eyes came back to the present. "I decided I'd do nothing, but I didn't let Nadelman know my decision right away. I let him think about it a good long time while he was tied up naked in the yard. And maybe I scratched him a little."

"A little?"

"After that day, I was known around Belsen as the Mohel. Everyone asked Nadelman how he was recovering from his second bris. The prick never came near me again." Micah sighed then. "But there's more to this story, habibi. Because humanity is slower to recover than lose."

He clapped his hands together and walked through the cloud of flour dust. He turned a white bucket over and sat on it, facing Geno. "I worked translating for the British until Berlin fell in May. Then a group of us, mostly Hungarians and Poles, started making our way east. Two women were in the group and to my shock, Lilia was one of them. She was bones, corasón. All bones and big eyes and rotted teeth. A womb burned out with chemicals. Her precious sister nothing but ashes in Poland. Yet walking along, she spoke of her family's restaurant in Budapest. Of a little bag of diamonds and gold a Christian family buried in their yard, waiting for the end of the war. She was going home with a little piece of hope. Then we were camping along the side of the road one night, and a group of Red Army soldiers found us. They held all the men at gunpoint and took turns with the women."

Geno felt his eyebrows pull low. "But they were on your side. The Russians were fighting with the allies by then."

"Presiado, the Russian men were insane with revenge and bloodlust. They conquered the Germans and felt everything they found in the land was rightfully theirs. Everything. They killed it, burned it, robbed it and raped it and felt no shame."

Geno remembered the rumpled, white-haired woman who served him matzo brei and felt sick.

"We started east again but Lilia didn't talk about hope or dreams or diamonds anymore. Just near the Hungarian border, another band of Russian soldiers found us. They took Lilia off the road into the woods. This time, habibi, I didn't do nothing. I guess my knife spared Nadelman because it had a much bigger job."

"How many were there?"

"Four. I cut two throats. The third I stabbed in the gut. The last I stabbed up the ass and when he screamed and fell over, I took the shit-coated blade and cut his cock off."

Geno stared, his mouth open as he took in the most heroic yet *psychotic* thing he'd ever heard. Thinking, *Dude, in all my fucked-up and twisted drawings, I never cut it* off.

Micah's head was shaking. "Thing is, habibi? Revenge isn't all that sweet. I'm not a terribly religious man. It was another luxury I left behind in Greece. But I know one day, God will want to have a little chat with me about those four men. And I'm not looking forward to it."

Christ, Geno thought, *and I thought being in the principal's office after cheating on a test was bad.* "What do you think he'll say?"

Micah rested his elbows on his knees and his floury palms opened to the ceiling. "I'm hoping when I'm judged, nineteen forty-two to nineteen forty-five won't be entered into the record. I wasn't alive then. I wasn't human. I wasn't *on* the record. I hope it's the things I've done since that count. I've tried to live a good life. Give more than I take. I haven't been perfect at it. When I found out Stavi's husband was abusing her, I turned back into my wartime self."

Geno's eyes widened. "Really?"

"He beat her up and she miscarried my only grandchild. Right upstairs by the ovens. It was a boy and she was going to call him Sam." Micah got up and walked over to the wall by the mixers, eyebrows furrowed as his fingertips moved in a small circle. "It's been patched. You can't see it unless you know what to look for, but I put her husband's head into the wall here. Then I broke his arm with the dough hook. Like I said, humanity is quickly lost, slower to get back."

He came back to sit on the overturned bucket again. On the radio, Dinah Shore was singing "What'll I Do?" Geno reached to touch the numbers on Micah's forearm and asked, "How many people know about what happened to you?"

"Not many." A tiny shiver went across Micah's shoulders and his hands curled into fists. "I used to be more willing to tell. In the years right after the war. But many people thought since I went willingly with Schultze, what happened with Nadelman and his gang wasn't much different. Wasn't so bad. Possibly I even deserved it. Or encouraged it." His hands slowly opened. "After a while, I figured they were right. So I stopped telling." The last words were swallowed up, his normally melodic voice tight and thin, worn down to dust.

"No," Geno said. "No, they were wrong. They lied to you."

The wrath of Caan filled his veins. He couldn't possibly have lifted Micah up onto his shoulder. Instead he tried to reach inside the old man, find the young boy who lived on spit and chances and pick *him* up. Hold him tight and tell him the truth.

"I'm telling you. I speak as one who knows. I say what happened with *both* Schultze and Nadelman was rape. And you didn't deserve it."

He crossed his wrists and laid his palms against Micah's. Their fingers folded down and they sat in silence. Elbows on knees, hands clasped as brothers and war mates.

"I still have so much anger in my heart," Geno said. "I think given the chance, I'd shoot Anthony Fox in the head and enjoy it."

"You lived through your own Auschwitz," Micah said. "Revenge is a luxury you can leave behind, habibi. Don't lose your humanity. You're too fine a boy to waste time getting it back."

The tears dripped out of his Geno's eyes and nose. Micah reached and brushed them away.

Geno closed his eyes at the human touch.

A survivor's touch.

A father's touch.

"You're too fine a boy," Micah said, followed by a long flow of Ladino. Geno couldn't understand all the words, but the tone around the endearments was clear.

Poor boy. You poor sweet boy.

My poor darling, precious boy.

You are strong and kind and humane and you are the only one around here with a lick of…

Realizing common sense and humanity were the same thing, Geno tipped over and fell into Micah's chest, burying his face in flour and muscle. He didn't weep. He just went home.

Micah rocked him, a hand stroking Geno's head. Inked numbers in his dusty skin. Strong arms and a stronger heart.

"Hijo querido," he said. "You and I know what it's really about."

JUNE

MOS IN ARMOR

*E*P's SPRING EXHIBITION was set for the end of June. Residents could show independent projects, or, for those who needed structure, work within a concept set by the staff.

Aedith came up with an idea using masks, calling it *Outside/Inside/Hidden*. She brought in a tall stack of blank, white masks, explaining it was the way they were stacked on the art store shelves that inspired her.

"The way one fits snug on top of the other," she said, demonstrating with two of them. "We don't just wear one mask, we wear many. First the mask we show to the outside world and under it, the mask we put over our feelings. Under that…" She lifted up the second mask, revealing the empty table. "What's under there? What's the thing we keep under layers of masks?"

Outside/Inside/Hidden would be a hands-on exhibit, meant to be touched and handled by viewers.

"Everyone get the metaphor?" Corley said, pointing around the table. "We're allowing this to be touched."

"I don't know, I can't quite grasp the concept," Juan said. "Can someone hit me over the head with it?"

The art room downshifted into the quiet energy of creative production. Geno painted his *Outside* mask a metallic black. Sections of jaw and cheek and brow precisely outlined in gold with a single-hair brush. He glued tiny nuts, bolts and washers along the contours of the face, then went over the whole thing with clear varnish. The end result was Mos in armor, a steam punk machine man.

The *Inside* mask Geno left virgin white, pristine and unadorned. Tears gathered in a silvery border beneath the eye holes. But instead of falling as droplets, they fell as tiny handcuffs. Then Geno dipped a brush in red paint and bounced it on his wrist, splattering the mask with blood.

"Whoa," Corley said, leaning to look. "That's…"

"Does it need something else?"

"No. Don't touch it, don't mess with it. Leave it like that."

Geno came up blank for the *Hidden* motif. He couldn't think of anything, until one day when The Thing stopped by. Geno was sitting in a creative sulk, cutting one of the plain masks into thin strips and watching them collect in a pile on the tabletop. He stopped. Slowly reached and hollowed out the center of the pile, pushing the plastic into a nest. He blinked a few times, then jumped up from the table.

"Don't touch that," he said to no one and everyone. "Nobody touch that. Be right back."

He ran across the lobby and barreled downstairs to the kitchen.

"I need an egg," he said to Stavroula. "Can I have an egg?"

"Sure," she said. "Scrambled?"

"No, no, I mean the shell. I just need the shells."

With her spatula she pointed to the metal basin holding a morning's worth of eggshells. Geno picked out two halves, rinsed out the goo and took them back upstairs. He trawled through the shelves and drawers of art supplies and found some yellow feathers.

He carefully glued the plastic nest together and arranged the shells in the hollow, adding a few snippets of yellow feathers. Then he backed away and took it in.

The broken, robbed egg in the henhouse looked exactly the way he envisioned.

But it was so sad.

For the first time, Geno wasn't sure he wanted this to be his hidden truth.

"It's fantastic," Stef said, coming to look.

"It's not done," Geno said. "Something's missing."

It took a few days and a morning of watching Max bury things in the sand table and dig them up again. Once more, Geno jumped up, heading to his room this time. He searched in a drawer for a box kept tightly closed and hidden away. Inside were pieces of cobalt blue sea glass he and Carlito picked up on the beach, the first summer after Analisa died. Little treasures scattered in the waves and sand for her two chicks to find.

Hey boys. It's me.

Geno pushed the smooth, frosted fragments around on the desk. He found two that were roughly teardrop shaped. Put together, they made a heart, which he carefully glued on the edge of one eggshell, as if it were spilling out.

"Wow," Stef said, arms crossed and chin nodding. "It's like I told you. They—"

"Didn't get the best of me," Geno finished.

The ups and downs of recovery could kill a guy. One day you were two floors shy of the top of the world, gazing at your strong, blue heart, thinking everything was going to be all right. You had a nice Italian dinner with Vern, listened to some great stories about Nathan in his youth, laughing hard through the bittersweet memories. You told Vern, finally, what his unflagging support meant to you, how you couldn't thank him enough. You got some solid, well-deserved sleep.

The next day, for no damn reason, you felt like garbage.

"No damn reason," Stef said. "You're sure about that?"

Geno's head bobbled back around on his shoulders before he flopped over his crossed arms on the table. "Not to state the obvious but I miss my family."

"Dude, just because it's obvious doesn't mean it's invalid. You're entitled to feel sad about a crushing loss. *Sad* barely begins to describe it."

"It's so fucking hard," Geno said. "And I don't mean hard like difficult. When my mom died, it's like all the softness went out of my life. Everything was either sharp or flat. It hurt like being cut with a razor and I had nothing soft to lean on or hide behind. My dad was there. He tried. But he broke. Something in him just unwound and hung loose."

"And your brother drifted from you as well," Stef said.

"The more I think about it, the more it seems like I've been lonely for a really long time. And when I look down the road toward the rest of my life, I don't know what I'm going to do. It's not fucking fair. I'll never be able… I'll never be in love."

"What makes you say that?"

Geno spread his hands. It was too obvious for words.

"You'll never be in love because you were raped?"

"It changes everything."

"So you're saying it changed one of two things specific to love. It either made you inherently unlovable, or it altered your willingness to love others. Which is it?"

Geno didn't answer.

"It wasn't a trick question," Stef said. "The answer is the truth in your gut. Are you unlovable because you were raped, or are you intensely cautious because you were raped?"

"Cautious."

Stef nodded. "Trust is going to be a thing with you."

"An issue."

"Bluntly, yeah. If we want to mindfully turn 'issue' inside-out, we could call it a cause. Or a value."

"I'm just…really scared," Geno said.

"Brother, if you weren't scared, I'd be concerned something was wrong. Tell me what scares you."

"Everything."

"Now that's being lazy," Stef said. "Try to name things. One thing. Pin it down."

"I'm scared I'll constantly be on my guard. Constantly fearful of being…"

"Being what?"

"Betrayed."

Stef circled his hand in the air, asking for more.

"Screwed over," Geno said. "Railroaded. Taken advantage of. Emotionally assaulted."

"Someone hurting you without your consent," Stef said.

"I guess."

"That's going to happen."

Geno's eyebrows pulled down.

"I make the confident prediction," Stef said. "Backed by all the money in my wallet, someday, someone you care for is going to hurt you. You'll like a girl and she won't like you back. Or she will for a little while, then dump you. Maybe after she sleeps with your best friend. I can't predict the details but I'm telling you, someone you love will let you down. Disappoint you. Maybe even break your heart. It'll happen. But then what?"

"I don't know."

"Play out the scenario. Hypothetically. You give some girl your heart and soul, your pain and secrets, and she shits on you. Then what?"

"I…"

"Worst thing that could happen?"

"I hurt."

"Is that the worst?"

"Yes. It is." It sounded lame but it was Geno's story and he was sticking to it.

"So then what do you do?"

"I don't know," Geno said, feeling like he was engaged in swordplay with a plastic knife.

"What did you do before you were raped? When you were hurting? Don't think too much. Say the honest, gut answer."

Geno shook his head. "I don't know, I'd talk to someone? Carlito. Or Chris. My mom or dad."

"So circle back. *Now* what's the worst that could happen to you?"

"I hurt and I have no one to talk to."

"Which is worse than just hurting?"

"Yeah."

"Can you push that a little?"

"What do you mean?"

"Equate hurting and having no one to something else that happened to you."

Geno swallowed hard. "It would be like being in Anthony's basement again."

Stef nodded.

"Helpless," Geno said. "And scared."

"That's right."

"Nobody coming."

"Nobody to rescue you."

"Yeah."

Stef let a few beats pass. "I don't know if this is answerable," he said. "But I'll ask. At any time during your ordeal, did you feel you were unworthy of rescue?"

"No," Geno said. Fast. It was out his mouth before his brain could mull it over.

"Never?"

"Not once."

"And now? Are you still worthy of rescue?"

"Yeah. But I don't have anyone."

"Which means?"

"I don't know. What? Stop *asking* me shit." Geno laughed, but with a shrill edge.

"It means you have to find your people. Hear me out a sec. I'm not saying losing your family is something you bravely and blithely move on from. It's not something you get over. What happened to you is horrible. *Is*, not was. This is still happening. It's unfair. It's inhumane. It's a tragedy. It hurts and it changed you. But it doesn't mean you are doomed to walk this earth alone. Or that you deserve to walk the earth alone. It *sucks* you have to build a new tribe. But it isn't impossible."

Geno stared into the distance. "I hate that I have to."

"Can you hate it and do it anyway?"

The question brought back days with Wayne. Learning to pull an attack close, shrimp out and run like hell. Heart behind your teeth but you did it anyway.

"Yeah," Geno said. "I think I can."

THE MOTHERS ALWAYS JUMP

*J*AV SAT AT his reserved booth at the Bake & Bagel, reading Neil Gaiman over his lunch. Geno came out from the back room and around the counter, his clothes and apron dusty with flour. He carried his own sandwich and a bottle of iced tea. "¿Puedo sentarme?"

"For a small fee," Jav said, then gestured to the bench across.

"So," Geno said. "Remember when I found your notebook and instead of returning it right away, I read it like a dick?"

"No, I don't recall that at all," Jav said. He picked up the napkin dispenser and pretended to throw it at Geno's head. "Dick."

"I'm sorry about that."

Jav shrugged. "It's weird in there."

"You wrote about me."

"Yeah, I wondered if you saw that. I hope you didn't think I was making fun of you. I have a funny way of looking at the world. I see names or situations and my weird head starts telling a story. That's all."

"I get it," Geno said. "I thought it was cool, actually."

"Yeah?"

A bit of quiet passed while Geno ate. "Random question for your weird head," he said. "Do you believe in an afterlife?"

"Kind of," Jav said slowly. "I envision it as the ultimate cocktail party where you get to talk to everyone you ever wanted and get all the answers to your questions."

"Like who killed JFK?"

"Did Atlantis exist? What were they pyramids really for? Area Fifty-One in Roswell, what was *that* all about?"

"I think after Q and A, you get to have a beer with your seventy-seventh great-grandfather."

Jav pointed at him. "See now that would be cool. Learning the history of your name. Imagine if you were led into a presentation room with this gigantic family tree."

"A guided tour of your genealogy."

"The ultimate documentary. Narrated by David Attenborough."

Geno crumpled up his napkin and dropped it on the empty plate. "Do you think everyone's happy there?"

"In heaven?" Jav wrinkled his brow over the question. "Huh. Happy? I don't know."

"I sometimes have a problem with that aspect of it. The way people say, 'He's at peace now' or, 'She's in a better place.' Pissed me off at my mother's funeral. Maybe it was a better place but who were they to say she was peaceful there?"

"So you're thinking maybe there's no physical suffering, but the departed feel sadness or regret on the other side."

"I guess I'm wondering, do they miss us?"

With his finger, Jav made patterns in some spilled sugar on the tabletop. "I was talking about my cousin with Stef once and he said, 'He must miss you like crazy.' I believed it. I mean I *could* believe it. I could believe heaven or whatever was a place where sadness still existed."

"See, I think about my mother," Geno said. "Watching from the other side while I was getting raped. I have this vision of her beating on the wall. The barrier. Whatever separates this life and the afterlife. Bashing her fists against it and screaming to get through."

Jav felt his eyes widen and his finger stopped moving. "Jesus."

"I can't accept she would be on the other side, floating in her state of eternal grace, just watching. She had to have been tearing the place apart. It's what mothers *do.*"

Stunned, Jav rubbed his fingertips together, watching the sugar crystals fall like snow. "I was skiing once," he said. "On line for the lift and up ahead was a mother and little boy, maybe six or seven. And he miscalculated getting on the chair and slid off before the bar was down. Just a few feet, he wasn't hurt. But then the mother jumped off too."

"Yikes."

"The attendant shut down the line, got them back on their feet. Everyone was fine, they were off on the next chair. The attendant looked at me, shaking his head and he said, 'The mothers always jump.'"

Geno laughed. "Right?"

"The dude was like, 'I've never seen one hesitate. No thought, they just go. The dads continue ahead and call back, *I'll meet you up there.* The mothers jump.'"

"It's what they do," Geno said.

"Then I'd have to agree with you," Jav said. "She must've been out of her mind. Whatever the afterlife is, she must've been tearing up the place."

Geno chewed on his bottom lip as he drew a deep breath in and out. "Weird, because as much as I hate envisioning her like that, I need it. I need her to have been that way."

Jav crossed his arms as the idea grew larger and more intense. "Wow, that's a powerful fucking image, man. A mother on the other side, whaling on the boundary and can't get to her children."

A moment passed, both of them staring into space, alone with their thoughts. "You ever think of telling your story?" Jav asked.

"What, like write a book?"

"A book. An article. An art show. Producing something."

"Maybe a radio story?"

"Sure," Jav said, as an idea he'd been kicking around suddenly crashed into a new idea. A *great* idea.

"Uh-oh," Geno said. "I think The Thing just showed up. You got that look going."

"Yeah…"

"Better write it down."

"No," Jav said. "No, this isn't a story. This is a phone call."

HIM HOLDING HIMSELF

*G*ENO CAME THROUGH the warehouse lobby, heading from the art room to dinner. Jav and Stef stood by the security booth. Their laughter echoed off marble and the sunlight from the front doors etched them in gold.

"Ah-ha," Jav said, pointing at Geno. "You. Come here. Got something for you."

"For me?"

"I'll be outside," Stef said, and with a wave, he left.

"Two things," Jav said. "One educational, the other not so much." From his messenger bag he took a small, buff-colored paperback, *Genghis Khan and the Making of the Modern World.*

"Nice," Geno said, laughing. "I will definitely read this."

Then Jav took out a small, leather-bound book. "And this is also for you. Because every man should have one."

Geno ran a thumb along the blank pages, strangely touched. "Thanks."

"Careful, don't lose the bookmark."

A business card was tucked in the spine.

Camberley Jones
Journalist & Storyteller
National Public Radio

"She's a friend of mine," Jav said. "I didn't give her your name or any details. I only said I knew a guy with an important story to tell. She said to give you her card. So I am."

"Wow," Geno said. "Okay." *Important* rolled around his head. Shedding its skin. Unfolding, unwinding and opening up.

I have an important story to tell.

"Thanks," he said.

Jav smiled and came in high for a handshake. Their palms smacked together, fingers folding down. A beat. Then Jav hugged him.

"Eres el más valiente," he said, rubbing Geno's head.

Geno was lying in bed that night when out of the dark, like a shooting star across Nos, he remembered Seth and the roller coaster that fell four hundred and fifty-six feet. *Straight down.*

"You must've been shitting your pants at the top," Ben said.

"Worse," Seth said. "I was so scared, I had a fucking erection."

Followed by the memory of Natasha, with her pink hair and piercings. "Maybe fear's another form of arousal."

Geno stared open-mouthed at the ceiling as pieces of his past joined hands with the present.

Was Natasha right?

As one, every particle in every fiber of his being replied, *Yes.*

Why else would the memory have imprinted on his brain, gone dormant and then revived right here, right now, when it would link up with everything Stef taught him and become truth?

It wasn't you. It wasn't your fault. It had nothing, zero to do with sex.

He believed it now. His body believed it.

Fear was another form of arousal. Fear and excitement were equal parts removed from normal.

And your dick doesn't know the damn difference, he thought.

You didn't get hard for him. Your body reacted without your brain's permission because you had all that shit in your bloodstream. Enough to kill someone with a weaker heart.

You survived because your heart is strong.

Geno floated in the serenity of long, slow easy breaths. The immaculate joy of believing your own thoughts. Feeling every square inch of his forgiven body press into the bedclothes. Aware of his skin and bone and muscle and hair for the first time in nearly a year.

It wasn't your fault.

His hand slid tentatively down the waistband of his sweats. It curled around his penis, small and cool and shy.

It's okay.

You're allowed.

His breathing stayed long and measured as he felt himself grow larger. Warm and tactile, with a give. Then harder, but still uncertain.

You're allowed.

His bottom lip retreated behind his teeth a little as his mind searched around for an image. It had been so long, nothing came to him. No female face from his past, no celebrity fantasy, no idealized dream-girl musings. Just his hand. The feel of him holding himself. Like coming home. His head quiet. No voices at his shoulder. No memory. Only bright golden light spilling out of his pores. Soft like soap. Luscious like butter. His skin glowing pink then red. Then with a pop, a bright marigold of yellow and orange behind his eyelids.

It was the tiniest orgasm he ever had. A squeezed hiccup. A weak spurt, barely anything.

But it was his.

And it had been so long.

He laughed weakly in the dark, the heat flowing over his skin and the bright light in his veins.

TWO SIDES OF ONE MAN

To: BMarino@gmail.com
From: Geronimocaan@gmail.com

Dear Ben,

It's been a while and I know there's a shit-ton to say after I disappeared.

You helped save my life and I never said thank you.

I told you a whole bunch of lies and I never said I'm sorry.

If it's not too late or too damaged, and you're not too weirded out, I'd love to meet up and tell you some truths. You deserve them. You were a good friend to me and I'd like to say so in person.

Take care,

Geronimo Caan
(FYI, most people call me Geno)

To: ChristopherMudry@gmail.com
From: Geronimocaan@gmail.com

Dear Chris,

Yeah, I know, I got some balls reaching out, after everything I said to you.

I'm sorry.

Under the shitty circumstances, I took aim and fired at the first thing I saw, trying to bring it down as low as I felt. And I'm so fucking sorry it was you. You trusted me with something and I used it as a weapon. You didn't deserve it. I'm really sorry.

If you weren't my friend, if you weren't sleeping over that night, if you hadn't put your backpack in my car, who knows how long it would've taken them to find me. You helped save me and I need to say thank you.

And I'm sorry.

I hope you're doing okay in Oregon. I hope it's a place where you can be yourself.

Take care,
G

After sending the two emails, Geno looked up the website of the Stockton Police Department, hoping their chief had an email listed. He did, and Geno started typing.

To: Chief@StocktonPD.com
From: Geronimocaan@gmail.com

Dear Captain Hook,

Discovered something interesting today. In stage productions of Peter Pan, the part of George Darling and the part of James Hook are traditionally played by the same actor. Two sides of one man. I know that seems random, but I've been thinking about you a lot lately. I never forgot that you got to me when my dad couldn't. That night and the days after, right up until the arrest, you were there.

I'll turn twenty-one on July 20, 2010. I'd like the first legal beer I buy to be for you. I hope this can happen.

Sincerely,
Mr. Caan

To: Geronimocaan@gmail.com
From: ChristopherMudry@gmail.com

G,

Thanks for your note. It was great to hear from you. I don't think a day goes by that you don't cross my mind one way or another, wondering if you're okay. Hoping to God you're okay.

Yeah, what you said that day hurt, but the circumstances were beyond shitty and it wasn't hard to put into context. I understand where it was coming from. But I also appreciate the apology. Not just for my own feelings, but because it shows me you're still the same decent guy I knew. Anyway, it's accepted and you're forgiven. We'll move on before it gets awkward. Wait, it's already awkward. Oh well.

School is awesome. Oregon's amazing. It's a whole other world and I feel like I found my people, you know? Like I can finally breathe and I'm ME for the first time in my life.

Let me know if you ever want to visit. There's a cool vibe out here on the West Coast. It's healing. If that makes sense.

Really good to hear from you, G. I hope I'll hear more. My number's the same so call or text if you want.

Be safe.
Chris

⁓

To: Geronimocaan@gmail.com
From: Chief@StocktonPD.com

Dear Mr. Caan,

It's on the calendar. MacClellan's Pub. Bring ID and don't be late.

Best wishes,
Capt. Daniel Hook
P.S. My twin brother is James Hook. He's a captain in the US Coast Guard. True story.

New Name, New You

A STREET FAIR WAS happening in Chelsea and the Bake & Bagel had a front row seat. Micah and Geno got up at three in the morning to make extra batches of bacon dough and the upstairs crew was double staffed. Jav came in to work behind the counter with Stavroula.

"I finished that book about Genghis Khan," Geno said to Jav during a rare lull.

"How was it?"

"I liked it. You know anything about him?"

"Only what I learned in school. Emperor of half the world. Badass motherfucker."

"When he was about fifteen, his father died, and the tribe kicked him out. Him and his mother and brothers and sisters. They wandered around in exile, starving. Then he was captured by his father's friends and they made him a slave."

"Wow."

Geno nodded. "I was surprised to learn how much of his youth he spent being hungry and a captive. Anyway, he finally escaped, and the escape earned him a reputation. Men began to join with him. They became his generals. That's how it started."

"With escape," Jav said.

"Yeah."

"And being known as something other than a slave."

They were quiet a little while, then Geno asked, "Do you believe everything happens for a reason?"

"I do," Jav said. "But not everyone gets the privilege of liking the reason. Of feeling the reason was worth the ordeal or the experience."

"Never thought of it that way."

Jav looked at Geno a long moment. "You're going to be a huge voice in the world."

"You think?"

Jav nodded. "I think your story has a lot of power. It can be the kind of thing that builds an empire."

Micah came upstairs from the dough room. "Komo etash, habibis. What can I do?"

"You kill the average guy," Jav said.

You have no idea, Geno thought.

Conversation turned to one of Jav's favorite subjects, names and the stories behind them. He was born Javier Gil deSoto but changed it to Javier Landes after 9/11.

"Because the voices told you to?" Geno said.

"No," Jav said, laughing. "Because I— Shh. Wait." He glanced up to the ceiling. "Did you hear that?"

"You're ridiculous," Geno said.

"I was born Michalis," Micah said. "Day I landed at JFK, an immigration officer pronounced it Micah. I liked the way it sounded. Liked the idea of having a new name. It's a reset button."

"New name, new you," Jav said.

"It's actually a practice in Kabbalah. Jewish mysticism. Changing your name after a serious illness or injury."

"No kidding?"

"I've heard that," Geno said. "You change your name to confuse the Evil Eye, make it hard to find you."

"Geronimo," Micah said. "Now that's a name."

"Funny, you know what occurred to me the other day?" Jav said. "Geronimo is both a battle cry and a cry for help."

Geno blinked as his mind looked over this revelation from all sides.

"Your boyfriend's back," Micah said, punching Jav's arm.

"I must be in trouble." Jav headed out and Geno finished wrapping up one more sandwich before he went out front as well. The bakery was full of talk and laughter and eating. Beyond that, outside, the fair was in full swing. A brilliant spring day, filled with sound and smell and joy.

Jav and Stef were huddled up on one side of a booth. Heads together, talking behind their hands and sneaking glances toward the far end of the counter.

Geno followed the covert looks and saw Stav, standing with her arms extended over the bakery case, her hands caught up by a tall, sandy-blond man on the other side.

Geno slid onto the opposite bench of the booth and asked, "Who's that?"

"My nephew's father," Jav said. "Roger Lark."

"The Treehouse Guy?" Geno said, a little too loudly and Stef swatted him.

"Shh," he said. "It's on."

"It's on?" Geno said, softer.

"We introduced them last night," Jav said. "It's so fucking on."

Geno faked a yawning stretch and glanced back. Stavroula and Roger were lost in each other, fingers clasped tight like they could never be torn apart.

"Look at them," Stef said, his hand wrapping around Jav's wrist. "Dude, I can't *believe* we didn't think of this before."

Jav leaned his head against Stef's as he looked. "I've never seen her smile like that."

Filled with a sudden, pure happiness, Geno got up and went behind the counter. He walked up to Stavroula and tugged on the strings of her apron.

"Why don't you take the day off," he said over her shoulder. He looked at Roger. "Hi, I'm Geno. Stavroula works for me."

The Treehouse Guy had grey eyes and an enormous smile beneath a big nose. "I'm Roger," he said, shaking Geno's hand. "Are you hiring?"

Blushing and dazed, Stavroula turned back to look at Geno, who eased the loop of the apron over her head, then put it around his own neck. "Get out of here. I got this."

Geno stood in the shop doorway with a cup of coffee, watching the fair. Tired to the point where it didn't matter anymore. Thinking about battle cries and cries for help. Names that hid you from the Evil Eye and voices that could build an empire.

He heard the click of a camera shutter. Turning his head toward it, he saw a girl. As the camera lowered, her face came into view. She was Asian, with a teal-blue streak in her long, black hair. Tight jeans and a flannel shirt. Her golden arms tattooed and a ring in her nose. A smile that began at the corner of her upper lip, then bloomed downward across her chin when she saw Geno staring.

She came closer, turning the camera around to show Geno the display. He leaned and looked at himself, posed in the doorway, strong-looking and contemplative. Ankles crossed under the hem of his long apron. Fit, tattooed arms in a black T-shirt. He looked good.

He looked at peace.

"Hope you don't mind," she said. "It was a nice moment. I went for it."

He minded. He would always mind cameras pointed in his direction. But it was a really good moment. He couldn't stop looking at it.

"Oh my God," she said.

Geno looked down at her. "What?"

"It's you."

"I'm sorry?"

Her mouth parted in an incredulous laugh, her eyes blinking rapidly. "I don't believe it."

"We've met?"

"You don't remember?"

"No, I'm sorry."

"It was earlier this year. Back in January. At a bar on the Upper East Side. We both saw a guy slip a roofie into a girl's drink."

Now Geno's mouth fell open. "Oh my God."

"It's you."

He touched his forehead, the night coming back to him. "Holy shit, I remember you."

"What's your name?" she said.

An impulse of the heart raced his brain to the finish line of his mouth. "Gen," he said. With a hard G.

"Gen?" she said. "Is that short for something?"

"Genghis."

One of her perfect eyebrows raised. "For real?"

Geno nodded.

She crossed her arms. "Your name is actually Genghis."

Geno laughed at his feet. "No."

She laughed too, easily, as if this were an inside joke they had for years.

"My name is actually Geronimo."

Her hand touched his bicep. "Okay, now you're messing with me."

He took out his wallet, drew out his driver's license and handed it to her.

She looked at it, then back at him. "I stand corrected. So Gen is short for Geronimo?"

"I was Geno for a long time. But I've been recently reinventing myself as Gen."

"How recently?"

"About thirty seconds ago." His chuckles were spilling out without control. "I'm sorry," he said. "I've been up since three. I'm a little punchy."

The hand not holding his license extended toward him. "I'm Tai. It's not short for anything and it's the name I was born with."

"It's nice to meet you. Again."

They shook. Both the grip and their eyes holding on.

"I'm so glad to see you," Tai said. "I'm not exaggerating when I say I've thought about you a lot all these months."

He wished he could say the same.

She handed the license back, with one last glance. "Caan," she said. "Genghis Caan. I get it."

"What do you think, too obvious?" He put the wallet back in his pocket.

"No, I like it. Genghis and Geronimo. Both warriors."

And one is a cry for help, Geno thought.

"Are you working all day?" Tai asked.

"No, change of shift should be coming soon and then I can leave."

"Hm. Well, if you happen to see me loitering around this block, casually taking pictures, it's pure coincidence."

The moment peeked around from behind Geno's back, pulling at his shirt tails.

"Okay," he said. "And if I happen to be carrying two sandwiches, it doesn't mean anything."

Tai's smile spread from top to bottom. "It'll be nice randomly bumping into you later."

Geno watched her walk away. A hand settled on his shoulder and squeezed, then moved to the back of his neck. Micah kissed his head. Keeping Geno tucked under his arm, they watched the fair go by.

EPILOGUE

I'M LISTENING

"IF YOU HAD to confess to one crime you've already committed," Geno said, reading from *The Book of If*. "What would you confess to?"

"Shoplifting," Tai said.

He looked up from the pages. "Really?"

She looked up from her laptop. "Hasn't everyone?"

"Not me."

She turned her head sideways, fixing him with one eye. "Never? Not one piece of bubble gum ever?"

"I don't think so."

"Well then, what's your confessed crime?"

"Forgery?"

Her brows arched high. "Like checks?"

"Like taking my brother's test for him."

"You're a pathetic criminal," she said, shaking her head. "Next question."

"If you were to be any famous person's personal masseuse, whose would you like to be?"

"Yours," she said.

"I'm not famous."

"Yet."

Geno closed the book and got up from his desk. He slung a leg over Tai's chair and wiggled behind her, sliding arms around her waist.

"Hey, you," she said, rubbing his head. She was editing the pictures that would be exhibited at the Lark Gallery next month, with proceeds going to Exodus Project's new crisis hotline. EP residents would be displaying their artwork as well, but the main focus would be Tai's collection, a photo essay inspired by Geno's story.

His chin on her shoulder, he looked at the images he helped create.

A hand cuffed to an iron bed frame. It was his own hand and a makeup artist added the blood and wrist wounds. A Milky Way galaxy was superimposed over the flat surface of the cuff. It was the picture Geno liked looking at the least, yet the one he was most proud of, because he'd gotten through the shoot without a Xanax.

Next came a series of black-and-white shots. Close-ups of his stoma scar, showing the progression of a new tattoo based on Geno's mandala self-portrait. First the scar alone. Then the star of David inked dead center, enclosed in a ring. His parents' names lettered around. The addition of more and more circles and symbols, spreading over Geno's abdomen and side. The tattoo was about ten inches across now. Maybe he'd add onto it, maybe he'd stop here. He hadn't decided yet.

The next picture was a small farmhouse in a wooded glade. It belonged to friends of Tai's parents and they were more than happy to let it be used. In the shot, Geno stood in the open doorway, a hand on either side of the frame. Totally silhouetted and light spilling all around his body. The house was white in real life, but Tai easily made it red on the computer.

An image of Geno's hands cradling two baby chicks in a nest of blue sea glass. (Tai spent three hours editing out the poop.)

A shot of Geno from behind, the viewer looking over his shoulder as he stared at Anthony's abandoned house in Heading.

A photo of him sitting before a mirror, forehead to forehead with himself, overlaid with stars. It was the only picture in the series that showed his face.

It took a little coaxing, but Stavroula Kalo agreed to pose as the woman banging on the barrier of heaven. She arrived at the shoot full of doubts, worried she wouldn't capture Geno's vision. But Tai was patient. The three of them worked together, talking and sharing and collaborating. Stavroula loosened up, began to trust herself, and with the help of a couple shots of tequila and some heavy metal music, she let rip and *nailed* it. In the final picture, her hair was wild and electric, her face and body contorted in a scream of helpless rage. It involved the most editing to create the otherworldly boundary, and the nebulas shooting out of Stavroula's fists. Tai still wasn't satisfied but Geno never tired of looking at it.

"This isn't comfy," Tai said, turning both legs to the side and scooching up into Geno's lap. She slid arms around his shoulders and hugged him, exhaling on his neck. His hands pressed into her skin, felt the give of her flesh and muscle.

He'd graduated from Exodus Project on July 18th, exactly fifty-four weeks after he pulled up to the curb outside Anthony Fox's house. He was still living at the facility while deciding what his next move would be. Rory Finch had shown him the attic floor of her townhouse on West 20th Street. It was filled with junk which could be moved. The ceilings were low and the bathroom was tiny. It wasn't a palace, but Geno was welcome to think it over.

He'd called Camberley Jones and they went for coffee. She sent him links to back episodes of *Moments in Time* and he listened to her tell other people's stories. He liked her voice. He admired her work. He trusted her compassion. He felt he could take the worn, dirty backpack holding his ordeal and put it in her hands.

Camberley was coming to the Lark Gallery to see the exhibit. Geno's stomach got all warm and nervous thinking of everyone who would be there. His fellow war mates from EP. The art room staff. Stav, Stef and Jav. Micah. Lilia and Rory. Vern and Zoë. Chris Mudry said he wouldn't miss it. Ben Marino said he'd be there yesterday. Jason Dahl said he'd move the Earth to come but couldn't promise. Ed Shaughnessey RSVPd yes. So did Captain Hook and Detective Mackin.

The tribe.

Geno ran his mouth along Tai's smooth hair. Their relationship was slowly unfolding like a love note. He still lived at EP, where there wasn't much privacy for them. She lived at home in Brooklyn, where there was no privacy whatsoever. But they hadn't yet reached a point where they wanted to close themselves behind doors anyway. They'd bared their souls, but not shown much skin. Not yet. Right now, they were telling an important story.

His hand reached up to touch the star of David on his gold chain. Beside it hung a new pendant, the Kabbalah Flower of Life, made up of dozens of overlapping circles. Stef gave it to him as a graduation present.

At the reception after the ceremony, Stef was a bit of a wreck. Geno had never seen him so vulnerable and reticent, poised on the edge of enormous emotion. He kept slipping away from the crowd, backing into a corner to be next to Jav for a few minutes. He stood still, chest expanding and contracting in deep breaths. Like he was taking hits off an oxygen tank. He found his smile, squared his shoulders and went back into the crush.

This matters to him, Geno thought. *This work is his life. He doesn't leave all of it outside his door, some of it always stays with him. It's the most important thing in the world.*

He glanced at Jav then, still in the corner, his eyes following Stef everywhere. *Well. Maybe the second most important thing.*

"Think you guys will get married?" he asked Jav later that evening.

Jav laughed down at his beer and scratched his temple. He wore Stef's winged ring on his index finger now. He had a new tattoo as well, a small goldfinch on his neck, up by his ear. Its wings spread in an arc of black, white and yellow. "Right now I'm deciding whether to give up the lease on my uptown apartment," he said. "Move downtown for good."

Geno bumped him with an elbow. "What's stopping you?"

"Fear."

"Of what?"

Jav's shoulders rolled. "It's scary when you hit it out of the park on your debut."

"Can you be scared and do it anyway?"

"You are so Stef's graduate."

Geno smiled. "It's not a bad thing to be."

"No, it isn't." And at that moment, standing tall and gazing across the crowded art room at Stef, Jav looked like a king. The J of his name morphing to X. Both conqueror and conquered.

"Well, you already put him in ink," Geno said, pointing to the bird on Jav's neck. "Now put him in writing. It's what you do."

A loud beeping chortle broke Geno's thoughts apart. The phone was ringing. Tai slid off his lap. He went back to his little desk and pulled on his headset.

"Empire Hotline. My name's Gen."

Silence.

"I'm listening," Geno said. "I'm here."

The sound of a long breath being drawn in.

Silence.

"Take your time," Geno said. "Whenever you're ready, I'll listen."

Another rush of air, followed by an exhaled sound. "Hi."

"Hey."

A sniff. More shaking breaths. But no words.

"How you feeling right now?" Geno said softly.

"Like I want to die."

"I know."

"I hurt so much."

"I know, man."

"Do you?" The guy's voice splintered.

"Yeah, I do. I was there and now I'm here. I know."

"Oh my God…"

"It's all right," Geno said, his voice shaking a little.

Tai reached a hand to him. He reached back and their fingers clasped. Squeezed once. Let go.

"Jesus Christ," the guy on the phone said. He was crying.

"It's all right," Geno said. "You think no one believes you, no one understands. But I swear, man. I do."

More crying. Violent, wet sobs. Like knives thrown at a wall.

"Take your time," Geno said. "Whenever you're ready, I'm listening…"

A BETTER MAN

*T*HE APARTMENT WAS quieter than dust when Stef got home from work.

"Hey bud," Stef said, crouching down for Roman. "So dark in here. Where's Javi?"

Roman trotted off toward the bedroom. Stef followed and saw Jav was asleep. *Seriously* asleep, the covers pulled up to his ears. He'd been up late with the last galley proofs of *The Chocolate Hour,* which was releasing next month.

Heading toward the kitchen for a beer, Stef saw the proofs were on the counter, stacked facedown except for the last page with Jav's picture and biography.

> *Gil Rafael is the author of four books. The short story collection,* Client Privilege, *includes "Bald," which was shortlisted for an O. Henry Award and made into the 2004 movie of the same title. His novella,* Gloria in the Highest, *and his full-length novel,* The Trade, *were both New York Times bestsellers. He has written articles for The New Yorker, GQ and Esquire magazines and appeared on NPR's Moments in Time.*
>
> *A native of Queens, Rafael lives in Chelsea with his partner Stef, who makes him a better man.*

The last line was circled in red with an arrow off to the side.

Are you sure about this? Jav's agent wrote. *We're making it official?*

Jav's handwriting answered below, in the blue ink of his favorite pen: *Putting it in writing.*

Next to the stack of proofs was a small, opened jar of Beluga caviar, scraped empty. A Post-it was stuck to the side, Jav's blue pen exclaiming, *Dude, this stuff rocks. We should keep it around all the time.*

"You moron," Stef said.

From out of the bedroom, Jav's voice called sleepily, "Get the fuck in our bed, Finch."

THE WIND

"The wind blows my tale out the door
And takes it to the furthest shore.
May it bring back a hundred more."

—Chilean Folktale

Afterthoughts & Resources

*I*T'S IMPORTANT TO POINT OUT the Model Penal Code (MPC) is not law in *any* jurisdiction in the United States. Currently, nearly all rape statutes in this country are gender neutral. Alabama, Georgia and North Carolina still use gender-specific terms for sexual assault, as does Article 213 of the MPC. It wasn't until 2012 that the American Law Institute began a multi-year project to revise Article 213, a project still ongoing as of this publication.

Geno Caan's interpretation of Article 213 is not accurate, but given the year (2006), his youth and his mental state, I feel his takeaways are valid.

In October 2015, the United Kingdom's Safeline announced the launch of #5MillionMen: the first dedicated National Helpline and Online Support service for the 5 million male survivors of rape and sexual abuse in the UK. The number is 0808 800 5005

In November 2016, Sweden announced the opening of a male rape crisis center, the first one specifically for men in the world.

RAINN (Rape, Abuse & Incest National Network) is the United States' largest anti-sexual violence organization. RAINN created and operates the National Sexual Assault Hotline (800.656.HOPE, online.rainn.org) in partnership with more than 1,000 local sexual assault service providers across the country and operates the DoD Safe Helpline for the Department of Defense. RAINN also carries out programs to prevent sexual violence, help survivors, and ensure that perpetrators are brought to justice.

Acknowledgements

ONCE AGAIN, I'VE REWRITTEN a little history and used a lot of literary license to achieve my ends. New York City purists will point out, rightfully, that the High Line elevated park did not open until 2009, and the Whitney Museum of Art did not begin construction on its downtown location until 2010. I'm aware of the historical inaccuracy. It was entirely intentional, as I felt I could back things up a few years without altering the space-time continuum. Still, I apologize for any offense I may have caused to longtime Chelsea residents.

I wrote most of *Finches* at my dining room table. I have to extend my thanks to the charms that showed up at the bird feeder outside the window. Especially on the days when I felt I'd bitten off more than I could chew. I'd look out to see a cluster of bright yellow goldfinches or red house finches, and it was like they were telling me, "You got this."

Rach Lawrence and Camille Barrineau were my twin towers during the writing. Often my Scylla and Charibidis. They lean hard on rough drafts and if the story breaks, they stick around to talk about it. Both push me to be better and I'm intensely grateful and privileged to have them as friends.

My editor, Becky Dickson, leans even harder on my work. I am running out of words to thank her for…everything, really. Mostly for teaching me to just say what I mean and tell the damn story. Then she does that *Thing* of slicing a bit from the end and making it the perfect beginning.

From within my always-awesome Army, I had a crack elite force of beta readers. They were invaluable in figuring out the pacing and various points of view. All their little understandings added up to a tremendous wisdom. I can only hope they are aware of the ownership they have in this novel and how grateful I am to share the process with them.

Daniella Chacón Araujo who fixed my horrible white New Yorker Spanish. And Astrid Heinisch who fixed capitals and cases in the German. Gracias and danke.

Tracy Kopsachilis reversed the color palette of *Larks* and produced original oil-on-canvas artwork to create a masterpiece of a cover. Colleen Sheehan took all the formatting worry out of my hands and made it beautiful.

Someone who deserves a lot more recognition than I've given is my massage therapist, John Scalzo, who's been with me for five books now. He's one of the most loving and kind souls I know, with amazing power in his hands. So much of this book came together while he was taking my neck, back and shoulders apart. We only recently discovered we come from the same hometown (although when I graduated high school, he wasn't born yet) and I don't think it's an accident he ended up on my team.

Emma Scott, my beautiful kaleidoscope of butterflies... Dude, I have no words and I know you'd tell me to save them for the next book anyway. I'm coming back to you, I promise. Let's always be us. Oh, and thank you for telling me it was continuum, not compendium. (What does that even *mean?*)

I get no compensation from the BBC for advertising *Planet Earth*. Seriously, if you've never watched this series, you need to. Wild ass. It's a thing. The coffee table book is awesome, too.

"You kill the average guy" is my Uncle Bill's line. I use it often.

My husband's parents met when they had summer jobs at Creedmoor Psychiatric Center on Long Island. They took great pleasure in answering "How did you two meet?" with "In the mental hospital." How could you not?

My daughter's interest in art therapy shaped Steffen Finch's brief mention at the end of *Larks*. While I sat and wrote at the dining room table this summer, Julie was often on the other side with her artwork. I'm not sure she knows how much it helped me, having her there. Or how much I enjoy being together, alone.

My son AJ is kind and his heart is strong. He slipped off the chair lift at Gore Mountain and I jumped after him. "The mothers always jump," the attendant said to me. AJ loves that story. And why not? I fell into the pool when I was four and my mother jumped in, fully dressed. It's what mothers do.

Thanks, Mom. And I'm sorry I scared you.

It's ridiculous how thrilled I was to use one of my dad's favorite jokes in a book. Oy, I'll Tell Ya Airlines has been making me giggle since I was twelve.

And JP, my curator and sailor, my most treasured friend and partner. You're the best thing that ever happened to me and loving you is the best thing I do.

Thank You

IF YOU ENJOYED *A Charm of Finches*, I'd love to hear about it. Please consider leaving a short review on the platform of your choice. Honest reviews are the tip jar of independent authors and each and every one is treasured.

If you're a Facebooker, join others who enjoyed my books in the Read & Nap Lounge:

LQRWRITES.COM/LOUNGE

Stop by my website

SUANNELAQUEURWRITES.COM

or look for me on Instagram at

@SWAINBLQR

Wherever you find me, all feels are welcome. And I always have coffee.

Suanne Laqueur

Also by
Suanne Laqueur

A Small Hotel

THE FISH TALES
The Man I Love
Give Me Your Answer True
Here to Stay
The Ones That Got Away
Daisy, Daisy

VENERY
An Exaltation of Larks
A Charm of Finches
A Scarcity of Condors
The Voyages of Trueblood Cay
Tales from Cushman Row
A Plump of Woodcocks

SHORTS
Love & Bravery: Sixteen Stories
An Evening at the Hotel

ANTHOLOGIES
Flesh Fiction

About The Author

A FORMER PROFESSIONAL DANCER and teacher, Suanne Laqueur went from choreographing music to choreographing words, writing stories that appeal to the passions of all readers, crossing gender, age and genre. As a devoted mental health advocate, her novels focus on both romantic and familial relationships, as well as psychology, PTSD and generational trauma.

Laqueur's novel *An Exaltation of Larks* was the grand prize winner in the 2017 Writer's Digest Book Awards and took first place in the 2019 North Street Book Prize. Her debut novel *The Man I Love* won a gold medal in the 2015 Readers' Favorite Book Awards and was named Best Debut in the Feathered Quill Book Awards. Her follow-up novel, *Give Me Your Answer True,* was also a gold medal winner at the 2016 RFBA.

Laqueur graduated from Alfred University with a double major in dance and theater. She taught at the Carol Bierman School of Ballet Arts in Croton-on-Hudson for ten years. An avid reader, cook and gardener, she started her blog EatsReadsThinks in 2010.

Suanne lives in Westchester County, New York with her husband and two children.

Printed in Poland
by Amazon Fulfillment
Poland Sp. z o.o., Wrocław

25350519R00309